John Clarke

BRIGHTEST *and* BEST

BRIGHTEST
and BEST

AMISH TURNS *of* TIME

OLIVIA
NEWPORT

SHILOH RUN PRESS
An Imprint of Barbour Publishing, Inc.

Print ISBN 978-1-62836-633-4

eBook Editions:
Adobe Digital Edition (.epub) 978-1-63409-559-4
Kindle and MobiPocket Edition (.prc) 978-1-63409-560-0

All scripture quotations are taken from the King James Version of the Bible.

Cover design: Faceout Studio, www.faceoutstudio.com

Published in association with the Books & Such Literary Agency, 52 Mission Circle, Suite 122, PMB 170, Santa Rosa, CA 95409-5370, www.booksandsuch.com

Published by Shiloh Run Press, an imprint of Barbour Publishing, Inc., P.O. Box 719, Uhrichsville, Ohio 44683, www.shilohrunpress.com

Our mission is to publish and distribute inspirational products offering exceptional value and biblical encouragement to the masses.

Member of the
Evangelical Christian
Publishers Association

Printed in the United States of America.

CHARACTERS

Ella Hilty
Jed Hilty—Ella's father
Rachel Hilty—Jed's wife, Ella's stepmother
David Kaufman—Rachel's son from her first marriage, Ella's stepbrother
Seth Kaufman—Rachel's son from her first marriage, Ella's stepbrother

Gideon Wittmer
Betsy (Lehman) Wittmer—Gideon's wife, who died five years ago
Tobias Wittmer—Gideon's son
Savilla Wittmer—Gideon's daughter
Gertrude "Gertie" Wittmer—Gideon's daughter

Lindy Lehman—sister of Betsy Lehman, best friend of Rachel Hilty

James and Miriam Lehman—uncle and aunt of Betsy and Lindy

Margaret Simpson—first-grade teacher at Seabury Consolidated Grade School
Gray Truesdale—Margaret Simpson's beau
Braden Truesdale—Gray's brother
Percival T. Eggar, Esquire, Attorney at Law
Ulysses R. Brownley—superintendent of Seabury schools
Deputy Fremont—deputy sheriff
Mr. Tarkington—principal of Seabury Consolidated Grade School

Amish Families:
Isaiah Borntrager Family
Cristof Byler Family
Bishop Leroy Garber Family
Joshua Glick Family
John and Joanna Hershberger Family
Aaron and Alma King Family
Chester Mast Family

CHAPTER 1

Geauga County, Ohio, 1918

Don't take another step!"

Ella froze. Her eyes flashed between the red rug on the floor in front of her and Nora Coates at the blackboard.

The schoolteacher's calico skirt swished softly as she came around the desk.

Ella relaxed her muscles but did not move her feet. "What's the matter?"

"You haven't been here in a long time, have you?" Nora stood six feet in front of Ella.

Ella Hilty was twenty-six, at least three years older than Nora. She left school after the eighth grade, half a lifetime ago, and had only occasional reason to be inside the one-room schoolhouse since then.

"The children all know how soft the floor is right there," Nora said. "The red rug reminds them, and they walk around the other way."

"Soft?" Ella echoed.

Nora grimaced. "*Rotted* is a more precise word."

Ella wasn't sure whether she felt the spongy floor yield beneath her weight or only imagined it.

"Nellie Watson put her foot through it a few months ago," Nora said. "I never heard such shrieking from a child of school age."

"I will step carefully if you would kindly advise me," Ella said.

"Take a long step to your left and you should be on solid ground again."

Ella turned her gaze to an open space under a window and

lifted her skirt just enough to accommodate the movement. Safely out of the danger zone, she squatted and lifted one corner of the red rug. Beneath it, the dank wood floor had caved in, splintered edges ringing the spot where Nellie Watson's foot must have sunk through.

"It's been wet from underneath," Ella said.

Nora nodded. "Three winters ago, during my first year teaching, Mr. King patched it, but it didn't hold."

Ella straightened the rug and stood. She understood now why Nora had asked for representatives of the parents committee to inspect the schoolhouse in the middle of July. There was time for repairs before the children returned to school in September.

"Did you attend school here?" Nora asked.

Ella nodded. She had lived in Geauga County, Ohio, all her life.

"The blackboard was new when I started," Ella said. Twenty years ago the new chalk had flashed white under the teacher's firm, quick strokes against the board. Ella had never seen anything like it. But she was six, had seen little of anything beyond the Amish farms, and only learned to speak English after she started school.

"The blackboard is still serviceable," Nora said, "but I wish one of the men would be sure it is properly secured. Sometimes the children lean on the chalk ledge when I ask them to come to the board to show their work. The creaks I hear are unnerving."

Gertie would do that. Gideon's daughter was newly six and due to begin school in a few weeks.

"I loved school." Ella moved cautiously toward the front of the room. She examined the strained wooden slats of the chalk ledge.

"Did you ever think of staying in school?" Nora's eyes brightened with curiosity.

Ella shook her head. Her parents never kept her from her books. She borrowed whatever she wanted to read from the small library in town. Besides, her eighth-grade year was also the year of her mother's death, and Ella took on housekeeping for her father. The youngest of eight children, she was the only one unmarried and living at home.

That was twelve years ago, and Ella was still the only sibling unmarried and living at home. Now, though, there was Rachel. Jed Hilty had a new wife.

Gertie Wittmer jumped unassisted out of her father's wagon. Gideon's impulse was to reach out and catch her, but she wouldn't want him to. She never did. Of his three children, the youngest was the most independent. Tobias was obedient, Savilla was sensible, and Gertie was independent. Perhaps this was because Gertie didn't remember what it was like to have a mother and the others did.

Gertie's small form hit the ground in a solid leap, and she grinned at him before running toward the schoolhouse. Perhaps he ought to warn Miss Coates to exercise extra firmness in helping Gertie adjust to the decorum of a classroom.

"Ella's here!" Gertie disappeared into the building.

His daughter's exuberance at the prospect of seeing Ella pleased Gideon. His own exceeded Gertie's, and for a moment he envied her freedom to express herself unconstrained. For obvious reasons, Ella was not part of the parents committee, which consisted of two Amish fathers and two *English* fathers. Both groups of children shared the schoolhouse, as they had for decades. Gideon had asked Ella to come, believing that a woman might see flaws in the schoolhouse that men would not.

Gideon looped the reins over a low branch of a flowering dogwood tree and followed his daughter into the school.

In the doorway, he held his pose. It was a long time after Betsy's death, when Gertie was a baby, before he saw Ella's loveliness. With an arm around his daughter, Ella raised her dark eyes toward Gideon, testing the softness at his core. Surely it was God's will that they should be together. Why else would a woman like Ella not have married years ago?

"Oh good, you're here," Miss Coates said.

Gideon's head turned toward the rattle of wagons behind him, bringing Aaron King and the two *English* fathers. They had six weeks to ready the building. Aaron's eyes would see the small flaws that could be remedied easily, but Miss Coates had already impressed on Gideon that the building needed more than fresh paint and polished desks.

The three fathers thumped in, their boots seeming heavy against the floor.

Walter Hicks rapped his knuckles against a vertical beam. "My boy warned me that things might be worse than we thought."

"Theodore is an astute young man," Miss Coates said.

Gertie ran a finger down the chalkboard and studied the resulting smudge.

Gideon glanced around. "Since we're all here, Miss Coates, perhaps you can point out to us particular matters of concern."

The teacher pointed up, above Walter's head. "I keep an extra bucket under my desk because every time it rains, that spot leaks. It got a lot worse in the spring."

"I've got a few spare shingles," Aaron King said.

Gideon watched as Gertie ducked under the teacher's desk and rattled the metal bucket.

"Gertie," he said, and the girl emerged and moved to one of the two-seater desks in ragged rows. She looked small sitting there, and the thought that his youngest child was beginning school knotted him.

Ella pointed at the red rug. "Did you know there's a gaping hole in the floor?"

Gideon was not surprised about the roof, but he had not heard about the floor.

"The windows need sealing," Miss Coates said.

Gideon crossed to a window and ran a finger along its edges. "They need a lot more than sealing." Even his slight touch broke off bits of the crumbling frame. It was likely the other five windows were just as dilapidated.

"When the wind blows in the winter, the entire building creaks," Miss Coates said.

"All buildings settle and creak," Gideon said, glancing at Gertie, who mimicked his movements on another window beside Ella.

"It's not that kind of noise," the teacher retorted. "It's the sort that makes one think the ceiling might come down. The students become quite distracted."

"How did it get to be so bad?" Walter Hicks wanted to know.

Aaron King shrugged. "One day at a time."

Robert Haney, the second *English* father, spoke for the first time. "We get busy with the summer harvest and then planting and then the fall harvest."

"And then the children are back in school," Miss Coates said. "You're all busy with your farms, but I do feel that for the safety of the children, this is the time for a concerted effort."

Gideon tilted his head back to inspect the ceiling beams. "Perhaps we should ask the school district for funds to build a new structure entirely. If we had the supplies we need, I'm sure the Amish families would be happy to build."

"One of your frolics?" Walter said.

Gideon nodded. With proper planning, the Amish erected barns in only a couple of days. A one-room school should not be difficult to organize.

"I doubt the district would underwrite the construction," Robert said. "I see in the newspaper all the time how the schools lack proper funding. And the process of requesting funds and awaiting a decision would take longer than we have before school begins again."

"Perhaps we just need to impress upon the authorities the extent of the need," Ella said.

"I've been trying and trying," Miss Coates said. "It's as if the superintendent turns and walks the other way when he sees me coming."

"Gertie," Gideon said, "come stand with your *daed*."

Walter Hicks leaned against a beam, as if to test its strength. The cracking sound pulled Gideon's heart out of his chest.

⤞✦⤝

"Watch out!" Gideon's voice boomed.

Ella lurched toward Gertie and snatched her up.

"No!" Gertie writhed in protest.

Ella held tight.

"Gertie!" The edge in Gideon's voice startled his daughter into compliance.

Ella held the girl in a viselike grip and stumbled through a maze of desks toward the back of the schoolhouse. Above her, the ceiling split open.

"I see the sky!" Gertie said.

Ella squeezed tighter, wishing she had a third hand for raising the hem of her skirt so she could see her feet and move faster.

"Ella! Gertie!"

Ella turned toward Gideon's frantic voice, a tone she had never heard from him before. She stumbled where two desks narrowed the aisle and shoved at one of them with her hip.

"I've got her," Ella shouted. "Everybody get out!"

Nora moved quickly. Mr. Hicks and Mr. Haney hesitated but headed for the door. Ella had her eye on the opening. Behind her, the front wall of the classroom groaned. In reflex, Ella turned her head toward the sound. The blackboard snapped off the wall on one end, rent down the center, and dangled.

Ella gave the obstructive furniture one last shove as the structure heaved. A fracture traveled above her head. Half the ceiling crashed down, strewing debris. Ella did not see the origin of the board that smacked the back of her head.

CHAPTER 2

Gideon shouldered past Aaron King and back into the school-house.

"Ella!"

"Here!"

Her voice led Gideon to the shelter Ella had found under a desk, her arms still clasping his daughter.

"Has it stopped?" Anxiety threaded Ella's voice.

"For now." Gideon squatted and reached to take Gertie from Ella. "Come quickly."

With his daughter over his shoulder, Gideon reached for Ella's hand, not caring who might see the affection between them. Only when they were safely out in the sunlight did he realize Gertie was limp against his neck.

"Gertie!"

The child made no sound. Gideon knelt to lay her on the ground and rubbed a hand over her face. "Gertie!"

"She was fine when I went under the desk." Ella knelt beside Gideon.

Gertie's intake of air came before she opened her eyes. Gideon exhaled his own breath.

"*Daed.*"

"I'm right here."

"I don't want to go to that school."

"Does anything hurt?" Gideon put a thumb under Gertie's chin and looked into her eyes, satisfied that all he saw was shock.

"No. Ella wouldn't let go."

"She wanted to keep you safe." Gideon turned grateful eyes to Ella. "Thank you. I would never have reached her in time."

"As far as it is within my power, I would never let anything happen to Gertie," Ella said.

Gideon looked carefully at Ella now. She was noticeably more scraped up than Gertie. Bits of wood stuck to her bonnet, and gray dust spattered her blue dress. "What about you? Are you hurt?"

She put a hand to the back of her head. "Something took a whack at me. I may have a bit of a headache tonight."

"Promise me you'll rest."

She nodded, and Gideon allowed himself to meet and hold her gaze.

"I want to go home," Gertie said. "Carry me."

"Of course," Gideon said. "First show me that you can move your arms and legs."

Gertie responded by moving all four limbs at once. "Now can we go home?"

Gideon slid his arms under Gertie's shoulders and knees and unfolded his stocky form as if she weighed nothing more than the wind.

Miss Coates stepped toward them. "I'm sorry. Even I did not realize the true condition of the schoolhouse."

"You're not to blame," Gideon said.

"If I'd had any idea, I would never have suggested that we meet inside."

"This will certainly make our case with the school district. It's time for a new building."

"It's definitely the strongest argument we could hope for," Miss Coates said.

Walter Hicks fell into step beside Gideon. "I will draft a detailed account of today's event and deliver it personally to the school superintendent first thing in the morning."

"Thank you, Walter." Gideon glanced at Ella again, looking for reassurance that she was unscathed.

Gideon carried Gertie to his wagon with everyone else following as if no one wanted to be left behind. "Can you sit up?"

Gertie nodded. "I just want to go home."

Gideon settled her on the bench of the wagon. If she got tired, she could lay her head in his lap as they drove home.

"Shall I take you home?" he said to Ella.

Miss Coates spoke. "I have my cart. I'll take Ella. You just look after Gertie."

"Yes," Ella agreed. "Take her home. Watch her closely."

"You're sure?"

"I'm fine." She brushed debris off her dress and straightened her bonnet.

Gideon noticed Ella moved more slowly than normal.

"*Daed*," Gertie said, "please, can we go?"

"Go," Ella said.

❦

The other three men left shortly after Gideon, leaving Ella and Nora Coates standing and staring at the building with its roof yawning open to the elements on one side.

"What should we do?" Ella asked. "Is there anything we should take out to keep safe?"

"I feel badly enough that you were all in the building on my account," Nora said. "I can't ask you to go back in."

"You wanted the men to see for themselves."

"I was not expecting the encounter to be quite this dramatic." Nora wrapped her arms around herself.

"I hate to think what would have happened with thirty-five children inside and you responsible for their safety," Ella said. "That would have been an unreasonable expectation—unfair to ask of you."

"Yes. From that perspective, what happened today is the lesser of two evils."

"There can be no argument now that we need a new school. Surely the superintendent will release the funds under these circumstances—and quickly."

Nora looked away. "I rather suspect he will propose another solution."

"What other solution could there be?" Ella gestured toward the building. "Even if the roof could be repaired, there are so many other things wrong."

"I don't know," Nora murmured. "I can't help but feel that there is a reason he has resisted all my requests for help before this. I

15

wouldn't have turned to the local committee if I thought the super-intendent would help."

Ella examined Nora's profile, unable to push away the sense that Nora had something else to say.

"What is it?" Ella stepped into Nora's gaze.

"I wanted to leave the school in good condition."

"Leave the school?"

"I'm not certain of anything," Nora said, "but I may not be returning to teach this fall."

Ella was certain Nora had not mentioned this possibility to the parents committee. Gideon would have told her if he'd known the school would need a new teacher. He would be responsible to help select another young *English* woman willing to appreciate the Amish ways.

"I haven't yet signed my contract for the new school year," Nora said.

"Don't you intend to?" Conflicting possible answers to the question swirled through Ella's mind.

"I must decide by the end of July," Nora said. "That would still give the committee a few weeks to hire another teacher."

"I didn't realize you were unhappy in your position."

"Oh, I'm not!" Nora was quick to respond. Then she smiled. "I'm rather hoping for a marriage proposal very soon. My beau knows that if I sign a contract we wouldn't be able to marry until next summer."

Ella fumbled for words. "That's. . .good news. I hope you'll be very happy." How difficult would it be to find a new teacher in just a few weeks—someone willing to teach in the middle of farmland and accommodate both *English* and Amish students?

"He hasn't asked me yet." Nora's laugh sounded nervous.

"But you want him to."

Nora's lips stretched into a smile. "Yes. Very much. I'm quite smitten, I'm afraid."

Ella recognized the sensation. She was quite smitten herself.

"You should teach," Nora said.

"I'm not qualified," Ella answered easily, seeing nothing to dispute. "I didn't go to high school, much less the teachers college."

"We've only met a few times," Nora said, "but I see something in you. You're qualified in other ways."

"I assure you I'm not," Ella said. She kept house for her father for eleven years before he remarried, and she gladly looked forward to running Gideon's household. She knew nothing about teaching.

"You always have a book with you."

Ella sighed. She would have to explain to Mrs. White at the library about the book she'd left in the collapsed building.

"There must be a way to demonstrate your capacity," Nora said.

Ella said nothing. She also was hoping for a marriage proposal very soon. Embarking on a teaching career was the furthest thing from her mind.

"How are you feeling?" Nora asked.

"Well enough, under the circumstances." The headache Ella anticipated had not yet materialized. She felt only a sting at the back of her head.

"Are you well enough to ride into town with me before I take you home?"

"Oh, I don't know," Ella said. "Haven't we had enough excitement for one afternoon?" Riding into town would take them miles in the wrong direction.

"I want you to meet someone." Nora raised her eyebrows with hope.

"If this is about teaching—"

"Just meet someone. A new friend."

Ella hesitated.

"We'll have a nice chat along the way. And I'll bring you home whenever you like."

"Well, all right." Ella had no need to hurry home. Rachel looked after the house now. If she wished, Ella only needed to be present for the family's evening meal.

Nora led the way to where she'd left her horse and cart. They climbed in.

"My beau has a Ford," Nora said. "As soon as he proposes, I intend to learn to drive it."

The horse began a casual trot toward Seabury.

❧

Margaret Simpson admired the three pristine erasers and set them an equal distance apart on the chalk ledge at the front of her class-room. Her list of ways she hoped to prepare for this year's class was lengthy, but she would have to accomplish many of the tasks at home. In the middle of the summer, the principal of Seabury's consolidated grade school allowed teachers limited access to the building. Margaret looked at her watch, knowing that any moment now the principal would stand in the doorway to her classroom and clear his throat. He was a stickler for rules, including the schedule on which he would open and close the building over the summer.

Few of the other teachers bothered to come into the building in the months when classes did not meet. Some had other jobs for the summer. Some helped on family farms. Some traveled. Margaret, though, seemed to have nothing more exciting to do than straighten her classroom and make lists. She decided to scoot out before Mr. Tarkington could make her feel that she somehow inconvenienced him. Pushing papers into the leather satchel she had carried since she entered teachers college eleven years earlier, Margaret readied to depart the building. She would do Mr. Tarkington the courtesy of stopping by the office to thank him for opening the building.

A few minutes later, Margaret stepped into the bright afternoon sunlight. July was not one of her favorite times of year in eastern Ohio, though January was far worse in the other extreme. At least she had mastered using fabrics and styles that allowed her clothing to breathe. She was grateful for the current fashions that did away with cumbersome underskirts and allowed shortened hems above the ankle. The new garb was far more practical than what Margaret had grown up with.

Outside the school, Margaret turned to look at it. Her first position out of teachers college had been a one-room schoolhouse in southern Ohio, but four years ago she jumped at the chance to teach in a larger—and newer—consolidated school. While she was confident she could capably teach any grade, teaching first graders was a good match for her. She shielded her eyes from the sun and looked over at the adjacent high school. From her classroom windows, when school was in session, she could see the older students coming and going from the high school. Every year they looked younger to Margaret.

Of course the students were the same age coming into high school. It was Margaret who aged. When she became a teacher, she never imagined she would still be teaching at age twenty-nine. She would meet someone, as her college classmates had. She would marry and have her own children.

It hadn't happened. And now Margaret did not know a single unwed woman her age with any serious expectation of marriage. Until a few weeks ago, Margaret would have—reluctantly—put herself in that category and focused on being grateful she had work she enjoyed. Now she was not sure.

Margaret's rented bungalow was only six blocks from the school. She owned a car because her uncle had given her one he'd tired of, but it was foolish to think an unmarried woman would own a home. The bungalow, with its low-pitched roofline and overhanging eaves, was no architectural wonder. It had come from the Sears, Roebuck catalog as a kit, arriving in a railroad boxcar. Her landlord had constructed it himself eight years ago. The home was cozy with a small second bedroom, but its best feature was the front porch shaded by an extension of the main roof. Except in the harshest winter months, Margaret enjoyed sitting on the porch with a book or her sewing.

Her shoes clicked down the narrow sidewalk in automatic movements.

When she saw him—as she hoped she would—Margaret slowed her steps to give Gray Truesdale time to catch her eye and cross the street to say hello.

Gray was the reason Margaret was not fully certain she would never marry.

She nearly melted the first time he spoke to her and was so tongue-tied that she could not imagine he would ever repeat the act of kindness. Or perhaps it had been pity for the spinster schoolteacher.

But Gray Truesdale had never married, either, and he was more than mildly eligible. At thirty-five, he owned a home that had not come from a kit. One of the first men to own an automobile truck, Gray did steady business in deliveries and home repairs.

Margaret liked a man who was not afraid of hard work.

She liked Gray Truesdale. He had spoken to her again after the initial social disaster, and gradually she relaxed and enjoyed herself with him. He made her tingle up and down. It was the oddest sensation, but delicious.

Now he waved and approached. "I wondered if I might run into you."

"And you have." She smiled.

"I might be in your neighborhood later," he said.

"Oh? When might that be?" The familiar exchange had become a litany between them.

"Around suppertime, I expect," he said.

"I expect I'll be taking a roast chicken out of the oven about then."

"Is that so?"

"Yes, I do believe I will be."

"I imagine it will be a juicy roast chicken."

"That's the kind my mother taught me how to cook."

Gray nodded. "Well, then, I'll certainly be mindful."

He tipped his black hat and backed away.

Margaret tingled.

⋯⊰✦⊱⋯

Ella recognized the neighborhood they turned into.

"Lindy Lehman lives on this street," she said.

"That's right," Nora said. "Do you know Lindy?"

"She's my stepmother's oldest friend." Ella did not add that Lindy was the sister of Gideon's deceased wife. Most *English* had enough trouble sorting out Amish relationships. The simplest explanation was best.

Nora's brow creased. "But your stepmother is Amish, isn't she?"

"That's right."

"And Lindy. . .is not."

"No. She chose not to be baptized and join the church, but she grew up among our people. Lindy and Rachel are still close friends."

"Is that allowed?"

"No one can force another person to believe," Ella said. "Officially Lindy was never a member of the church, so she has done nothing wrong by leaving."

"She has quite a workshop behind her house."

"I've seen it," Ella said. "She's talented. Her birdhouses are popular all over Geauga County."

"It's an unusual occupation for a woman, don't you think?"

"She used to spend a lot of time watching her grandfather."

"He was Amish?"

"Yes, but he didn't see the harm in a girl learning to use a few tools."

"Perhaps I'll order one of her birdhouses," Nora said. "I wonder if she knows Margaret Simpson across the street."

"Is that who you want me to meet?"

Nora nodded. "She teaches at the consolidated grade school. If anyone could help you become a teacher, it would be Margaret."

Ella held her tongue. Nora did not understand how complicated the notion was—or that Ella and Gideon were talking of marriage.

Nora pulled her horse alongside an automobile parked in the street in front of a bungalow.

"That's Margaret's car," she said. "I confess to envy. I feel so old-fashioned to still be driving a horse and cart."

Ella gave an awkward smile.

Nora blushed. "I meant no offense. I respect the ways of your people. I know you don't use cars. But I have my eye on the future. I just don't know how Margaret affords an automobile of her own. Maybe the town teachers earn a higher salary than the rural teachers."

Envy was not entirely unfamiliar to Ella, though she had no aspirations to the *English* ways.

"There's Margaret now." Nora guided her horse to the side of the street.

Margaret stood on her front porch and waved. Nora and Ella walked up the brick path to the bungalow. Nora made introductions.

"I thought you two would enjoy meeting," Nora said. "Margaret is a wonderful teacher and a good friend."

"Do you have a child in Nora's class?" Margaret asked Ella.

"I'm not married," Ella said, "but she's been the teacher for my stepbrothers, and I have friends with children in Nora's school."

Nora sighed. "Or what's left of my school."

Margaret's eyebrows went up.

"The schoolhouse is in serious need of repair," Ella explained.

"We need funding," Nora said. "Do you have any influence with the superintendent?"

"Me?" Margaret said. "I've been in the county for four years, and Mr. Brownley barely knows my name."

"I don't want to leave the farm families in the lurch," Nora said.

"It will be hard enough to find a teacher if I don't return, but now they need a new building."

"I wish I could help," Margaret said. "I have absolutely no influence on these decisions, but I do have a fresh pitcher of cold lemonade."

Ella silently admitted her thirst. July days seemed to bring perpetual thirst. And she liked Margaret Simpson. She smiled acceptance of the hospitality.

CHAPTER 3

Gertrude, please don't play in the dirt." James Lehman's tone was kind, but he mustered a firm expression. He knew this child well. If he gave her any reason to believe his request lacked conviction, Gertie would dawdle until one of the endless tasks on the Wittmer farm distracted him.

"I'm not playing," Gertie said. "I'm experimenting."

"Then I suggest you experiment in the grass. "You know your *aunti* Miriam doesn't like you dragging dirt into the house at suppertime."

Gertie tossed her stick aside and rose from the crouch that already had left an inch-high gray ring around the hem of her dress. She moved to the grass, where she would be content to lie on her back and squint at the clouds.

Gideon came around the corner of the barn, wiping sweat on his sleeve.

"How is she?" he asked.

"She hasn't said a word all afternoon about the school falling in," James said. After six days, Gertie was beginning to believe not all schools were like the one she'd visited.

"Good. No nightmare last night either," Gideon said.

"Sit in the shade for a few minutes." James gestured to the empty outdoor chair beside him, part of a set he'd made several years earlier. "The heat will get the best of you."

Gideon dropped into the chair and glanced at Gertie sprawled on the ground. "Where are Tobias and Savilla?"

"I sent them both to the woodpile to make sure Miriam has enough for the kitchen stove for a few days."

"We could eat a cold supper more often, you know." Gideon lifted his hat and ran his fingers through limp, damp hair. "Miriam is the one who suffers most when the kitchen heats up."

"There's no talking to her when she makes up her mind to cook," James said. "Now Savilla wants to learn, which gives Miriam more reason."

Smiling, Gideon nodded. "I don't know what I would have done without you these last five years. After Betsy died. . ."

"Hush. Betsy was our niece. We loved her and we love you." James turned his gaze across the property to the *dawdihaus* Gideon had built when James and Miriam arrived to help with the house and children after Betsy's sudden death. Without children of their own, James had imagined he and Miriam would live into their old age in the farmhouse across the state that they had occupied since they were newlyweds. Miriam was the one to say they ought to move so they could care for Betsy's family.

"I'd like to have Lindy out more often," Gideon said. "My children should know their mother's sister better than they do."

"She comes if you ask."

"I know. But I also know Miriam tends to fuss even more when Lindy is around."

James laughed. "Are you suggesting I should handle my wife? What would she do with herself if she didn't have you to fuss over?"

"Put her feet up and get the rest she deserves."

James had to admit Miriam looked ragged recently.

"Still no news from the superintendent?" James asked.

Gideon pushed out a slow breath. "It's been a week since Walter Hicks took that letter into town. You'd think that this close to the beginning of school the board would act quickly."

James nodded. "They could have a special meeting or something."

"We need to make sure no one goes in the schoolhouse."

James scrunched up his face. "Who would go in there? Everybody knows half the roof fell in."

"I wish I could be sure," Gideon said. "I put up a sign and roped off the front entrance, but you never know."

"I'll go by in the morning on my way into town. I promised Lindy to help her with some deliveries."

"I've heard some call you 'Wagon James,'" Gideon said. "Do you ever say no to a delivery?"

James shook his head. "Not if I'm sure it will help folks if I deliver. A man wants to be useful."

"I should get back to the barn. One more stall to muck. Shall I take Gertie with me?"

"I've already pulled her out of the dirt over there." James gestured. "I might as well look after her until supper."

Gideon paced over to the patch of dirt. He looked up at the scene before him and back to the dirt. "It's a drawing of the horse pasture."

"How can you tell from scratches in the dirt?"

"It's not scratches. She drew what she saw. The fence is perfect."

James got up to look for himself. "Why would Gertie do such a thing?"

Gideon rubbed a boot through the dirt and scattered the stick drawing.

Gideon could tell from the timbre of the approaching clatter that the horse pulled a cart on the brink of repairs.

"It's Miss Coates," he said.

"Maybe she has news from the superintendent."

"Maybe. She's smiling."

In the sunshine-blanketed grass a few yards away, Gertie sat up. "I said I don't want to go to that school."

"Gertie," Gideon said, "go inside and see if Miriam needs some help."

Gertie obeyed without hesitation, as if to impress on her father that she wanted nothing to do with the teacher or the school.

Miss Coates pulled her cart up alongside the barn and got out. Her face beamed. "Since you're the head of the parents committee, I wanted you to be the first to know."

"I appreciate your taking the trouble to come all the way out here," Gideon said. "Good news from the school board, I hope."

"Oh, I'm afraid I have no word on the matter of the schoolhouse. This is another matter, but not unrelated. I've accepted a proposal to be married in a few weeks. Obviously under these circumstances, I won't be continuing as teacher."

Gideon nodded. Obviously. A stone settled in his stomach.

"Congratulations," he said. "I hope your marriage brings you every happiness."

"Thank you," Miss Coates said. "I came as soon as I could. I wanted you to have every available day to begin the search for a new teacher. She'll have to be approved by the district, of course. I'm sure the superintendent will have some names for you to correspond with. I've already submitted my resignation."

"I'll contact him immediately." Perhaps this second line of inquiry would prod the superintendent to release funds for the new school.

"I hope your little girl has recovered from the events of last week," Miss Coates said.

"She's not too keen on school right now," Gideon said, "but I'm sure she'll be fine."

Miss Coates hoisted herself back into the cart. "I won't take up any more of your time. If I can help with the search in any way, please do let me know. I won't be moving away for another two weeks."

The horse trotted out of the farmyard. With a grin still on her face, Miss Coates offered a final wave.

Behind Gideon, the back door of his home opened. Miriam stepped out.

"What was that all about?" she said.

Gideon sighed. "We don't have a school building, and now we don't have a teacher, either."

"Miss Coates is getting married." James sidled over to his wife and kissed her cheek.

Miriam tilted her head and lost her gaze in James's eyes.

Pangs of loss heated Gideon's belly. He had hoped to have fifty years of Betsy looking into his eyes that way. She'd been gone five years, and now he hoped to have a long life with Ella, but still grief washed through him in odd moments.

⸎

Even after being out of school for twelve years, Ella still cultivated the rhythm of opening a book every day and expecting to learn something interesting. The Seabury Public Library had a small but varied collection, and Ella sometimes checked out her favorite books every few months, either to read them again or simply because she enjoyed having them within reach on her bedside table. Since her father's marriage to Rachel, who gladly shared household chores, Ella had more time than ever to absorb what the library offered.

She was running a finger along a shelf of bird and wildlife books on a Monday morning when a pair of green eyes startled her by staring back at her over the tops of the books. She gasped.

"Hello, Ella."

The voice was familiar, but Ella could not place it immediately. Margaret Simpson came around the end of the aisle.

"Oh, it's you," Ella whispered. "I'm afraid I didn't recognize you just by your eyes!"

Margaret chortled and then shushed herself. "I was hoping they might have some new animal books I might share with my students. But first graders need illustrations, and scientists seem to prefer lots of big words."

Ella flipped through the books in her arms. "This is my favorite book on birds. There are lots of words, but the drawings are delightful."

Margaret took the book and opened it in the middle and turned a few pages. "Mmm. *Birds of Geauga County.* I see what you mean. Your favorite, you say?"

Ella twisted her lips sheepishly. "I check it out four times a year."

Margaret handed the book back to Ella. "I'll let you enjoy it again now, but I'm going to remember it when school begins. I suppose you heard about Nora Coates."

"Yes, Mr. Wittmer told me. He's on the parents committee."

"I rather think that the condition of the schoolhouse will be more formidable than finding a new teacher. Recent graduates of the teachers college will be eager to go wherever there is a position available."

"I hope so," Ella said. "We only have six weeks to sort it all out."

"What else do you like to read?" Margaret lowered her voice further, glancing toward the librarian at the desk.

"Recipe books. Agriculture. Veterinary medicine. Waterways. *The Farmer's Almanac,*" Ella said. "Occasionally some American history, particularly biographies of some of the presidents."

"Goodness. I love your curious mind. I have a small library of my own at home. You're welcome to borrow anything you'd like."

"Thank you."

"I suppose you've read all the great novels. *Jane Eyre? David Copperfield?*"

"I don't generally read fiction." Ella had never read a novel.

"I'm sure we can find a story you'd like."

"I don't want to put you to any trouble." Ella did not want to imagine explaining to her father—or to Gideon—that she was idly passing the time with an *English* novel. It was one thing to read for edification or to form useful skills, but another to indulge in a story that was not true.

"The next time you're in town, feel free to knock on my door."

"You're kind." Ella clasped her stack of books against her chest. "I'd better check out and be on my way. I need to. . .well, I should. . .be going."

She stepped quickly toward the desk. Margaret Simpson was perfectly nice and seemed determined to be friends—which was what unnerved Ella. She hadn't had an *English* friend since Sally Templeton when they were fourteen years old.

"Three yards of plain white cotton fabric," Miriam said. "Watch as the clerk measures it out. Don't let him cut it short."

"I won't," James said.

"If you forget the *kaffi*, you'll have nothing to drink with your breakfast tomorrow."

"I won't forget."

"There are two baskets of eggs on the back porch for you to take in for store credit. You know what the price is on those, right?"

"I do."

"Blue thread. Two spools. The girls are outgrowing their dresses again."

"On my list."

"And don't forget to stop by Lindy's and see if she's finished painting the rack I asked her to make."

"I won't forget."

James found Miriam's fussy, bossy moods endearing. It would bother some husbands, but he appreciated her mind for details to keep both Gideon's home and their own *dawdihaus* running smoothly. He supposed that if they'd had their own children, Miriam would have focused her fussing on them. But they'd had Betsy and Lindy and their brothers and sisters to dote on, and now they had Betsy's children.

It was already hot even before midmorning. James filled a jug with water to take in the wagon.

"No rest for the weary," Miriam said.

That was what James feared. He hoped Gideon would marry Ella soon. At least when fall came, all three children would be in school for the first time and Miriam's days would ease.

CHAPTER 4

On the beige settee with green and blue tapestry pillows, Margaret sat in her front room with hands in her lap and feet flat on the floor. Almost flat. One toe wiggled in rhythm with the ticking second hand of the clock on the mantel. She refused to give in to the urge to open the oven too soon. Patience would yield impeccable golden crusts, steam rising from the precise vents she had cut in the tops before sliding two pies into the oven side by side.

Tick. Tock. Tick.

A fine red thread ran through the weave of the pillows. Margaret seldom looked at them closely enough to notice it.

Tick. Tock. Tick.

The minute hand circled the clock face seven more times before Margaret popped up and pushed through the oak door into the kitchen, where the woodstove blasted intolerable heat. Temperatures on the first of August were beastly on their own. In past summers, Margaret was content with a cold plate of cheese and fruit for her supper. Her kitchen table always had half a dozen books on it, and food she could pick up with her fingers was more convenient while she read.

That was before Gray Truesdale.

Margaret took the two blackberry pies from the oven and transferred them to the cooling rack, though she had no intention of letting them cool. She wrapped each one in a fresh white towel purchased at the mercantile only four days ago. She and Gray could cut into one tonight—still warm—and she would send the other home with him.

He stopped by two or three evenings a week now. Margaret couldn't be certain he would come tonight, but she would be prepared. It was Thursday, a day he seemed to favor. She moved the coffeepot to the heat of a front burner.

Perspiration dripped from both temples. Taking a handkerchief from her skirt pocket, Margaret dabbed at the moisture while she walked through the house. The front porch would be cooler, and if Gray didn't see her sitting in her swing on a fine evening, he might think she would not welcome a visit.

Across the street and two houses down, Lindy Lehman knelt in a flower bed. When Lindy glanced up, Margaret waved. Tomorrow evening she would wander over with a friendly offering of leftover pie.

Margaret heard the grind of Gray's truck, though it had not yet come into view. Several neighbors were outside their homes. If they were paying attention, they would soon realize that Gray's visits held a pattern. What the neighbors might think of a male visitor to a woman who lived alone was a dilemma Margaret had not faced before.

She didn't care. This might be her last chance.

Gray's truck was not loud or irregular. Margaret doubted anyone else would recognize the pitch of its engine from three blocks away, but her ears were peculiarly attuned to the sound. He eased to the side of the road down the block, exited, let the door fall closed without slamming it, and plunged his hands into this pockets for a casual stroll toward Margaret's porch.

Her chest heated up just with the thought of him, and his scent filled her mind from yards away.

"Evening," he said, turning up the brick path in front of her home.

"Evening." Margaret gave the swing a slight push, determined not to appear too eager.

"It's a fine night."

"Quite lovely."

Gray reached the bottom of three broad steps, set his foot on it, and leaned on his knee. He was a tall man, and fit. When he removed his hat, dimming rays of sunlight brightened his brown eyes.

"I was just about to have some pie," Margaret said. "I wonder if you might want to sit on the porch and have a slice."

"That's the most hospitable offer I've had all day." Gray took two slow steps up the stairs.

Margaret stood and smoothed her skirt, trying to will her heart rate to slow. "I'll only be a minute."

By the time she returned with a tray of pie and coffee to set on the low table beside the swing, he sat on what Margaret had come to think of as Gray's side. He slowed the sway to take a plate from her and wait for her to sit next to him with her own pie. Margaret played with her fork for a moment while Gray filled his mouth with steaming fruit and crust.

"Mmm. You make a fine pie, Miss Margaret Simpson."

"Why, thank you."

Gray started the swing again, a gentle, fluid wobble in rhythm with the motion of his fork rising and falling. They sat in shadows now.

"I trust you know that I come around for more than your cooking," Gray said, his eyes looking straight down the length of the porch.

"I rather hoped that was the case." Beside him, Margaret pushed a clump of blackberries first one direction and then the other. "Would you like some coffee?"

"In a minute," he said. "There's something I'd like to ask you first."

"Yes?" She felt his eyes on her and turned her head to meet his gaze.

"I wonder if I might express my growing affection for you."

Margaret's breathing stilled. *Affection.*

Gray set his pie plate on the tray and took Margaret's. Had he seen her tremble? She hoped not.

"If I have your kind permission," he said, "I would very much like to kiss you."

"You do," she whispered.

Gray laid three long fingers at the side of her chin and leaned toward her. Margaret hadn't been kissed in years, and no other beau's kiss had been as delicious as this one. Gray lingered long enough to be convincing, but not so long as to raise alarms as to his intentions.

"I'll go to bed a happy man tonight."

❧❀❧

Whether or not Gray slept, Margaret did not know. As many times as she closed her eyes determined to sleep, each time she shut out the shadows of her bedroom, she remembered his kiss.

It was good to know she had not turned into a dried-up spinster who could not make a man feel something.

Growing affection. That was the way he put it. Not pity for her age. Not convenience because he didn't know another suitable woman. Affection.

Still glowing from her dreams, Margaret rose early on Friday morning, dressed carefully, gave thanks for her breakfast, made notes about what she must accomplish—no matter how distracted she was—and walked six blocks to Seabury Consolidated Grade School. The principal offered two hours this morning for teachers who wanted to enter the building.

Margaret carried her leather satchel, which contained the composition book she used for her lesson plans, a set of colorful alphabet cards to attach to the classroom walls, and a rag and tin of vegetable soap with which she would polish the desks in the room. Every six-year-old deserved to find school a cheery, welcoming place on the first day of a robust educational career.

She had reached the desks in the third row when footsteps sounded in the hall.

Good. It was time other teachers joined her determination to have classrooms ready when school resumed. The building's custodian had mopped and scrubbed the rooms thoroughly in June after school let out and undertaken a list of minor repairs, but it was up to the trained teaching staff to be ready at the first bell.

The footfalls ceased right outside her classroom door, and Margaret looked up from her task. Immediately, she abandoned her vegetable soap and stood erect.

"Good morning, gentlemen," she said.

Principal Tarkington stepped into the room with the school district superintendent, whom Margaret had met only once or twice in a room full of other teachers.

"Mr. Brownley asked me for a recommendation," the principal said, "and I have suggested he speak with you."

"Of course," Margaret said, though she could not imagine what the superintendent would need her help with.

"I have some telephone calls to return," Mr. Tarkington said, "so I'll leave you two to talk."

"Thank you, Mr. Tarkington." Margaret watched him pivot and leave the room.

Mr. Brownley began to pace along the wall of windows.

"I've received some correspondence," he said. "In responding, I require the assistance of a competent teacher dedicated to the principles of a sound public education, and Mr. Tarkington assures me that you meet this description."

"I've been teaching for nine years." Margaret rotated slowly to follow the path the superintendent was taking across the back of the classroom. "I believe I am accomplished in my profession."

"I'm glad to hear you sound confident. That is just the disposition I seek."

"I'm happy to help."

Brownley crossed his wrists behind him and paced along the opposite wall. "Have you much experience dealing with resistant parents?"

Why didn't the superintendent simply say what was on his mind?

"Occasionally I have met parents who do not understand the importance of regular school attendance," Margaret said.

Brownley nodded.

"And if a child presents a disciplinary challenge, I find it constructive to win over the parents to offer a united front in resolving the matter."

"Excellent." Brownley pulled papers out of his suit jacket. "I have here two items of correspondence signed by Mr. Gideon Wittmer and others."

"Mr. Wittmer?"

Brownley raised an eyebrow. "Do you know him?"

"Not exactly. I met someone who knows him."

"Then you will not be surprised that these particular parents have children in one of the outlying one-room schoolhouses."

"A school which is in need of both repairs and a teacher," Margaret said.

Brownley's face brightened. "I must say I had not expected you to be so informed on the matter."

"I'm afraid that is the extent of my knowledge."

Brownley pulled out the chair from behind Margaret's desk and sat down. "It's a delicate matter."

Margaret waited.

"This is the letter requesting funding for a new schoolhouse." He laid one sheet of paper on the desk and positioned a second beside it, precisely one inch apart. "And this is the letter asking for names of teachers the local parents committee might correspond with about the open position."

"I understand that these are considerable challenges," Margaret said, "given the limited time before school opens."

"If only it were as simple as that."

Margaret waited again.

"We will not be rebuilding the school, Miss Simpson, nor looking for a new teacher."

"Oh."

"Mr. Tarkington tells me you are one of his best teachers. Surely you can appreciate that these circumstances suggest that now is the right time to integrate these pupils into the consolidated school."

"We have a fine grade school. And the high school is excellent as well."

"I agree. And I'm confident that we can accommodate the thirty or so students being displaced by closing their school." Brownley folded the letters and returned them to his pocket.

"Of course I wish to be helpful," Margaret said, "but I feel unclear as to what you are asking of me." These were administrative matters. Shouldn't the superintendent and the principal work out the details of the transition?

"Mr. Tarkington tells me you can be quite persuasive."

Once again, not knowing how to answer, Margaret waited.

"Some parents may resist our plan," Brownley said. "I would like you to persuade them of its virtues."

"Me?"

"You did say you wanted to help. This will be a significant change for all of the families affected, but the Amish families in particular will need to understand that they must comply with this decision."

Margaret gulped.

Ella sat in a wooden yard chair she did not quite trust. It dated back to the early days of her parents' marriage, and it creaked. The sound was ordinary, especially for the age of the chair, but after the creaking and groaning of the schoolhouse ceiling before it caved in, she would have preferred a chair more respectful with its silence. She looked up from her book about the health of chickens and saw her stepbrother crossing the farmyard.

Stepbrother was not a word that settled naturally in her mind yet. She used it readily enough to describe members of other families, but attaching a first-person possessive pronoun to the word complicated its meaning. *My stepbrother.* She avoided saying the phrase, instead referring to both David and Seth by their names in conversation.

David was a nice enough boy—a young man. He was nearly fifteen, out of school, nearly ready to begin attending Singings and consider courting. If he had any objections to his mother's decision to marry Jedediah Hilty, Ella never heard him voice them. Yet he seemed to walk around wrapped in a secret Ella could not decipher. She wasn't even sure she wanted to. Her mind was full enough of her books and Gideon and Gideon's children.

Ella expected David would walk past her to the barn or into the house. He might nod or lift his hand in a brief wave. Instead, he shuffled toward her. She had already caught his eye, whether she meant to or not, so she couldn't ignore him now.

Silent, he stood beside her for a moment and stared down.

"How are you, David?" Ella said, wishing she could go back to her book.

"I'm fine."

He said nothing more. His eyes were not fixed on his feet, as Ella had supposed, but on the stack of books on the ground beside the chair.

"Do you like to read?" she asked.

He nodded. "Do you mind if I look at the books?"

"Go ahead."

He squatted and went through her pile. "You read a lot about animals."

"I like to understand how to take care of them," she said, "or just to enjoy them."

He had his hand on *The Birds of Geauga County.* "What's your favorite bird?"

Ella twisted her lips. "I love the sound of a mourning dove, but I like the name of the American coot."

He smiled. "I like the chimney swift for the same reason."

Now she smiled. "I didn't know you liked birds."

"They're interesting from a scientific perspective."

This surprised her. "You like to read about science?"

He nodded. "Sometimes. There are a lot of things I want to understand better. Not just science."

"What are some topics you're curious about?" This was by far the longest thread of conversation Ella and David had ever exchanged.

He tilted his head. "The war."

"The war in Europe?" Ella's heart spurted.

"I'm not supposed to be curious about that. But I am." He shuffled through the books again. "Do you have any novels?"

"No," she said slowly. "I don't read novels."

"Oh. Okay."

She let a beat pass before asking, "Do you read novels?"

"Only two or three. My *mamm* doesn't approve. She says only the *English* read them."

Ella closed her book around one finger.

"There's so much world out there." David stacked the books neatly. "I don't know why I'm supposed to be afraid of it."

"I don't think the point of our ways is to be afraid."

"Never mind." David stood up.

"David—"

But he was already walking away.

CHAPTER 5

Three days later, Margaret opened her composition book to a fresh page and smoothed it down against Gideon Wittmer's simple polished oak dining room table. Margaret could feel the solid crafts- manship of the chair she sat in and admired the smoothly sanded end tables in the front room and the braided rug that brought warmth to the wood floors.

Three days earlier she had never been on an Amish farm, and now she tried not to stare at the two bearded men in plain black suits. Though the two *English* fathers were clean shaven and dressed in the more familiar coveralls of farm laborers, their expressions matched the stern expectation of Gideon Wittmer and Aaron King.

"Thank you, Mr. Wittmer, for inviting us into your home," Mar- garet began. "Obviously we face some challenging changes."

On Friday, right after her meeting with Mr. Brownley, Margaret had driven her Model T out to the old school and seen the shambles for herself. She did not blame the school board for deciding against repairing or rebuilding.

"Why didn't the superintendent come to talk to us himself?"

It was Walter Hicks who voiced the question all four men must have been thinking. *What he really means is why did he send a woman?* She could hardly speak aloud the responses clanging in her mind. *Because you won't like his answers. Because he doesn't take your proposal seriously.*

"Mr. Brownley asked for my assistance, and I am glad to give it." Margaret spoke with more conviction than she felt.

Gideon cleared his throat. "Perhaps it would be best if you put forth Mr. Brownley's response in a clear manner."

"Yes, of course." Margaret laid a pen across the blank page in her composition book. "The board feels it will be in the best interest of the children and their families if they ride the bus and attend the well-respected consolidated schools in Seabury."

There. She'd said it. She refused to cower.

"They won't build us a school?" Robert Haney sounded stunned.

"I'm afraid not," Margaret said.

"We'll appeal the decision," Walter said. "There must be due process for an appeal."

"As a matter of procedure," Margaret said, "I'm sure there is. If you'd like, I'll find out the schedule of the school board meetings. But I must say that I believe there is little point in the effort. From an economic perspective, the decision is quite firm."

Margaret scanned the four faces, looking for glimmers of acceptance, even excitement. Surely they knew that other one-room schools around the county had been closed. The board's decision could not have come as a complete surprise.

"The schools are well run with a faculty of qualified teachers," she said. "We are broken into grades, which allow individual teachers to become specialists of sorts with particular ages. The benefits for the children will be innumerable."

Robert Haney grunted.

"The district will send a bus." Margaret forged on. "The children will have adult supervision from the moment they get on the bus in the morning until the moment they get off in the afternoon."

"It's a long day for the little ones," Walter said.

Margaret answered, "I find they adjust quite well and enjoy the additional subjects we are able to offer in the consolidated school."

Walter scratched the back of his neck. Robert twisted his lips to one side. Margaret adjusted her hips in the chair and looked at Mr. Wittmer and Mr. King.

Aaron King finally spoke. "Do you teach the basics?"

"We give students a strong foundation for learning," Margaret said.

"So the basics."

"And so much more."

Gideon's eyes widened. "We are accustomed to discussing the curriculum with the teacher. Miss Coates knew us well."

Us. The Amish. The *English* fathers would come around. The Amish parents would need more persuading.

"Why don't you come for a tour?" Margaret said brightly. "You can see for yourself the quality of education your children will receive. We can do it on Friday, if that's convenient."

❧❀❧

"Are you sure I should be here?" Trailing behind the others four days later, Ella whispered to Gideon. "I'm not one of the parents."

Gideon could not take her hand to reassure her with the others watching, though he doubted anyone would be surprised when they announced their intention to marry. James and Miriam would be delighted that Gideon had found happiness again after Betsy. Jed Hilty would be relieved that his daughter would be taken care of. Others would find it fitting that Gideon's children would have a mother again. Aaron King's wife had come along for the tour of the school, so Ella was not the only woman.

"You'll be a parent," Gideon whispered back. Soon, he hoped. She would mother his three, and they would have more *boppli* together.

The Kings had readily agreed that Ella should join the tour, not because she was a parent, but because she read so many books. Since the Amish did not have a teacher of their own to evaluate the school, Ella was the next best thing. She could look around and know exactly what the students would be learning.

When Ella's steps slowed, so did Gideon's. They tilted their heads back to look at the three stories of sprawling brick with sober columns of white-framed windows.

"It looks so official," Ella said. "It's as big as twenty school-houses."

Gideon counted twelve windows across on each story, including a double-width door at the center of the ground floor, which the Kings were very near. He wished Walter or Robert had come along for the tour. They might not have any more experience than he did with large schools, but at least they were *English* and might interpret the philosophy behind the school. But Walter said he didn't need a tour to know he would do what the law said, and one of Robert's horses went lame and he didn't want to leave her.

Aaron and Alma King stopped just short of the door, both of

them turning to gauge Gideon and Ella's progress. A moment later, the visitors stood four abreast looking at the door.

"Do we ring a bell or just go in?" Alma scanned the oversized door frame.

"Why do the *English* have to build everything so big?" Aaron scuffed one shoe against the sidewalk.

Gideon stepped forward and rapped on the door.

"They'll never hear that," Aaron said.

Gideon knocked again, harder.

"Try the knob," Alma urged.

Gideon turned the brass bulb, and the door creaked inward. The click of an *English* woman's step reassured him.

Margaret Simpson's smile was unnaturally broad. "Come in!"

⤞⋇⤝

"We pride ourselves on our commitment to prepare students to participate fully in twentieth-century life," Margaret said as she led them down the main hall that cut through the building.

Ella caught Gideon's eye. Pride? No Amish parents would want their children learning pride, and the year printed on a calendar meant far less for a full life than friends and family. Ella held no grudge, though. The Amish had been in Geauga County a long time, but Margaret Simpson had not. She lived and worked in town and had never taught an Amish student.

"The library is right down here," Margaret said.

Ella could not help but perk up at the racks of books that greeted them a moment later.

"The children are permitted to check out three books at a time, and the teachers are free to select volumes to keep in their class-rooms to supplement a unit of study."

The grid of walnut tables at the center of the library looked inviting. Ella could imagine herself finding a quiet spot and spreading out a stack of books.

"Who helps the children select appropriate reading material?" Gideon asked.

"The librarian gets to know the children, and of course the teachers will know if a book is beyond a child's ability."

Savilla would follow the rules. And Tobias was old enough to know that he ought not to pull a novel off the shelf. It was Gertie who—once she learned to read—would soak up everything in front of her. Once Ella and Gideon were married, she would have to watch carefully what came home in Gertie's book strap.

They walked farther down the hall. Margaret gestured toward two heavy cabinets.

"These are the art cupboards," she said. "We don't have an art teacher yet, but the grade-level teachers are encouraged to nurture artistic expression. I'm sure we'll be delighted to discover what artistic talent your children will bring into the school."

Ella and Gideon glanced at each other. Art certainly was beyond the Amish basics. Sketching a design for a building or a quilt top was a matter of practicality to accomplish the task, but nurturing artistic expression was another.

They continued down the endless hall.

"The music room is way at the back," Margaret said, "so as not to disturb any of the classrooms. All our students learn to read music and sing harmonies. Once they are in the sixth grade, they may take lessons on a musical instrument. We have a delightful man who comes in, and the music store on Main Street offers instruments at reasonable prices."

Margaret pointed out the paved playground behind the building. Why children would want to play on such an unforgiving surface befuddled Ella. Then she took them up a staircase to classrooms on the second floor.

Margaret was overeager, in Ella's opinion. They went into several classrooms, representing different ages, where Margaret pulled textbooks off shelves and flipped them open.

Mathematics. Literature. Science. World history. Health and hygiene. Geography. Modern inventions. Great works of art.

Ella could not help thinking of David. He was too old for grade school now, but what might he have thought if presented with these options when he was still in school?

Ella paid close attention to Margaret's explanations, moistening her lips every few minutes in concentration. Alma King bore a steady, intense scowl. Aaron looked overwhelmed. Gideon asked a few questions about some of the books. Margaret did her best to answer them, but Ella could see that her responses tightened the tension in Gideon's expression.

Margaret was friendly and talkative and enthusiastic, all qualities Ella easily admired.

But when the superintendent sent Margaret to talk to the Amish parents, he might just as well have put her on a train blindfolded.

⚜

The tour had not gone well. The expressions on the faces of her four Amish guests told Margaret that she'd said all the wrong things. For days afterward she reviewed the conversation. She was so determined to impress them, and make them *want* to send their children to the consolidated school, that she hadn't heard the true questions folded into the polite inquires.

School would begin in four weeks. And if the Amish children did not arrive on the first day, Margaret would have both Mr. Tarkington and Mr. Brownley to answer to.

Perhaps it was not too late. Perhaps she could still persuade the Amish parents that she wanted to make their children's transition as smooth as she possibly could.

For this reason, on the Monday morning after the tour, Margaret made sure she had plenty of gasoline in her Model T and headed for the Amish farmlands and the nearest *English* neighbors. She did her best to calculate the miles and judge how long the children would be on the bus. The most outlying farm could be farther than she realized. She didn't yet have a list of the students the grade school expected. For now, she made sure she knew where the hidden turnoffs were and where to look for the clusters of farm buildings that might mark the homes of students who would venture into an intimidating new school in one short month.

It was intimidating even for the Amish parents. Margaret should have seen that before now.

Her satchel on the seat beside her held the true mission of the morning.

Margaret pleased herself by finding the road to Gideon Wittmer's farm more efficiently than she had the first time she visited. A man—not Gideon—tugged a reluctant calf out of the barn and into the pasture. Perhaps she had confused herself after all.

She shut off the engine of her car. "Have I found the Wittmer farm?"

"Yes, you have." The man lifted his head and pushed his straw hat about an inch off his forehead.

"I recognize you," Margaret said. "You're the gentleman who comes to help Lindy Lehman with deliveries of the beautiful birdhouses she paints. They call you Wagon James."

"I won't deny it. Lindy is my niece—my brother's daughter. I'm James Lehman."

"I'm Lindy's neighbor, Margaret Simpson."

A screen door slammed closed, and Gideon appeared on his front porch.

"Good morning, Mr. Wittmer."

"Good morning, Miss Simpson. Thank you again for the tour of your school."

Your school. Not *the* school. Margaret resolved not to read anything into Gideon's choice of pronouns. She picked up her satchel and got out of the automobile as gracefully as she could.

"I have a bit more information from the superintendent," she said, reaching into her satchel. "This is a letter about the bus route and where the children will be picked up."

Gideon took the envelope from her but did not open it. "I appreciate the trouble you've taken to bring it all the way out here."

"No trouble at all." Margaret straightened her hat. "Mr. Brownley thought perhaps the communication should come to you first as the head of the parents committee. I imagine letters will go out to everyone very soon."

Gideon nodded but did not speak. The silence thickened, leaving Margaret feeling exposed.

"Do you have any questions?" she managed to say.

"You've been kind," Gideon said.

"I want to be helpful." She pointed at the envelope. "There's a map with the letter. Mr. Brownley asks that you verify the locations of the farms with school-age children."

"I will."

"If there's any discrepancy. . ."

"I'll make sure he knows. Thank you again for coming."

He had dismissed her. Margaret was backing up toward her car now, suddenly anxious to be on her way. The dust cloud her tires stirred up as she drove off the farm made her cough.

CHAPTER 6

Every chair in Gideon's front room was occupied. Six additional straight-backed wooden chairs from the dining room formed a back row against one wall. James Lehman was not a father, but he was interested in the education question that would affect the entire congregation. He leaned against a door frame at the rear of the assembly.

So far Chester Mast did most of the talking. Now he pounded his fist into his thigh. "How can we expect our children to grow up untainted by the world if we send them into this worldly environment?"

John Hershberger agreed. "Neither the setting nor the companions are Christian. If our children go to this school, we lose them to the world."

"The world is changing," Cristof Byler said.

"Not for the better," Chester shot back.

Gideon showed the palm of one hand to the gathering. "We must speak in an orderly manner so that all may hear." He was one father among many. If he were not on the parents committee, he gladly would have yielded leading this meeting to one of the others.

"Let every soul be subject unto the higher powers." Joshua Glick quoted Romans 13. "For there is no power but of God: the powers that be are ordained of God. Whosoever therefore resisteth the power, resisteth the ordinance of God."

"Train up a child in the way he should go: and when he is old, he will not depart from it." Jed Hilty responded to Romans with Proverbs. "It is the God-given role of parents to train up the children God gives us."

"We've been sending our children to the state's schools all along," Joshua said.

"But we knew the teachers. We oversaw the curriculum and knew what she was teaching." Cristof Byler hung his head as if in grief. "What will happen to our children if they are exposed to the world to the degree that the *English* propose?"

"Isaiah," Gideon said, "we haven't heard from you."

With twelve children, some married with little ones of their own and some still in school, Isaiah Borntrager was sure to have an opinion.

Isaiah spoke softly but with an unyielding tone. "We can teach our children everything they need to know to follow the Lord without involving the *English*."

"So you are in favor of defying the authorities?" Gideon asked.

"I am in favor of obeying God's ordinances to bring up my children in the admonition of the Lord."

"There could be trouble if we do as you suggest," Gideon said.

"It seems to me," Isaiah said, "that there will be trouble for us no matter what we do. Either we rile the authorities or we risk losing our own children to the *English* ways."

Silence.

The range of posturing and opinions collected in Gideon's home came down to Isaiah's two realities.

James pushed away from the door frame. "I am not a father," he said, "so I do not face the decision the rest of you face. I know you will also consider the good of the congregation. Several weeks remain before the start of school. Let us make it a time of prayer, beseeching the Lord for wisdom."

Men around the room nodded.

The front door opened, and six-year-old Gertie crossed through the room to find her father.

"The mailman brought a letter," Gertie whispered into his ear. "He told me it looked important and that I should give it to you immediately."

❧

The chickens raised a ruckus at the sound of an *English* automobile crunching through the gravel lane leading to the Hilty farm. Ella let a basket of wet laundry thud to the ground below the clothesline and shaded her eyes to assess the arrival. A flash of green told her the vehicle belonged to Lindy Lehman. Ella walked out to meet the visitor.

"Did Rachel know you were coming?" Ella said as Lindy closed the driver's door behind her.

"It's a surprise." Lindy walked around to the rear of the car.

"She'll be glad to see you under any circumstances."

Lindy opened the trunk, and Ella gasped at its contents. "It's beautiful!"

Lindy grinned. "David's birthday is coming up. I thought I'd bring him an early present."

Ella lifted the birdhouse reverently. She would know one of Lindy's birdhouses anywhere—the construction without nails, the precise cut of the openings, the rich hues of paint colors harkening to traditional Amish dyes.

"I only recently discovered how much David knows about birds," Ella said. Together they ambled toward the house. "I met your neighbor recently, too—Margaret Simpson."

"A friendly sort, wouldn't you say?"

"Very."

"I suspect she has a beau." Lindy chuckled. "It's sweet to watch the way he drops by casually to sit on the porch. I'm not sure what they'll do when the weather snaps."

Ella smiled. "The Amish find ways to court without much fuss. I suppose the *English* can do it as well."

Lindy turned up one corner of her mouth. "Sounds like the voice of experience."

Ella blushed.

"Gideon's been mourning my sister a long time." Lindy held Ella's gaze. "You'll make him happy. Betsy would have wanted it."

"Thank you, Lindy," Ella said. "I do love him."

Ella had never spoken to Lindy about courting. Had Gideon? Maybe it was James or Miriam.

They meandered around the side of the house.

"Will you have a booth at the auction?" Ella asked. "It's coming up soon."

"Same as last year," Lindy said. "Once I sell what I have, I'll close up and enjoy the rest of the day."

Ella pulled open the back door. "Rachel?"

Rachel appeared promptly—and dropped her jaw at the beauty of Lindy's creation.

"For David," Lindy said.

"He's out in the barn with Jed," Rachel said, "but he's going to love this."

"I heard about the school board's decision." Lindy arranged the birdhouse on the kitchen table.

Rachel sank into a chair. "I don't know what to think. At least Seth is twelve. If Jed decides he should go to school, he'll manage. I feel sorry for the parents who have little ones to put on a bus by themselves."

Like Gertie. At least she would have her sister with her, but Savilla was only nine herself.

"Consolidation might be a good thing," Lindy said.

Rachel popped out of her chair and snatched a dish towel off the pie rack. "Of course you would say that."

Ella winced.

"I'm only trying to see the positive," Lindy said. "It's going to happen, so why not find the good?"

"You chose not to join the church." Rachel's voice sharpened. "We agreed years ago you wouldn't try to turn me *English* as well."

"I'm not! Please, Rachel, let's not quarrel."

Ella decided now would be a good time to slip out and walk out to the mailbox on the road. Lindy and Rachel had been best friends all their lives. Whatever they had to work out between themselves, they would do it without an audience. Normally Ella would walk briskly out to the road. Today she took her time, and when she returned she would resume hanging the wet laundry.

The mailbox contained only one letter, addressed to Jedediah Hilty with a return address showing the school district's office on Main Street in Seabury.

❧

Gideon sent Gertie back out to play in the yard and set the envelope in his lap as he listened to the continuing discussion among the men. He had hoped that gathering the men to talk would guide them all to a decision of one mind and heart. Instead, the reasons for and against complying with the school district's ruling splintered the conversation. Gideon felt the tension hardening like bits of concrete spattered on a wall. The bumps might never be smoothed again.

Each time Gideon glanced down at his lap, the return address on the letter taunted with more insistence. As Chester Mast and Cristof Byler went back and forth, Gideon fingered the edge of the envelope. With one thumb, he tested the seal and found it loose. Raising his eyes to watch John Hershberger's face as he again lamented the undesirable influences the Amish children would face, Gideon slid a finger under the flap and slowly pulled out two sheets of paper, one a letter and one a form.

The voices faded away as he read the words on the page.

"Gideon."

He looked up to see James with eyes full of questions.

"Is this a letter that pertains to our discussion?"

Gideon gave a slow nod. "I imagine each of you will find one in your mailbox."

"Then perhaps you should read it to us now," Isaiah said.

Gideon licked his bottom lip and held the page in front of him.

"Just read it," Aaron King urged.

Gideon should have exercised the self-discipline to leave the envelope unopened until the men had left his home. He needed time to think. They had come to no helpful conclusion on what to do about the consolidated grade school. The instructions in this letter would slash all hope of reaching a peaceful agreement.

"Gideon," James urged.

Gideon cleared his voice.

"Dear Mr. Wittmer,

"This letter reminds us all of the decision of the State of Ohio to establish a compulsory age for education. State law requires students to remain in school until they have reached the age of sixteen. It is our hope that this will encourage more of our young people to complete the requirements for a high school diploma, which will in turn equip them for meaningful employment and successful lives as productive citizens.

"You are receiving this letter because our records show that you have a child or children who may meet the academic requirements of entering the ninth grade or above, or because our records regarding the ages of your children may be incomplete.

"*The enclosed form should be used for enrolling your son or daughter in Seabury High School. Please return the completed form at your earliest convenience. Previous school records will be used to determine ages, assess achievement, and make sure of compliance with state law. Students transferring from the recently closed school may be asked to take an examination before final grade placement.*

"*We look forward to providing your child with a strong educational foundation.*

"*Yours truly,*

"*Ulysses R. Brownley, Superintendent.*"

The silence lasted only as long as it took for Gideon to fold the letter along its creases. Then the room exploded around him.

⸙

Ella walked past the laundry basket one more time. The letter looked too substantial to risk its welfare out in the yard while she hung wet shirts.

Inside, David's eyes were wide with pleasure and gratitude. He rotated the birdhouse a quarter turn to admire a fresh angle. Lindy and Rachel seemed to have put aside their nascent quarrel.

"I'll take it upstairs for now," David said, "until I decide where to hang it."

"Please take your boots off before walking through the house," Rachel said. "I've just cleaned the floors."

David sat down and began to unlace one boot.

"I brought in a letter for *Daed*." Ella handed the envelope to Rachel.

"From the school board," Rachel said. Though it was addressed to her husband, she tore off one end of the envelope and scanned the contents.

"What is it?" Lindy leaned forward, elbows on the table. "More information on the bus route?"

"This is ridiculous," Rachel said. "They can't do this to us."

"What is it?" Lindy repeated.

Ella had never seen Rachel's face so pale, her jaw so set.

Rachel returned the letter to the envelope. "They want children to stay in school until they are sixteen. They claim it is state law."

Ella's eyes went to David, who yanked off his boot and then froze his motion.

"I'll be going to high school," he said.

Wonder shimmered in his voice.

"You most certainly will not," Rachel said. "You're turning fifteen next week. You finished the eighth grade a year ago. Do they expect you to become a child again?"

"It's state law," Lindy said. "It's happening everywhere. The schools in town are good, solid schools."

"What possible reason would I have for sending my able-bodied son back to school?" Rachel glared at no one in particular. "Even when he was ten or eleven, the teacher said he was working well above other students his age. Besides, Jed has already come to depend on David's help around the farm. He does the work of a man."

David slowly unlaced his second boot, his eyes down. "I'd like to go to the high school."

Ella stiffened and Rachel spun.

"You're a child," Rachel said. "You'll do as you're told."

"You just said I was a man." David lifted his eyes now.

Ella's head suddenly felt as if it were clamped in a vise. Slowly the pressure squeezed, one notch at a time.

"I'm sure you can talk about this," Lindy said, moving to put one hand on David's shoulder.

"There's nothing to talk about," Rachel snapped.

"It would only be for a year." Lindy's voice was hardly above a murmur.

"Jed will have something to say about this," Rachel said. "I cannot imagine he will see the need for a fifteen-year-old to go to school."

Ella slipped out the back door for the second time that morning. Rachel and Lindy. Rachel and David. Lindy and David. Jed and Rachel. Jed and David. It was not Ella's place to interfere in any of these relationships that had deluged the quiet Hilty house when her father and Rachel married. Even if it were up to her, she had no advice. Soon—she hoped—Gideon's children would be her focus.

At the laundry basket, Ella lifted a damp shirt and snapped it through the air before pinning it to the line. In a few months she would be hanging Gideon's shirts.

CHAPTER 7

M̲argaret carried her neatly typed report along Main Street toward the superintendent's office. With Seabury Consolidated Grade School and Seabury High School on adjacent lots, Mr. Brownley might easily have his office in one of the two modern buildings rather than farther down Main Street. Without doubt, the handful of remaining one-room schools in the rural county around Seabury would soon be closed and students integrated into the schools in town, so he could administer from one of the main buildings.

She had done what she could with the Amish, answering more questions than they knew to ask, inviting them for a tour, and making sure they had the information needed for sending the children to school on the first day. She had written an account of her encounters with the Amish. Only time would tell whether she had persuasively alleviated their hesitations. The report did not contain her own hesitations or the self-chastisement over what she might have said differently.

A few minutes later, on an ordinary sunny August Wednesday morning, Margaret stood in front of the superintendent's desk as he leafed through the pages of her report.

"This is a good beginning," Mr. Brownley said. "I see several opportunities here for strengthening your alliance with the Amish as we move forward."

Alliance? Margaret would not have used that word in describing her only partially successful course of action.

"What is your next step?" Mr. Brownley removed his black-rimmed reading glasses and raised his gray eyes to Margaret.

"Is my report lacking?" Margaret said, confused.

"On the contrary."

"Sir?"

"I am not unaware of the special nature of a relationship with the Amish," Brownley said. "You've done well at communicating the stipulations of the law. Inviting their prominent parents to tour the school was a good strategy to help them prepare for the transition. But we do need to be sure they complete the transition. I suspect that even after the first day of school on September 9, we will discover we do not have uniform compliance."

"Yes," Margaret said, "I would agree that not all the parents will accept the new schools at the same rate."

"And this is why we need you to continue as an intermediary. We must have compliance. It will not be acceptable for us to turn our heads when we are aware of children who become truants."

"I hardly think it will be a case of children deciding to become truants."

Brownley waved his hand. "The end result will be the same. Whether by their choice or their parents', they'll be truant, and I will not tolerate the rate of truancy in my district that might result if the Amish children are not in their assigned classrooms."

"What about the children who are not Amish?"

"Some of their parents may resist, but they will come around. They will understand the law and adapt. The Amish may understand the law and defy."

"Is that not a harsh judgment? They have done nothing wrong so far."

"September 9, Miss Simpson. That is the day that matters. Then we will know where we stand with them. I want you to make sure we accomplish our goal."

Margaret tilted her head. "Perhaps you can be more specific in your instructions to me."

"You've shown yourself capable, Miss Simpson." Brownley rose, paced to the door, and opened it. "I look forward to your reports. Shall we say twice a week for now?"

Margaret swallowed hard. She could not force the Amish parents to send their children to school. Keeping her jaw from slackening in shock required intentional manipulation of her facial muscles as Margaret exited the building and stepped again into the sunlight. She turned vaguely in the direction of her home, walking slowly with the wide brim of her hat angled toward the sidewalk and seeing people's shoes rather than their faces.

When the sound of a pair of men's work boots fell into step with her creeping pace, she looked up.

"Gray!"

"Good morning." He smiled. "It's my good fortune to be hauling for the mercantile today, or our paths might not have crossed."

Margaret stopped walking and looked into Gray's expectant expression. Her lips opened and closed several times without producing sound.

"Margaret, are you all right?"

She gripped her satchel with both hands. Still no words came.

Gray put a hand to the side of her face, transferring his comforting warmth and sureness. Something calmed within her.

"Mr. Brownley has asked—assigned—me to continue as an intermediary with the Amish families. He has some concern they may not send their children to school. I have no idea on God's green earth what he thinks I could do about it if they don't."

Gray took her elbow and they resumed walking. "Surely he could send a man. It would be more authoritative."

Margaret bristled against the collar of her dress.

"Be firm," Gary said. "Utterly firm. It's not a personal matter. There is no question of a choice, and they must come to understand that truth. You've given them the instruction they need, and they must comply with the law."

Gray sounded as if he had been reading the same manual as Mr. Brownley. Yes, it was the law. But was there no room for humanity?

They made the turn that would take them off Main Street toward Margaret's home. Gray had pulled her hand through his elbow and covered it with his palm. The sensation stirred her.

Someone to care for her. Someone to protect her. Just when she had—nearly—talked herself out of thinking she minded missing that experience.

Margaret let out a slow breath. The Amish controversy would not always hang between them. Perhaps it did not matter if their impulses diverged on this matter. One way or another, the issue would resolve and have nothing to do with Margaret in the future. She and Gray would be all right. There was no need to openly disagree on a passing concern that would not involve them for the long run.

❧

The bishop arrived.

Although Gideon had not spoken directly with Bishop Leroy Garber since the collapse of the schoolhouse, he was not surprised that the head of the church's district would turn up on his farm while he worked with Tobias and James to make sure disease or unmanaged pestilence did not endanger the fall harvest. It was only a matter of time before the bishop, who had no school-age children, would have heard from parents who did about the impending enforcement of state law.

"*Gut mariye.*" Bishop Garber dismounted his horse in the middle of a row of wheat, careful to still the animal before its hooves wandered into Gideon's crop.

Gideon brushed his hands against his trousers, loosing bits of soil in a black spray. "I'm sorry I have no refreshment to offer you out here."

"No need. I won't keep you from your work for long."

"What can I do for you?"

The bishop glanced at Tobias, whose eyes had lifted to the exchange.

"Tobias," James said, "let's check the plants in the next row."

Gideon tipped his hat forward a quarter of an inch in thanks as James led Tobias out of listening distance.

"I do not face the decision you face," the bishop said. "My children are over sixteen. But those who are married with their own children will face the dilemma soon enough."

"It's difficult to know what the right thing is," Gideon said. "I'm sure parents will seek your counsel as bishop."

"They already have. That's why I've come to you."

"I have no clear answers, Bishop."

"Perhaps not. But what is certain in my talks with other parents is that they are looking to you. Your name comes up in every conversation. They will follow your lead."

"Bishop, I don't ask for such a role. I am only a parent seeking to please God and do what is best for my children."

55

"That is just what any of them would say. But they seem to think you will help them find that point of intersection."

"How can I help them find what I do not see clearly for myself?" Gideon rubbed an eye with one palm.

"We see through a glass darkly," the bishop said, "but we still see."

"I will rejoice when light banishes this particular darkness," Gideon said.

"Someday you will be nominated to be a minister."

Gideon's gaze snapped into focus on the bishop's face. "We are only talking about school."

"You are a leader, Gideon. People recognize that. Your leadership on this question will be your ministry."

"I do not seek it."

"None of us ask to be ministers or bishops. God chooses us. If he chooses you now, you must serve."

⌖

Margaret festered for two days over how to do what the superintendent asked of her. School would begin in just over three weeks, and she had looked forward to pleasantly preparing her classroom, refreshing the lesson plans she had used successfully for the last four years to teach six-year-olds to read, and closing out the summer by canning the vegetables from her garden and the bushels of fruit the mercantile sold at irresistible prices this time of year.

Making sure the Amish children turned up where the state expected them to be on September 9 was not something she knew how to do. Nor did she know what the consequences would be if she failed.

On Friday morning, she once again checked the fuel gauge in her Model T. Armed with a list from the superintendent's office of names and addresses of students they believed should enroll, she cranked the engine of her car and began to roll through the spidery miles of farms, hoping a strategy would take form in her mind as she drove.

Gideon Wittmer came to mind again and again. The only two Amish fathers Margaret had met were Gideon and Mr. King, and between the two of them, Gideon seemed the clear choice for reasonable alliance.

Not *alliance*. Margaret shivered against the word again. It sounded too much like the alliance of nations fighting the war in Europe. She did not want war, not in Europe and not in Seabury.

Conversation. That was a better word.

Margaret turned her car toward the Wittmer farm. If she was going to please Mr. Brownley, she would have to start somewhere.

"He isn't home," an elderly woman said when Margaret knocked on the Wittmer front door.

Peeking around a corner was a pair of bright green eyes in a suntanned face framed by blond hair under a gossamer headpiece, the sort all the Amish women wore. Margaret could not remember what they called them.

Margaret smiled at the little girl and said to the woman, "Do you know where I might find Mr. Wittmer?"

The woman waved a hand first one direction and then the other. "He had some errands to do, some people to see."

"Maybe I could visit another day—soon," Margaret said. "It is rather important that I speak to him."

The little girl came out from around the corner and tugged on the woman's sleeve. "*Aunti* Miriam, *Daed* told me he was going to visit Mr. King, but he would be home for lunch."

Margaret glanced at her watch. It was nearly noon now. She had the Kings' address on her list, showing several grade school children and a high school student.

"Thank you." Margaret beamed at the child. "You look like you're old enough to start school."

"First grade!"

"That's just the grade I teach. Perhaps I'll be your teacher."

The woman put a hand on the girl's shoulder. "Gertie, please go set the table."

"I'm not trying to cause trouble," Margaret said once Gertie went into the kitchen.

"I'm sure you mean no harm," the woman said. "I'm sorry I couldn't tell you where Gideon is. You know these roads. He could be anywhere."

"I understand. If you would tell him that Miss Simpson was here, I would be grateful. I'll try again another day."

Margaret drove toward the King farm, and her intuition was rewarded with an approaching Amish buggy. She pulled to the side of the road and waved. The buggy slowed, and she could see the driver was Gideon Wittmer. Margaret got out of her car and waved again.

"Miss Simpson," Gideon said from the seat at the front of the boxy buggy.

"How fortunate to run into you," she said. "I was hoping we could speak for a few minutes."

"What can I help you with?"

"I'm considering forming a Parents Committee for United Schools." The idea had sprung to her mind only moments before. "You've seen for yourself the quality of our school. Perhaps you would be so kind to serve on the committee and help other parents on the outlying farms to feel comfortable with the consolidated schools."

Gideon's fingers twisted in the reins while his horse waited patiently for instructions. "I think you'll find the *English* parents will appreciate having more information. You could organize another tour and invite anyone who is interested."

"Excellent idea! And the Amish parents?" Margaret held her breath. "As a member of the committee, you could be an invaluable partner, a bridge between the new school and the Amish parents."

He gave a guarded smile. "I'm afraid I can't help you with that."

CHAPTER 8

The late summer auction was Ella's favorite. The spring frolics, held when the ground softened into a milder season, were too muddy for her liking. But the last week of August was perfect. Rarely was there rain, and the edge had come off the peak of summer temperatures. The bustling Saturday brought out all the Amish families in the district and many curious *English* looking for a bargain to showcase in their homes.

Gideon would likely spend most of the day in the auction ring, where horses, harnesses, hitches, plows, binders, and buggies would be sold. Gideon was looking for one new horse. He had his eye on one from the line Aaron King bred, a two-year-old Belgian workhorse. The bidding would be competitive. Aaron's horses always fetched a good price.

Ella preferred wandering among the large quilts, handmade furniture, baked goods, canned foods, and crafty household items. From year to year, she knew who would have the best home-canned apple pie filling to save for the middle of winter or who had a piecework quilt for sale two years in the making. The price an *English* woman would pay for an Amish quilt stunned Ella every time. Ella walked the rows of tables and booths, looking for that irresistible item she might want to bid on. She had little money of her own, but she wanted to contribute. The money raised today would go into the fund that Amish families could count on in a time of illness or financial difficulty.

A flash of familiar red-gold hair caught Ella's eye a few yards ahead. "Lindy!"

Lindy paused, and Ella caught up with her.

"How are things at your booth?" Ella asked.

"Brisk." Lindy looked over her shoulder. "I got a spot in the main aisle this year."

"That's good! I predict that you'll sell out by lunchtime."

Lindy chuckled. "I hope so."

"Who's watching your booth now?"

"David's there. He has a good head on his shoulders. He won't let anyone talk him into a price I wouldn't take."

"I'll be happy to help if you need an extra pair of hands."

"Thanks. I'll keep that in mind." Lindy pivoted and walked backward for a few yards before turning around again. "My neighbor Margaret said she asked Gideon to be on a committee and he declined."

Ella sighed. "It's so complicated!"

"Is Gideon going to send his children to school?" Lindy glanced over her shoulder.

"I don't think he's made up his mind." Ella's gaze followed Lindy's shifting line of sight. All she saw was a buzzing crowd, a mix of Amish and *English*. She didn't recognize everyone, but who could on a day like this? A couple of tall *English* men who resembled each other carried a set of tent poles and a bundle of canvas. The auctioneer strode past with a megaphone in one hand. An Amish woman cradled a quilt as if it were her firstborn child. Everything Ella saw seemed normal for the day.

"I suppose I should get back to David," Lindy said, glancing the other direction.

"Lindy, what's wrong?" Ella asked. "What are you looking for?"

"I'm not sure," Lindy murmured. "I just get a funny feeling sometimes."

"What kind of feeling?"

"As if I'm being watched."

"There are hundreds of people here," Ella said.

"I know. It's just a feeling. Sometimes it happens in town, too." Lindy shook her head as if in a shudder. "Don't pay any attention to me. There's my booth."

Ella looked up to see David standing out in front of the booth with several other Amish boys near his age. She slowed her pace as she followed Lindy.

"My *daed* says I will go to school, but only for one year," a boy said. "He doesn't want to get involved in trouble, but I think it's silly."

"Mine will keep my brothers and me home," another boy said. "And I'm glad. I'm too old for school! My brothers know everything they need to know to help on the farm."

Ella loitered on the fringes of the booth as Lindy patted David on the shoulder in thanks and took her place among her display of colorfully painted birdhouses, children's toys, and quilt racks.

The boys were nearly unanimous in their opinion that it was ridiculous to think they needed to go to high school. One after another, they voiced the same opinion.

Everyone except David, who said nothing.

⊱❦⊰

James watched his wife's face gladden at the array of goods around them. The six pies she baked for the auction sold within minutes of putting them on display. It was the same at every auction, whether spring or late summer. Everyone new Miriam Lehman's pies were the best in Geauga County.

A few moments ago, they had been arm in arm. Now Miriam had slid her arm out of his elbow to lean her head toward Mrs. King's, both of them pointing at quilts hanging from a web of lines strung between poles. James smiled, letting her go without protest. She deserved this day of pleasure and friendship, and he was glad to give it to her.

They were fourteen and finishing the eighth grade when they first began to look at each other with particular interest. They weren't even old enough to go to Singings, but they knew. James was certain first, and Miriam a few weeks later. They were young, but they would be together.

They were sixteen when they began going to Singings, and James refused to offer a ride home to any other young woman. Miriam was the one for him.

The day after her eighteenth birthday, they married. His father helped him acquire a small farm. Someday, James had thought, he would expand the acres. Someday, when he and Miriam had a houseful of children, sons and daughters, the promise of the future.

Then the children did not come.

At the beginning of December, James and Miriam would celebrate their forty-fourth anniversary and a life together that unfolded differently than either of them imagined in those early years.

They were *aunti* and *onkel* to dozens of children, the offspring of their siblings. Betsy and Lindy had always shone luminous even among their own siblings. While James still wondered what it might have been like to raise children of his own, his heart was at its most tender when he thought of the sisters.

One passed and the other chose the *English* world.

Still James loved them both.

Margaret draped the quilt over the end of her bed.

She hadn't intended to purchase anything more than a few token jars of tomatoes to supplement what she had grown in her own yard, but when she saw the precise arrangement of green, blue, and purple triangles and flawless stitching, suddenly she wanted the quilt more than anything else she saw all morning.

Margaret had gone to the Amish auction accompanied by her ulterior motive—to understand more about these puzzling people who might—or might not—be the subject of considerable drama in sixteen short days. If they kept their children out of school, Margaret was sure the blame would be assigned to her failure to persuade them. If the first day of school passed peacefully, it would be no doing of Margaret's. She had no delusions of sincere victory because she had no conviction of the merits of the challenge.

The superintendent said he wanted a woman's touch in the matter. A woman's touch was personal and warm. What good could come from a heavy-handed approach? Margaret would work her way down her list of names and addresses and pay a call to each family, beginning Monday.

The quilt looked lovely in the bedroom, though Margaret would take some time deciding if it should have the place of her bedspread or instead be arranged casually on the back of the reading chair she kept beside the bed. What to do about the Amish conundrum was much more pressing.

Conundrum. Not a very friendly word.

Ice cream. Ice cream would soothe a ragged day, and making it would give her body something to do. Margaret lit the stove and pulled eggs and milk from the icebox and sugar and vanilla from the pantry. She stirred and mixed, her taste buds already anticipating a sensation still hours off.

The knock on the door, just as she took the mixture off the stove, startled her. That Margaret heard neither the approaching engine on the street nor the footsteps on her porch stairs testified to her preoccupation. At the front door, she glanced through the slender pane of glass and saw Gray Truesdale—and regretted she had not looked in the mirror before she left the bedroom and exerted herself in the kitchen. Smoothing her hair with one hand, she opened the door with the other.

Of course she was glad to see him, though befuddled how she had lost track of the likelihood that he would call tonight.

"I was in the middle of making ice cream," she said.

"I'll help," he said.

Margaret pointed to the wooden ice cream maker situated decoratively in the corner of the porch, and Gray bent to pick it up and carry it into the kitchen. He held the inner canister while she poured the mixture in and then added the dasher before securing the lid and handle.

"I hope you have plenty of ice," he said. "And salt."

"Both," Margaret said, "though I should have chipped off the ice before I began."

Gray smiled and rolled up his sleeves. "I'll do it."

She watched as he opened the bottom of the icebox and chipped enough ice to fill the wooden bucket far more efficiently than she could have. Effortlessly, he carried the assemblage out to the front porch, positioned himself on one knee, and began to crank. The muscles in his arms rippled in a captivating rhythm, and Margaret felt heat rise in the back of her neck at her inability to turn her eyes away from the movements of his lanky frame.

"I went out to the auction today." She forced herself to do something other than gawk at this man who had come into her life ten years later than she would have liked.

"I was there, too." He looked up. "Working with my brother."

"I didn't realize you had a brother."

"All my life." Gray grinned.

"Perhaps I'll meet him someday."

"I hope so." Gray's expression sobered. "He's my only family."

"Your parents?"

"Gone long ago. I'll tell you about it someday. Not tonight."

Margaret sucked in one cheek. Gray was thinking of their future.

"What kind of work were you doing today?" she asked.

"Helping to set up some tents. I left my brother on his own to get them down, but he'll be fairly paid for the extra work."

Gray cranked.

Margaret watched in admiration.

"I wanted to ask a question," he said.

"Of course."

He cranked.

She admired, hoping he did not see the unabating blush.

"Tomorrow is Sunday."

"Yes, it is."

"Church is at eleven."

"Yes, it is."

"I'd be pleased if you'd allow me to call for you at quarter till."

"I'd be pleased if you would," she said.

He cranked.

She made herself look away.

"Then I look forward to the Lord's Day all the more."

"Likewise, I'm sure."

He cranked. They made small talk—what they had seen at the auction, the fine weather, the headlines in the newspaper out of Cleveland about the war in Europe and spreading influenza. Gradually, the cranking slowed.

"It will have to sit for a while," Gray said.

Margaret crossed to the corner of the porch and unfolded a rug to lay over the ice cream maker.

"I have blackberries," she said.

"Is that so?"

"I mean, if you might like to come back after supper. We could put blackberries over the ice cream."

"Well, I believe that would be quite delicious and convenient."

She watched him saunter back out to his truck, already savoring what his kiss would taste like later that evening.

Ella stroked the nose of Gideon's new horse, hoping he had not paid too dearly for her. It was a buggy horse, though, not the workhorse she had expected him to purchase.

"I'll make sure she's well broken in before you need to use her," Gideon said.

Ella raised her face, confused.

"I have an extra cart I'll sand down," he said. "You'll always have a horse and cart available for visiting or shopping or whatever you need it for."

His eyes met hers, and she fell into them. "Gideon. . ."

"It's time, isn't it?" he said. "If you'll have me, I would like to be your loving husband."

"Of course I'll have you!" Ella's heart raced. The crowd around them lost its color, the vibrancy of the day fading in the illumined moment.

"I'll care for you, provide for you, and do my best to bring happiness into each of your days."

"Gideon. . ." She wanted him to kiss her.

He cupped her elbow and nudged her around the back side of the makeshift stable behind the auction ring, and she waited while he glanced in both directions before removing his hat and dipping his head to oblige her wish—which he evidently shared. Ella hoped Gideon's kiss would always draw her to him as it did now.

"Your father will have no objection, will he?" Gideon whispered when he broke the kiss.

"None whatsoever."

"I could speak to him today, if you like."

"As soon as possible, please."

"Wedding season is only two months off."

"We can be one of the first couples to publish our banns." What a relief it would be to talk openly about their relationship. They could speak to the bishop and set the date for the first Thursday in November, as soon as the harvest season was finished. Rachel would gladly take on the role of mother of the bride, and Ella's siblings would come from their scattered farms for a joyful day.

Gideon kissed her again, this time lingering in a delectable recognition of the decision Ella had waited so long for. He was hers.

CHAPTER 9

W hat sort of small gift of friendship might she take to Amish families as she visited? Sampling at the auction had convinced Margaret she could not compete with their jams or jellies, and their baked goods tempted her to beg for recipes that had never been written down. She wandered through the mercantile on Monday morning considering whether packets of stationery might be appropriate for the mothers, or perhaps flower seeds to put away for next spring.

I should have asked Lindy. She used to be one of them.

Margaret picked up two packets of stationery with matching envelopes bundled together in wide ribbons. She would start with two families today. If the gift seemed to cause offense, tomorrow she would try something else.

At the counter, as she counted out the necessary coins, she was startled to see Mr. Brownley enter the store.

Their eyes met.

"Good morning," Margaret said.

"Good morning." Brownley's eyes shifted to look down the long center aisle. "Have you seen the deputy sheriff? I was told he came in here."

The clerk pushed a button and the cash register opened. "He's in the back. Saw him looking at the hammers. Said he'd be right up."

"I told him I would just be a minute and he disappeared," Brownley muttered.

"Is everything all right, Mr. Brownley?" Margaret asked.

"Everything is in hand, Miss Simpson. The sheriff and I decided to pay a few calls on the farms, that's all."

"I'm about to do the same thing," Margaret said. "I thought perhaps a gentle, personal approach—"

"School starts two weeks from today," Brownley said. "I've decided we need a firm approach, one that makes the law clear."

Margaret's jaw dropped. She clenched it closed immediately. "Did I misunderstand your instructions to me?"

"I was clear, was I not?"

"I thought so. But now you seem inclined to handle the matter yourself."

Deputy Fremont plunked money on the counter, and the two men exited the mercantile.

Margaret scrambled after them. "May I inquire about the nature of the calls you plan to pay?"

Deputy Fremont laughed. "My badge is all the explanation most folks need."

Margaret hustled to keep pace with their strides.

"I thought we'd take my automobile," the sheriff said. "It will look more official."

"Good, good. Makes a strong statement."

"Mr. Brownley," Margaret said, trailing them, "might I have a word?"

"You can come along, Miss Simpson." Brownley nodded at the deputy. "She won't be any trouble."

"Mr. Brownley, please." Margaret's pitch rose. "Ought we not act in concert on the matter? Is this really necessary?" Had he expected that in less than a week she would be able to report that the Amish families had promised compliance? Indignation rose at the insult of his assigning a task to her and nevertheless acting on the matter without so much as a consultation. He would never have treated the efforts of a man so trivially.

"As I said," Brownley replied without pausing his step, "you may come with us if you wish. But the matter is settled. Deputy Fremont suggested that a visual reminder of the strength of law might prove effective, and I think he has a point. He's certain the sheriff over in Chardon would agree. We can be done with this matter once and for all."

So this was Deputy Fremont's idea. Despite the abundant

Amish population in his district, apparently he understood their peaceable ways even less than she did. Margaret ignored the deputy's cockeyed grin.

"We can't possibly know who will turn up on the first day of school," Margaret said. "Maybe all of them will."

"Unlikely," snapped the deputy.

When they reached the deputy's vehicle, Margaret thrust herself between the officer and the superintendent. "I must forcefully remonstrate against this decision. Give me time. I will bring you a report as we agreed."

"I've changed my mind," Brownley said.

"Then the task you described is no longer incumbent upon me?"

Brownley shook his head. "I didn't say that. I'm sure the softer side of a woman will have its place, but you cannot have expected I would abdicate my responsibility and leave the matter entirely in your hands."

Fremont leaned against the hood of the car to crank the engine. Brownley nudged Margaret aside and opened the passenger door.

"What's our first stop?" Fremont asked when the engine caught.

"Now here's where you can help, Miss Simpson," Brownley said. "Who is the most influential Amish father?"

Margaret hesitated but finally said, "Gideon Wittmer." He was influential, but Margaret's brief encounters with him also led her to believe he would hold his own. The deputy's vehicle would have no bearing on his response.

"Where's his farm?"

"I'm coming with you." Margaret avoided Brownley's eyes, instead pushing past him to climb into the backseat.

⊱✦⊰

The boys were out back, throwing pebbles toward the side of the barn to see who could land one closest to the structure without striking it. From his kitchen window, Gideon watched Tobias competing with Jed Hilty's boys.

"We'll all be kin before too long." Jed toyed with his mug and sipped his coffee. "I couldn't be more pleased that you and Ella will wed. You'll give her a fine home. And with only sons of her own, Rachel never expected to be mother of the bride."

"Ella will appreciate her advice." Gideon returned the coffeepot to the stove. "I'm no help. When I married Betsy, her mother and sisters arranged everything, right down to how many roast chickens we needed for the meal."

Jed chuckled. "I have three other daughters. I've learned that weddings are a good time to let the womenfolk take the lead."

"The boys get along well," Gideon said, looking out the window again.

"Seth gets along with everyone," Jed said. "David is peculiar at times, but they are both good boys. Their father would have been proud."

"Will you send them to school?" Gideon had not intended to be so blunt, but with only two weeks left of the summer break, the imminent need to find his own answer to the question had begun to round the corner of polite conversation.

"Seth is only twelve," Jed said. "He just finished the sixth grade, so he should take two more years."

"But at the *English* school?" Gideon turned his gaze to the eyes of his future father-in-law. "You've decided that this is right and pleasing to God?"

"I've decided Seth will handle himself well and learn what he needs to learn. He's not a troublemaker, and he won't want to disgrace his mother."

"And David?"

Jed sighed. "Fifteen years old. I see nothing he will gain from returning to school after he's been out for a year. Rachel agrees."

"He's not even close to his sixteenth birthday."

"No, but I can't see how the *English* will find reason to bother themselves about Amish children who have already left school. It makes no sense for them to return to the rolls."

"I'm glad to hear you say that," Gideon said. "Tobias is only thirteen, but he'll soon be fourteen. I'll need him for the harvest, but then he can go to school over the winter. I'll take him out again when I need him for the early spring planting. He won't want to go back next year."

Gertie burst into the room, coming from the front of the house.

"*Daed*, two *English* men are here." Gertie's eyes widened. "Savilla said to find you right away."

Gideon swooped up Gertie and strode through the house. Jed's boots thudded right behind him.

"Savilla!" Gideon called as soon as he was on the front porch. The girl ran toward him, leaving two men standing alongside the fenced pasture.

"I heard them talking," Savilla said. "It's about school."

"And the lady who was here before came again," Gertie said.

Gideon eyed the parked car, recognizing it as a vehicle that belonged to the Geauga County sheriff's department. He set Gertie on the porch.

"Savilla, take your sister in the house," Gideon said, "or go out to the *dawdihaus* and visit Miriam."

"Is everything all right?" Savilla took Gertie's hand but looked over her shoulder at the visitors, who now fixed their stares on her father.

"I'm sure it is," Gideon said. "We'll talk about it later."

Jed kept pace with Gideon as they walked across the rolling front yard toward the fence.

"I'm Gideon Wittmer," Gideon said. He nodded at Margaret Simpson, the only one of the three visitors he recognized. "What can I do for you?"

"We just want to make sure you understand the law," said the uniformed man.

Margaret stepped forward. "This is Deputy Fremont and Superintendent Brownley. There's nothing to worry about."

"I'm not worried," Gideon said.

So this was the superintendent behind the forceful correspondence made to sound friendlier than it was.

"I'm Mr. Hilty," Jed said. "Is there something you need from us today?"

The superintendent flipped a few papers. "Jed Hilty. I don't see the Hilty name on our list of students."

"I've received your letters. I have stepsons who might be on your forms," Jed said. "Kaufman."

"So you both understand the new laws?" the deputy asked.

"We've read your letters," Gideon said.

"Do you have questions?" Margaret asked. "This would be a good opportunity to have them answered."

"No questions," Gideon said. The more he looked at Miss Simpson, the more nervous she seemed.

"Good," said Mr. Brownley. "Then can we expect your full cooperation?"

⥼⥽

"Rachel told me the happy news." Lindy embraced Ella in the middle of a Seabury furniture store that frequently carried Amish craftsmanship.

"*Danki!*" Ella made no effort to contain her smile.

The last two days had been a whirlwind. Though her engagement to Gideon would not be published to the church officially for weeks, already the news buzzed.

"When Betsy married Gideon," Lindy said, "he became my brother. I suppose your marriage will make you my sister."

Ella swallowed a lump that formed in an instant. "You're so gracious to me. No one can take Betsy's place, but I'm going to do my best to love her family as she would have."

"I know you will. And you can count on me for help. Just let me know what you need."

Ella glanced at a crate Lindy had set on the floor.

"Toys." Lindy leaned toward Ella and spoke behind her hand. "The owners discovered that they sell more furniture if children find a toy to play with while the parents shop. And even if they don't buy furniture, they almost always buy the toy."

Ella giggled. "I only came in to look. I'm not sure Gideon realizes how much space my books take."

"Let me make you a bookcase," Lindy said. "It will be a wedding present."

Lindy glanced over her shoulder, first in one direction and then the other.

"Are you still having that strange sensation?" Ella asked.

Lindy nodded. "I was sure someone was following me just now on the street. I was anxious to get inside. But if I don't know who is following me, how do I know the person is not in the shop now?"

Ella looked around the store. She saw an *English* couple with a small child, who likely would soon discover the treat of Lindy's well-crafted toys, and an *English* man standing in front of a dining hutch and nodding at the salesman's explanation of its features. At the back of the store, a woman wearing a light wool dress bent over an oversized ledger. They could have been in any shop in town.

"You don't see anything odd, do you?" Lindy asked.

Ella shrugged. "I guess not. Everyone looks ordinary."

"I'm probably just on edge. I get a thing in mind, and then it won't leave." Lindy waved off the thought. "I can't even describe who it is I feel watching me. Don't pay any attention to me."

Ella now turned her face toward the window that looked out on the street, where people went about their business in unremarkable ways. Some stopped for a glance in the shop's window, which featured a small table and chairs set attractively, but most walked briskly past on their way somewhere else. No one seemed to loiter.

"I'd better let the owner know the toys are here," Lindy said. "Then I'll be on my way and try to keep my spooks to myself."

CHAPTER 10

Seething irritation tarnished the shine of exuberance Margaret usually felt on the first day of a new school year. When she accompanied the deputy and superintendent to the Wittmer farm, she had nursed a frantic hope that she might buffer the encounter. Instead, Gideon's refusal to say with certainty that all three of his children would be in the consolidated school incensed both officials, sending them charging off to other farms with an even more stern approach. Margaret's efforts to coax and cajole yielded no satisfaction for anyone. When the trio returned to town, after being stonewalled at four farms, Mr. Brownley insinuated that if the Amish children did not attend school, he might have to reconsider her principal's assurance that she was a highly capable teacher.

Margaret made the rounds, introducing herself to mothers and leaving small gifts that seemed feebler with each visit, and at the end of two weeks she still had no clear inclination of what the Amish would do. In fact, she had growing doubts that even the *English* families would cooperate until after the fall harvest when they no longer needed the unpaid labor of their children.

On September 9, Margaret was outside the school even before Mr. Tarkington arrived to unlock the building. The classroom was ready. She had nothing else to do but wait for her students, but she wanted to be in an environment where she was certain she could maintain order.

Margaret straightened books. She had refrained from unburdening herself with Gray Truesdale on the Amish matter. He was a strong man. He would want a woman who could manage her own affairs.

She checked the chalk in the long tray running along the base of the blackboard, making sure a fresh piece was positioned every eighteen inches, and thought about Deputy Fremont. If ever a man knew nothing about children!

Raising the lid to every desk, Margaret ensured she had placed a sheet of art paper from the art cabinet in the downstairs corridor for each child. Her students were six-year-olds, and children who enjoyed school were more likely to learn their words and sums. Art on the first day would help set the tone.

She imagined the bus rumbling out to the farms and stopping at the designated corners to collect the children, beginning with the most outlying acres and gradually moving back toward Seabury. How many would get on?

She picked up the pages of her attendance list and seating chart and tapped them to precision at the corners.

Children are resilient, Margaret reminded herself. This would not be the first time she had students who were uncertain about entering a classroom. Very, very few failed to adjust to the classroom structure and expectations. First graders from the farms would be learning the same reading and spelling and arithmetic they would have learned had their one-room school not collapsed. There would just be a few other subjects as well.

Running a finger down the list of names, Margaret settled on the last alphabetical entry. *Wittmer, Gertrude.*

~※~

"I want to go."

David's tone was respectful, controlled—and more adamant than Ella had supposed him capable of. Why had she not noticed before this how tall he was?

"Seth will go." Jed replaced the Bible he used for morning family devotions on the shelf. "You will stay here on the farm. I can't spare you."

David spread his feet, bracing his stance. "I've lived here less than a year. You always got along without my help before this."

"I've made my decision." Jed adjusted his glasses on his face.

"What about my decision?" David said. "You never even asked me what I thought was right to do."

"We'll work in the south pasture today," Jed said.

Seth stood at the door running one thumb and forefinger along his suspenders while gripping his metal lunch bucket in the other hand. Ella glanced at Rachel, who averted her eyes from the quarrel brewing between her husband and son. Ella didn't blame her. She had no wish to watch it boil over, either. Up to this point, David had not outright defied Jed. Ella sprang up from her chair, crossed the room, and put a hand on Seth's back to guide him out the door before closing it behind her.

"What is your *daed* going to do?" Seth asked.

"What he thinks is best because he cares about both of you." Ella's answer was swift and honest. "You don't mind if I walk with you to the bus, do you?"

Seth shrugged. "I know the way."

"Of course you do. But it might help your mother if she knew that the arrangements the *English* made have worked out."

Seth was a mild child, without the complexity that pulsed under David's usual outward respect of his elders. He would do whatever would be easiest for his mother.

Seth's designated bus corner—and David's, were he allowed to attend school—was three-quarters of a mile down the main road at the end of the Glicks' lane. To attend the one-room schoolhouse, Seth had walked more than twice as far last year. Still, Ella hated to think of him standing on the side of the road on a dark, frigid morning when winter came, wondering if the bus would be on time.

Mrs. Glick stood at the corner with two of her children. Ella tried to remember how old they were—was it seven and eight or eight and nine? The girls were so alike in size and coloring that Ella had trouble keeping them straight.

The Mast boys were there also, their lunch buckets already set aside to free their hands for tossing pebbles into a small creek across the road. Seth shrugged out of his jacket to join them with his superior aim. Ella contemplated their ages as well. At least one of them was older than fourteen and headed for the high school.

"David is not coming?" Mrs. Glick stood with her daughters on either side of her, arms around their shoulders protectively.

Ella shook her head.

"What a difficult day," Mrs. Glick said. "We will pray for God's care for all our hearts."

"He does not fail us," Ella said. She peered down the road in the direction Gideon would come from. His three children were also assigned to this bus stop. Ella's head pivoted between watching Seth, who showed no sign of trepidation about attending an *English* school, and watching for Gideon.

When her vigilance was rewarded and Gideon's buggy swayed into view, Ella let her breath out. She hadn't known what to think. They spoke of the question every time they saw each other, yet she hadn't been sure he would put his children on the bus. His horse clip-clopped toward Ella, and she made sure to have a smile on her face, both for Gideon and for the children.

Gertie and Savilla jumped out of the buggy in matching green dresses, black aprons, and braids securely pinned against their heads under their *kapps*. Tobias took his time. From the buggy bench, Gideon's eyes settled for a few seconds on each of the assembled children.

Ella approached the buggy.

"David didn't come," Gideon said.

"He wanted to."

"Jed has said all along that he saw no benefit in taking the boy out of the fields when he already finished his book learning."

"And you," Ella said. "You're here with all of your *kinner*."

The head of every student and adult at the corner turned toward the clattering of an unfamiliar vehicle, all of them curious about the *English* bus. The front end looked like most of the vehicles that rumbled down this road from time to time. A black hood housed the engine, with an open bench behind the steering wheel. The bus stopped in the middle of the intersection.

Mrs. Glick's girls broke away from the stance they had held so dutifully. Curiosity widened the eyes of all the children. Even the older boys abandoned their pebble tossing.

"It looks like a cage in a wagon," Gertie pronounced.

The comparison was apt. A sturdy wagon base spanned the wide rear axle, and wooden framing rose from the wagon—where she presumed there were benches—to the roof above. On a fine day like today, canvas flaps were rolled and restrained up against the roof. When winter came, they could easily be let down to offer protection from the elements. It would still be very cold.

Ella had once ridden in an automobile, but she doubted any of the children gawking at the bus had. A few hands pushed out from the interior, followed by faces looking over the horizontal timbers of the wagon's framing.

The Byler children, Ella noted, and the King children. The Henderson boy, an *English*, grinned as if he had never done anything so exciting in his entire life. Ella recognized a couple of *English* girls who rolled their eyes at the silliness around them. The bus would make one more stop, closer to town, for the last of the children assigned to this bus. At least one other bus would make a separate route picking up children who lived in the opposite direction from town.

The bus driver lumbered off his bench and down the one step to the ground. He consulted a sheet of paper. "Let's see, Glick?"

"Here," the two girls chimed.

"Climb aboard." The driver pulled a pencil from over his ear and made two check marks. "Kaufman?"

Seth raised a hand.

"Should be two," the driver muttered. "Seth and David."

"I'm Seth. My brother is not coming." Seth placed one foot on the step and hoisted himself into the bus.

Ella's stomach clenched as she watched the *English* cavern swallow the unsuspecting boy.

"The superintendent is not going to like this." The driver pursed his lips and drew a careful circle around David's name. "Mast?"

The oldest students of the corner clambered aboard.

"Let's see," the driver said. "That leaves Wittmer. Three."

Ella sucked in a breath and held it.

⊱✿⊰

Gideon bent over and spoke to his young daughters. He had made his peace with this moment. Savilla was a sensible child. Gertie was simply relieved that she did not have to go to the school that had collapsed around her. She was younger and more impulsive than Savilla, and as much as it seemed impossible that his youngest was old enough for school, Gertie was ready.

"Savilla, you are the older one," he said, looking into their matching green eyes. "You must look after Gertie. Do you understand?"

"Yes, *Daed.*" The girls spoke in unison.

"You do as you're told. Follow instructions. Remember your manners. Don't lose your lunch pails."

"Yes, *Daed.*"

With his hands on their shoulders, Gideon turned his daughters around. They held hands as they got on the bus, Savilla patiently waiting for her small sister to manage the high step into the bus. Gertie immediately stuck her head out and waved.

The driver consulted his list again before looking at Tobias. "You the Wittmer boy?"

Tobias nodded.

"Let's go, then. We have a schedule to keep."

Tobias looked at his father.

Gideon cleared his throat. "Tobias will not be attending school. He is needed on the farm."

The driver tapped his paper. "I can't do anything about the Kaufman boy who didn't show up, but Tobias Wittmer is standing right in front of me. He needs to get on the bus."

"He's not going. I'm his father, and this is the decision I've made."

"The law says he needs to go to school."

"The law does not know my boy," Gideon said. "He was one of the brightest students in our school. Miss Coates said he was doing eighth-grade work two years ago. I need his help, and the consolidated school will not teach him what he needs to know to farm."

"I'm not in charge of what they teach," the driver said. "I'm just supposed to get the students to school."

Gideon looked up at the sun. "As you said, you have a schedule to keep."

The driver puffed out his cheeks and shook his head while he carefully circled Tobias's name. "You'll be hearing from the principal."

CHAPTER 11

Gideon." Ella put a hand on his arm.

"It's all right."

His eyes fixed on his little girls, Gertie hanging out of the bus to wave enthusiastically and Savilla trying to tug her sister back to safety. Ella forced herself to wiggle her fingers at the girls. Whatever she felt at their departure into the *English* world, even for a day, must be magnified in Gideon's heart.

"Not too late to change your mind," the driver said. "Be a law-abiding citizen."

Gideon shook his head.

"Are you sure?" Ella asked.

"No. Yes."

The bus's engine roared to life and the driver put it in gear. Ella's vision clouded with the dust the oversized tires thrust into the air, and she covered her mouth to cough.

"Gideon Wittmer, what have you done?"

Mrs. Glick. Ella had nearly forgotten she was there. Simultaneously, she and Gideon turned to face their neighbor's bulging eyes.

"You stood right here and watched me put my children on that bus." Mrs. Glick scraped her shoe through the dirt. "My little girls."

"My little girls are also on the bus," Gideon said.

Mrs. Glick pointed at Tobias. "The other boys got on, and some of them are older than your son."

"I cannot cross my conscience," Gideon said.

"What will the other fathers think?" Mrs. Glick jabbed a finger in Ella's direction. "And Jed Hilty! Did the two of you decide together to do this?"

"We talked about it," Gideon said, "but I don't make another man's decision."

"I know Mrs. Mast didn't want those boys to go on the bus. What are you going to say to her about keeping your boy home?"

"I do not imagine we will discuss it," Gideon said. "The matter is between Mrs. Mast and her husband."

"But the law!"

"There are new laws about education," Gideon said, "but there are also laws about religious freedom. Isn't that what brought our ancestors to America two hundred years ago?"

Mrs. Glick huffed and tied her bonnet in a firm knot before pivoting and stomping toward her home.

"Maybe she's right, *Daed*."

Tobias's voice surprised Ella, and she riffled through her memories of the last few weeks for any sentence she'd heard him speak on the subject of school or a remark Gideon might have passed on about something his son had said. She came up with nothing.

"It's all right," Gideon said.

"But *Daed*. . ."

Gideon put an arm around his son's shoulders, as Ella had seen him do countless times in the last few years.

"Are you saying you want to go to school?" Gideon asked.

Tobias hesitated. Ella could not tell whether he was considering disagreeing with his father or simply wanted Gideon to be safe.

"We'll talk more at home," Gideon said. "Why don't you drive the buggy home? I'll see you there. I feel like a walk."

Tobias looked from Gideon to Ella before shuffling toward the horse and finding the reins. Ella watched him put the buggy into motion and drive past them before reaching for Gideon's hand.

He squeezed her fingers. "It's all right."

"You keep saying that," Ella said.

"It's true."

"But it's risky." Slowly they began to walk toward the Hilty farm. "You're breaking the law."

"So is your father."

"I know." Her voice caught. "I'm worried about both of you."

"We are in God's hands."

"What if there are consequences?"

"The authorities are blustering," Gideon said.

"How can you be certain?"

He lifted one shoulder and let it drop. "Perhaps I'm not. But why will they concern themselves with Amish young people? We pay our taxes, and they leave us alone. That's the way it has always been. They are blustering for the sake of their own people, not for us."

Ella pressed her lips together. Gideon made a good point. The Amish population in Geauga County was fairly significant, but no one had ever disturbed their way of life. They lived on their own farms, took care of each other, and asked little of the *English*. Why should the *English* care now?

But the deputy had been to see Gideon with the superintendent. Official correspondence reminding everyone of the laws had arrived in the mailboxes of all the Amish families.

"What if they press the issue?" Ella said. "What if you're wrong and they do care?"

"Then I will be wrong about that," Gideon said, "but I will not be wrong about our right to express our religious beliefs. Even the *English* laws protect that."

"I'm nervous, Gideon."

"I know."

"I wish I could be as calm as you are." Ella sighed. "I should get home. Rachel and *Daed* and David—I don't know what to think."

"Seth will be all right."

"It's David I'm worried about."

☙❖❧

At the sound of the bell, students who had attended Seabury Consolidated Grade School the previous year responded by jostling out of their social groups and into grade-level lines. Margaret's job in this annual first-day ritual was to assist and redirect any students who seemed uncertain what to do. She ambled through the recess play area while students scrambled into formation and spoke quietly to children who looked confused about the procedure, pointing toward the lines they should join. These children were in three categories: first graders starting school, older students who were new to the district, and Amish, with their expansive, startled eyes sponging up the motion around them and the details of the building before them.

"Look at them." A seventh grader jeered at two Amish boys in his line. "I'll bet they don't even know how to read."

"That's enough," Margaret snapped. "In this school, we show respect for all our students. Is that understood?"

"Yes, ma'am." The boy looked at his feet.

Margaret turned to the Amish students. "Welcome to our school. I would love to know your names."

"Seth Kaufman," one said.

"Jacob King," the other said.

"You're both in Mr. Taylor's class. You'll enjoy him and learn a great deal."

"*Danki*," Seth said.

Jacob elbowed him and whispered, "Speak English."

"Thank you," Seth said.

The last straggler found a place in the fourth-grade line, and Margaret marched alongside the first graders to greet her own students. The daily entrance into the school always began with the youngest classes. Margaret led the wobbly line of six-year-olds through the main hall on the first floor, up the stairs at the rear of the building, and into her classroom. There, she stood at the door greeting children and pointing to where they should sit. She'd already memorized the seating chart. Now she simply needed to connect faces with the names.

Richard. Franklin. Patricia. Molly. Mary. Elbert. Gertrude.

"You're the lady who was looking for my *daed*," Gertie said.

"That's right," Margaret said. "I remember you. How lucky I am to be your teacher this year."

"*Daed* says there is no such thing as luck. Only *Gottes wille*."

Beside Gertie, a thin Amish boy nodded his head, and his hat bobbed.

"Well, if it's *Gottes wille* for me to be your teacher, I am even more pleased." Margaret turned to the boy. "You must be Hans Byler."

The boy nodded again.

"I thought you two might like to sit next to each other," Margaret said, pointing. "I have two seats for you right there in the second row."

Margaret was glad Gertie and Hans had each other. Altogether six Amish students were supposed to enter the high school, and twenty-six were due to transfer to the consolidated grade school. But Margaret was certain she did not see that many outside as the lines formed. Not nearly that many. Her stomach soured at the impending conversation with Mr. Brownley about her failure in the assigned task.

Once everyone was seated, Margaret put a smile on her face and turned to welcome the first-grade class of 1918.

CHAPTER 12

Mamm, school is fine." Seth tucked the cloth napkin around the ham sandwich in his lunch pail and pressed the lid into place.

"You would tell me if something is not right," Rachel said.

"I would tell you. It's been a week, and everything is fine. I listen to the teacher, I do my work, I come home. It's not so different."

Ella tapped the loaf on the bread board. If she wrapped it now, it might still be warm when she arrived at the Hershberger farm. She had plenty of stew left from yesterday to feed the Hershberger family, which had grown last week with the birth of their newest daughter.

Seth picked up a mathematics textbook. "I have to go or I'll miss the bus."

His lips brushed his mother's cheek as he aimed for the back door. Before the screen door slammed closed, Jed came through it into the kitchen with a sigh he made no effort to disguise.

Rachel looked up. "What's wrong?"

"David has gone off already."

"The barn?" Rachel said.

Jed shook his head.

"Stables?"

"No."

"He'll be waiting for you in the field."

Ella glanced up at her father's doubtful expression and tucked a jar of strawberry jam into the food basket she was preparing.

"Every time I turn around, I've lost David," Jed said. "He doesn't come back for hours."

"He'll settle down," Rachel said. "He knows how important harvesttime is."

Ella spread a clean flour sack towel over the top of the basket. "Is it still all right if I take the buggy to the Hershbergers'?"

Jed nodded. "Please give Mrs. Hershberger our congratulations."

As Ella drove, she prayed. Thanksgiving for Seth's smooth adjustment to the new school. Mercy for David to accept Jed's decision. Grace for Rachel's palpable anxiety. Wisdom for Jed—and Gideon—if the *English* made trouble. Her prayers took her to the Hershberger farm.

As she lifted her basket from below the driving bench, the children's voices clattered through the open windows. The latest birth brought the number of children to eight. The oldest was about Seth's age. Walking toward the house, Ella cocked her head, trying to remember whether Seth had mentioned that the Hershberger boy was in his class.

She climbed the steps to the porch, listening to the cacophony of one child's wail and another's plea for maternal attention, while an older child's voice warned a sibling to get down off a stool.

Ella paused as she raised her knuckles to knock. At least four of the Hershberger children were school age, perhaps five. The bus would have come to their stop at least half an hour ago. Why were so many of them at home? She knocked, and a mumbling shuffle progressed toward the door. When it opened, Ella looked into the eyes of the eldest Hershberger daughter.

"*Gut mariye.*" Ella hid her speculations behind a smile. "Congratulations on your new baby sister."

"*Danki.* Please come in." The girl had a firm grasp on a four-year-old's shoulder. "I'll tell *Mamm* you've come."

She left Ella standing alone in the front room while she hurried down the hall toward the kitchen at the rear of the old farmhouse. A few minutes later, Joanna Hershberger appeared with an infant in her arms.

Ella smiled again. A boy and a girl, school-age, eyed her from across the room.

"I've brought some food," Ella said. "There's plenty for all of you to have a good meal. You only need to warm the stew."

Joanna tilted her head toward the oldest girl, who stepped forward to take the basket of food from Ella's arms. When she left the room, several other children trailed after her, curious about the pot's contents.

Ella turned to Joanna and put her arms out. "May I?"

"Of course." Joanna laid the sleeping infant in Ella's arms.

"Are you able to rest?"

Joanna shrugged. "Not at this age. But I will have her on a schedule soon."

Ella glanced toward the kitchen. "Your oldest daughter seems helpful."

"I don't know what I'd do without Lizzy."

"I'm sure you miss her when she's in school," Ella said. "Are they just out for a few days while you welcome your babe?"

Joanna looked away at nothing in particular. "John has decided our children will learn at home. I will teach them."

So far Ella had seen nothing to suggest organized lessons in progress—or organized anything. She returned her gaze to the baby in her arms, who yawned but did not open her eyes.

"The Borntragers also will teach their children at home," Joanna said. "We can work together on the lessons. We'll begin soon."

Ella nodded noncommittally. Her father. Gideon. John Hershberger. Isaiah Borntrager. Who else was defying the new laws?

Gideon, Aaron King, and Cristof Byler huddled around the harvesting equipment in Gideon's alfalfa field. The mid-September morning brought an overcast sky. Gideon hoped it would burn off soon.

Cristof braced his foot against a stationary wagon wheel. "Don't you think it would be better if we're all of one mind?"

Gideon puffed out his cheeks in a slow exhale. "The men I've talked to seem to have made up their minds."

"What about the bishop?" Aaron said. "In all these weeks, I haven't heard him say anything."

"Why don't we meet with him?" Cristof raised his eyebrows.

"I've spoken with him," Gideon said. "He came to see me. He understands the complexity of the question."

"A church vote, then," Aaron said.

"And what would we vote on?" Gideon said. "Forbid our children to go to school in town? Let the younger ones go, but not the older ones? What about pupils who have already finished the eighth grade, and now the *English* want them to return to school? Whatever we decide, the *English* will find fault. No, I don't think a church vote is the right course."

"Then tell us what you suggest." Cristof crossed his arms over his chest.

"The apostle Paul reminds us that as far as it is up to us, we should live at peace with all men—including the *English*."

"They will only recognize peace if we do what they say we must," Cristof said.

Aaron squinted his eyes. "I think Gideon has something else in mind."

Gideon nodded. "The school board meets tomorrow. We can go to them—the entire board—and ask for an exception to their rules. We can assure them we want our children to have the education they need for the way we live—and we can provide it ourselves."

"But we don't have a teacher," Cristof said. "We don't even have a school."

"One thing at a time," Gideon said.

"It won't work." Cristof grunted and turned away.

"One thing at a time," Gideon repeated.

❦

"One thing have I desired of the Lord, that will I seek after; that I may dwell in the house of the Lord all the days of my life, to behold the beauty of the Lord and to enquire in his temple."

The words of Psalm 27 wafted through James's mind as his wagon reached the highest peak of the rolling hills, and he held the horses for a moment so his spirit could inhale the view. The tinge of red creeping through the leaves announced the turn of the season. The sun's glare still made him shade his eyes, but without summer's ferocity. The lake reminded him he had promised Tobias a fishing day before the weather turned too cold for an early morning outing when the fish were biting. What was missing was the white wooden tower of the old schoolhouse. Instead, James saw the hole in the roof and the slight slant of the entire building. Would the *English* have moved all the children to the schools in town if the rural structure had remained sound? Or if Miss Coates had not left to marry? The change likely was only a matter of time.

Movement caught James's eye. A figure moved to the back of the schoolhouse with a ladder. The roofline was lower in the rear. Miriam had made James stop scaling roofs a long time ago, but it was fairly simple to get on the school's roof from the back. James urged his horses forward full speed, down the sloping ground toward the schoolhouse.

"Isaiah Borntrager, what in the world are you doing?" James scrambled off his bench and stomped over to the base of the ladder. Isaiah was two-thirds of the way up.

"There's no such thing as an Amish man who doesn't know how to build," Isaiah said. "We manage to keep our homes standing. Why shouldn't we keep the school standing?"

"Half the roof fell in, Isaiah. Come down from there."

Isaiah took another step up.

"This outside wall is not trustworthy," James said. "It won't hold your ladder."

"God is trustworthy."

James sighed. He did not think this was what the scriptures meant when they spoke of trusting God.

"Isaiah," James said, "come down. Let's talk about this."

"I'll gladly accept any help you feel led to offer," Isaiah said, turning to look down at James over one shoulder, "but I'm through talking. I am a man of action."

"Does your wife know you're doing this?"

"This is not her decision."

"Just what do you plan to do when you get up there?" James gripped the rails of the ladder and braced his feet.

"Today I'm just looking around to see the true condition," Isaiah said. "Then I'll make a plan. I'm not going to sit around waiting for the state to decide what is best for *my* children. If you don't want to help, go on home."

Having seen what Isaiah was doing, James could hardly drive off now. He gripped the ladder more tightly, realizing that Isaiah's decrepit ladder was in no better condition than the school's roof. James fixed his eyes on Isaiah's left foot as it tested the next rung. James saw the step give more than it should have.

"Watch out!"

The rung cracked. Isaiah lost his balance. The ladder surrendered its purchase on the side of the building. Isaiah let go. James's sight filled with the mass of stubbornness dropping straight toward him. The last thing James saw was Isaiah's hat flying off his head.

Then James was on the ground, and Isaiah was on top of him.

～✦～

"What was I supposed to do?" James winced.

Miriam dipped a cotton cloth in a bowl of warm water and dabbed the scrapes on her husband's cheek again. "Isaiah could have killed himself falling off that ancient ladder—and you."

"I don't think he'll try that again."

"Unless he gets a new ladder," Miriam said. "Are you sure you don't need a doctor?"

James took the cloth from Miriam's hand and probed under his beard for a spot where he suspected the skin had split. Already his shoulders, hips, and knees ached from the sudden surprise of Isaiah's weight dropped on him. James pushed out of his mind the image of what might have happened if Isaiah had been alone when he fell.

"No doctor," he said. "I may be moving slowly for a few days, though."

"Then we'll move slowly together."

James watched Miriam as she carried the bowl of water to the sink. The spry gait she'd had since girlhood was diminished. Miriam's neck bent at a tired angle.

"Disagreeing with the *English* is no excuse for doing something foolish," Miriam said. "But we can always count on Isaiah Borntrager to be rash."

"Things were simpler when we were in school."

"That was a long time ago, old man." Miriam winked.

She started calling him *old man* on his twenty-fifth birthday, which came fifty-six days before hers. Now, James supposed, he more obviously fit the description.

The *dawdihaus* door opened, and Gertie tumbled in.

"I'm sorry, little one," Miriam said. "I didn't bake cookies today."

"That's okay. My friend Polly shared the cookie her *mamm* put in her lunch bucket."

"That was generous," James said.

Gertie climbed into James's lap, as she did every day after school. "What happened to your face?"

"God gave me this face," James said. "Maybe I got the leftovers because He was saving the best parts for you."

Gertie giggled and leaned into James's sore right shoulder.

"How was school?" James smothered his wince.

"I like school," Gertie said. "I can read twelve words now. Pretty soon I'll know enough to read a whole book to you."

"That will be great fun." James kissed the top of her head. "And the bus?"

"Polly's teaching me songs to sing on the bus."

"Oh?" Over Gertie's head, James caught Miriam's eye.

"They're not like the songs we sing in church," Gertie said. "They go fast, and they rhyme, and we do hand motions."

James changed the subject. "Did your teacher give you an assignment to do before you go back to school?"

"She said we should choose a book at home and see if we can find three words we know and read them to our families."

James tried to picture Gideon's small shelf of books. At least half of them were in German. Gertie might have to find her words in a seed catalog.

CHAPTER 13

With their black hats still on their heads, a row of Amish men sat straight-backed in the downtown Seabury building where the school board held its announced meetings. James was among them. Gideon planned to speak on behalf of the group, but he mustered the men to produce a presence that would let the board know they were earnest in their petition. He was not one man speaking on his own. Even the bishop had come in support. This was not one or two fathers disgruntled with the new regulations. It was an unsettled community that wanted to find peace again.

Gideon was warned he would have to wait until the call for new business was announced, and the board would not have a great deal of time to hear him out. James countered with advice that Gideon be prepared to hold the floor. His statement should be carefully thought through. While he might make notes, Gideon should be ready to look the board in the eye and speak convincingly.

The assembly opened with a dry reading of the minutes of the previous board meeting, followed by a motion to accept them. A spattering of *English* parents shifted in their seats, as if to get comfortable for the coming proceedings. Then the board resumed discussions of matters of old business: the budget, one unfilled teacher position, the refreshments committee for the fall harvest dance for the high school students, a new format for report cards, new tires for one of the buses, a delayed textbook order. Why the school board let the topics remain unresolved from week to week, or month to month, confounded James. The decisions did not strike him as complex—nothing approaching the significance of an unsafe rural building that technically belonged to the district or the consequences of its closure for the families it had served for more than three decades. Twice James turned his head slightly for a glance at Gideon. If Gideon was becoming as impatient as James, he did not show it. Well habituated by lengthy church services, the Amish men barely moved for two and a half hours.

"Do I hear a motion to adjourn?" the superintendent finally said.

"So moved," said one of the board members.

Instantly, Gideon was on his feet. "I believe you have overlooked new business."

Ulysses Brownley blinked at Gideon. "The hour is late. Perhaps at our next meeting."

"With all due respect," Gideon said, "we requested in advance to be heard at tonight's meeting, and we have patiently waited for you to consider your weighty matters, although all of us will have to be up before dawn to tend our animals."

Brownley cleared his throat. "Very well. We will now consider new business, but only briefly. What is the matter you wish to put before the board?"

"We wish to present our reasons for requesting an exception on religious grounds to the new educational regulations."

"We do not make the state laws, Mr. Wittmer," Brownley said. "We are only charged with enforcing them at the local level, in one small school district."

"Nevertheless, I wish to make our case," Gideon said, "in the hope that we might continue to work together for suitable education of our children as we always have."

Good for you, Gideon. James turned up one corner of his mouth.

Gideon stepped out of the row of men and centered himself before the members of the board arranged across the front of the room.

"True education," he said, "cultivates humility, simple living, and submission to the will of God. We train for life both in this world and in the next. We do not see school and life as separate spheres. The highest form of religious life is our community life, and we guard carefully against any threat to our community."

Brownley leaned back in a wide black leather chair and pulled out his pocket watch.

Gideon was undeterred.

"So long as schools were small and near our farms, we have gladly worked with teachers the district so generously provided to find a meeting of the minds. In this way, we have considered both what was needful for our children's participation in our life together and what the state offered for their good."

"Mr. Wittmer," Brownley said, "perhaps you can get to the point."

"I have four points," Gideon said, calmly ignoring the scowl on Brownley's face. "First, we believe that it is in our children's best interest to attend school close to our homes, where they can easily help with the farmwork that is foundational to our way of life.

"Second, we would like our children to receive instruction from teachers committed to and respectful of our values. This will require special qualifications that may not coincide with those the state would measure.

"Third, our children need only basic skills in reading, writing, and arithmetic. All other training should be conducive to our religious life. These goals do not require that our children remain in school after the eighth grade.

"And last, our children need to be trained for our way of life, not the *English* way of life. Our hope is not that they achieve earthly success, but that they are prepared for eternity."

James wanted to stand up and clap. Gideon's late nights formulating his thoughts had yielded a polished presentation in which he did not look down at his notes even once.

"Since the form of education is an expression of our religious life," Gideon continued, "we respectfully request that the board relent and allow our children to attend school close to home and in a manner that allows for parents to consult freely with the teacher for pupils up through eighth grade. After that, our children will withdraw from school."

James watched the superintendent's face as he made a show of consulting his pocket watch once again.

"We will take it under advisement," Brownley said, "with the reminder once again that our duty is to execute state law, not formulate it. Now, I will once again entertain a motion to adjourn."

Gideon allowed himself a sigh of relief.

He could have said far more, but Ulysses Brownley had heard enough for one evening. The seed was planted. By God's grace, it would grow.

Aaron King clapped him on the back. Joshua Glick shook his hand. Grinning, John Hershberger dipped his head toward Gideon. Jed Hilty gave a satisfied nod. Cristof Byler looked red in the face from holding himself back, but he had held to the agreement that only Gideon would speak for the group. Even Isaiah Borntrager was pleasantly composed. Amid the unspoken congratulations, it was James's eyes Gideon sought, and his reward was a smile that said James could not be more pleased.

At the front of the room, board members whispered in huddles before dispersing. Spectators trickled out of the meeting room.

"I'll get the buggy," James said.

"I'll be out in a few minutes," Gideon said. His mind needed two minutes of quiet before the spirited ride home. The men would return together to Gideon's home, where they had left their rigs. No doubt the conversation would be animated. Isaiah and Cristof and John would unfurl all the words they guarded during the school board meeting.

Gideon slipped down the corridor and turned into a side hall where he hoped to lean against the cool brick wall and catch his breath.

His refuge dissipated before he could close his eyes and utter a prayer of thanks. Heavy footfalls made him stand up straight.

"Mr. Wittmer." It was Brownley.

"Yes?" Gideon moistened his lips.

"The laws exist for a reason," Brownley said, his words a snarl.

"We are peaceful, law-abiding people," Gideon said. "But we take our faith seriously."

"Education and religion do not mix."

"I beg to differ."

"I'm warning you," Brownley said. "If you and your ragamuffin friends persist in this dissent, you must do things properly. Go through channels."

"I believe that is what we were doing tonight," Gideon said. His neck suddenly ached. "Is not the school board the right authority to meet with on the question of education? If we should go elsewhere with our concerns, we welcome your counsel."

"Don't placate me," Brownley said. "I can manage my own school district. You'd be wasting your time pressing the question. The law is clear. I will provide you a printed copy in its entirety upon request."

"That won't be necessary," Gideon said.

"I notice that your son is on our truancy list." Brownley shook a finger. "Send that boy to school starting tomorrow and I will instruct the teachers to go the extra mile to help him catch up. The same offer stands for your friends who are breaking the law."

Gideon pressed his lips together and said nothing.

"I will be monitoring the attendance reports personally. If these children do not turn up in school soon, you will face the full consequences under the law."

Gideon exhaled softly. "Perhaps we should arrange a meeting to discuss our concerns when the hour is not so late."

"Discussions will not change the law, Mr. Wittmer. Put your children in school."

❧❧❧

"He's gone again," Jed muttered as he walked past Rachel, who rummaged through the vegetable garden looking for autumn squashes. Pulling overgrown bean plants from the fence two rows down, Ella stiffened at the irritation in his voice.

"Where?" Rachel said.

"He doesn't leave me notes," Jed snapped. "I asked him to throw down some hay in the barn, and he left the job half done. I haven't seen him in hours."

"It's never been like David to act like this," Rachel said. "I don't know where he could be going."

Ellie busied her eyes searching for dry beanstalks to pull, but she could do little to divert her ears.

"I can't watch him every minute of the day," Jed said. "Nor should I have to. He's fifteen and capable of doing a man's work."

"Perhaps you should talk to him again."

"And say what? I've said it all before. Would he have defied his father this way?"

Ella held her breath. Rachel gave no answer.

"I have to see to the hay myself. The animals shouldn't suffer because of David's willfullness." Jed grunted and tramped out of the garden.

Ella yanked another bare stalk and tossed it in the pile. Either Rachel refused to see the obvious or she was more naive than Ella thought. It could not be coincidence that David's odd behavior began the same week school resumed session. He was not gone every day, nor all day, but his absences roughly coincided with the same hours Seth was legitimately off the farm to attend school. How David was getting to Seabury and back, Ella didn't know. But she did not have be an *English* professor to know where he was spending his lapsed hours.

Looking over the waning vegetation, Ella gave her stepmother a flimsy smile, grateful in the moment that it was not her place to advise what Rachel should do with her recalcitrant son.

"I told Joanna Hershberger I'd bring some cotton cloth she could use for the baby," Rachel said. "I don't think I'm up to taking it. Will you go?"

"Of course. I'm almost finished here."

Ella waited for Rachel, sniffling, to finish collecting squash and haul the basket toward the house before raking through the soil at the base of the spent bean plants and returning the rake to the tool shed. She went to the well to pump water over her hands, her mind muddled over whether the Hershbergers had made the right choice to keep their children home.

News of Isaiah Borntrager's impulsiveness had spread through the farms in the last ten days. Jed had driven over to the abandoned school to see for himself the further damage Isaiah's shenanigans had caused. On James's behalf, Gideon had taken a horse and ridden out to speak privately with Isaiah before mounting freshly painted signs on the old school warning off additional disturbance. If the school district did not do something soon, Gideon told Ella, he would gather a crew to safely dismantle the structure before anyone else got hurt. Gideon's report of the school board meeting two days ago—and Mr. Brownley's hostility afterward—did not suggest the board members were concerned with the decrepit building.

Ella fetched the cotton from the house and hitched up the open buggy. She would use it for as many days as the weather remained fine. Winter would come soon enough and necessitate enclosed transportation.

The Hershberger infant seemed no closer to a routine than the last time Ella visited, and Ella saw no books or papers to indicate schooling was under way for the older children. In fact, the baby screamed over much of the brief conversation Ella had with the tiny girl's exhausted mother, who gave one distracted instruction after another to her eldest daughter about the care of the younger ones. Ella's presence only added to the chaos, and she did not stay long.

When Ella went past the school on her way home, she paused to gaze on the broken shell, still stunned to see what had become of the school she had loved. Most of the teachers came straight from the teachers college and only stayed two or three years before marrying or moving to a more progressive school. As a pupil, Ella was always curious about each new teacher who arrived with untarnished energy and dedication. Only one of them ever expressed exasperation with Ella's barrage of questions about what they read or her perseverance to complete the work of a higher grade level.

Tobias and Savilla had experienced this school, where teachers found ways to feed the minds of the Amish pupils without crossing their parents. Gertie's impressions of school were in the hands of Margaret Simpson, who was a kind individual but who believed in progressive education. The old school stirred warm memories. The new school reminded Ella more of a sleeping, unpredictable monster.

A black-capped chickadee settled on a haphazard pile of crumbling roofing, its orange-hued sides shimmering in the September sun as it dipped its head and pecked, searching for edible tidbits. Ella wondered if David had seen this bird.

Ella sighed. *David. This is not the way.*

CHAPTER 14

T he wagon coming toward Ella could only be Aaron King's. His hitch had been unbalanced for years, causing the team to pull slightly to the right. Aaron insisted it was hardly any trouble to compensate with the reins and saw no reason to repair or replace the hitch. Trying not to laugh at the spectacle, Ella gave him wide berth in the road and returned his wave.

Aaron carried a full load of lumber, some of it hanging precariously off the open back end of his wagon. Ella scrunched her face.

Aaron's barn was fairly new, raised at a frolic only three years ago. The last time the church met at his home, Ella hadn't noticed it was in need of repairs—certainly not enough to explain the size of the load in his wagon. Besides, he was headed east, not south toward his farm. Curious, Ella turned her cart around in the road and urged her single horse into a canter to keep Aaron in view. With each turn he took, Ella became more persuaded of his destination.

The Mast farm.

Ella followed Aaron to the west end of the Mast farm, to a pasture Chester had left fallow the last two years. Her eyes widened at the view.

Two buggies, three wagons, and a total of nine men and older boys. They descended on Aaron's wagon to unload. Chester had been the boss at the last two barn raisings. Now he glanced at each piece of lumber and pointed to where it should be laid.

Ella glanced across the Mast acres. The crew was a long way from the house or barn, and the shape taking place before her eyes was too large for an ordinary outbuilding.

A gasp caught her by surprise. Chester strode toward her.

"Keep your eyes in your head," he said.

Slowly, she rotated her head to look him in the eye. "You're putting up a school." The layout was identical to the collapsed building.

"We won't get it up today," Chester said. "We need a lot more lumber, and some glass for the windows, and a woodstove. But yes, a school."

"But. . ." Ella did not know how to finish her sentence. She swallowed. Did Gideon know about this?

"Gideon did a fine job speaking to the school board," Chester said, as if reading her thoughts, "but I know a stubborn face when I see one. That Mr. Brownley has no intention of altering an iota of his plan."

"Surely he will not sit idle and let you build a school."

"I don't require his permission. It's my land. I'll build whatever I want on it. The building won't belong to the *English*. It will belong to us, and we'll use it as we see fit."

Ella's heart boomed. "You're very bold."

Chester swung his arm wide at the other fathers and sons. "We are bold together—bold in obedience."

The men's movements were fluid, cooperative, effective. Aaron's load had not been the first to arrive. Already four trestles were laid out, ready to answer the call to hold up a roof.

"It's a fine place for a school, wouldn't you say?" Chester beamed. "A quiet corner with a view of God's goodness, but close enough to the road that it will not be difficult for our families to reach."

Ella nodded. Chester had chosen well. Pupils could come out of school and look toward an expansive sky with a band of deciduous trees fluttering against the horizon. Mast wheat would rise in golden rolls before their eyes to the east, and Borntrager cattle would dot the verdant pasture to the west. Amish children would know that the land was God's generous gift and learn their role in caring for it.

"It will be lovely," she said. "Truly. But Mr. Brownley will still consider our children truants. We won't be authorized to hold classes."

"We do not need the state's approval to educate our children. We are perfectly capable."

"But we don't even have a qualified teacher."

"We'll find one. And when we do, we'll be ready."

James Lehman entered the Seabury Consolidated Grade School without fanfare. No bell. No knocker. He pushed open the oversized door and went in. The interior of the school resembled many *English* buildings constructed in the last decade or so and matched what James expected.

Standing in the main corridor, he sought his bearings. Tasteful signs in modern script announced the purposes of the rooms or gave cryptic instructions. ART. MUSIC. LADIES. GENTLEMEN. PRINCIPAL'S OFFICE THIS WAY. CLASSROOMS ABOVE. PLEASE USE STAIRS AT REAR.

James was not there to speak to the principal, and he was not curious about *English* art or music lessons, which would have no relevance for the Amish children. He wanted to see Gertie in the setting that seemed to make her happy, look in on Savilla because she seemed less happy, and take Gideon a report.

He passed the office—where he saw no one in attendance anyway—and followed instructions to use the broad rear stairs. On the second floor, another set of scripted signs gave pertinent information. It was not hard to find the one that said, GRADE 1, MISS SIMPSON. James turned the knob, and the door opened easily.

Chalkboards, desks, books, a globe, cheery letters and pictures of animals attached to the walls. It looked like any classroom ought to, but was brightened by a bank of electric lights.

The woman at the front of the room paused with her chalk in midair. "Can I help you?"

"Miss Simpson?" James said.

"That's right."

"Then I'm in the right place." He stepped into the room.

"Sir—"

Gertie squealed, slid out of her seat, and hurtled toward him. "This is my *onkel* James."

James warmed with the enthusiasm of the introduction and received Gertie's hug, lifting her the way he would have after school in the *dawdihaus*.

"Is Gertie needed at home?" Miss Simpson set down her chalk.

"All is well at home," James said. "I only wanted to see for myself."

"Class is in session," Miss Simpson said. "If you'd like to come back after school, I will be happy to answer any questions you have."

James surveyed the rows of desks and the pairs of eyes of their occupants. On one side of the room, a little boy squirmed. At the back, two little girls leaned their heads together and snickered.

Did they snicker at Gertie that way? Which one was Polly?

He set Gertie down and turned back to Miss Simpson. "I won't disturb you. I'll stand in the back."

The teacher's jawline tightened, but her voice retained its cordiality. "The principal did not mention to me that I should expect a classroom visit. I might have been better prepared."

"I haven't spoken to the principal," James said. "I only wanted to observe the class." The request seemed unremarkable to James. At the old school, he stopped in three or four times each year. Others did the same. The children were part of the church community. Why should adults not be interested in their surroundings?

"Gertie," Miss Simpson said, "would you mind taking your seat, please?"

Gertie tilted her head back to look at James, who nodded. Smiling and waving over her shoulder, she returned to her seat next to Hans Byler.

Miss Simpson took several steps closer to James. "I'm afraid that without Mr. Tarkington's knowledge—and approval—I cannot invite you to stay."

Why did he need an invitation? He was already there.

"You see," she said, "our policy is that visitors should make arrangements through the office."

"I was in town on other matters," James said. "It's on my way home."

"I understand, but I must ask you to leave. Make the proper arrangements, and you will be welcome to visit another time. It's in the best interest of the children."

"I don't require any special attention," James said. If she had simply let him go to the back of the room when he came in, the children would have forgotten he was there and her penmanship lesson would be well on its way to completion.

"I'm afraid I must ask you to leave," she said. "I have the principal to answer to on the matter."

It was the most ridiculous thing James had heard in a long time. Why would the school discourage families from knowing what happened in the classroom? But Miss Simpson seemed like an earnest young woman trying to do the right thing, so he nodded in reluctance.

⚘

Margaret drew lunchtime recess duty. She welcomed the brisk breeze on her face, though she could not help raising her hands to be sure her hair remained tucked into its bun. The rumble of Gray's truck bounced around her ears, and for a moment she thought she had let her imagination go too far. Then a truck pulled up to one of the wide doors at the rear of the building, and Gray emerged from the cab. He looked up, caught her eye, and smiled. Margaret wanted to wave, but she could not bring herself to do it in front of a playground full of children and teachers. Gray opened the back of his truck and began lifting out desks. She'd heard one of the upper grades needed additional seating. Even from this distance, Margaret saw the muscles in Gray's forearm ripple and had to avert her eyes.

Miss Hunter, from the third grade, sidled up to Margaret. "Did you hear what those people are doing?"

"What people?" Margaret pointed at a boy. "Elliott Lewis, you keep your hands to yourself."

"Your friends the Amish," Miss Hunter said. "They're in the office now."

Margaret's brow furrowed, and her heart sped up. "Who?"

"I don't know their names. You might, since you visited them."

Margaret returned her gaze to Gray, who now pushed a cart stacked with four desks toward the entrance.

"Go see," Miss Hunter said. "I'll watch things out here."

"I'd better get the door for that delivery," Margaret said, already stepping away from the playground.

She reached the door just in time to hold it open for Gray. Circumspect, he nodded his head in appreciation and pushed the cart through.

"Where do you suppose these go?" he said.

"Someone in the office will want to deal with them," Margaret said. "This way."

Until now, Gray's courtship and Margaret's work were separate spheres orbiting her life but not crossing paths. It was oddly delicious to see him in the middle of the day, his nearness fluttering her heart as usual. Walking beside him down the wide corridor, she forced herself not to hope he would kiss her, as she would have at home. That was simply out of the question here. She took a deep breath and clicked her heels along the tile a little more energetically.

The door to the school office was propped open. Simply walking down the hall with Gray had been enough to make Margaret forget Miss Hunter's remark that there were Amish in the office. Now she tried to absorb the scene. Mr. Tarkington stood with hands in his suit coat pockets, scowling at two sets of Amish parents. Margaret fished around in her brain for their names. The Masts and the Borntragers.

"I'm afraid that is not how things are done," Mr. Tarkington said.

"Is it against the law?" Chester Mast asked, holding his gaze on the principal.

The principal opened his mouth, closed it, and finally formed a sentence. "I'll have to check the regulations and consult with the superintendent. This is highly unorthodox."

"You've been telling us to put our children in school, so we are here to do that," Isaiah said. "In the eighth grade."

"But these pupils have already completed the eighth grade. They belong in the high school next door." Mr. Tarkington turned to Chester Mast. "I was under the impression that your son was already studying in the ninth grade."

"And now he's going to study in the eighth grade," Chester insisted, "along with the Borntrager boy. They'll soon catch up on the lessons."

"I imagine so," the principal said, "since they completed the eighth grade two years ago."

"The law says they have to go to school," Chester said, "but I don't believe it says what grade they have to be in. These children will go to the eighth grade."

Tarkington scoffed. "Do you intend to retain them in the eighth grade until they reach sixteen years of age?"

This possibility had never occurred to Margaret.

"I'm going to need a signature for my records," Gray said. "I can't just leave the desks in the hall."

Margaret turned to him, one ear still cocked toward the commotion in the office. "Will it suffice if I sign? Mr. Tarkington has his hands full."

"I suppose." Gray handed her a sheet of paper and a pen. "I'm glad not to be in his shoes. They seem like stubborn people who are not about to do what he wants."

Margaret scribbled a signature. Superintendent Brownley was not going to like this any more than the principal did.

"They're not stubborn," she said. "They want what is best for the children."

Unconvinced, Gray exhaled through his nose as he lifted one of the desks off the cart and lined it up against the wall. "It would be a lot easier for everyone if they just did what they're supposed to do."

Margaret already anticipated a summons to the superintendent's office and a mandate to talk some sense into the Amish.

CHAPTER 15

In the eleven months since Rachel and her boys entered the Hilty household, Ella had become accustomed to the sound of an automobile rattling down their lane. Lindy Lehman turned up at unpredictable intervals and was always welcome. This time, though, instead of the engine's revolutions slowing and its intrusive tumult tapering as it approached the house, the car roared at high speed.

Ella stood in the yard on Monday with a large basket of straw, getting ready to freshen the henhouse. She started to wave but opted to step out of the way as the car veered toward the spot she occupied.

Lindy braked hard and the car lurched to a halt.

And Ella saw David hanging his head on the passenger side of the bench.

Lindy got out. "I hope Rachel is here."

Ella nodded. "What's wrong? Is David all right?"

"It's best if I talk to Rachel."

"Go on in."

Lindy glanced at David. "I'd better stay here. Would you ask Rachel to come out, please?"

"Of course." Ella brushed straw off her hands.

David had begun to squirm and his fingers gripped the door handle.

"Stay right there, David." Lindy's tone made no allowance for discussion.

Ella found Rachel in the boys' bedroom upstairs, changing the linens on their beds. Rachel dropped the pillowcases and raced down the stairs. Ella followed, determined to keep silent but unable to turn away from the commotion. Obviously David had left the farm again early Monday morning. Where Lindy found him was the curious question.

"David!" Rachel said, startled.

"You can get out now," Lindy said.

"You're supposed to be in the field with Jed." Dread seeped through Rachel's voice.

"He was a long way from the field," Lindy said. "David has something to tell you."

David opened the door now and got out of the car. "I'll go to the field now."

"David," Lindy said. "You know what you need to do."

"Can't you just let me go find Jed? Isn't that what you all want?" Ella's gaze snapped up. David's complexion flushed.

"Sneaking around is not the way," Lindy said. "You have to talk to your mother."

David exhaled heavily. "There's an assignment due in my literature class. If I don't turn it in today, I'll get a zero."

School. Just as Ella thought.

"Literature class?" Rachel echoed. "You've been leaving Jed with all the work so you could go to that *English* school?"

"I *like* school, *Mamm*," David said. "What is so wrong with wanting to learn?"

Rachel calmly pivoted to face Ella. "Would you please take the cart, find your father, and tell him it's urgent that he come to the house?"

Twenty minutes later, Jed had little to say as Ella drove the cart back from the field where he had abandoned his tools and tasks to answer his wife's summons. When they reached the house, Lindy's car was still there. Ella stopped the horse long enough to let her father out of the cart before pulling alongside the stable to unhitch the buggy and send the horse into the pasture.

She grimaced slightly as she opened the back screen door, which tended to both creak and slam. The kitchen was empty. Voices wafted from the front room. The worn state of her shoes made little sound as she crossed the kitchen linoleum and leaned against a wall to listen.

"How many days have you been to school?" Jed demanded.

"I don't know," David mumbled. "I haven't been counting."

School started only two weeks ago. Based on his absences from the farm, Ella reasoned David had been to school at least half the time.

"Why would you contradict my express wishes?" Jed said.

"What about *my* wishes?" David said.

"David!" Rachel's tone was sharp with warning. "Don't speak to Jed that way."

Ella peeked into the front room. David slumped deep into the davenport.

"Where did Lindy find you this morning?" Jed leaned forward, hands on knees.

"Does it matter?" David said.

"I want to know."

"I hitched a ride into Seabury."

"I saw him getting out of a car," Lindy supplied. "He should talk to you. A calm conversation would be better than sneaking around."

David huffed and turned his face to Lindy. "Can't you see where this is getting me?"

"I hope it will keep your relationship with your mother honest," Lindy said.

"So you're on her side."

"I'm not on anybody's *side*—"

"You could have fooled me."

Rachel choked back a sob. "David, please."

"I'll fix some *kaffi*." Lindy stood. "Perhaps we all need a moment to calm down."

"Yes," Rachel said, "and I have coffee cake."

Ella looked from the coffeepot on the stove to the cake on the counter.

"I don't need cake and *kaffi*," David said. "I want to go to school and turn in my literature paper. It's the first real grade of the year."

The pleading in his voice pierced Ella. How much had David been holding inside all these months?

"David's right," Jed said. "We don't need cake and *kaffi*. We have work to do."

"Jed, please," Lindy said. "Let's figure this out."

"Your friendship means a great deal to Rachel," Jed said. "But I am her husband. We have already talked about this and made our decision."

"But David—"

"David will not go to school."

Ella grimaced. Her father was not an unreasonable man, but once he made up his mind, he rarely saw the purpose in revisiting the same question.

"He's fifteen," Jed said. "He's capable in the fields, and I need him. If he wants to read in his spare time, he is free to do so. I've never kept my own daughter from her books as long as the work was finished."

David rolled his head against the back of the davenport.

Jed stood. "Come on, David. We've lost enough of the morning already."

Ella ran her hand across her face. *David, David, David.* The boy did not know what he was up against.

Jed strode across the room, opened the front door, and waited. David unfolded his reluctance into a shuffle and followed Jed out. Lindy turned to embrace Rachel.

Ella lit a burner on the stove and filled the coffeepot with water. Lindy entered the kitchen alone.

"Where's Rachel?" Ella had supposed they would both come.

"I told her I would bring *kaffi*."

Ella scooped ground coffee into the percolator receptacle. "You did the right thing by bringing David home."

Lindy shrugged one shoulder. "It doesn't seem to have done any good."

"He shouldn't be sneaking around." Ella set two slices of coffee cake on a plate and nudged it down the counter toward Lindy.

"I agree. But he'll do it again."

"Maybe not," Ella said, though she thought Lindy was right.

"Jed should let David go to school. He'll be sixteen in a year anyway."

"What if he wants to stay in school long enough to graduate high school?" The coffee started to bubble.

"He'll be old enough to decide," Lindy said. "I wasn't in school, but I was sixteen when I knew I wouldn't stay with the Amish."

A fork shook in Ella's hand. "Is that what you think David wants? To leave the church?"

"I haven't asked him," Lindy said, "and I won't. But I've known him all his life, and I've never seen him behave this way. Rachel and Jed have to listen to him and find out what's in his heart."

Ella removed a tray from a cupboard and arranged the cake plate and two coffee cups on it.

"Are you going to say that to Rachel?" Ella said, tucking two napkins under the edge of the plate.

Lindy paused before saying, "Rachel means a lot to me. I want her to be happy."

CHAPTER 16

A glance at the sun told James he was running later than he planned, but he wouldn't leave the farm on Wednesday morning without kissing his wife. He stroked the horse's nose, with an unnecessary warning not to gallop off with the loaded wagon, and started toward the house.

As he rounded the corner of the barn, a fleeting sound—a faint footfall—made him pause and look over his left shoulder. But he saw nothing unexpected. His biggest canvas tarp secured the lumpy load he was taking into town. He was transporting two end tables, the usual assortment of eggs in a range of colors, and a carefully packed quilted wall hanging Miriam had just finished. The mercantile owner now kept a list of customers who were interested in Amish handiwork. Most likely he wouldn't even put Miriam's latest creation on display, because it would sell before his best customers could answer their phones to learn it was there.

James turned back toward the *dawdihaus*, where he hoped to find Miriam with her feet propped up after the morning skirmish of getting the girls readied and to the bus stop on time.

Miriam looked up as James entered. "Will you be long today?" she said.

"I don't expect to be. I'm just stopping at the mercantile and then on to Lindy's." He could have sanded down and refinished the end tables himself, but Miriam had insisted they ask Lindy to do it and pay her a fair price.

"Good." Miriam nodded.

He kissed her and ambled back out to the wagon to take up the reins. At least the bus had come and gone. If the road was clear, he might make up for lost time and still be at the mercantile when the owner opened the doors.

When James took the wide turn onto the main road, something in the load softly slid and came to a stop against the side of the wagon. He scowled, trying to think what he had forgotten to tie down. He hoped it was not the crate of eggs. Few things were more aggravating to clean up than broken eggs. And if the eggs soiled the wall hanging—James refused to dwell on that possibility.

The mercantile came into view. Two women and a man stood on the sidewalk awaiting its opening. James pulled up as close as he could and tied the horse to the hitching post. Pacing along the side of the wagon, for the third time that morning he heard a sound he couldn't place. The bottom of a brown work boot now protruded from under the tarp.

James swiftly untied the corner of the canvas and flipped it back.

"David, what in the world are you doing here?"

"I needed a ride," David said. He retrieved a book that had escaped his grasp and scooted out of the wagon.

"Does Jed know where you are?"

David avoided James's eyes.

James exhaled. "This is about school, isn't it?"

David's gaze went down the street in the direction of the schools.

"Answer my questions, please," James said.

"Yes, I'm going to school," David said. He looked James in the eye.

"Have you snuck into my wagon before?"

David twisted his mouth and nodded. "You usually go into town on Wednesdays."

The boy was right. James nearly always went on Wednesdays, with other days determined by needs of the household or neighbors.

"I can't imagine you only sneak off to school on Wednesdays," James said.

"I'm also getting very fast at running," David said. "And the *English* are curious enough that they'll almost always stop to pick me up if I put my hand out."

"I see," James said. "You are defying your father."

"He's not my father!"

"He's your mother's husband, and you live in his house."

"I'm not seven years old."

"This is not our way, David."

"I'm late." David pivoted and sprinted down the sidewalk.

❧

Margaret led her ragtag line of first graders down the rear stairs of the grade school with firm instructions that they hold the railing and watch the feet of the pupil ahead in the line. At the base of the stairs, she directed them to line up quietly outside the music room. As soon as the older students came out, the little ones would go in. And then she would have forty minutes to catch her breath while the music teacher had charge of her class.

When the last of the first graders straggled into the music room and the teacher clapped her hands for the students' attention, Margaret raised the hem of her skirt to take the stairs more swiftly. Before the time came to fetch her class again, she wanted the arithmetic lesson to follow to be fully organized, including a set of problems on the board.

Voices in the upstairs hall startled her.

"So it turned out high school was too hard for you." A boy's voice cracked mid-taunt. "Maybe if you took your hat off, you'd be able to think better."

Two other voices laughed. Margaret hustled her upward steps.

"Look at the big lug," the first boy said. "He can't even think what to say."

More laughter.

Margaret entered the upstairs corridor. Why these eighth graders were out of the classroom was unclear, though one of two Amish boys had his hands on a rolling wooden cart stacked with books.

"I hear they don't fight," an *English* boy said.

"Let's find out." A second boy pulled back his fist and swung at Elijah Mast, hitting him squarely on the jaw. Thrown off balance, Elijah stepped back but made no move to retaliate. Only a few months short of sixteen, he was taller and broader than any of the *English* boys. Margaret had no doubt he could have put them on their rumps with one swift movement.

A boot slammed into Elijah's shin, causing another step back.

"Stop!" Margaret shouted. She closed the yards between herself and the boys. "This will stop immediately."

The *English* boys cowered at having been caught. Margaret turned to the only one she had not witnessed actively bullying.

"You go get Mr. Tarkington immediately," she said. "And be sure you come back with him."

Relief and shame mingling in his face, the boy darted down the hall toward the stairs.

"Are you all right?" Margaret said to Elijah, who had his hand on his jaw now.

He nodded. The boy with the cart, Luke Borntrager, shuffled his feet.

"I'm sure Mr. Tarkington will want to speak with both of you," Margaret said, "but for now why don't you go back to your class?"

The cart was in motion within seconds. Margaret was certain Elijah and Luke could ably defend themselves if they had chosen to. She glared at the bullies.

"Let's see, you're taller than your friend. Does that make you better?"

"No, ma'am," they mumbled, eyes on their feet.

"Or does your black hair make you better than his blond hair?"

"No, ma'am."

Margaret glared at the boys. "Different is just different. It's not better or worse. The two of you are old enough to understand that."

Mr. Tarkington's feet thundered up the stairs, followed by the more reluctant steps of the third boy.

"Down to my office, all three of you," the principal said. "This is inexcusable."

Margaret exhaled relief for the moment.

"Miss Simpson," the principal said, "I'll speak to you later for a full accounting of the facts."

He left with the boys. Margaret leaned against the wall. How could the Amish children learn anything if they felt a constant dread of mistreatment? Perhaps their parents were right. Perhaps it would be better for everyone if they had their own school where they could practice their peaceful ways without threat. On the other hand, why should they be removed from sight in order to be safe?

Margaret would tell Mr. Tarkington what she had seen, but she doubted the boys would face serious consequences. More likely, blame would be laid at the feet of the Amish parents who put their older children back in the eighth grade.

None of this was fair.

❦

James took his rig down Lindy's quiet street and drove to the back of her lot, where her workshop sat behind the small house. With another needless playful warning to the horse, he strode to the workshop door and knocked.

No answer came. She might be in the house or on an errand of her own, or she simply might not have heard him. James turned the knob. The wide door opened.

James stifled the impulse to call Lindy's name. Something was off. Taking care where he stepped, he entered the workshop and softly closed the door behind him. Two drawers from a half-stained dresser lay splintered on the workshop floor. The contents of a tool shelf were clustered on one end. A bucket of blue paint lay on its side, the dense liquid settling into its own irregular shape on the sloping floor.

James stood still, his ears attuned to a slight noise across the workshop. He saw no one and crept toward it.

At the last minute his eyes flicked up to the board swinging down toward his head, and he raised an arm to block the stinging blow.

Someone gasped.

James turned toward his attacker.

"*Onkel* James!"

James grimaced. First Isaiah Borntrager fell off a ladder and landed on top of James. Now his own niece took a swing at him with a two-by-four. How would he ever explain to Miriam the bruise certain to form on his arm?

Lindy let the board clatter to the floor.

"What happened?" James asked.

Lindy blinked several times. "I went out for a few minutes. When I came back, the door was ajar. I'm sure I closed it when I left."

"Did you lock it?"

She shook her head. "I have too much Amish in me to lock a door, I guess. When I heard someone outside again, I got scared."

"Well, it's just me. I didn't see anyone else outside." James picked up the pieces of one of the dresser drawers.

Lindy groaned. "I'll have to make all new drawers."

"I can help you with that." James looked around. "Other than the obvious damage, is anything missing?"

Lindy's eyes took slow inventory of her workshop, and she let out a cry. "My best carving tools were on that shelf."

James put an arm around her shoulder.

"I had three carved birds ready to sell in the Amish crafts store." She broke away from him and went to her workbench. "My bird-house templates! They're gone!"

"All of them?"

"Every single one. I had them out because I was going to cut some pieces today."

James righted the paint bucket. "I'm sorry this happened to you."

"The quilt rack!" Lindy said. "I was painting birds on the side pieces for Mrs. Tarkington."

"She'll just have to understand," James said.

"I don't even understand," Lindy said. "I do just enough work to support myself. My prices are fair. I mind my own business. I'm a quiet neighbor. Why would anybody do this to me?"

"We should get Deputy Fremont over here," James said.

"I have never liked him," Lindy said.

James understood. He did not much like Fremont, either, especially after his strong-handed approach to the Amish in recent weeks.

"I know," he said, "but he is the law."

CHAPTER 17

Gideon's here," Rachel said the next day, her gaze out the front window.

Ella sprang to her feet. Gideon's buggy swayed down the lane toward the house.

"Tell him the celery is coming along nicely," Rachel said. "We should have plenty for the wedding."

Ella smiled and picked up her shawl. She doubted Gideon cared about the details of the traditional wedding celery, but it was sweet that Rachel was monitoring its progress. Ella stepped out onto the front porch in time to watch Gideon wrap the reins around a fence post and amble in her direction. She would spend her life with this man, loving him, loving his children, loving the *boppli* they would have together. If God ever smiled, surely He smiled now. The day was golden.

"Do you have time for a walk?" Gideon asked.

"Of course." Ella descended the steps. "Let's go out to *Daed's* fallow field."

Once they were away from the house, Gideon took Ella's hand.

"I want to ask you about an idea," he said.

Gideon might not care about celery, but they had other wedding details to work out. They still had to choose their attendants and finalize the date.

"Shall we try to see the bishop?" Ella said.

"I know you want to marry soon," Gideon said.

The pressure in Ella's chest was immediate. "Don't you?"

"Maybe we should let others go first. After all, we'll have our whole lives."

Ella said nothing but kept walking. Obviously she did not know Gideon's mind as well as she thought.

He squeezed her fingers. "We will find the right date. I am not having doubts."

"Then what?"

"I would like to see the school question settled first—or at least take myself out of the crux of it."

"How will you do that?"

"First I have to do what I think is best for my own children. I want you to teach my daughters at home."

"I heard about what happened to Elijah Mast," Ella said. "But nothing like that is going to happen to Gertie and Savilla."

"I pray not," Gideon said.

"They like school and have made friends."

He nodded. "I am not going to give up with the school board. If other children hear their parents talking at home about the Amish 'problem,' as they like to call us, how can we know what might happen? It's my duty as their father to keep them safe."

"I understand." Questions flooded Ella's mind. Would Gideon keep the girls home temporarily? Would he get their lessons from the teachers at the school? Did the girls want to study at home? Why did he think she knew the first thing about making lesson plans or what a first grader and a fourth grader ought to be learning?

"Besides," Gideon said, "I am not comfortable having them in the *English* school. They will be attracted to *English* ways."

"But you teach them our ways at home," Ella said. "They will always know truth." She banished the image of David's rebellion rising in her mind.

They walked a few yards in silence.

"Do you have hesitations about teaching them?" Gideon asked.

"I don't know very much about teaching." The intrigue of teaching collided with the reasons Gideon asked it of her.

"But you understand a great deal about learning," he countered. "You are more than capable of teaching them to read and do basic math and enough history to know where they come from."

"I suppose so."

"If you are going to be their mother—and I hope they will see you that way—then it is fitting that they learn from you."

"But what about the laws?" Ella said. "You've already been warned to put Tobias in school."

Gideon shrugged. "I didn't do it, and nothing happened."

"You may be asking for trouble by taking the girls out."

"I made our case with the school board that the Amish can teach our own children. We need to show this is true. If they are watching me, that's all the more reason I need your help."

Ella moistened her lips. "Can I think about it?"

As much as she loved learning, Ella had never seriously considered teaching. Why should she? The one-room school always had an *English* teacher—and not one who had been out of school for twelve years.

"Prayerfully consider it," Gideon said. "I won't say anything to the girls until we're sure."

❧

"Did you hear what I said?"

"Mmm?" Margaret lifted her eyes to Gray's face across the table at the modest restaurant on Main Street.

"I was saying what a fine September we've had," Gray said. "I suppose October will bring a change in the weather."

"Yes." Margaret turned up the corners of her mouth. "I believe October is my favorite month of the year."

"I'll take note."

They were seated at a table near the window for an early supper, before darkness fell. Margaret could not quite see well enough from this distance to discern the two figures across the street.

"Margaret."

Gray's voice recaptured her gaze.

"I'm sorry," she said. "What did you say?"

"You've barely looked at the menu. Shall I order for you?"

Margaret dropped her eyes to the printed sheet in front of her. "Yes, please. I'm sure it's all delicious."

"You seem quite distracted," Gray said. "If you're not feeling well, I'll take you home."

"I feel fine," she said, resolving to pay better attention. "Quite hungry, actually."

"Would you like to tell me what's on your mind? It might help to talk about it."

She looked out the window again. "One of the pupils in Miss Hunter's class has missed more than a week of school due to illness. In fact, she's missed more school than she's attended this year so far. We're all starting to be concerned."

"I would think so. That's a long time for a child to be ill."

"The odd thing is, I'm fairly certain that's her across the street with her father."

Gray turned his head. "Where? I don't see anybody but that Amish man and his buggy."

"Yes, that's him."

"How can you be sure? They all look alike."

Objection rang in Margaret's ears, but she said nothing. A girl in a dark gray dress began to skip, only to be reprimanded with one gesture from her father.

"She doesn't look sick to me," Gray said.

Nor to me.

Gray laughed with abandon.

"What's so funny?" Margaret said.

"That Amish man is *lying* to the school authorities."

"Let's not jump to judgments," Margaret said. Perhaps the girl had been sick and was now recovering. Her parents might be keeping her home as a precautionary measure. Across the street, the girl climbed into the buggy—without assistance—and disappeared into its dark interior.

"You can see with your own eyes," Gray said. "That child is fine. There's no reason she shouldn't be in school tomorrow."

"Tomorrow's Friday. They may decide to let her finish out the week resting at home and start fresh on Monday."

"Or it may be a ruse."

The horse began to pull the buggy away from the curb.

"Let's not let the Amish problem come between us," Gray said. "Let's enjoy our baked fish and roasted red potatoes."

Amish problem. Margaret bristled at the phrase, although Gray was not the first person in town to use it. Still, it soured her stomach to think that he would adopt it. These were children. They were not a problem.

"Of course," she said. "That sounds delicious."

His features crinkled with his smile, his eyes dancing as he looked at her. Margaret wasn't sure any man's gaze had ever warmed her at the core the way Gray Truesdale's did. The disadvantage of not asking him to take her home right then was the interminable wait for his lips to find hers before the night was over.

❧❦❧

Monday was art day. As the fourth week of school opened, Margaret selected art supplies from the cupboard in the downstairs corridor, arranged them in a basket, and carried them up to her classroom. This would be the first real art project of the year, other than some simple coloring with Crayolas. Up until now, Margaret focused on introducing a solid curriculum of reading and arithmetic as she assessed each pupil's ability. The children had been working hard for three weeks. They deserved to spend the last hour of the day exploring what they could do with charcoal pencils on thick paper. Art was required in the consolidated curriculum, and Margaret was determined to demonstrate its value to dubious parents.

When the primers were stowed and the oil cloths draped over desktops, Margaret held up one of the hand mirrors she had brought from home.

"Take turns with the mirrors," she said. "You can hold them for one another. Draw what you see in the mirror. It's called a 'self-portrait of the artist.'"

Margaret's expectations were appropriately low for what the completed projects would look like. She was more interested in observing the process of the children's efforts. They were only first graders, after all, and it was only the beginning of the school year. Most of them still struggled to control their thick pencils even to form the letters of their names.

Around the classroom, giggles and groans, jubilation and frustration greeted Margaret. She walked up and down the aisles, complimenting the effort her pupils made and touching their shoulders in encouragement. Lopsided eyes, uneven ears, disproportionate noses, oddly shaped faces—whatever the result, Margaret buoyed her students in the process of looking carefully and moving the charcoal with control.

She reached Gertie Wittmer's desk beside Hans Byler. Hans's project looked like most of the others around the room.

"I can't do this," he said.

"All I ask is that you try," Margaret said.

"But mine doesn't look like Gertie's."

"Why should it? *You* don't look like Gertie."

Hans laid the charcoal down. "Gertie, show Miss Simpson your picture."

Gertie had turned her drawing upside down. "I'd like to see it," Margaret said.

Slowly, Gertie flipped the paper.

Margaret's eyes widened. Gertie's features stared up from the desk. Margaret lifted the paper at the edges.

"Gertie, this is wonderful!" Margaret had never seen a six-year-old produce such a recognizable self-portrait, even the reflection of light in her eyes as it bounced off the mirror. "I can't wait for your father to see this."

Gertie reached up and tugged on a corner of the drawing. Margaret released it, lest the paper tear.

"Don't you want your father to see this?" Margaret asked.

Gertie shook her head.

"Why not?"

Gertie shoved the paper into her desk but did not answer Margaret's question.

"All right," Margaret said. "But please be careful with it. I'll collect them when everyone has finished."

Jed's voice carried up the stairwell.

"It gets dark earlier every day," he said. "David is not carrying his load. Before school started, he never once complained about working alongside me."

"He still doesn't," Rachel said. "I haven't heard him say one word of criticism or complaint about helping you."

"Then why is he never around to do it?"

Upstairs, Ella tucked folded towels into a narrow cupboard. The conversation was becoming tiresome. Her father had always been one to mutter. It was his way of getting something off his chest. In the old days, though, Ella never would have discerned his downstairs grumblings if she were on the second floor of the Hilty home. Lately Jed's voice rose. It was hard not to hear Jed and Rachel having a slightly different version of the same conversation every few days.

Ella padded to her room and softly closed the door to block the voices. In a moment, Rachel's would break in disappointment, and Jed would either promise to be more patient with David or pull the front door closed behind him with more force than necessary.

David got up early and stayed up late to keep up with barn chores. He never missed a family meal. Some days he turned up on the farm shortly after lunch. What could her father do? Tether David to a post to physically prevent him from leaving? Ella supposed his comings and goings depended on what was happening at school—when he had an exam or an assignment due. Vaguely she wondered what high school must be like. Perhaps if she had attended high school, she would feel more prepared for what Gideon asked of her now.

She shook off the thought. Savilla and Gertie were nine and six. How difficult could it be? The half-collapsed schoolhouse still contained shelves of textbooks. Gideon would find a way to get what she needed—if she agreed to his request.

CHAPTER 18

The children concentrated on copying short sentences Margaret had written on the chalkboard. On the desk in front of her lay her attendance book, her grade book, and a stack of lesson plans. Soon she would divide the first graders into two groups, a smaller group who seemed on the path to independent reading and might even be ready for second-grade primers by February, and a larger group who were mastering reading at a more predictable rate for six-year-olds. Margaret made notes on a pad as she considered each child's progress, gazing out the windows along one side of her classroom from time to time. Outside, russet and bronze had displaced variegated green on most of the trees, and the sky, while still dazzling, was less glistening than in the summer months. October had arrived, and seemed to rush into full flame by its second day. Margaret had not been making conversation when she told Gray it was her favorite month. She looked forward to the season's change every year.

She scanned the classroom to make sure no child faltered in the task, knowing that some would produce more legible papers than others. Little tongues stuck out the corners of several mouths, and other children scrunched their faces in concentration, but everyone's pencils were making regular contact with paper. Her eyes turned to the view outside, soaking in the autumn colors that framed the high school next door. A flash of black caught her eye and she looked more closely, finding a dark-clad Amish boy hustling up the sidewalk, approaching the front door of the school. Out of reflex, Margaret looked at the clock in her own classroom. The boy was considerably late for the start of the school day. He seemed in a hurry, though. Perhaps he had a good reason for his tardiness. He slipped through the door.

"That was David."

Margaret startled to see Gertie standing at the desk. "Do you know him?"

Gertie nodded. "I'm going to have a new *mamm*, and that's her new brother."

Margaret blinked, waiting for the puzzle pieces to fall into place. "Who is going to be your new mother?"

"Ella Hilty. I can't wait."

Hilty. Margaret visualized the list of Amish students she had studied several times. Jed Hilty was listed as stepfather to David and Seth Kaufman.

"David is not supposed to go to school," Gertie said. "I heard my *daed* talking to my *onkel* James."

From Margaret's brief glimpse of David, he certainly appeared young enough that he belonged in school, and he carried a bundle of books. She pulled her eyes from the window and focused on Gertie.

"Do you have a question?" Margaret said.

"I'm finished." Gertie produced a neatly scripted page of sentences. "Do you have something else I can copy?"

"Of course." Margaret rummaged beneath the papers on her desk and produced a reading primer the class had not yet begun. "Try this."

Gertie took the book. "It looks easy."

The girl sauntered back to her desk. Margaret had not noticed any of the children watching where she gazed, but if any of them would, Gertie would. She was bright, observant, talented, hardworking, and eager to please. Margaret made a mental note to speak with Gideon Wittmer about his remarkable child.

⊱⊰

The next afternoon, Ella pushed open the library's heavy door, her arms overflowing with this week's curiosity. Tucked in between her usual topics were two frayed textbooks bearing stamps inside the front covers as evidence they had once belonged to the same college that had supplied teachers to the one-room school for the last three decades. Both addressed the topic of preparing to instruct young children. When she discovered them, Ella felt as if she had made the winning bid on an auction for one of Miriam Lehman's full-size quilts. She signed them out and stacked them between her other selections, hoping she would be able to get them up to her room before anyone wondered what they were. Ella had kept Gideon waiting for nearly a week. Soon he would ask her for an answer. Perhaps these books would help her know if she was making the right choice.

Outside, Ella held the books against her chest while she traipsed to the end of the block and around the corner to where she left her horse and cart thirty minutes earlier. Stops at the mercantile and the post office had justified the excursion into town. The number of children on the sidewalk told Ella the schools had just let out. Soon it would be time to begin preparing the evening meal, a task she and Rachel shared amiably. She secured her books under the cart's bench, beside the mercantile bundle wrapped in brown paper, and gave the mare a friendly greeting. The horse nickered, and Ella smiled. She would miss this horse once she moved to Gideon's home, but his new animal awaited her there.

If only they could settle on their wedding date.

Ella climbed up to the bench, raised the reins, and took the cart into the slight traffic of Seabury. Down the street, the adjoining schools loomed as a reminder of the decision she had yet to make about the future education of Gideon's daughters. For the most part, the premises showed signs of the end of the day—few vehicles or horses nearby, a forgotten lunch pail, papers tumbling in the breeze when they were supposed to have boarded the bus with their owners.

In a small lot added last year to accommodate the increasing number of automobiles that teachers acquired, an engine cranked to life. The sound demanded Ella's attention. She recognized the car as Lindy's and started to lift her hand in a wave. When she saw a passenger leap over the side door and into the seat, though, Ella stilled her hand.

David.

At lunchtime, her father came in for the meal but said David preferred to stay in the field. He had claimed he wasn't hungry and didn't mind the extra work, telling Jed he would finish the task and there was no need for him to hurry back.

Ella couldn't hear what David now said, but Lindy's laugh in response floated on the breeze and made Ella's stomach clench. A minute later, the car rumbled past Ella. If either Lindy or David noticed her, they gave no indication. Lindy accelerated in the direction of the Amish farms.

"Let's go, girl," Ella said to her horse before clicking her tongue and raising the reins. Quickly, she urged the mare to a trot and then to a canter. A full gallop seemed inadvisable with the rickety cart in tow without risking the collapse of an axle or a wheel spinning off.

Apparently Lindy enjoyed fast driving. Ella couldn't keep up. With a sigh, she slowed the rig.

Lindy had done the right thing the day she brought David home when she found him in town. Was she now abetting his deceit?

❧

James held a folded list in his hands. The girls were already home from school, and he had accomplished few of his intentions for the day.

Inspecting the fences, examining the shoes on all the animals, going into town to check on Lindy, and a half dozen other tasks remained unattended. The list was too long to accomplish in one day, but he had expected better progress.

But Miriam was slow and pale, and James had insisted after breakfast that she take it easy. All day long she fussed around the *dawdihaus* despite his repeated encouragement that the items on her own day's list could wait.

"Please lie down," he said now.

"I should see about the girls." Miriam started to push herself out of her chair.

"Tobias is looking after them."

"I haven't even started supper."

"We'll find something." James put a hand on Miriam's shoulder with gentle pressure. "The bedroom is right over there. If you get out of the chair, the bed is the only place I will allow you to go."

"You're getting bossy, old man." Her words protested, but her eyes moved to the bedroom.

"I'll sit with you," James said.

Miriam nodded. James held out a hand to help her up and walked with her to the bedroom, where she sat on the bed and removed her shoes. James pulled a chair to the side of the bed and held her hand as she stretched out. Within three minutes her breathing deepened and evened.

James released her hand but made no move to leave the room. He did not want her to wake and find him gone from the *dawdihaus*, or to wake and become too ambitious about the evening meal.

Besides, he welcomed time to sit still before the Lord and clear his heart and mind.

Even after all these weeks, parents remained in disbelief that the old school was gone. Building a new one seemed a risky venture without official approval to hold classes. The school board was no friendlier toward the wishes of the Amish than it had been two months ago. Discovering David in his wagon and the vandalism and theft in Lindy's workshop rattled James. Even Gideon, with his propensity for sensible decisions, was conflicted.

The quiet life James and Miriam had enjoyed together for nearly forty-four years seemed elusive now.

The bedroom window allowed just enough outside light to read for a few minutes. James reached to the nightstand for his Bible and turned to Proverbs.

"The name of the Lord is a strong tower: the righteous runneth into it, and is safe."

James murmured prayers that he would see the strong tower.

Gertie's self-portrait lay protected by a large envelope on Margaret's automobile seat. For three days she had stared at it multiple times each day, and every time she was equally astounded that a child Gertie's age could produce something so remarkable. Margaret was tempted to go to the library and see if she could turn up information on the childhood works of some of the world's great artists. If the request was too specific, Mrs. White, the librarian, might know of a volume she could request on loan from a Cleveland library.

She could not believe that any parent would not want to know about such an exceptional ability. Gideon was entitled to see for himself what his offspring could do. Imagine what Gertie might accomplish with proper training, perhaps even private lessons.

Margaret certainly did not have the ability to teach Gertie what she deserved to learn.

If he had a telephone, Margaret could have called and arranged a proper meeting. Instead, she hoped she would at least find him home.

She stopped her car at what seemed like a respectful distance from the house and barn and crunched along the gravel for the remainder of the distance on foot. Just as she reached the front porch, someone called her name. Margaret turned to see Gideon beside a well pump at the side of the house, wiping his hands on a towel.

"Mr. Wittmer," she said. "I hope you are well."

"Very well, thank you," he said. "And you?"

"Very well also. I was hoping I might have a few minutes of your time."

"Is Gertie giving you trouble?"

"Oh, goodness, no. She's a delightful child—probably my best student, though I'll have to ask you not to repeat that to any of the other parents." Her laughter sounded more nervous than she meant it to.

"I'm glad to hear that." Gideon gestured toward two chairs on the porch, and they sat. "Are you here on behalf of the school district?"

Margaret took a seat and arranged her skirt. "I wanted to show you a piece of your daughter's classroom work."

Gideon took the envelope Margaret offered and unwound the string that held the clasp closed. The art paper slid out into his lap.

"Miss Simpson," he said, "who drew this?"

"Why, Gertie did! That's what's so remarkable. I've never seen such talent in a child of her age."

"I see." Gideon stared at his daughter's face but did not pick up the paper.

"Mr. Wittmer," Margaret said, "I daresay I was expecting a good deal more enthusiasm for Gertie's effort. She's seemed averse to presenting it to you, but the more I looked at it, the more I thought you should see it."

"Miss Simpson," Gideon said, "this is an example of why the Amish need our own schools."

"I beg your pardon?"

"A six-year-old should not be asked to choose between pleasing her father and pleasing her teacher."

"I assure you, I had no intention of putting Gertie in such a position." Margaret's heart pounded. What was he accusing her of?

"Gertie made the picture because you asked her to, but she knows that our people do not use graven images."

"And I assure you I do not teach my pupils to worship idols." Margaret's back straightened. "A charcoal drawing is hardly a golden calf, Mr. Wittmer."

"Gertie's dolls do not even have faces, Miss Simpson. Images may create pride or attachment to something other than God. In the future, I would appreciate it if you would find other work for Gertie to complete while the *English* students study art."

"Surely not!"

"Please understand, Miss Simpson. We both want what is best for Gertie."

"Yes, we do," Margaret said as she stood up. But how could anyone think it was best for a little girl to deny a talent that could have come only from God?

CHAPTER 19

Friday morning breakfast and family devotions proceeded just as they did any other day of the week. Antsy, and with one eye on the clock, Seth jiggled his knee while Jed read from his German Bible. David sat still, but with an expression that suggested to Ella he wasn't hearing much of what came out of Jed's mouth. Rachel watched her sons more than she did her husband. Jed calmly refused to rush. This had been the pattern for weeks, ever since the start of the school year.

At the "Amen," Seth popped out of his seat, kissed his mother's cheek, grabbed the books bundled by a strap of leather, picked up his lunch bucket, and dashed out the door to catch the bus.

"We'll do as we did yesterday," Jed said to David, "but to the east in the field."

David nodded. "There's no need for both of us. I'll go."

"Thank you," Jed said.

Ella took control of her jaw to keep it from going slack. Did her father really think David intended to go out to the field?

She watched David slip his arms into a lightweight jacket and arrange his hat on his head before going out the back door and disappearing behind the barn.

Ella took her shawl off its hook and straightened her prayer *kapp*. She would leave the cart behind this morning. The route was uncertain, but Ella was determined to follow David's movements. As quietly as possible, she saddled a horse and led it out, going behind the stable. David was gone, as she expected he would be, but the grassless ground around the barn bore no evidence that David's footsteps had turned toward the fields of crops. Rather, he had rounded the barn and angled off toward the main road. From the house, his movements would be unseen.

On her horse, and from a distance, Ella followed. Once David entered a plot of vegetation, footprints were harder to find, but Ella was certain David would emerge on the road. She could take her own path and find him. This time, since he was on foot and she was on horseback, she would have the advantage of speed.

Ella reached the road and stilled the horse, waiting and scanning in both directions.

One minute passed, and then two. Perhaps David had found the road ahead of her after all and was already out of sight.

Three minutes, then four and five. Ella nudged the horse forward slowly. Movement in the bushes drew her attention to one side.

At last.

David broke through and, startled, halted.

"What are you doing here?" he said, shifting his books to the other arm.

"I wondered the same thing about you," Ella said. "I saw you get in Lindy's car after school the other day."

He said nothing, instead starting to walk and peering down the road in hopes of an automobile's arrival.

"Are you waiting for Lindy now?"

"No."

"Is she helping you?"

He pressed his lips closed.

"David, this is not right."

He raised his eyes to meet hers now. "I'm not giving up school."

"But sneaking around—it's defiance. It comes from pride."

David shrugged. "I'm hardly sneaking anymore, am I? Everyone knows. My *mamm* pretends she doesn't, but that's only to make herself feel better."

Ella blew out her breath.

"Besides," David said, "as long as I show up at school, I keep Jed out of trouble. They won't come after him for not enrolling me. I'm doing a good thing."

"Disobeying his wishes is *helping* him?" In all the discussions about the new school laws, this was the most convoluted logic Ella had heard. "You can take my horse and go home before anyone realizes you're gone."

"I have a math test this morning. I can't afford another zero in that class because of an absence."

David waved his hand at an approaching automobile, which slowed. Ella didn't recognize the driver. Of course, she knew only a few people in Seabury. David showed no hesitation about the process of finding a ride. He leaned in the open car window, exchanged a few sentences with the driver, and got in.

Gideon decided to see for himself. Ella had been the first to tell him about the school Chester Mast was intent on building, but it hadn't been long before other parents wondered what he thought. At the last church gathering—in the spacious Byler home—Gideon could hardly eat his midday meal without an interruption every two bites from someone seeking his opinion. It was time to ride out and see what Chester was up to. If the construction seemed unrealistic, Gideon would escape forming any opinion at all. On the other hand, if it was progressing in a convincing manner, the existence of a new school building might signal to the school board that Amish families meant business about their children's education.

Hammers clattered in ragged rhythm, ringing across open land and becoming louder as Gideon approached. He recognized the wagons and teams. Cristof. Isaiah. John. Chester Mast was guiding a boy a year or two older than Tobias to find the right angle before he hammered. Gideon remembered the boy had begun the school year riding the bus with his girls. Gideon would try to remember to ask Savilla later if he still attended school. Isaiah Borntrager was up on a ladder—a more secure one than he had dragged to the shambles of the old school, Gideon was relieved to see. John Hershberger was perched on a high beam making sure a joint aligned perfectly.

"You here to help?" Chester approached Gideon.

Was he? Gideon scanned the scene again and slid off his horse.

"Where do you need help?" Gideon said.

Chester's curly brown beard shifted as his mouth shaped a grin. "Somebody has to make sure Isaiah doesn't kill himself up there."

Gideon nodded. Heights had never bothered him. He rolled up

both sleeves as he strode toward the ladder. As he walked, he spied one more wagon he recognized, and its owner was unloading two buckets of nails from the back.

"James," Gideon said.

James looked up. "You found us." He set the buckets at his feet.

"I didn't know you would be here," Gideon said.

"Just trying to do my part," James said.

"But building a school?"

"There's no law says Chester can't build on his own property," James said. "We can be ready when the time comes."

Gideon worked his lips out and in. The only reason his girls were still in the *English* school was that Ella had not yet decided to take on the challenge of teaching them. He could hardly blame the other fathers for making their own preparations.

"I thought you were going into town with some of those tables Joshua Glick builds," Gideon said.

"They're popular at the furniture store." James nodded toward the load in his wagon. "I'll be on my way soon."

"I don't see Joshua here."

"Nope. He's still quoting Romans. Says what we're doing is rebelling against a God-ordained government."

Gideon certainly did not feel rebellious. Why would God ask him to hand his innocent little girls over to the *English* world, where they learned to make graven images and sing frivolous songs? If the school would stick to a simple education, perhaps the brewing conflict could have lost its heat before now. Instead, Gideon saw no way to avoid contentiousness. Perhaps he was a rebel after all.

"Will you check on Lindy while you're in town?" Gideon asked.

"I may stop in to see the deputy, too," James said, nodding. "I'm not persuaded he's even trying to find out what happened at her workshop."

"Tell Lindy to come for supper one night," Gideon said. "The children would love to see her."

"I will."

James reached into his wagon and extracted a hammer. "If you're with us, you're going to need this."

Gideon grasped the sanded wooden handle. His goal had been to persuade the school district the Amish needed their own school with a teacher who understood their ways. Chester was right to forge ahead. It was an act of faith that God would bless their obedience.

~☙~

"I've spoken with Mr. Brownley."

Margaret stiffened against her will and met Mr. Tarkington's eyes. He had come to her classroom door in the middle of the day and asked her to step into the corridor.

"I'm sure you are aware that the Amish problem has not resolved."

Why did everyone insist on labeling the situation the *Amish* problem? The Amish were not the ones who changed the unspoken agreement by which everyone had lived side by side for decades.

"First they refused to enroll some of their children," Mr. Tarkington said. "Then they put some of them back in grade school when they clearly belong in the high school. Now too many of them are absent too often, claiming they are ill."

"I read in the newspaper that influenza is spreading," Margaret said. "The soldiers are bringing it home from Europe."

"Now, Miss Simpson, your tendency to give people the benefit of the doubt is a charming trait," Mr. Tarkington said, "but we both know that influenza is not ravaging the Amish farms."

"It might be."

"We've only had three cases in all of Seabury," he said, "and those were in households where family members had visited Cleveland."

"The paper says they may close the schools in Cleveland. We should not take it lightly."

Mr. Tarkington cleared his throat. "Let's not be distracted from our own matters. Mr. Brownley would appreciate it if you would once again do what you can to gather reliable information."

"I rather thought I disappointed Mr. Brownley with my previous efforts."

"Then you shall have a chance to redeem yourself," the principal said.

"These things take time to sort out," Margaret said. "We need to find common ground through understanding each other."

"The sheriff's office is losing patience."

"I will see what I can do," Margaret said, though she had little idea of what that might be. Her meeting with Gideon Wittmer over his daughter's artwork made plain that the Amish notions about education were more entrenched than she had judged.

Margaret stepped back into her own classroom, where she had left the children reading silently. Her eyes went to Gertie Wittmer and the empty seat next to her. After perfect attendance since the beginning of the year, Hans Byler now had missed two days.

Gertie turned a page. If the girl knew anything about Hans, or about other students whose attendance was becoming erratic, she showed no sign. The other teachers would allow Margaret to look at their attendance records, which might tell her whether the principal and superintendent were reacting in a more extreme manner than the evidence suggested.

At the end of the school day, Margaret lined up her class and led them out the front door, where some met their parents, others scattered on the street to walk home, and others found their buses. Margaret scanned the flow of students out of the school, looking for patches of black and the rich hues of Amish dyes, and counted. It did seem as if there ought to be more Amish students.

Margaret crossed the pavement to the line of buses and caught the elbow of the oldest Amish student in the school.

"Yes, Miss Simpson?" he said.

"I hope things are well with your family," she said.

"Yes, ma'am."

"And. . .your neighbors? Is there any sign of influenza?"

"None that I've heard of," the boy said.

"Good." Margaret glanced around. "I notice some of the children have not been in school. Perhaps some other illness?"

The student shrugged.

"And you?" she said. "Should we discuss with your father returning to the high school?"

"My *daed* has made his decision. It is not my place to challenge it."

"I see. So the children who are missing school are simply doing what their fathers have decided?"

The bus engine howled. The boy looked over his shoulder at the idling vehicle.

"Go on," Margaret said. "Don't miss your bus on my account."

CHAPTER 20

Margaret festered all weekend. Even Gray Truesdale's invitation for a Saturday afternoon stroll did not banish from her mind the Amish *dilemma*, as she preferred to call it. Even that seemed a harsh word. *Conundrum? Mystery?*

By Monday, Margaret had resolved to do whatever was within her power.

On Tuesday, she decided to start with the deputy sheriff. If the county sheriff was as impatient as Mr. Tarkington led her to believe, then perhaps reasoning with Deputy Fremont would buy her more time. She gave her pupils one assignment after another to work independently while she scratched arguments and wording onto sheets of paper, crossed out, revised, and finally memorized. As soon as the children were safely dismissed after school, Margaret braced her shoulders, lifted her chin, and walked to the local sheriff's station. If Deputy Fremont would not listen, she would take her car to Chardon the next afternoon and deal with the county sheriff himself.

Deputy Fremont kept Margaret waiting so long she was ready to pound on his desk. By the time she had his attention, she remembered almost nothing of the reasoned arguments she had spent the day preparing and instead blurted out her frustration.

"I will deal with this matter," she said. "I am here only to ask you to communicate to the sheriff in Chardon that he need only wait with more patience for a favorable outcome."

Deputy Fremont chuckled as he stood and picked up his jacket from the back of his chair.

"You can't seriously think we are going to overlook the exceptional level of truancy among the Amish children."

"I will speak to the fathers and make clear that they must comply with the law," she said. "The children can come to school while the families make their case within appropriate legal parameters."

"I have my instructions," he said.

"And what would those be?" Margaret saw no benefit from the deputy screeching his tires onto Amish farms again with blustering threats.

Deputy Fremont picked up a stack of papers from the corner of his desk. "These are official notices of fines that are the consequences of Amish flagrancy."

"Amish flagrancy! Can you not see the hyperbole in such a term?"

"I suppose you are entitled to your opinion." The deputy picked up the crank that would start his automobile. "But frankly, it has no bearing."

Margaret stood and leaned over the desk. "Are you truly going to inflict fines over a matter that might yet be solved by conversation?"

"The time for conversation is past."

"The time for conversation is never past."

He laughed again. "Miss Simpson, you were supposed to help the Amish consolidate. You failed. Now it's time for me to do my job. I represent the sheriff's office. My duty is to enforce the law, not to turn my head the other way."

"I must protest!"

"If you like." He gripped the papers in one hand. "I have work to do, starting with Mr. Wittmer. I think you were right when you pointed us to him as the most influential of the fathers. If we set an example with him, the others will come in line soon enough."

Margaret swallowed and composed herself. "Deputy Fremont, perhaps if you and I work together, we could be more effective."

He shook his head. "I have my orders from the sheriff."

Deputy Fremont strode past Margaret and into the street, his papers in one hand and his crank in the other.

Margaret trailed after him, but once outside, she turned sharply toward home. She would take her own automobile out to the Amish farms.

She had not counted on finding Gray Truesdale standing on the corner where she needed to turn toward her bungalow. His back was to Margaret, and she halted her steps before he twisted around. If only she could ask for his help. If only she could ask anyone's help. But right now Margaret could not afford further delay. This was no time for flirting or explanations or wondering if he was going to kiss her.

Gray's head began to rotate, and then one shoulder dropped.

Margaret pivoted, retraced her steps for half a block, turned down the wrong street, and muttered sincere prayers that Gray would not decide to go to her house—at least not before she could arrive, get her own crank to start her car, and pull away in a direction that would allow her to avoid eye contact. It wasn't that she meant to deceive him, but only that she had no time to be polite.

Moments later she cranked the engine and put the full weight of her foot on the pedal. There was a reason her uncle had given her this old car, though. It wasn't fast enough for him, and at the moment, neither was it fast enough for Margaret.

By the time she arrived at the Wittmer farm, Deputy Fremont and Gideon were squared off in front of the barn. Margaret braked with a lurch and leaned against the door, willing it to open smoothly. She groaned when she saw the official yellow form already in Gideon's hand.

"Deputy, please," Margaret said, approaching the men.

"I've done my duty here," Fremont said. "I have several other stops to make, and my wife would like to have me home for supper."

"I refuse to believe we cannot have a reasonable conversation about this matter," Margaret said.

"Miss Simpson," Gideon said, creasing the paper, "your assistance is not necessary."

Heat flushed through her face. "I represent the school in this matter."

"It's a matter for the law now," Fremont said. He shuffled through the remaining papers. "I will move on. Mr. Hershberger's children haven't been to school at all. Mr. Borntrager, Mr. Mast, Mr. Byler. Yes, I think I've got everyone sorted out."

Gideon seemed far calmer than Margaret felt.

"I think you'll find the fine modest," Fremont said. "I would hate for matters to escalate, so I'll remind you to take note of the date specified on the form. We'll need to see all the children properly enrolled and attending regularly by that date. And I stress *regularly*."

The deputy marched to his car. Margaret fixed her eyes on Gideon, who disappeared into his barn.

⋙✦⋘

Gideon murmured the "Amen" and closed the Bible. He had chosen to read, "Children, obey your parents" from Ephesians the next morning not to assume a disciplinary posture but as a gentle reminder to his three children that he had their best interests in mind.

"Gertie," Gideon said, "please go check and see if we missed any eggs last night."

"But I do that after school," Gertie said, fumbling to tie her *kapp* under her chin.

"Today I want you to do it this morning." Gideon looked into Gertie's eyes, her mother's eyes, and waited for the protest to pass through the muscles of her face.

Savilla slid off the davenport, her eyes focused on the clock on the mantel. "I'll get the lunch buckets. Hurry up, Gertie."

Gideon put the German Bible on the shelf. On most school days, the girls would be six minutes away from leaving for the bus stop. Savilla hated to be late for anything and knew well the consequence for missing the bus.

Tobias stood up. "I noticed the stalls need mucking. Shall I do that today?"

Gideon nodded. "This morning, please. After midday, Aaron King will come to help us get the last of the hay into the loft."

Tobias nodded and left.

Savilla returned with two lunch buckets. "I forgot where I left my shawl."

"What do I always tell you about that?" Gideon said.

"Hang it on the hook." She set the lunch buckets on the floor next to the front door. "I think I left it on my bed."

Four minutes.

Savilla's steps on the stairs were light, rushing, scampering. She returned with the shawl over her shoulders and took custody once again of the lunch buckets.

Three minutes.

139

"Gertie's taking too long," Savilla said.

"We're all right," Gideon said.

"No, we're not. We'll be late."

"It's all right, Savilla."

"If we miss the bus, you'll have to take us to school, and I know you're busy." Savilla stuck her head out the door. "Gertie!"

"Savilla, please sit down."

"I can't, *Daed*. It's time to go."

"I asked you to sit down."

She plopped into a chair, her eyes shifting between the waiting lunch buckets and the ticking clock.

Two minutes.

"We're going to have to run," Savilla said. "Gertie doesn't like it when I tell her to run for the bus."

"You won't have to run," Gideon said.

"I don't understand why you asked Gertie to get eggs in the morning. She dawdles."

"We'll just wait for her."

One minute.

Gertie burst in, breathless. "I looked in all the nests and there's not a single egg."

Savilla popped up, and Gideon motioned she should sit again.

"I need to talk to both of you," he said.

"Your eyes are not smiling, *Daed*," Gertie said.

"I've made a decision," Gideon said. "I've decided that the two of you will learn at home from now on."

Savilla's eyes widened. "We're not going to school?"

Gideon shook his head. "I think it's best for you to stay on the farm and study here."

"But who will teach us?"

Gideon brightened his tone. "Today you will have a school holiday! Play outside. Get some fresh air."

Gertie squealed her delight.

Savilla scowled her doubt.

❦

When Gideon's buggy approached, Ella set aside the bird manual and leaned on the fence to wait for him.

"I took the girls out of school," he said.

"I thought you might," Ella said. "I was at the Hershbergers' when the deputy arrived with the papers yesterday. He said he had already been to your farm."

"I will pay the fine, but I will not be bullied into sending my children to a school that thinks so little of them that they would make no effort to understand their home."

"Miss Simpson seems very nice." Ella's heart pelted her chest. This conversation could have only one end.

"She's quite pleasant." Gideon nodded. "But she is one teacher, and despite her intentions, she seems to have no voice in the decisions."

Ella swallowed. Living alone or having a job or even owning an automobile did not mean *English* women were equal to their men. Lindy had said as much many times. But once she decided she didn't want to marry, Lindy chose to live among the *English*. Better to be an *English* old maid than an Amish one, she reasoned. Ella wasn't so sure. Margaret Simpson did not seem to be any better off for her *English* upbringing and independence.

"I'll do it," Ella whispered.

Gideon raised his eyebrows.

"I'll teach the girls," Ella said. "I won't have any idea what I'm doing, but I'm willing to muddle through if you are."

Gideon's brow wrinkled. "I want you to be certain."

"I am." And she was.

CHAPTER 21

I'm old enough to decide." David spoke with surety two days later. "If I'm old enough to do a man's work on the farm, I'm old enough to decide I want to stay in school."

"But if you go to school, you won't be here to do a man's work," Jed said.

"David, no," Rachel said.

"I'm going to live with Lindy. She's like an *aunti* to me. You always tell me that."

Ella held her breath. The breakfast she'd swallowed a few minutes ago threatened to work its way up. When she saw Lindy pick David up after school, she never imagined it would come to this. At least David waited until after morning devotions and Seth's departure, sparing his brother this scene.

"I already packed," David said. "I don't mean to hurt anybody. If you want me to, I'll come home on Saturdays and work from dawn to dusk."

"That won't be necessary," Jed said.

Rachel blanched. Ella's stomach sank.

"Lindy has been my friend since we were small girls," Rachel said. "I can't believe she would do this to me."

"I haven't talked to her about it yet," David said. "But she'll say yes."

Ella's eyes flicked up. With his bag packed, David seemed certain.

"I'll ask her not to," Rachel said. "She'll know I don't approve."

"Then I'll go somewhere else," David said softly. "I'll find a place to camp, or get a job after school and rent a room."

"You would really do that?"

David met his mother's eyes. "Wouldn't you rather I be with Lindy? I know Lindy would rather know I'm safe."

Ella forced some air out of her lungs, wishing David had waited two more minutes until she'd at least left the room, if not the house. She could have been cleaning the henhouse or sweeping the porch or mixing bread dough or on her way to Gideon's. Anything but listening to this. Slowly she stood up from the end of the davenport.

David stood as well, and without speaking he climbed the stairs. Ella crept out of the room and hovered at the doorway to the kitchen.

"Are you going to just let him go?" Rachel said to Jed. "You didn't even try to stop him."

"He has made up his mind," Jed said.

"Don't you think of him as your own son?" Rachel said, her pitch rising. "Would you let your own fifteen-year-old son do this?"

"When we married, I took responsibility for the boys," Jed said. "But he already runs off half the time even though he knows our decision. How do you propose that I make him stay?"

"Forbid him to go."

"And if he goes anyway?"

"He's my son, Jed. He's going to the *English*."

"Lindy went."

"But my son! It's different."

David's footsteps returned, heavier. Above his mother's eyes, he caught Ella's gaze.

She shook her head. David bent to kiss Rachel's cheek and went out the front door with a duffel.

꙳

Younger men arrived to scramble up the ladders, hoisting shingles over their shoulders in a way that made James's shoulders ache just watching them. Chester Mast had driven all the way to Chardon to order lumber and supplies. The school would be finished soon. Already, while the roof crew enclosed the top of the building, others sealed windows in their frames, whitewashed the walls and floor, hammered in shelves, and sanded the wall where the chalkboards would hang.

Today's effort had been a sort of frolic among the men and any boys not in the *English* schools. Earlier progress came from a few men at a time turning up to do what they could between the long hours of their harvests, but all agreed that a frolic that brought nearly twenty men together would speed them to the finish line. The chalkboards would be the last large pieces to transport, once they arrived.

The women were at the Glicks' with a promise to arrive with lunch for everyone when the hour came. James had dropped Miriam off with a crate full of ingredients.

With his hands crossed behind his back, James stood at the rear of the school and imagined the room alive with children. Gertie and Savilla. Hans and the other Byler children. All those Hershberger girls whom James couldn't quite tell apart. The Glicks. The Borntragers. The Kings. Jed Hilty's stepson. The names of others in the church district drifted through James's mind.

Cristof Byler sidled up. "It will be a fine school."

James nodded. "What do the *English* think?"

Cristof laughed. "Not too many *English* school authorities come out this way. Chester's boys are in school—for now—so they have no reason to visit his farm."

"Will you take your children out?"

"Just as soon as we have a teacher. I'm already keeping Hans home some of the time. Gideon says he's working on finding a teacher."

A new voice spoke. "James."

He turned toward Isaiah Borntrager.

"The women sent a message," Isaiah said. "Miriam collapsed."

The pressure in his chest stopped James's breath.

"They said you should come," Isaiah said.

James gulped air. "Of course."

He strode to his buggy, checked the hitch and reins, climbed to the bench, and put the rig in motion.

At the Glick farm, three women hovered over Miriam on the front porch, one fanning her, another urging her to sip water, another arranging a pillow behind her head in the deep Adirondack chair. James nudged his way past them and knelt in front of his wife.

"What are you doing here, old man?" Miriam said.

She grasped a glass of water, and James was relieved to see it did not wobble in her grip.

"What happened?"

"I felt a little tired, that's all."

"She nearly passed out," Mrs. Borntrager said.

"I'll take you home." James put one hand behind Miriam's back to help her up.

"I promised you lunch," she said.

"I'm not hungry."

"I'll find something at home."

"You're going straight to bed." He took the water glass out of her hand and handed it to Mrs. Borntrager.

As soon as they arrived home, James once again pulled a chair up to the side of the bed to insist that Miriam rest. He would have to talk to Gideon about expecting less from Miriam with the main house and children. Surely Gideon would marry Ella in a few weeks, and the pressure would ease on Miriam. And he would have to be more direct with Miriam. It was no sin to admit she was tired.

Forty-four years. James wanted forty-four more with his bride.

Saturday brought the men together again for a morning of finishing work. Gideon tied his horse to a tree and hefted his toolbox out of his buggy.

"Where's James?" Cristof wanted to know. "I was hoping he would help us sort out what we need to build the desks."

"He can't leave Miriam," Gideon said. "She'll refuse to rest if he's not there to make sure she does."

"Then he is where he should be," Cristof said.

"We should talk to Lindy Lehman about the desks," Gideon said. "She's a better carpenter than most people realize, and she'll appreciate the need for simplicity."

"I can't get used to the idea of a woman carpenter. It's not fitting."

"You have one of her birdhouses in your yard."

"That's different."

"Only in size."

Joshua Glick broke into their conversation. "Gideon, I just heard that you took your children out of school."

"That's right." Gideon gripped his toolbox with both hands and looked Joshua in the eyes.

Joshua gestured to the nearly finished school. "Someday we'll have a school. In the meantime, though, we should obey the law."

"In my mind," Gideon said, "the question has become more complex."

"Perhaps we should all pull the children out of the *English* schools," Cristof said. "If we were united, it might send a strong message."

"It would get more of us in trouble," Joshua insisted. "Several men have already been fined."

"It's a small amount," Gideon said. "The deputy is blustering more than anything."

"The Bible tells us to live in submission to the government," Joshua said. "Are the apostle's words not clear?"

"They are," Gideon said.

Cristof spoke. "Maybe the time has come for a church vote."

"No." Alarm spurted through Gideon's gut. "Asking for a vote would only inflame matters further."

Joshua kicked at the dirt. "People look up to you, Gideon. You should set an example."

"Perhaps I am," Gideon said.

"I mean an example of doing the right thing," Joshua said.

"Perhaps I am," Gideon repeated.

"That's right," Cristof said.

Gideon began to wish Cristof would go find something else to do.

"Joshua," Gideon said, "you are in favor of running our own school, aren't you?"

"I am—when it's legal."

"That may take some time." So far Gideon had not been able to persuade the superintendent to grant him an appointment to discuss the matter calmly. He was quite sure cooperating to make an Amish school part of the district had not entered Mr. Brownley's mind.

"We have to go through the proper procedures," Joshua said. "While we wait, the children should be in school."

"And what becomes of our children in the meantime?" Gideon said. Gertie's self-portrait took form in his mind, along with the frivolous novel Savilla had been assigned to read. How would a book called *The Secret Garden* prepare Savilla for a quiet life on an Amish farm?

Ella happened to glance out the window of her second-story bedroom and saw the automobile before she heard it. She dropped her dust rag on the small desk and leaned toward the windowpane. Three seconds later, she pivoted and flew down the stairs.

"Rachel! Rachel!"

"In the kitchen," came the answer.

"Where's my *daed*?" Ella burst into the kitchen, where Rachel held a long wooden spoon and stirred coffee cake batter.

"I'm not sure. He left right after breakfast." Rachel tilted her head in question. "What's so urgent?"

"The deputy's car is coming down the lane."

Rachel dropped her spoon, spattering batter on table and floor, and raced out the back door calling her husband's name.

The knock came on the front door. Ella smoothed her apron and focused on not hunching over as she answered it.

"Hello," she said, stepping out onto the porch.

"It's a fine Monday morning," Deputy Fremont said.

Superintendent Brownley was with him this time. His gloomy scowl was the only expression Ella had ever seen on his face.

"We are thankful for each day God gives," Ella said.

"Is your pa here?" Deputy Fremont asked.

"My pa?"

"Or whatever you people call your father. Jed Hilty. I need to speak to Jed Hilty."

"It's a large farm and it's harvesttime," Ella said. "I'm not sure I can say where he is just now."

Rachel came around the corner of the house, her faced blanched but her spine extended, her shoulders back.

Good for you. Ella liked seeing determination in Rachel.

"Are you Mrs. Hilty?" Fremont asked.

"I am. May I be of assistance?"

"Can you tell us where your husband is?"

"No, I can't."

"Can't or won't?" Mr. Brownley muttered.

Rachel returned his stare but said nothing.

Brownley cleared his throat. "Would you give your husband a message?"

"Of course."

"We're pleased he has cooperated and we see David Kaufman in school, but his attendance has been erratic."

"I'm certain it will improve," Rachel said.

"I understand you are the boy's mother."

"Yes, I am."

"Then you can appreciate the gravity of the situation."

Gravity? Ella thought. That seemed a severe word.

"Your son's attendance borders on truancy. He's often late or leaves the building early without authorization."

"As I said, I believe you will see improvement," Rachel said.

"Your husband has the opportunity to be an example of coop-eration that other parents can emulate."

"I'll tell him you said so."

"Thank you."

Ella stood on the porch and watched the two men retrace their steps to the deputy's automobile, crank the engine, and roar off the farm.

Only then did Jed appear.

"*Daed!*" Ella met her father's eyes. Had he been there all along?

"I couldn't find you anywhere," Rachel said. "The horses were all here. I thought you must have walked out to one of the fields."

Ella believed Rachel had looked diligently for her husband. Surprise burned its way through Ella's chest. Jed had not wanted to be found. Had he seen the car coming even before she did?

Rachel gave a rapid account of the conversation.

"I have half a mind to take Seth out of school," Jed said.

"But he's only twelve," Ella said. "Seventh grade."

"They wanted David and now they have him," Jed said. "Are we also going to give them Seth?"

Why should Seth be a pawn to trade with the school district, one boy for the other? Ella's father had backed down so easily at the moment of David's ultimate defiance, but now he would take a sweet, earnest, contented boy in exchange? Ella pressed her lips together to keep disrespect out of her words.

"Other families are teaching their children at home. Your Gideon, for instance."

Ella swallowed.

"If you can teach Gideon's girls, you can teach Seth."

Ella found her voice. "I'm not even sure I can do a good job with the girls. Seth's lessons would be more advanced. It might be too much."

Jed looked again at the empty lane where the car had been before pacing across the yard to the barn.

CHAPTER 22

In church the following Sunday, Gideon mulled over the reality that so far the bishop had not publicly addressed the education of Amish children. He supposed the *English* would call it the "elephant in the room." By now any member in church could look around the congregation and know which decision each family had made, including his.

Joshua Glick had been right. As soon as word got out that Gideon was keeping his girls home from school, other households did the same. No matter how many times Gideon said that he did not judge another man's conscience on the matter, other fathers seemed to look to his example.

Yet the closest any of the ministers had come to preaching on the subject was to choose a Bible passage exhorting kindness to neighbors, as they might have done at any Sunday worship service of the year.

Gideon bowed his head, making a prayer of the final hymn.

Where shall I go? I am so ignorant. Only to God can I go, because God alone will be my helper. I trust in You, God, in all my distress. You will not forsake me. You will stand with me, even in death. I have committed myself to Your Word. That is why I have lost favor in all places. But by losing the world's favor, I gained Yours. Therefore I say to the world: Away with you! I will follow Christ.

Gideon made sure Tobias remained with the men to transform the benches of worship into tables for a meal in the King barn. He was glad for his coat this morning, and grateful that the next Sunday service was scheduled in a heated home large enough to accommodate the congregation. A juicy, steaming morsel of pork dangled from his fork on its way to his open mouth when Gideon felt a little hand thudding against his back. He turned to see Gertie. The girls were supposed to be eating with the women, under Ella's supervision. Miriam was home ill.

"*Daed*," Gertie said, "Katie Glick said that you're going to jail because I'm not in school. I don't want you to go to jail."

Gideon swung his legs over the bench so he could take her in his lap. "I am not going to jail."

"Promise?"

"Only God can promise. You know that."

"I'll go to school, and I won't draw any pictures or sing any songs. I'll only read the alphabet and do my sums."

"Don't you like learning at home with Ella?" Gideon said.

"Yes, I do. She makes everything interesting."

Gideon nodded. "Then let's keep doing that."

"But you'll go to jail, *Daed*!"

"I'm not going to jail." He kissed the top of her head. "Now go find Ella and finish your lunch."

The men around the table chewed silently, some of them staring at Gideon as he picked up his fork.

"She might be right," Aaron King said. "We could all go to jail."

"The fine was barely more than the cost of cotton for a child's dress," Gideon said. "It's hardly a foreshadowing of jail."

"I've been thinking," Chester Mast said. "Perhaps our children should all be in school for now."

"Chester!" Gideon's jaw dropped. "You're the one building a school on your own land."

"And I intend to see it used someday—sooner rather than later. My boys have been out of school the last few days, but I'm going to send them back tomorrow with a proviso."

Gideon lifted both eyebrows. The clinking of forks ceased.

"Some of the subjects the older children study are beyond what any of us regard as necessary, so in those subjects I will instruct my sons not to complete the assigned work."

Isaiah Borntrager laughed. "Chester Mast, you have spoken the word of the Lord."

Hardly. Gideon ran his tongue across his bottom lip while he thought.

"Health, world governments, art, other frivolous classes—my boys will be present in class, and I cannot control what falls on their ears," Chester said. "But I do have a say in what they focus their minds on, and it will not be these subjects."

"Gideon, what about you?" Aaron said. "Will you send your children back to school with these instructions?"

Gideon pictured Savilla's copy of *The Secret Garden.* Gertie's graven image was hidden in his dresser. He might need to present it to the school board as an example of unacceptable instruction.

"No, I don't think so," he said.

Gideon opened the accounts ledger lying at the center of the desk in the small alcove where he kept his papers. A shadow fell over the paper, and he looked up.

"May I interrupt you?" James said.

"Of course. How is Miriam today?"

"That's what I want to discuss," James said. "It broke her heart not to be well enough for church yesterday."

"Everyone asked after her."

"I will stay home and make sure she rests," James said. "But she will not want to stay down long."

Miriam was like her niece in that way. Right up until the week that Betsy died, Gideon had urged her to stop trying to do everything on her own.

"I want to help," Gideon said. "What can we do for Miriam?"

"A few changes will make things easier for her," James said. "Small things that she won't argue against."

"Whatever you have in mind."

"First," James said, "I want to put up a railing. We have only two steps up into the *dawdihaus*, but I would feel better if she had a railing."

"That's a simple thing," Gideon said.

"And I want to bring a comfortable chair into your kitchen," James said. "She needs to be able to get off her feet but still keep an eye on the stove."

"There's plenty of room under the corner window," Gideon said.

They should have done it years ago.

James scratched his head. "I'm concerned about the stairs up to the bedrooms, but I can't think of a way to keep her from going up and down."

"I'll talk to her," Gideon said. "I'll say the children are old enough now that there's no reason to coddle them. They can carry up their own laundry, and I'll put a broom and a dust rag in the hall closet. Miriam won't have to go upstairs."

"She'll be suspicious," James said. "She won't like the idea of the children doing her work."

"It won't be her work. It will be their work from now on." Gideon paused. "Do you really think she'll be all right, James?"

James looked out the window. The delay in his response caused an extra heartbeat in Gideon's chest.

"James?"

"I'm sure it's temporary," James said. "She needs more rest. But she will always think taking care of somebody else is more important than taking care of herself."

"I can ask Ella to stay around more," Gideon said. "She doesn't have to run off the moment the day's lessons are finished."

James nodded. "Miriam enjoys Ella."

"And Ella enjoys Miriam."

When Gideon and Ella married, Miriam could really let go of daily responsibilities. Miriam would respect Ella's new role to manage the house and children. Ella had ably managed her father's home for eleven years. She had learned well from her own mother and older sisters the skills she needed for cooking and gardening and canning and milking. At the same time, Gideon had no doubt that Ella would enjoy having Miriam nearby for advice or companionship, someone to sit with on the front porch and snap peas or husk corn, without letting Miriam exhaust herself.

Perhaps James was counting on this scenario, and counting the weeks until the date Gideon and Ella would arrange with the bishop.

Looking back, Gideon could not imagine how he would have managed during the last five years without James and Miriam, and he hoped they would feel no compunction to leave when he married again. Their departure would leave a gaping hole in his children's hearts. But they had taken on the care of three young children at an age when most people were enjoying grandchildren, not running after toddlers.

Miriam deserved the rest that the union between Gideon and Ella would bring her.

The plan suffered from one consequential complication.

How long would Gideon's kitchen table serve as adequate space for daily lessons with two girls?

"Where's Miriam?" Gertie asked.

"She's resting." Ella tapped the primer page. "Can you sound out the next sentence?"

"She's been resting since Saturday," Gertie said. "That's three days. When is she going to be finished resting?"

Savilla sighed. "When she's feeling better, silly."

"Don't call me names."

Ella gave Savilla a warning eye.

"Sorry," Savilla muttered, lowering her gaze back to her own book about the nocturnal habits of small animals.

"Are you going to make us lunch?" Gertie asked.

"I suppose so," Ella said. Lunch was several hours away.

Gertie swung her feet under the table. One shoe came into contact with Savilla's shin.

"Ow!" Savilla glared at Gertie.

Ella wasn't sure she had ever seen that expression on Savilla's face before. Perhaps both girls were always on their best behavior around her, cautioned by their father to mind their manners. Now that she was teaching them and would soon be living with and caring for them, she was bound to see another side to their relationship.

"Keep your feet to yourself, please," Ella said.

"That's not what Miss Simpson says." Gertie folded her hands and placed them in her lap. "She says, 'Hands and feet, nice and neat.'"

After nearly ten years of teaching, Margaret Simpson would have a long list of pithy reminders for classroom behavior.

"Miss Simpson always asks how the bus ride was," Gertie said.

"That's thoughtful of her," Ella said, tapping the page again.

"Then she makes sure everyone has a lunch bucket. She doesn't want anyone to be hungry at school."

"She's very kind."

"Can we pack lunch buckets?" Gertie looked up, hopeful.

"We don't need buckets, sil—" Savilla cut herself off. "We're sitting right in the kitchen. We can have lunch with *Daed* and Ella and James and Miriam."

"Let's concentrate," Ella said. "Then you can surprise everyone with the new words you learned."

Gertie put a finger under the first of three simple sentences on the page. Ella watched the girl's delicate lips go through the motions of finding the right formation for a *p* sound and silently add the other letters before pronouncing *put*.

Gertie looked up. "Are we going to have a chalkboard? At school we had a chalkboard."

"We could ask your *daed*," Ella said, "but since it's just us, we can use paper."

Savilla closed her book around a finger. "May I go in the other room to read, please?"

Ella nodded. "You can tell me later about any parts you didn't understand."

It would be impossible for anyone to concentrate through Gertie's chatter. Savilla tucked in her chair, as she always did, before leaving the room with relief.

"Miss Simpson gave us silent reading time," Gertie said. "We were supposed to use it to try to sound out new words."

"Would you like to have silent reading time, Gertie?" Against the left side of Gertie's head, her coiled braid sagged, and Ella reached over to adjust a pin.

The child shook her head. "I didn't like that part. It was more fun when we got to talk."

Gertie missed the other children, a factor Gideon may not have taken into consideration in his decision to keep her home. Margaret Simpson's classroom was in an *English* school, but she was an experienced, qualified teacher. Margaret would know what to say right now to encourage Gertie to focus on the task before her. While Gertie had been in school for just a few weeks, Margaret's class was her only experience of formal instruction. No wonder she measured the experience of sitting at the kitchen table with Ella against being in the classroom of a trained teacher.

"Let's read for fifteen more minutes," Ella said. "Then you can decide whether you would rather work on sums or handwriting while I see how Savilla is doing."

They were just two sisters in two grades, and already Ella wondered how the teachers in the old one-room schoolhouse had managed with thirty or forty students spanning eight grades.

CHAPTER 23

Margaret packed the leather satchel she carried between home and school. Today's teachers meeting had not been on the Thursday afternoon schedule. Mr. Tarkington came around to the classrooms only an hour ago requesting that teachers remain after school. Margaret had escorted her pupils to their waiting buses and returned to her classroom to pick up her things, planning to leave as soon as the meeting concluded. Gray would be waiting for her at the diner for lemon cake and coffee.

The music room was the only space in the school that would accommodate the assembled staff—other than the gymnasium, which would swallow speech in its cavernous hollow and throw back the echo of children playing. Margaret walked through the abandoned upstairs corridor, still chasing from her mind the voices of her own students. She'd had near perfect attendance that day. Only Gertie Wittmer was missing. Her desk still held her books and pencils and the oilcloth she used during art projects, but Margaret suspected Gertie would not be back. Hans Byler still attended—usually—but he looked lonely now when he turned his eyes to the empty desk beside his. Gideon had not formally withdrawn his daughters, but both girls were gone. That was no coincidence.

She should have done something. But what?

Allowing herself an indelicate audible sigh, Margaret shook off the thought. After Deputy Fremont slapped fines and hissed threats at the Amish fathers, Margaret considered herself relieved of responsibility to coax cooperation from them. She had never been one to play the fool, and if she had the opportunity, she would tell the school superintendent exactly what she thought of his tactics.

Mr. Tarkington cleared his throat to open the meeting. "It has come to my attention that some student grades are falling."

Margaret raised one eyebrow. The principal called a special meeting for this? Every year some students struggled. Competent teachers knew what to do.

"I have four of them in my class." Mr. Snyder taught the seventh grade. "I've spoken to Mr. Vaughn at the high school. The same thing is happening there."

Miss Hunter gave voice to Margaret's question. "What exactly is happening?"

Mr. Tarkington pushed his lips out. "Those of you teaching the younger grades may not have observed what is happening in the older grades."

"If they would simply turn in their work," Mr. Snyder said, "the grades would correct. As it is, I will have to give failing grades for the first quarter."

"I understand," Mr. Tarkington said, "that these students refuse to complete work, but only in certain subjects."

"Let me guess," Margaret said. "Assignments are missing in health and hygiene, literature, and world geography. At the high school, we might add higher mathematics, world history, art, and music."

Mr. Tarkington checked notes jotted on a sheet of paper. "That is correct."

"And the pupils you're referencing are Amish students," Margaret said.

"That is also correct."

"The Amish are not accustomed to those subjects," Margaret said. "I would go so far as to guess that the parents of these students would say that the subjects are not relevant to salvation or the practice of their religion."

Mr. Tarkington shifted his weight. "I'm a churchgoing person. I would venture to say that every person in this room is. But we offer an education that prepares students for the modern century. While we certainly hope to impart proper moral values to our students, our direct aim is not the furtherance of religion."

"I think you'll find the Amish don't make that distinction," Margaret said.

"Nevertheless," the principal said, "our task is to ensure the pupils conform to the standards we have established."

Margaret's mind withdrew from the discussion that ensued. The law said the children had to be in school, and many families complied. But just as the law did not say which grade they must enroll their children in, neither did it specify that the children must earn passing marks. Failing marks would ensure both that the students would not learn the objectionable material and also that they would not advance to higher grade levels. Margaret's lips curved in slight admiration at the ingenuity of the Amish strategies.

❧❦❧

"I'll feel better if I see for myself that David is all right."

Rachel's determination greeted Ella as she pulled the buggy onto the Hilty farm after spending most of the day on lessons with Gertie and Savilla. Ella relaxed the reins in her hands but did not get out.

"Right now?" Ella asked. There was barely time to go into town and back before supper.

"The meal is in the oven," Rachel said, "with enough wood for a slow heat. I don't want to wait another day. I hope you'll come with me."

Ella offered a smile and a nod. Rachel climbed into the buggy, and Ella signaled the horse again. Tomorrow would make two weeks since David's departure. Perhaps it would help Rachel's recent temperament if she saw for herself that David was safe and cared for.

Rachel fidgeted all the way into town, and although Ella infused her words with optimism and cheerfulness, Rachel did not settle. Any mother would want to know her child was looked after, but at least half of Rachel's nervousness might be in anticipation of what she would say to her old friend under circumstances neither of them would have imagined when they were girls—or even a few weeks ago.

After a while, Ella abandoned attempts at easy conversation and concentrated on coaxing better speed from the horse. Finally they turned onto Lindy's street. Ella let her eyes linger for a moment on Margaret Simpson's bungalow, wondering if Margaret missed Gertie as much as the little girl seemed to miss her. Ella tied the horse up in front of Lindy's house, and she and Rachel paced to the back of the lot where Lindy's workshop sat.

"What was that?" Rachel hurried her steps.

"I didn't hear anything," Ella said, trying to keep pace.

"There it is again," Rachel said.

Scraping and scuffling. It could just be Lindy pushing a piece of furniture across the room.

Thud.

A splintering sound.

A yelp.

The door of the workshop opened, and a man darted out and across a patch of grass before disappearing behind the neighbor's thick hedge. Ella caught a glimpse only of a blue shirt. She didn't recognize the man.

Rachel and Ella burst into the workshop. Splintered against the far wall were the remains of several birdhouses. A bookcase lay on its back, the bottom shelf kicked out of place.

"Lindy?" Rachel called.

A moan. A foot.

Rachel cleared the debris and found her friend, taking Lindy's face in her hands. "Open your eyes! Talk to me!"

With a sigh, Lindy complied. "Did you see him?"

"Who was that?" Rachel asked.

"I don't know." Lindy raised a hand to her head. "I've already got an egg on my scalp."

"Who would want to do this?" Ella scanned the shambles.

Lindy pushed herself upright, leaning on one arm and delicately exploring her ankle with the other. "He came in and went crazy before I could ask what I could do for him. I tried to stop him, but he pushed me, and I tripped."

Ella righted the bookcase. Rachel knelt beside Lindy and pushed up the woolen trousers to examine the injured ankle.

"I'll never get used to seeing you in men's trousers," Rachel said.

"I only wear them when I work." Lindy winced under Rachel's touch.

"It's already swelling," Rachel said. "Do you have ice in that *English* kitchen of yours?"

"The ice man was here just yesterday." Lindy exhaled.

Ella stepped around Rachel to the other side of Lindy. "We'll help you up and into the house."

Gingerly, they got Lindy to her feet. Immediately it was clear she guarded the ankle against her own slight weight as she leaned on Rachel and Ella.

"We'll go slowly." Ella glanced toward the open workshop door. A flash of blue, on the sidewalk in front of the house, made her blink twice. The man moved out of view.

Why would he come back?

"What is it?" Rachel said, following Ella's gaze.

"Nothing," Ella said. Lindy was hopping at a painstaking but tenacious pace, and Ella would not suggest they should now follow a distraction from her care.

Ella was sure it was the same man. She didn't recognize him, but she would know him if she saw him again.

            ❧

Gideon regretted the action as soon as he put it in motion, but it was too late to stop the hay from tipping off the end of his pitchfork in the loft onto the man standing below him in the barn the following day.

Deputy Fremont sputtered. "Are you looking to give me a reason to issue an additional violation? I will write up as many fines as you'd like to pay."

"I doubt it's a crime against the state for a man to move alfalfa hay into his own stalls," Gideon said. He may have regretted the action, but he had not yet repented of the sentiment.

"I'll ask you again to come down," Deputy Fremont said.

"As you can see, I'm busy." Gideon stuck the pitchfork into a broken bale but restrained himself this time.

"You're going to want to look at this closely." Fremont picked hay out of his uniform.

Gideon doubted that.

Fremont waved a paper. "Apparently our last communication two weeks ago was not sufficiently clear. Rather than put your boy in school, you took your girls out."

Gideon wiped perspiration from his forehead with one sleeve. "It was clear enough."

"Then it was not sufficiently persuasive."

"There's a bench along the tack wall," Gideon said. "You can leave it there."

"Whether you look at it now or later, it's not going to change."

"I didn't expect it would."

The deputy stomped across the barn, found the bench, laid the paper down, and dropped a worn rein on top of it. Gideon threw down a generous shower of hay.

Fremont left the barn door wide open. Gideon waited for the sounds of the automobile engine coming to life and tires spitting gravel before he climbed down the ladder.

The fine was much stiffer this time—no slap on the hands. He was penalized for each child separately, and now he had three truant children rather than one. He scratched the top of his head while making mental calculations. He did not yet know the market price he would receive for the portion of his harvest that he did not need to keep for his own family and animals. Some of the repairs he planned to make over the winter might have to wait. His children were worth the price.

For others, though, the choice might be more difficult. The Hershbergers already were heavily mortgaged. Fines for four children would be beyond John's means. And Isaiah? Chester? Gideon was not sure.

❧✣☙

The lessons were finished for the day, and the girls had gone to the *dawdihaus* to cheer up Miriam, promising to heed Ella's warning not to be rambunctious. They could offer to read to Miriam, Ella had suggested, or ask her to tell a story about when she was their age, but they were not to ask for cookies or a game. Stew was on the stove, and corn bread cooled on the counter.

Ella debated looking in on Miriam. She seemed more rested than she was a week ago and unlikely to accept coddling for much longer.

The back door opened, and Gideon came in.

He glanced around. "Where is everybody?"

"Tobias is in the barn with James, and the girls are with Miriam," Ella said.

A silly grin crossed Gideon's face. "Good." He leaned in to kiss her on the mouth, something he never did when the children were within sight.

She would never tire of the taste of him.

"Let's go for a ride," he said.

Ella tossed the dish towel in her hands onto the table and reached for her shawl.

"What will you do about the fines?" she asked as the buggy rumbled onto the main road.

"Pay them," he said.

"You can't just keep paying fines," Ella said. "They're sure to get steeper."

"I have a plan." Gideon clicked his tongue to speed the horse. "Did James get into town to check on Lindy today?"

Ella nodded. "The doctor says it's only a bad sprain. Lindy needs to stay off her feet for a few days."

"Then it will be handy to have David around," Gideon said. "I hope he's helping with the chores around the house."

"Rachel wishes he would come home, and I don't blame her. Someone has broken into Lindy's shop twice. How is Rachel supposed to know David is safe? Lindy could come, too. I'd be happy to help look after her."

"But David won't come home, will he? Not unless Jed agrees to let him go to school."

"No."

"Then it's better that he is with Lindy for now."

"I don't understand why anyone would want to hurt Lindy— twice." Ella exhaled. "Rachel is organizing meals. James will make deliveries."

"Good."

She leaned forward, realizing Gideon's route. "Are we going to the new school?"

Ella hadn't seen the construction since it was hardly more than framing. The Mast farm was far enough off her usual routines that she did not cross their fields often.

A few minutes later, Gideon eased the rig to a stop in front of the one-room school and helped Ella out of the buggy. He held open the door to the building. Even in the waning afternoon, windows channeled light inside.

"The blackboard is up!" Ella said.

It was pristine, still rich in its slate hues, unclouded by layers of chalk smeared across the surface. Desks were lined up in precise rows, not yet subject to the jostling of squirming children. Three different sizes bore witness to the mixed ages the room was meant to serve. The simplicity and efficiency of the space beckoned beauty.

"All we need is an Amish teacher," Gideon said, "and I think I know someone who would do a wonderful job."

Ella's eyes widened. "You can't mean me."

"Of course I can."

"I haven't even got my legs under me with the girls. I wouldn't know what to do with an entire school."

"Of course you would. You'd figure it out, just the way you figure everything out."

"It wouldn't be legal," Ella said. "I'm not qualified."

"Let me figure out that part." Gideon took both her hands. "Just tell me you'll think about it. And it would only be temporary. I'll correspond with the teachers college and impress upon them the urgency of finding a suitable candidate as soon as possible."

CHAPTER 24

No, you are not going to work today." James could be adamant when he chose to be. "I brought strudel, with biscuits and pot roast for later."

"*Aunti* Miriam's pot roast?" Lindy's face brightened. "With mashed potatoes, peas, and gravy?"

"That's right. Enough for you and David to eat two or three times."

"Just like she used to make on Sundays, but it's only Saturday."

James had tried to persuade Miriam to prepare something simpler, but she brushed him off and began peeling a mound of potatoes. James adjusted the pillow under Lindy's swollen ankle.

"Tomorrow Mrs. Borntrager will bring a roast chicken," he said, "and the day after that Mrs. Mast has in mind a casserole."

"Did you arrange all this?"

"Rachel did," James said.

"I suppose everybody knows David is staying with me."

"You know how it is." James handed Lindy a mug of steaming coffee. "Word gets around on the Amish farms."

Lindy looked down into the dark liquid. "I suppose she came on Thursday to make sure David is all right. Now she'll think I can't take proper care of him."

"A better question is whether he's taking proper care of you." James moved Lindy's crutches within reach of her chair.

"David's already cleaned up most of the mess in the workshop," Lindy said. "He's out there now, trying to cut pieces for birdhouses. I had customers waiting for the ones that. . ."

"Your customers will understand," James said. "You need rest. No work."

After extracting a promise that Lindy would remain in the house and not try to hobble out to the workshop, James returned to his wagon. He let the horse clip-clop slowly while he worked his jaw from side to side, thinking. Rachel and Ella had insisted Lindy telephone the sheriff's deputy to see the wreckage in the shop for himself, but his examination had not gone beyond a cursory inspection. So far Deputy Fremont had not seemed compelled to investigate.

James took firmer control of the reins and steered the rig toward Main Street, where he parked in front of the local sheriff's office and went in.

Deputy Fremont looked up. "Mr. Lehman, isn't it?"

"That's right," James said. "I'm here to make an inquiry on behalf of my niece, Lindy Lehman."

Fremont reached for a folder at one end of his desk. "Simple breaking and entering."

"Don't forget that Lindy was physically harmed," James said. No doubt the *English* had a word for a crime in which someone was injured. "Do you have any suspects?"

Fremont shrugged one shoulder. "Not much to go on."

"Ella Hilty saw a tall man wearing a blue shirt and dark trousers," James said.

"That describes half the men in Seabury." Fremont scanned James from head to toe. "Probably *all* of the Amish farmers as well."

"Why would an Amish man break into Lindy's shop?"

"Why indeed?"

Heat flashed through James's neck. "You are going to look for this man, aren't you?"

"As I said, there's not much to go on. Perhaps if there's another crime that fits the same pattern, we'll have more information to work with."

The same pattern? Lindy's shop had twice suffered wreckage. Another episode in the same pattern would put her at risk a third time.

"I have other pressing matters," Fremont said. "Perhaps if your people would abide by the law and send their children to school, Seabury would return to being a peaceful town."

James swallowed his response. The smirk on the deputy's face made James wish he had a bale of hay to pitch down on his head.

Ella spotted David approaching from the corner on Monday after school and slowed her movements so she would be pulling the stew of chicken and potatoes out from under the buggy bench just as he reached Lindy's property line. She made sure to catch his eye.

"Hello, Ella." David shifted his books, hanging by their leather strap, to the other shoulder.

"You look well." Ella focused on the details Rachel would want to know. His face retained its round shape with color perched high on his cheekbones. In fact, David looked better than Ella had seen him since he first moved to the Hilty farm a year ago.

"Everything is fine," David said. "That's what you can tell *Mamm.*"

"Why don't you tell her yourself? Better yet, come by and show her."

David's head turned toward the clatter in the tree in Lindy's front yard. "Barn swallows," he said.

"They won't be around much longer," Ella said, eyeing David. "I'll miss them."

"The school library has a book about winter birds. I might check it out."

"I'd like to see it," Ella said. "Bring it when you come by."

David's gaze rotated back toward Ella. "You know I can't do that."

"Of course you can. We all want you to. . .visit."

"I offered to help on Saturdays. Your *daed* made it clear I needn't come."

Ella exhaled softly. "Your *mamm* wanted to see you the day Lindy got hurt. That's why we came."

"It's good you were here. *Gottes wille.*"

"Yes." She paused. "Rachel seemed unsure where you were, though."

They had called the doctor and waited with Lindy until he came. Then the sheriff's deputy came for a disinterested look around. And all the while, Rachel festered over why David had not come straight home from school that day.

"I was bird-watching," David said. "I told Lindy. She probably forgot because of everything that was going on." He let his bundle drop off his shoulder, unstrapped it, and pulled a sheet of paper from between the pages of a book.

Ella admired the sheet. "It's a brown thrasher. Did you do this drawing?"

The muscles around David's mouth twitched in a suppressed grin. "Does it really look like a brown thrasher?"

"I recognized it, didn't I?" The head was slightly elongated and the angle of the wings not quite right, but David had captured perfectly the downward angle of the beak and placement of the yellow eyes, along with dark spots on the white breast.

"It's the first time I tried sketching one. That's why I remember it was that day. When I got home, Miss Simpson from across the street was sitting with Lindy."

"Miss Simpson was kind enough to look after Lindy when Rachel and I needed to go home."

"I've already been over to thank her."

The stew pot grew cumbersome in Ella's hands under a wave of guilt. She knew the church's position on high school as well as David did, but somehow she could not bring herself to wish he would give it up.

"Come and see your mother," she said quietly.

"That would only cause her distress when it was time for me to leave." David buckled his books together again.

"What about church? We'll be at the Garbers' next time."

He met her gaze. "You know what that would be like."

Stares and whispers. Side glances. Heads shaking in sympathy and then bowed in fervent prayer for Rachel and her rebellious son.

"There's Lindy now," David said.

Ella looked up. Lindy stood framed in the front door, light from within outlining her form bent over two crutches. Ella followed David to the door.

⚹

Margaret sat on the front porch with an untouched slice of cherry pie in her lap and her fork slack in her fingers. She looked in both directions down the quiet street. A week after coming home and finding a sheriff's car parked in front of Lindy's house, Margaret remained unsettled. Locking her doors at night and when she was away from the house, which she had never done since arriving in Seabury, was insufficient assurance that the vandal would not return to the vulnerable block. Every evening, as she checked on Lindy and scanned the neighborhood, she saw nothing to alarm her, but she could not shake off images of Lindy's white face that night.

"Penny for your thoughts," Gray said, his plate already cleared of all but the slightest indication of what it had held.

Margaret scraped her fork along an edge of pie crust. "I'm still thinking about Lindy. Deputy Fremont doesn't seem to have done anything to make sure it won't happen again to someone else."

"You're safe," Gray said.

"I'm sure Lindy thought she was safe."

"But she took in that boy."

Margaret raised her eyes from her pie plate to Gray's face, shadowed just outside the feeble beam of the porch light. "What do you mean?"

"She took in that Amish boy."

"He's her best friend's son, and he wanted to go to school."

Gray shrugged. "It's a warning."

"A warning! That's ridiculous." Heat fired up the sides of Margaret's neck.

"It's best if folks stay out of the Amish problem."

"I wish people would stop calling it that!" Margaret set her plate on the side table with too much force, and the fork clattered to the porch floor.

"Whoever broke into Lindy's shop wants her to stay out of the business of what happens with the Amish." Gray gently lifted Margaret's hand and wrapped his long fingers around it.

No matter what Margaret's mood, when he did that, yearning shivered through her. A man's touch. A husband. A family. A future.

"It's a matter for the sheriff," Gray said. "It's better if everyone leaves it be. Then there won't be any trouble."

"David Kaufman is a perfectly nice young man," Margaret said. "Why should anyone think he would be trouble?"

"He belongs at home with his parents," Gray said, as if it were obvious.

Margaret flushed, uncertain whether the sensation rose from fury at Gray's words or the touch that made her tingle.

"I'm glad," Gray said, "that you're not in the middle of that business anymore. I can rest more easily knowing there is no reason anyone should target you."

"They're children," Margaret said. "I still have Hans Byler in my class."

"Do your job," Gray said, "but there's no reason to be personally involved."

"It's my job to care about the welfare of my pupils."

"You wouldn't be the excellent teacher you are if you didn't care," Gray said. "But sometimes you have to draw a line. Let the authorities handle this. The fines should bring all the families in line."

Margaret's heart sank a fraction of an inch. How could a man whose hands and lips made her go soft at the center also spike distaste at the back of her throat?

"I'd like to escort you to church on Sunday," Gray said. "May I?"

In the evening's obscurity, she could not see his eyes, but she smelled the cherry pie on his breath and felt the stroke of his fingers on the back of her hand.

CHAPTER 25

T he answer came to Ella during the family's Friday morning devotions after her father's brief meditation on Isaiah 26:3: "Thou wilt keep him in perfect peace, whose mind is stayed on thee: because he trusteth in thee."

In the last week, since Gideon asked her to take on teaching the Amish students temporarily, Ella had gone out of her way three times to pass by the new school building on the Mast farm. Each time she paused to pray, wanting only *Gottes wille.* If she took on this challenge, God's will must be certain in her heart. On the Wittmer farm, gradually, Gertie had settled into the new routine, and Savilla remained as steadfast in her work as she was in most things. The time they spent on lessons seemed more efficient each day, and Ella began to see how it would be possible for her to rotate between groups of children learning at different levels.

When she opened her eyes on Friday morning, Ella felt the peaceful certainty she had sought all week. Seth was soon out the door to catch the bus—perhaps for the last time—and Ella was soon on her way with the family's buggy.

This time she entered the one-room school with her mind buzzing with plans. She started at the back of the classroom, pulling the larger desks slightly farther apart. Memories of being in the seventh and eighth grades with inadequate space for lengthening legs had come to her in the middle of the night. Then she re-spaced the front desks, resolute in tolerating the jagged aisles in exchange for the certainty that no child would have to wrestle with whether to admit she couldn't see the board. On the teacher's desk—her desk—at the front of the room sat a tin of new chalk. Ella took out a piece, reached high, and began printing letters, capital and small in pairs, across the top of the chalkboard. She worked carefully but efficiently, the same approach teaching would require. Tomorrow was Saturday. The girls would not be expecting her for lessons, and Ella could spend as much time as she needed preparing the classroom. She stood at the back now, pleased with the start she had made. The mercantile would have packages of paper, and the students would know to bring pencils. A bookcase at the front of the room awaited textbooks, which Gideon had promised to retrieve from the old school after he shored up a beam for safety.

Ella had not said anything to her father yet. She supposed she ought to ask his permission; she was not a married woman yet. But Jed would support an Amish school. He would see all the reading Ella had done in all the years since she left school herself as divine preparation for this moment. Like Esther in the Bible, she was called "for such a time as this."

Her wedding day was less than two months off. Gideon believed God would provide a teacher who could begin right after Christmas. Ella would burn the candle at both ends helping Rachel scrub down the house in preparation for the wedding while also planning lessons, but Rachel would be grateful to have Seth out of the *English* school. *All things work together for good to them that love God and are called according to His purpose*, Ella reminded herself.

If she wanted to catch Gideon before he left the house for his own work, Ella couldn't dawdle all morning in the schoolhouse. She gave the door a satisfied tug behind her and put the horse into a canter.

Miriam was standing on Gideon's porch shaking out a rug when Ella arrived.

"The girls are ready for you," Miriam said. "I told them to wait in the kitchen and not to make you spend half the morning looking for them."

Ella smiled. Savilla would be doing exactly as she was supposed to be doing. It was Gertie who might wander off distracted by any one of a hundred things.

"I'd like to see Gideon first," Ella said.

"I think he's working on his papers."

Ella stood behind Gideon's desk in the alcove for nearly a full minute before her presence disturbed his concentration. He met her gaze, and his eyes crinkled.

"You're going to do it, aren't you?"

"It makes my heart pound in terror to think of it, but yes, I want to try." She would be married in a few weeks. If she did not try now, she would never have another chance to find out if she could manage a classroom.

Gideon stood, and Ella was certain he wanted to be alone as much as she did. But neither of them would risk one of the children—or Miriam or James—finding them in an embrace.

"I'm nervous," she said. "Civil disobedience has never been my strength."

"But obeying God has always been your strength," Gideon said. "Can you start on Monday?"

Three days—only two if she did not count the Sabbath.

Ella nodded. "Eight o'clock." She would be ready, even if Savilla and Gertie were still her only students.

❧

The dispassionate warning in Gray's tone the evening before lingered in Margaret's mind for most of the night. She doubted he wished harm to anyone and believed he wanted her to be safe. He simply saw no reason for the sheriff or the school officials to concern themselves with what became of the Amish.

Gray had never mentioned conversing with any of the Amish men. He had helped them set up for their auction, and most likely that had not been the first time. Certainly he would have no occasion to speak to an Amish woman, but if he ran into one of the men in the hardware store or the mercantile, would he greet him? Could he truly hold himself so separate from the Amish that he could not at least nod his head and say good morning?

It wasn't so easy for Margaret. She had been to the farms. She had shared small gifts with the mothers, met with the fathers, and kept a protective eye on the children while they were in school. Margaret had tried telling herself they weren't her responsibility—just what Gray was saying. All her efforts to befriend the Amish and understand their ways were undercut by Superintendent Brownley's impatience and Deputy Fremont's utter lack of humility.

Mr. Brownley had asked her to take on a task and then ensured she would fail.

Yet when Margaret stood in her classroom every day and looked at Hans Byler, she thought he was the bravest little boy she had ever known. He was the youngest and smallest of all the Amish children in the school, and since Gertie Wittmer had stopped attending, he was alone in the classroom with his black suspenders and bowl-cut hair under straw hat. Nearly every day, as Margaret took attendance and checked off twenty-four names of children who resembled each other and one who did not, she thought of Jesus' parable of the shepherd who left ninety-nine sheep to find the one lost lamb and carry it home on his shoulder.

On Friday after school, Margaret walked home, changed into more comfortable shoes, and took her car out. In her own mind, she could not think what to do for the Amish children. Never one to consider prayer confined to church walls—or any walls—Margaret wondered if God might yet show her what to do and give the courage to do it. No matter what Gray Truesdale thought.

A sign, she murmured. *A sign.*

She drove out toward the Amish farms, trying to remember details of the turns she had taken when the summer sun was still high in the sky, even at this hour of the day, and optimism propelled her awkward attempts at befriending families she understood almost nothing about. The superintendent might just as well have assigned her to make sure the Creoles of Baton Rouge, Louisiana, reported to school in Seabury, Ohio. She'd fumbled the job. They all had. The only difference was that Margaret would take another approach if she had a fresh opportunity.

The automobile whizzed through an intersection. Margaret was a hundred yards down the road before recognition niggled at her. *Intersection* was an overstatement. It was only a narrow lane that came up on one side from a farm.

An Amish farm. She couldn't remember the family's name. The faces of two older boys floated through her mind. Mace? Macky? Mast? Elijah Mast had been the boy attacked in the upstairs hall at school.

That was it. But something looked altered.

She told herself it was only the bare branches, whose leaves in full summer bloom would have hidden untold details. But it was more than that. A flash of shiny whitewash had caught her eye, and she distinctly remembered the Mast house as being a nondescript gray.

Margaret braked, turned the car around, approached the lane, and navigated into it.

And there it was, in the corner of a fallow field. A one-room school that looked like so many dotting the Ohio countryside, except this one was brand new.

Outside, an Amish horse, still hitched to a buggy, nuzzled the ground in the shade. Realization dawned. Margaret shut off her engine, stunned. At least four minutes passed before she felt her breathing was under control and her heart would not explode through her sternum. Fumbling for the handle on the driver door, Margaret slid out of the automobile.

At the school's door, with her fingers on the knob, Margaret filled her lungs. She had dared to ask God for a sign. Was this it?

"Hello?" she called before the door was fully open.

"In here," came the response.

Margaret stepped into the immaculate room and stared into the face of Ella Hilty.

"Your people have built a school!" Margaret said.

"I won't try to deny it." Ella spread her arms wide.

Margaret envied the excitement in Ella's voice.

"On the day I first met you, Nora Coates was trying to persuade you to be a teacher," Margaret said. "But. . .I'm confused."

"But I'm not qualified," Ella said. "It's all right to say it. I know that truth better than anyone."

"So you've found another teacher?"

"Not yet," Ella said. "Gideon is making inquiries. I'm only going to fill in for a few weeks so the students don't lose ground."

"I want to help." The words tumbled past Margaret's lips before her mind caught up with their meaning.

Ella's eyes widened.

⋅⋘❈⋙⋅

The benches were loaded in the wagon to be taken to the next home that would host worship in two weeks. The young people were organizing a walk along the river and probably would not be back until it was time for the evening's Singing. With a basket of empty dishes hanging from one arm, Miriam was herding Gideon's daughters toward the buggy, while Tobias and James hitched it to the team of driving horses.

Standing beside his buggy and clutching her shawl around her shoulders, Ella offered Gideon a smile across the yard. It was time.

Gideon touched the elbows of Isaiah Borntrager and John Hershberger.

"Ready?" Isaiah said.

Gideon nodded. He had waited until the last minute intentionally, preferring to avoid a lengthy discussion. Persuading other fathers what they must do was not on his mind. He only wanted to be sure they all received the same information upon which to base their decisions. They would meet in the barn, but they would not be there long enough to need seats.

"The school is ready," he said a few minutes later. "Classes will begin tomorrow. For now Ella Hilty will teach, until I hear from the teachers college about someone who might come in the middle of the school year."

Gideon glanced up and saw Bishop Garber enter the barn.

"I cannot afford any more fines," Aaron King said. "I'll have to leave my children in school in town until we're sure everything is in accordance with the law."

"I understand," Gideon said. "I respect the decision of your conscience."

"I don't see how the *English* are suddenly going to leave us be," Joshua Glick said. "They'll only see this as more reason to object to our ways."

"Maybe so," Gideon said. "But we have to prove we can manage a school on our own."

"My *kinner* will be there," John Hershberger said.

Gideon nodded. Mrs. Hershberger was sure to be relieved of the expectation that she should manage lessons along with eight children, including a colicky baby. His eyes went from one man to the next, and he was fairly sure what each one would say. Opinions had not changed much over the last two months.

"We're not here to argue today." Gideon said. "Every man has to decide for himself, though I'm sure if any of you wants to talk, the bishop would be happy to help."

The bishop nodded.

"And of course you can talk to me privately," Gideon continued. "Today I only want some idea of how many children Ella should expect tomorrow. It's only fair that she know. Now raise your hand if you intend to send your children to an Amish-run school beginning tomorrow."

John Hershberger's hand shot up. Gideon smothered his chuckle and waited for others, mentally tallying the number of school-age children each man had.

CHAPTER 26

The morning, the first Monday in November, still carried the overnight chill, and Ella poked at the wood in the potbelly stove once again to coax new flames to cast their heat into the schoolhouse. She smoothed her apron and adjusted her *kapp*, but she wasn't ready to throw off her shawl. As long as she was cold, she presumed the children would be cold, so the fire was warranted.

Unless it was her nerves that drained the heat from her body.

Ella had wound the clock on her desk as soon as she arrived, but she checked it again now. At the center of the desk, where only she would see it, was the day's schedule—or at least Ella's best guess about how the day might go. The wide, high windows welcomed abundant morning light, but lamps stationed around the room were at the ready, their bases filled with oil.

Moistening her lips for the umpteenth time that morning, Ella paced down the center aisle to look out the window on the front of the building. She was determined to welcome her pupils individually as they arrived. Gideon estimated she might have sixteen or seventeen, but it was hard to be certain. Fathers might change their minds in either direction—put their children on the buses as usual, or send them to Ella even though they had not raised their hands when Gideon asked. Sixteen students would not include everyone up through eighth grade, but it was a solid beginning.

John Hershberger was first. Four children scrambled out of his buggy. Ella mentally rehearsed the girls' names: Lizzy, Katya, and Esther. Or was Katya the youngest one? Panic surged up her throat, and Ella took a deep breath. Miriam had told her three times that

Esther was the youngest of the four school-age Hershbergers. Ella didn't know why she had such trouble remembering. The lone Hershberger boy was simple, named for his father but called Johnny.

James arrived with Gertie and Savilla, and Ella was grateful for the familiar faces. Isaiah Borntrager came, and then the Bylers. Seth loped over the hill, and the two Mast boys were the last to appear, though their house was within view.

They all looked startled to Ella, and with good reason. At best, some of them learned the previous afternoon that the school would open, but others learned only that morning at the breakfast table or intercepted on their way out the door to meet the bus. Several arrived with books in their arms—books someone would have to return to the school in Seabury.

The older ones knew what to do in the one-room school. The Mast boy walked straight to the stove and satisfied himself it was performing, and Ella supposed this had been his task in the old building. Lizzy Hershberger settled her stair-step siblings according to where children of the same ages would likely sit.

By three minutes after eight, Ella stood behind her desk, returning the stares of fifteen pairs of eyes.

"*Gut mariye*," she said.

"*Gut mariye*," came the unison response.

"This is an important day for all of us," Ella said, "and you might have been expecting a very different day when you woke up this morning. I want each one of you to know how glad I am to see you here, where we can help each other learn. I hope you'll be patient with me, and I promise to do my best to be patient with you. If we're kind and respectful, we can enjoy a wonderful school together."

Ella had meant to reassure the children, but as she listened to the words she had rehearsed a dozen times, her own pulse slowed. She believed what she said.

"I need time to get to know you," she said. "If you are fourth grade or older, please take out two sheets of paper and a pencil. While I listen to the younger ones read, you may work on an essay that will help me discover your abilities. On the board, you'll see three questions. You may choose the one that interests you the most and construct an essay with at least three supporting points. If you are in grades one, two, or three, please gather around my desk, and we'll take turns with the primer. Are there any questions?"

No hands went up. Instead, older students shuffled papers as they began their work, and younger ones shuffled their feet as they took places around her desk. Today would be language skills. Tomorrow she would find out what arithmetic skills the pupils had mastered.

A little hand tapped Ella's shoulder, and she smiled at an earnest face. "Yes, Gertie?"

"May I read first?"

"Thank you for volunteering," Ella said, pressing open a primer along the binding.

"And then Hans," Gertie said.

Ella's two youngest students seemed equally satisfied to be together once again.

❧

After dropping the girls off at school, James took a team of two horses and his wagon into Seabury. Rather than the mercantile or Lindy's workshop, though, his first destination was the Seabury branch of the county sheriff's office.

"I wondered what news you had about the man who attacked Lindy Lehman." James looked Deputy Fremont in the eye and braced his feet shoulder-width apart. "It's been ten days."

Fremont poised a fountain pen over an official-looking sheet of paper. "Unfortunately, ten days is plenty of time for the trail to go cold."

"May I ask whom you have interviewed?" James asked. It seemed to him Deputy Fremont had done nothing but throw ice on the trail to ensure it went cold.

"Your niece and a couple of neighbors. No one saw anything helpful."

"What about Ella and Rachel Hilty?"

"The Amish women?" Fremont used his pen to sign his name on a form.

"The witnesses," James said.

"I beg to differ," Fremont said. "On the afternoon of the incident, they both confirmed that they did not see the attack as it happened."

James set his jaw. "They might have seen something they did not realize was significant."

Fremont looked up again. "Shall we make an agreement? You do your job, and I'll do mine."

If James felt even minimal assurance that Deputy Fremont would in fact perform his duties, this conversation would be unnecessary.

"The matter has nothing to do with you," Fremont said.

"Lindy Lehman is a family member."

"You're not her husband or her father," Fremont said. "Neither are you a witness to the events in question. I'm afraid if you want information, you'll have to read it in the newspaper like everyone else."

Or I can uncover the information myself. Never in his life had he read an *English* newspaper, nor was he in the habit of gambling his money on long odds.

James left the sheriff's office determined not to return but equally determined to discover who would hold a grudge against someone as mild-mannered as Lindy.

He pulled up to her workshop a few minutes later, prepared to load and deliver items she had ready. Seeing her through the glass of the locked door, he knocked. Lindy hobbled on one crutch to let him in.

"David made me promise to lock myself in," Lindy said. "And my neighbor Margaret was on his side. I couldn't defy them both at one time."

"Don't apologize," James said. "Under the circumstances, he's right."

"What circumstances?" Lindy said. "We don't know what happened or why."

"Your shop was vandalized twice. You were attacked."

"I choose to think it was a vagrant who won't be back." Lindy settled herself on a stool and picked up a paintbrush. "Not when he knows somebody other than me might have gotten a look at him."

"Just how good a look did you get?" James asked.

"I didn't see his face, *Onkel* James. I told you that already."

"But you might have had a sense of how tall he was. Maybe you saw his boots, or noticed a limp."

"I wish I could tell you any of that," Lindy said, dipping her brush in blue paint and touching a birdhouse with the delicate point. "I guess I'd say he was taller than average. But I didn't notice his hat or his boots or anything else. I'll take Ella's word for it that he was wearing a blue shirt."

"Think carefully, Lindy," James said. "Any detail could be important. Maybe he was left-handed. Maybe his knee creaked."

Lindy laughed. "You sound like an *English* police officer—and a better one than Deputy Fremont."

Gertie would ask more questions than Deputy Fremont. James kept this thought to himself.

"Feel free to look around," Lindy said, "but I just want to get back to normal, and I'm not going to live in fear. That's not the way of our people, is it?"

"No, it's not." Her use of "our people" softened him.

"Are you still going to make my deliveries today?"

"Of course."

"I left my list in the kitchen." Lindy set down her paintbrush and reached for her crutch.

"I can get it," James said.

Lindy shook her head. "I can do it. While I'm gone, you can start with the two quilt racks for the furniture store."

James clasped his hands behind his back to squelch the impulse to offer support to Lindy's elbow—she would only swat him away—but he watched to be sure she safely crossed the patch of grass between the workshop and the house. Then he turned to her workbench before pacing to the wall used to shatter birdhouses ten days ago. James had seen the damage for himself. Now he wished David had not followed instructions to clean up the mess. Almost certainly Deputy Fremont would have overlooked a meaningful remnant, if there was one.

James carried a quilt rack out to the wagon and secured it. Before returning to the second one, he glanced across the street, unsure which house belonged to Margaret Simpson.

❧❦❧

Ella had not known exhaustion and exhilaration to be twins before, birthed from the same labor.

At two thirty in the afternoon she stood at the school door saying good-bye to her students, making sure they had collected shawls and lunch buckets and primers. Lizzy corralled her sisters and brother for a long walk home, the Mast boys shot off toward their house, and the Byler children's mother showed up with a buggy to collect them. Ella admitted relief to herself when she saw Gideon's buggy clattering down the lane.

Ella bent over and tied the strings to Gertie's prayer *kapp*. It was a preventive action. Gertie had a tendency to run out from under an untied *kapp* when she was set free outdoors. Savilla chased her sister, and both girls were in their father's arms a minute later. Gideon looked over their heads, his face a question. Ella watched as he helped his daughters into the buggy and then ambled toward the school. Ella slipped back inside the building.

"I'm sure you had an extraordinary first day." Gideon caught her hand and closed the door behind him.

Ella blew out her breath. "I think it went well, but I'm sure the girls will give you their opinions."

Gideon put his hand against her cheek. "You are so brave. I could not admire you more."

She breathed in his scent, holding it until her lungs begged for a fresh exchange of air.

Gideon glanced out the window. Ella followed his gaze. Two faces leaned out of the buggy and fixed on the schoolhouse.

Gideon laughed. "If we take two steps to the left, we'll have time for one short kiss before they burst out of the buggy to see what is taking so long."

Ella tugged his hand and took two steps.

CHAPTER 27

J ames had not meant to spend so much of the day in Seabury, but Miriam was the last person he wanted to disappoint, so he stood in the line at the mercantile waiting to pay for three spools of black thread. A markdown on canned beans caused an unusual midafternoon glut at the counter.

Four people ahead of him in line at the counter inched forward. Then three. Then two. Then one. With each ding of the cash register, James slid forward a couple of feet. Then a tall man stepped in from the side, nearly putting his boot down on James's toe.

"I ordered those long screws three weeks ago," the man said to the clerk.

"I'm sorry, Mr. Truesdale," the clerk said. "They haven't come yet, but they should be here any day."

"I'd better not find out that you didn't put the order in immediately."

"The order went in. It just takes time to get the length you asked for. They probably have to come from Chicago."

The man thumped the counter with both palms. "I'd think you would have figured out how to use the telephone by now. You're not the Amish, after all."

Truesdale looked down his long nose at James and brushed past him.

"I apologize," the clerk said to James. "That's Braden. His brother, Gray, is a much more pleasant person."

James set the thread on the counter and watched the man exit the store before handing the clerk his coins. By the time James reached the sidewalk a couple of minutes later, he saw no evidence of Braden Truesdale's presence.

Across the street, in front of a narrow house painted brown with yellow trim, a sign announced the business within: PERCIVAL T. EGGAR, ESQUIRE, ATTORNEY AT LAW. James worked his lips in and out a few times before tucking the thread under his wagon bench and crossing the street. As far as James knew, no member of the Geauga County Amish had ever engaged the services of an attorney. The Bible clearly said that true believers ought not sue each other in the courts of unbelievers, and right living kept them on the right side of the law.

Until now.

James came into Seabury more than most of the church members. Until a few weeks ago, he never paid much attention to the yellow and brown house. Lately, after two rounds of fines and the audacity to open their own school, James wondered how much trouble the Amish fathers might be in.

In the front room of the brown house, a young man at a typewriter looked up at James.

"I'd like to see Mr. Eggar," James said.

"Is he expecting you?"

"No, sir."

The secretary raised an eyebrow at the hat still on James's head and his simple black wool suit coat with no lapels or pockets.

"I'll see if he has time to meet you now." The young man straightened his rimless glasses as he stood.

James suspected this would be the attorney's first meeting with an Amish man. If nothing else, curiosity might secure the meeting.

James watched the gray suit disappear through an inner door, speculating that the attorney's private office had once been the dining room of the house. Perhaps the upstairs was still in use as a residence. Electric lamps testified that the structure had been modernized. James eyed a chair, unsure whether to take the liberty of sitting down.

The inner door opened. The young man returned.

"Mr. Eggar will see you," he said, gesturing that James should go in. As soon as James crossed the threshold, the secretary quietly closed the door behind him.

James was relieved to see a man of more maturity rising from a large desk and coming around it to shake his hand. Immediately he liked the friendly light he saw in Mr. Eggar's eyes and the firmness of his grip as he guided James to a high-backed chair upholstered in reddish-brown leather.

"Now, this is unusual," Mr. Eggar said, taking his seat behind his desk. "But if a man like you has need of my services, I give you my word that I will listen carefully."

The grace of God appears in needful moments.

⛓

The buses arrived and departed barely half full, making Margaret think that school administrators had underestimated from the start both the number of rural Amish students attending the one-room school in the past and the tenacity of Amish parents to influence the education of their children. The buses still carried students who were not Amish, but it seemed that each week fewer straw hats and prayer *kapps* dotted the view of children lining up at the buses. Margaret stood on Monday afternoon with other teachers making sure the bus pupils were accounted for before the engines roared. The afternoons were cooler now, and the drivers had lowered canvas siding on the wood frames of their buses to cut the wind.

"Have you none of them left in your class?" Miss Hunter, the third-grade teacher, said.

"None of whom?" Margaret said. She refused to cater to the tendency to speak of the Amish students as *them*.

Miss Hunter rolled her eyes. "You know what I'm talking about. You still have an Amish boy in your class, don't you?"

"Hans," Margaret said. "He was not in attendance today." She pictured him in Ella's classroom and hoped he got to sit next to Gertie.

The last of the buses pulled away from the school, and the teachers drifted into a huddle where they could brace the afternoon's brisk breeze together.

"The school district ought to give them what they want," Mr. Snyder from the seventh grade said. "Give them their own school. Things could go back to normal around here."

Margaret pressed her lips closed. If the other teachers did not yet know that the Amish had built themselves a school, she would not be the one to tell them. She only found out three days ago herself.

"I had not noticed the Amish children were particular trouble,"

Margaret said. Gertie and Hans were quite sweet.

"That's because you teach first grade," Mr. Snyder said. "You don't have to contend with older students not doing their work, or pupils who are obviously too old for the classes they are in. They're bored, and it's not my job to entertain them when they belong in the high school."

"Still, they deserve an education," Margaret said. "We have to admit that some of our students have been distinctly unwelcoming."

She stopped short of expressing her opinion about the general insufficiency of Mr. Tarkington's response to pupils who taunted the Amish children. He hauled offenders to his office, but Margaret suspected nothing of consequence transpired once they got there. She'd seen the smirks on the faces of students as they emerged from the principal's office.

"It's all an unnecessary distraction," Mr. Snyder said.

"The teachers in the one-room schools had no trouble accommodating a variety of students." Margaret thought of Nora Coates.

"That's hardly the same as teaching in a town school," Miss Hunter said.

Margaret's spine straightened, but she pushed down the retort forming on her tongue. "It's getting chilly out here," she said, turning toward the building.

Mr. Snyder might well be right that the Amish students would be better off in their own school. On that conclusion he would find common ground with Amish parents regardless of the position the superintendent and principals took. It was Mr. Snyder's reasons that were convoluted. Margaret could find no agreement there. Viewing the Amish students as an inconvenience to established comfort infuriated Margaret.

Margaret's offer to help Ella Hilty was sincere. For the sake of the children, she had to figure out how to carry out her word.

❧

Gray grinned at Margaret across the bench of his truck three days later.

"At this time of year," he said, "you never know how many pretty days we'll have left."

"Thank you for inviting me for a drive." Margaret dipped her head in a manner she hoped was coy, though she wasn't sure. "The fall colors are spectacular."

"We could drive all the way to Cleveland if you like." Gray's eyebrows raised in question.

Of all his endearing expressions, Margaret liked this one best. "What would we do in Cleveland?"

"Have supper," he said. "Then we'll see."

It was tempting. Ride all the way to Cleveland with the smell of him swirling into her every breath. Walk down the street holding hands. Stare into his brown eyes over the flame of a candle and not care who might think she was behaving in an unseemly manner. Feed him pie off the end of her own fork.

But the papers were full of news of influenza. They might not even find a restaurant open to serve them.

"It'll be dark soon," Margaret said. "Maybe we could just find a spot with a nice view and watch the sun go down."

He stopped at a corner and looked to the west. "I know a spot, if you don't mind driving past the Amish farms."

Her stomach soured. "Why would I mind? It's beautiful countryside."

"I would think you'd get enough of them at work."

"Get enough of them?"

Gray accelerated the truck into motion again. "Don't get testy. I was only thinking of you."

"I'm sorry if I sounded testy." Margaret stared straight ahead.

"I understand if it's a sensitive subject for you."

His tone was tender. She wanted to believe him.

"The sooner Brownley and Fremont knock some sense into them," Gray said, "the sooner things will be easier for you."

"Things are not difficult for me. Every school year has its challenges, but I'm grateful for any experience that makes me a better teacher."

"Did you know they built their own school?"

Against her will, Margaret's gaze snapped in Gray's direction. He met her eyes for a moment before turning back to the road.

"You did know, didn't you?" he said.

She wouldn't straight-out lie to him. "Yes, I did. I didn't realize it was common knowledge yet."

"I don't know that it is," Gray said, "but it will be soon enough.

Fremont got wind of it today. He went livid as an angry bee."

Margaret stifled a groan.

"They're causing a lot of trouble, Margaret. A lot of people are spending time and attention they ought to be using on other things."

She said nothing. She could see Gideon Wittmer's farm in the distance.

"They have to consolidate," Gray said. "It's the only way to let everyone move on. It will be better for everybody."

"The Amish don't seem to think so."

"They'll be made to see."

Gray Truesdale was a gorgeous man in any woman's eyes. Margaret was sure of that. That he would court her all these weeks was a phenomenon beyond her ability to explain. When his eyes latched onto hers, a loveliness surged through her that she had not known was within her. If they could just ride out this storm, perhaps the stone forming in her gut at this moment could soften again.

Or perhaps that was something she told herself when she ached for one more delicious moment, one more tantalizing kiss, before hope turned to vapor.

"Would it distress you if I changed my mind about taking a drive?" she said. "I think perhaps I should spend the evening in after all."

"I've upset you," he said, contrite.

"I wouldn't be very good company tonight," she said. "As you can imagine, I have a lot on my mind."

Gray pulled to the side of the road and turned the truck around. They rode in silence back toward town, but when he reached across the bench for Margaret's hand, she gave it to him.

In front of her house, he parked and walked around the truck to help her out.

"I'd like to escort you to church on Sunday," he said, "and then we can have dinner with my brother. It would please me if the two of you met."

Margaret hesitated.

"We can set all this aside for a day, can't we?" Gray said, putting a finger to her chin to turn her face up. "A Sabbath?"

Margaret swallowed hard. "I would be delighted to meet your brother."

CHAPTER 28

Margaret disliked the stares. This was not the first time she had arrived at church with Gray. Two hundred people turned up at this church every Sunday morning. Why should it raise eyebrows when two of them chose to sit together?

"Good morning, Margaret."

The cheery voice belonged to Mrs. Baker, who had been the first person to speak to Margaret on her first Sunday in town, four and a half years ago. At the time, Margaret thought her friendly and welcoming. Over the years she had realized Mrs. Baker simply liked to know everything that went on.

"Good morning, Mrs. Baker," Margaret said. Gray's light touch on her elbow steered her away from the encounter.

"People are starting to whisper about us," Gray said into Margaret's ear.

Margaret was well aware. People whispered if she and Gray sat together in church, and they whispered if they did not. She had not meant for her relationship with Gray, as ill defined as it was, to come under speculation. Rumors would fly if she broke it off with him—or if she didn't.

They sat in Gray's regular pew. When she came on her own, Margaret sat on the other side of the sanctuary and farther back. Everything felt odd from this perspective. The minister's voice intoned more deeply. The organ swells sounded reedy. The angle of the light coming through the front windows washed out the faces of the choir. The scent of flowers on the altar tickled Margaret's nose. More than once, as the choir sang an invocation and the minister announced the opening hymn, the urge to flee to the comforts of her own habits circulated through Margaret's veins.

And then the congregation stood, and Gray opened a hymnal and placed it so they could both see it. Margaret's mouth moved, but little sound came out. Instead, she was enthralled with the notes coming from Gray. He sang the most exquisite tenor harmonies, earnest and confident and the sort of lilting sound Margaret could listen to for her whole life and never tire. Margaret had not heard Gray sing outside of church. What else did Gray sing other than church hymns? Folk songs? Love songs? Ballads? Opera? Perhaps nothing.

As the third stanza began, Margaret tried to sing more robustly. Her voice was no match for Gray's.

Perhaps she was no match for Gray at all. Her stomach solidified every time they talked about the Amish. They never disagreed about anything else that Margaret could remember. It wasn't that she thought husband and wife must agree on every point. But if Gray could think as little of the Amish as he seemed to, who else would he be willing to dismiss for his own convenience?

Once Gray knew that Margaret intended to help Ella Hilty get the Amish school running smoothly, that could be the end of them.

And perhaps it should be.

If they stopped now, they might maintain a sincere friendship without expecting more from each other. Margaret would find a way to gradually see less of Gray. She would get used to being on her own again, as she had so long expected to be, and his attentions could turn elsewhere.

If only she didn't love having him near.

After church, Margaret took the arm Gray offered for the stroll to his brother's house. During the weeks of their casual courtship, the only time Gray had spoken of his brother was the day of the auction.

"What does your brother do?" Margaret asked. "When he's not setting up tents."

"Whatever he likes," Gray said.

"Is that a way of saying his employment is. . .unstable?"

"You might say that. He used to run the old farm after our parents. . .but he ran it into the ground. I had to insist he sell and move into town. Sometimes I hire him to help me, but he's picky about what he's willing to do."

Under her fingers, Margaret felt the muscle of Gray's arm stiffen.

"I'll warn you. Braden is Braden," Gray said. "A little rough around the edges. Don't take him too seriously."

"It's kind of him to have us for Sunday dinner."

"He knows I've been courting someone. I wanted to wait until you and I knew each other better before introducing Braden."

Margaret fought the grimace her face seemed determined to form. She never should have agreed to meet Gray's brother, not under the weight of doubt that they were meant for each other.

They ambled toward a gray-shingled house on a corner.

"Here it is."

Gray knocked on the door and then patted Margaret's hand while they listened to the shifting footsteps inside. When the door opened, Margaret stared into the familiar features of Gray's face. The eyes were a lighter brown, but they were set at the exact distance from the nose as Gray's—the same slender nose with its gentle slope. The black curly hair was cut slightly longer than Gray's with more flecks of gray, but the widow's peak notched the forehead in the same spot.

Margaret's breath caught and she glanced at Gray.

"Are we twins?" Gray said. "No. Just one stubborn combination of genes."

Margaret smiled through the doorway at the man who had not yet spoken.

"Braden," Gray said, "I would like you to meet Miss Margaret Simpson. Margaret, this is my older brother."

"Please come in," Braden said. "It may take me a few minutes to get everything on the table."

"I would be happy to help," Margaret said, stepping into a hall that ran through the lower story of the house, with a parlor and dining room on one side and—she supposed—the kitchen on the other side at the back, behind a room with a closed door.

"Not necessary," Braden said, turning to walk to the back of the house.

Gray nudged Margaret's elbow. They stepped into the parlor, and he leaned in to whisper, "I warned you he's rough around the edges."

Margaret looked at the adjoining room, where a table had been laid with a level of care that suggested a woman's touch.

"Is Braden married?" she whispered.

Gray rolled his eyes. "Goodness, no."

Braden emerged from the kitchen with a platter of sliced ham in one hand and a bowl heaped with mashed potatoes in the other.

"I told her there were only three of us," Braden muttered, setting the dishes on the table.

"Her?" Margaret said

"The housekeeper," Braden said. "She never listens. She made two vegetables. Who needs two vegetables?"

Braden disappeared into the kitchen again.

"Let's sit down," Gray said, gesturing to the table. He pulled a chair out for Margaret, and she arranged herself in it.

Braden returned with two hot vegetable dishes. "If things are overcooked, it's her fault. I only followed the instructions she left to put everything in the oven."

"It all looks lovely," Margaret said.

Braden grunted and sat down.

"I agree," Gray said. "You should try to hang on to this one, instead of chasing her off like all the others."

Braden glared at Gray. The fire in his eyes startled Margaret.

"I could say the same to you," Braden said, glancing at Margaret. "Are you going to hang on to this one?"

"If meeting you doesn't frighten her off," Gray said, "I just might."

Margaret's legs were ready to bolt, but her mother had been a stickler for manners, so she concentrated on keeping her feet flat on the floor under the table.

"Let's eat," Braden said.

"Margaret likes to return thanks before a meal," Gray said, bowing his head.

Margaret bowed also, listening to the simple prayer of blessing for the meal that Gray spoke. When he finished, Braden picked up the platter of meat and offered it to Margaret.

"I heard about the trouble on your street," Braden said. "Twice now, isn't it?"

"Yes." Margaret guarded her response as she laid a slice of ham on her plate.

"You should be careful," Braden said. "I would hate for any harm to come to my brother's friend."

❧⊕❦

Gertie and Savilla gripped the sides of Ella's cart while she rumbled to Gideon's farm after school on Monday. Each day, it felt more and more natural to spend her afternoon hours with Gideon's family, and the children had gotten used to having her there, even Tobias. The wedding was less than six weeks away. Ella found comfort in establishing some routines now, before she married Gideon. The adjustment in December would be easier for everyone, including Miriam. Ella pulled around to the side of the barn and unhitched the cart to let the horse graze in the pasture. The girls ran ahead into the house. By the time Ella got there, Savilla stood in the kitchen with her face scrunched up.

"What's the matter, Savilla?" Ella said.

"It's almost three thirty," Savilla said.

"Yes, that's right." Ella set a stack of books on the counter.

"Look at the food."

Ella glanced around the kitchen. Two winter squash from the garden. Eight potatoes, three of them cut in half. A plate with half a beef roast.

"It looks like Miriam is getting a head start on supper," Ella said.

Savilla shook her head and picked up a cut potato. "This is turning brown. She wouldn't leave food around to turn brown." Savilla touched the roast. "And this isn't cold. If she had just taken it from the icebox, it would still be cold. She hasn't been here in a long time."

Apprehension shivered through Ella.

"*Aunti* Miriam always has a snack out for us," Savilla said. "Milk and cookies or some strudel."

Savilla was right.

"Go see if she's upstairs."

"*Daed* told her the upstairs was our responsibility now," Savilla said.

"Let's just make sure," Ella said. Miriam could be stubborn.

While Savilla scampered up the stairs, Ella stepped out on the back stoop to scan the yard. Miriam could have decided to hang sheets to dry, pull overgrowth from the depleted vegetable garden, or do something else equally innocuous.

Savilla thundered down the stairs. "She's not anywhere in the house."

Gertie's shout came from the *dawdihaus*. Ella and Savilla raced across the yard and burst into the small home where James and Miriam lived and ran through to the bedroom.

"She won't wake up," Gertie said.

Ella gulped air. "Has she said anything?"

"I can't understand what she's saying," Gertie said. She thumped Miriam's shoulder.

Miriam lay on the bed, pale, but beginning to thrash against the quilt.

"Napping," Miriam said. "Just. . .a few minutes."

Ella touched Gertie's shoulder to nudge her out of the way. "Miriam," she said, "are you feeling unwell?"

"No," Miriam said, trying to push herself up on one elbow.

Ella looked into Miriam's unfocused eyes. "Perhaps you should rest a little longer."

"I'll make supper," Miriam said. "It will just have to be simpler than I planned."

"I'll look after supper," Ella said. "The girls and I will start by making you some soup."

"Soup is for sick people," Miriam said. "I may be a tired old woman, but I'm not sick."

"We'll find something else, then. But you don't have to worry about it." Ella turned to Savilla. "Can you finish chopping the potatoes?"

Savilla nodded.

"And Gertie," Ella said, "you can set the table for supper. I'll be there in a few minutes."

"Is *Aunti* Miriam coming?" Gertie asked.

"Shh," Savilla said, grabbing Gertie's hand. "Come on."

Miriam was sitting up now. Ella debated between encouraging Miriam to lie down again and taking her to the main house where Ella could keep an eye on Miriam and the girls at the same time.

"How about some tea?" Ella said.

"James will want *kaffi*," Miriam said, rubbing an eye with one hand.

"*Kaffi*, then," Ella said. "I'll make a pot here and you can take a cup over to the main house."

The door opened, and a man's footfalls approached.

"James?" Miriam said.

He appeared in the doorway. "What's going on in here?"

"I took a nap," Miriam said. "Ella and the girls are determined to make a fuss."

Ella exchanged a glance with James.

"Well, if you're tired," James said, "you should have a nap. You know I'm always telling you that."

"It's nothing." Miriam leaned on James's arm and stood up. "How were things in Seabury today?"

"Our prayers for peace have been answered at last," James said. "The war in Europe is over. The armistice was signed this morning in Paris. It's all the *English* are talking about in town."

Miriam put her hand over her heart. "Many mothers and fathers will be glad to have their sons home again in one piece."

"I was just going to make *kaffi*," Ella said.

James smiled. "*Kaffi* is always a good decision."

Miriam threw off James's supporting arm. "I'll make the *kaffi*."

CHAPTER 29

Are you sure you'll be all right on your own?" James evaluated the features of his wife's face. Extra lines fanned out from the corners of her eyes, and the color of her cheeks lacked its usual height.

"Old man, just go," Miriam said. "Did you think I wouldn't notice that you've neatly arranged the day so I won't be alone for more than thirty minutes?"

That much was true. James had invited the group of Amish parents, both fathers and mothers, to meet at the new schoolhouse after the students left on Tuesday afternoon. Ella would stay for the meeting, but the children would go home from school and Tobias would stay within shouting distance while he did the barn chores. If something happened, Tobias could take a horse and gallop for help.

"Well, if you're sure." James kissed Miriam's cheek.

"I was tired yesterday," Miriam said. "Can't a person take a nap without everyone declaring it a medical emergency?"

It was not just one nap. It was more and more naps. It was lost color in the face. It was a slower walk than James had ever seen in his spunky wife. But he knew when to keep his thoughts sealed.

"I'll try to make the meeting short and to the point," he said before leaving.

His extra moments with Miriam meant that when James arrived at the schoolhouse, parents already milled, awaiting someone who would take charge. Ella was dragging the smallest desks out of the way and encouraging parents to take seats in the desks large enough to accommodate them. Aaron King had thought to bring three of the church benches and was setting them up around the perimeter of the room.

"Shall we start as soon as everyone has a seat?" Ella asked.

The one person James most needed was nowhere in sight. James would have to do his best and hope the guest would still turn up.

Gideon took a seat in the front row, and Ella sat beside him. Behind them others quieted. James stood and faced the assembly and cleared his throat.

"We would all agree," he began, "that the children of our church district are the future of our congregation. As a church, our obligation to them is to prepare them for eternal life in the kingdom of God. For this reason, the nature of their education is important to all of us."

James paused and glanced out the windows behind the rows of parents. He assumed his guest would arrive in an automobile. The row of horses and buggies would assure him he had found the right location. James wasn't sure how much further into the meeting he could go on his own.

"Although I am neither a father nor a minister," James continued, "I want the best for our congregation. I want to know our children are on the path to salvation and not ensnared by worldly ways. For this reason, when Chester Mast began building this school that shelters us now, I was happy to help. Some of you have chosen to send your *kinner* here for Ella Hilty to be their teacher. Others are concerned about *English* retribution if your children do not attend their schools."

The sound of an automobile caused a few heads to turn. James breathed relief.

"I have taken the liberty of speaking to an *English* attorney," James said, "and I'm happy to see that he has just arrived. My hope is that he will help us understand the *English* system more fully."

A car door slammed. Restless parents squirmed to see who would enter the building. James paced to the back of the room and opened the door.

"Thank you for coming," James said softly.

"I'm sorry I'm late," Percival Eggar said. "These farm roads and oak trees all look very much alike. You really do 'live apart.' "

James led the way to the front of the room. "This is Mr. Percival Eggar," he said. "I met with him last week in his office, and I am confident that he can help us understand the risks and consequences of the choices fathers face as individuals, as well as our congregation, as we look for a way to stand together."

Percival set a briefcase on Ella's desk. "In my office, Mr. Lehman laid out for me the events to this point—the notices from the school district, the pressure to enroll your children in the consolidated schools in Seabury, the fines as a consequence of noncompliance, and the decision to open and operate this school as a private institution not subject to the regulations of the school district."

Isaiah Borntrager raised a hand. James acknowledged it.

"Why do we need an attorney?" Isaiah said. "They're our children, and we'll do what we think is best for them."

"I'm only here," Percival said, "to help you understand your legal standing. I'm afraid the fines you've paid are only the beginning of your exposure."

"The United States is a place of religious freedom," Chester Mast said. "That's all we're doing with opening this school."

Percival pointed at Chester. "That is exactly right. But the right to practice religion in a manner that conflicts with established law is bound to cause complications of interpretation."

"Don't we have a right to believe what the Bible says?" John Hershberger said.

"Of course you do," Percival said. "The question is whether we can establish that your actions with regard to the education of your children fall into the category of religious belief. Some would argue that you are free to believe as you choose, but you still must obey the law."

"If we hand our children over to the *English* school," Chester Mast said, "we will lose the next generation of our church. We can't separate how we interpret the Bible from how we educate our children."

"James," Aaron King said, "did you invite this gentleman because you believe we should take formal legal action? You know the way of our people is to stay out of the *English* courts."

James nodded. "I do know. I hope and pray for a peaceful solution without compromising the Word of God."

"They may not do anything more than occasional fines," Cristof Byler said. "As long as we pay them, they'll have no reason to bother us."

"What about those of us who cannot afford the fines?" Aaron King said. "Don't you think we'd like to have our children in our own school as well?"

Percival took a step forward. "I believe you should have that right, and I'm willing to help you fight for it."

A lull descended as the hope offered by Percival's pledge trickled through the assembly.

"If there can be peace in Europe," James said, "surely there can be peace in Seabury."

Isaiah grunted. "But at what cost did the peace in Europe come?"

Gideon twisted in his seat. He wanted to see the faces of the other parents. Before today there had been no discussion of involving an *English* lawyer. James had made these arrangements on his own, but when Gideon discovered what James had done, he did nothing to discourage assembling parents. This moment would be one they all remembered—the moment they did or did not engage the services of someone outside their own community.

Another *English* automobile announced its presence. While Gideon admired—from afar—the usefulness of a gasoline engine, it seemed to him that the *English* with all their education ought to find a way to make it less noisy. The sound was unnatural.

When Gideon saw who it was, he jumped up. A moment later, Superintendent Brownley shoved open the door.

"What in tarnation is going on here?" Brownley demanded.

"May we help you, Mr. Brownley?" Gideon said, calm and smooth.

"We'll shut down this school," Brownley said. "You've wasted your time and materials in building it."

"If that's what you've come to say," Gideon said, "you can be assured we have heard you."

Brownley strode along the side of the room. "What is this meeting about?"

"It's a private meeting," Gideon said, "on private property."

Brownley's eyes scanned the group. "It may not be illegal to build a structure on private property or to use it for private purposes, but you can be certain that using this building to keep pupils out of school will have repercussions."

"Duly noted," Gideon said.

"Furthermore," Brownley said, "whoever is posing as a teacher is in a precarious position."

Involuntarily, Gideon glanced at Ella, whose face paled.

"This so-called teacher will find herself in the middle of legal action if she continues without credentials," the superintendent said. His eyes settled on Ella. "The state establishes certain minimal standards for all teachers."

"Mr. Brownley," Gideon said. "If you would be so kind as to make time at the next meeting of the school board, I'm sure we would be happy to continue this discussion in an appropriate setting."

"Don't threaten me!" Brownley said. "Remember that I have the law on my side."

Percival Eggar stepped between Gideon and Brownley.

"What are you doing here?" Brownley asked.

"I will be representing the parties present. In the future you may address your concerns to my office."

"You?" Brownley scoffed. "Are you telling me that the Amish are engaging legal representation?"

"We had not quite worked out the details of our arrangement before your unseemly interruption," Percival said, "but now is as good a time as any."

Brownley glared.

Percival turned to the assembly. "I would be honored to represent anyone present in this room on the questions of compliance with recent changes in education regulations as they pertain to the free expression of religious conviction. I'm sorry that I was not able to meet each of you individually before our conversation was disrupted, but if you would like to accept my representation, I ask you to signal your intention by standing."

Gideon, already standing, stepped forward.

"This is absurd," Brownley said.

Chester Mast stood, followed by Cristof Byler. Jed Hilty. Isaiah Borntrager. John Hershberger. Joshua Glick. Aaron King. One by one, every man in the room rose. Gideon worked hard at smothering a grin. The wives joined, standing with their husbands. Whether parents were sending their children to the schools in Seabury, keeping them home, or taking advantage of Ella's tutelage, they were united on this question. They welcomed an *English* of Percival Eggar's education and standing in the community to their side.

CHAPTER 30

Brownley glowered, first at Percival, and then at the fathers on their feet as most of the wives present also stood.

Was this what it was like to feel proud? Gideon had of course been pleased with the accomplishments of his children from time to time. When Tobias helped to deliver a new calf. When Savilla baked bread for the first time without consulting a recipe. When Gertie, only a few weeks ago, sounded out an entire verse from the morning Bible reading in German, even though at school she was learning to read English. But in those instances, and many others, he reminded himself of the border between *pleased* and *proud*. If he was proud, even of his children, he might begin to think himself better than others. But at this moment, seeing the parents of his congregation voting bodily, Gideon crossed the border. He was proud of their courage, proud of their resolve, proud of their resistance against their own inner fears.

Ella stood with the parents. This gave Gideon pure pleasure.

Percival gripped Brownley's elbow and turned him toward the door. "I'm sure you understand the need for confidential conversation with my clients," he said, walking Brownley out. "You and I will have ample opportunity to speak reasonably and honorably about the matter."

Gideon caught James's eye. If James had asked him in advance, Gideon might have cautioned against involving an *English* man of the law. But the trust Percival Eggar had engendered in a room full of Amish strangers was testimony that James had done well.

Percival closed the door behind Brownley and paced back to the front of the room.

"You all have work to do and families to care for," he said, "so I want to make efficient use of our time. Mr. Lehman has given me a basic understanding of the dilemma you face and the range of responses represented in this room. I am happy to meet with any of you individually if you seek counsel about your particular circumstances. For now, I invite questions that may be of interest to the group as a whole."

If Gideon were not sitting in the front of the room, he could have seen which hands were going up.

Percival pointed at a hand. "Yes?"

"What if we can't find a teacher the state will accept?" Joshua Glick asked. "I want my children to go to an Amish school, but I also want it to be according to the law."

So far, the Glick children had remained in the Seabury school. Joshua was one of the more cautious Amish fathers.

"I understand Mr. Wittmer has already begun making inquiries on that matter," Percival said, "and on your instructions I will prepare additional documents and send them with a courier to the teachers college."

Murmurs of approval circled the room.

"May I also suggest," Percival continued, "that we explore alternative methods for how Miss Hilty may be properly credentialed for the position."

Ella sucked in her breath beside Gideon. He slid his hand off his lap and let it rest on the edge of the chair until his little finger touched hers. Their wedding was only weeks away.

❧

The fury on Mr. Brownley's face had punched the breath out of Ella, and now Mr. Eggar was suggesting she formalize her role as a teacher. She had only promised Gideon a few weeks. Her permanent promise to him was to be his wife.

Less than an inch of Gideon's hand touched Ella's, and for only a few seconds, yet she took comfort. He was near. He understood. Perhaps James had neglected to mention her betrothed state to Mr. Eggar. Even an *English* attorney would know that a woman would not continue to teach after her marriage.

"Miss Hilty has only begun teaching. Do I understand correctly?" Percival said, glancing at Ella.

Ella nodded.

"Other than formal education," Gideon said, "she is well suited to the task. Before beginning to teach here, she taught my daughters at my home for several weeks, and I saw daily the leaps in their learning."

Percival nodded. "We may need you to testify to that effect."

Testify? Ella's brows furrowed against her will.

"My girls love her," John Hershberger said. "Lizzy and Katya said Miss Hilty is every bit as good as Miss Coates was."

"Miss Coates?" Percival said.

"The *English* teacher we had until a few months ago," Gideon explained. "John is right. Ella has a curious mind and understands the needs of our children."

"Ella has done nothing wrong," Isaiah Borntrager said. "She hasn't lied about credentials she does not hold. All she has done is choose what is best for our community, something the state has no interest in."

"The state would argue they have the best interest of your children in mind," Percival reminded the group.

"Has the state met our children?" Isaiah countered. "Has the state worshipped in our services? How can the state have the best interest of our children in mind?"

"All good points." Percival nodded. "And we may be able to raise them in an argument about the exercise of religious liberty. At the moment, though, the superintendent would argue that as an untrained teacher, Ella is in over her head."

Ella's breath came in gasps at irregular intervals when she could no longer hold it in. She *was* in over her head, with only her instincts and love of learning to rely on. The day would come when a bright student would ask a question to which she did not know the answer, or a second grader would be unable to grasp the basics of borrowing to subtract and Ella would have no new strategies to help him master the concept. She supposed that teachers who attended the teachers college learned how to handle these challenges. They learned methods of instruction and ways of making proper lesson plans that kept them ahead of the questions their students would ask.

In truth, Ella was not sure she had made the situation better by agreeing to teach temporarily. In the eyes of the law, the Amish families had dubious standing as it was. If Chester Mast had not begun building the schoolhouse in which they all now sat, perhaps this moment would not have come.

"But if we focus on finding a state-qualified teacher willing to teach Amish children according to our values," James said, "Ella will not have to face these hurdles at all."

Thank you, James. Ella relaxed her spine. *Let's stay focused.*

Gideon shifted his weight in his chair and lifted his hand, ready to ask the looming question. "What can the state really do if we do not send our children to the schools in town—especially the older ones who already completed the eighth grade?"

"I pledged to Mr. Lehman that I would be candid and honest with all of you," Percival said. "It's almost certain that the fines will grow increasingly burdensome. I know that some of you already choose to keep your children in the town schools for that reason, so I will look for grounds to challenge the legality of the fines."

"And beyond the fines?" Gideon asked.

Percival gave a slight shrug. "The laws are new. This kind of case is untested. I can only tell you what is possible within the current language of the law, not what is likely in the eyes of a judge or jury."

By the time the meeting ended, Gideon felt as if he had harvested an entire field of alfalfa hay without even the help of his team of workhorses.

Percival Eggar lingered to answer individual questions and collect a few coins from each man who wished to avail himself of the offer of legal representation. James would have explained to Mr. Eggar that farmers struggling to pay the fines imposed on them by the state would not have unlimited funds for an *English* lawyer's fees, but Gideon trusted that James had come to a manageable agreement or he would not have invited Percival to meet with the parents in the first place. The few dollars Percival collected that day only ensured each family would benefit equally from the outcome of the legal case.

The legal case. The phrase springing up in Gideon's mind astonished him. Along with Cristof and Chester, John and Aaron, Joshua, Jed, Isaiah, and the others, Gideon was party to a legal case with the potential to wend its way through *English* courts.

After asking their questions and establishing themselves as clients of Percival T. Eggar, Esquire, Attorney at Law, the parents drifted out of the schoolhouse. James walked Percival to his waiting automobile.

Alone in the building, Gideon blew out his breath and offered Ella full-faced encouragement.

"It will all work out." Gideon met Ella's uncertain gaze.

"Maybe the children should have stayed in the town schools for now," Ella said. "There would not be so much at risk."

"There might be less legal risk," Gideon said, "but what of the risk to our children if they spend their days in the *English* world?"

Ella shuffled to a row of desks and began to straighten them. "We don't know what the authorities might do to the children."

Gideon joined her in straightening the room. "Why should they do anything to innocent children? Their argument is with the parents. They understand that minor children do not make these decisions for themselves. The fathers are all doing what they think best. The children are safe."

"And me?"

Gideon almost did not hear Ella. When her whispered words sank in, he abandoned the task of cleaning up and lifted her hands from the bench she pushed against a wall.

"You are not alone," he said.

Ella let out her breath. "But I am unqualified. Am I breaking the law by doing the work of a teacher?"

"You *are* a teacher," Gideon said. "You may not have a piece of paper sealed by the State of Ohio, but you have courage and faith and natural gifts. You have the support of your community. Even Miss Simpson has offered to help you."

Ella shook her head. "I don't want to get her in trouble."

"Miss Simpson strikes me as a person who makes her own decisions," Gideon said.

Ella met his eyes. "If we are to marry on December 19, our banns should be published in a few weeks. Rachel has pages and pages of lists to be sure the house is ready."

Gideon nodded. "We have all the way to January to find a teacher, and now we have Mr. Eggar to help."

Ella dropped her eyes again, but Gideon tipped her face up to kiss her. She was not the only one eager to marry on December 19. He wanted her in his arms and in his home, her face the first he would see in the morning and her lips the ones he would kiss each night.

❦

Margaret was late getting home from school that afternoon. The Amish *quandary*—the word she was trying out this week to describe the conundrum of Amish and townspeople trying to understand each other—weighed down her shoulders like a row of cement bricks. This was enough of a distraction to put her behind in planning her lessons and correcting the papers of her pupils. Gray's entrenched attitude that the Amish *problem* was not her concern magnified the distraction, and his brother's veiled warning unnerved her. As a consequence, while her pupils did quiet independent work, Margaret was spending too much time mentally muddling her way out of the cage she found herself in.

A blur in her peripheral vision made Margaret turn her head just as she reached the walk leading to her home, and she paused to turn her head and fully discern the sight.

Braden Truesdale skulked across her side yard, cutting through the garden that had yielded the last of its autumn bounty and heading toward the front of her lot.

"Braden!" she called as he came to the edge of the house.

His head jerked up, startle flickering through his eyes. The flour sack over his shoulder bulged in peculiar angular points.

"I didn't know you came through my neighborhood," she said, approaching him. Gray had never given a clear answer about Braden's employment, so Margaret could think of no good reason for him to be in her yard.

"Never know where I'm going to be," he said, tightening his grip to seal the sack.

Were his words a simple statement or another veiled warning? And what in the world was in that flour sack?

"I'll walk with you," Margaret said with false brightness. "I'm on my way to pay a call on a neighbor."

Braden pressed his lips into a tight, straight smile and nodded. Margaret watched his glance and followed his cue, turning back in the direction from which she had come.

"Is your workday nearly finished?" Margaret asked.

"Just about."

Margaret let herself fall back a half step and eyed the bag. The bulge in Braden's muscle, even under his shirtsleeve, suggested the bag carried items of weight. Books? Candlesticks? Jugs? The sour sensation in Margaret's stomach bubbled up through her throat.

"Here's my stop," Margaret said, across the street from Lindy Lehman's house. "Now that we're acquainted, I'll see you another time, I suppose."

"S'pose."

Margaret stepped into the street to cross to Lindy's. Braden marched toward Main Street. Margaret walked slowly, perusing his progress, before approaching Lindy's workshop. She could not always keep her neighbor's property safe, but on this one day, she could make sure Braden Truesdale did not stop there. Unless he had already been there and she'd caught him in a circuitous departure.

Gray would never believe her if Margaret told him she suspected Braden was responsible for the burglary and vandalism of Lindy's shop. But in that moment, Margaret was as certain as if she had witnessed the acts herself.

CHAPTER 31

J ames wandered down Main Street on Wednesday afternoon in no particular hurry. With Gideon's assurance that he intended to stay close to the house and barn today, James had taken his wagon into town with items from several Amish farms to trade for credit at the mercantile, and then picked up birdhouses, quilt racks, and toys from Lindy to deliver to the furniture store that kept her items on hand to attract customers who appreciated Amish craftsmanship. He caught her just before she left for a shopping trip in Chardon. With his tasks complete, James left his horse and wagon with the blacksmith at the edge of Seabury to reshoe the mare and relished the idea of an unhurried walk in the brisk fall air.

When James had enough of studying the *English* display windows and trying to fathom what the women found so compelling about the rising hemlines and the attraction of homburg hats and striped waistcoats for men, he moseyed toward the hardware store. Browsing there was never without benefit. James bypassed the aisles of electrical gadgets, which seemed to take up more space every year, and instead inspected the latest unadorned tools and work gloves that would serve a practical purpose. He had a hammer in his hand, testing its weight, when the voices from the next aisle wafted over the bins of nails and screws.

"Deputy Fremont is on his way now," one man said.

"What for this time?" his companion responded.

"Don't know for sure. My wife just talked to his housekeeper. He was in such a hurry that he left half his lunch uneaten."

"The Amish farms, you say?"

James's breath stilled.

"The paperwork came through, I guess."

"Paperwork?"

"The housekeeper didn't see all the details. Just saw a few names. "Hilty. Hershberger. Wittmer. Several others, I think."

"More fines, I suppose."

"I think the law has something more in mind this time. He just needs a judge's signature. If those families can't take proper care of their children, then the state will."

The hammer clattered out of James's hand and he bolted up the aisle, past the counter, and out the door.

At Percival Eggar's office, James burst through the door. The bespectacled secretary looked up, startled.

"I need Mr. Eggar," James said. "It's an emergency."

"I'm afraid he isn't here," the young man said. "He went to Cleveland today."

Cleveland!

"When is he due back?"

"I'm afraid I couldn't say. His instructions were that I should close the office at six o'clock because he did not expect to return before then."

James wheeled back out to Main Street. The blacksmith was a good mile and a half away, a distance not in the least daunting under leisure circumstances, even for a man James's age, but more fearsome when every moment was of the essence. James set off with a brisk pace and soon forced himself to trot. If he could get back to the farms soon enough, he could warn the others. There were dozens of places to hide on the farms where Deputy Fremont would never think to look. James covered the distance in eighteen minutes.

"I need my rig," James told the blacksmith. "I'll have to bring it back another day."

"I just got all the shoes off the mare."

"I'll have to take her anyway."

The blacksmith shook his head. "You know better, James. You can't take a horse used to being shod out barefoot and expect her to handle the roads between here and your farm. She'll be far too tender."

James sighed. The man was right.

"How long will it take?"

"Now, James, you know the answer to that. I haven't begun to clean the hoofs yet, and I'm not going to rush and risk an ill-fitting shoe. It's not fair to the horse and won't do you any good in the end, either."

Right again. "Then I need to borrow a horse. I don't even need a saddle." He could leave the wagon and ride bareback.

"Look around," the blacksmith said. "I don't have any to spare. I'm not running a livery."

James rubbed his temples. Lindy was gone in her car to Chardon, where she sometimes took orders and collected supplies. "I need a ride in your automobile. It's an emergency."

"The wife took the car to go visit her mother. I thought it would make things easier if I taught her to drive, and now she gallivants all over the place."

James blew out his breath. "Can you keep the mare overnight, then?"

"What's going on, James?"

"I'm not sure," James said. "I just know I have to get home."

When he was a young man, James had been a strong runner. He used to win all the races at the frolics by several strides. He prayed that his muscles would still know what to do all these years later.

⚜

Maybe James was right. Maybe Miriam was just feeling her age and refusing to accept the limitations it brought. Miriam was in the kitchen when Ella walked home with Gertie and Savilla. Still-warm cookies adorned the table beside a jug of milk from that morning, and Miriam was in the midst of slicing onions, celery, and squash on a cutting board at the counter. A chicken in a roasting pan was ready for the oven. Still, it seemed to Ella that Miriam was moving slowly, with slumped shoulders in need of rest. Ella would feel better if she could talk to James. She left the girls to enjoy their snack and chatter with Miriam and went in search of James.

"He's not here," Gideon said when Ella found him in the barn. "He went into town for the day. I imagine by now the blacksmith has finished with the mare and James is on his way home."

"Miriam needs to slow down," Ella said.

"I know. James knows. Even Miriam knows," Gideon said. "I had to stop her churning butter this morning. If she would take it easy for a few weeks, she could get properly rested."

"And I'll be here in a few weeks," Ella said. "She won't have to feel like she's responsible for everything around the house."

Ella expected immediate agreement. Instead, Gideon's gaze shifted.

"Gideon?"

"You're right," Gideon said, meeting her eyes again. "Another woman on the farm would take the load off of Miriam."

Another woman. Ella hated the distance in Gideon's choice of words. His face gave nothing more away. Ella pulled her thoughts back to James.

"Would you mind if I took your small buggy and went to look for James?" she asked.

"You know you're always welcome to the buggy," Gideon said, "but James will be home well before supper."

"I have an odd feeling about all this."

"I'm sure everything's fine. I knew it would be a long day away for James. That's why I promised to stay close to the house."

"I can't explain it, Gideon. I just want to go see if I can meet him on the road. Besides, I'd like to talk to him about Miriam without worrying that she's going to come into the room."

"She does have an uncanny way of appearing when we're whispering behind her back," Gideon said. "I'll hitch up the buggy for you."

With the reins in her hands a few minutes later, Ella took the team out to the main road and turned toward town. She did not push the horse for speed. Rather, her impulse was for care in what she noticed. James might have turned off somewhere with a delivery Gideon was unaware he planned to make, or perhaps he had detoured to give someone a ride home from Seabury. As she drifted along the side of the road, leaving ample room for passing automobiles whose drivers would be frustrated by her strolling pace, Ella leaned forward to look down the lanes for any sign of James's rig.

An approaching driver leaned on a horn—unnecessarily, since Ella was not impeding his path. The vehicle's high speed, churning up dust and gravel, alarmed Ella. When she saw it was one of the sheriff's cars, her heart lurched. Close behind was a bus similar to the ones the children rode to school in town. But the canvas sides of the bus were rolled up, and Ella could see that it was empty. The two vehicles seemed to be keeping pace with each other. Ella stopped her buggy as she watched them pass in the other direction.

"Why should they do anything to innocent children?" Gideon had said barely twenty-four hours ago. *"The children are safe."*

Ella was not so sure.

She scanned for a spot in the road wide enough to turn the buggy around. The horse's ears lay back as it pulled toward the edge of the road.

"Whoa!" Ella tugged on the reins, wary of going into the shallow ditch.

To Ella's relief, the horse stopped. Only then did she hear the moan. She jumped out of the buggy.

James lay in the ditch with a lump the size of a chicken egg swelling out of his forehead.

"James!" Ella knelt beside him.

He moaned again. Ella looked around. Where was his wagon? Had the mare spooked at the speeding sheriff's car and bus?

"Too fast," James said. "I went too fast but not fast enough."

"You're not talking sense." Gently, Ella touched the lump on his head.

"I got dizzy," James said. "I was running too fast."

"What happened to your horse?"

"At the blacksmith's." James labored to catch his breath. "She had no shoes. I wanted to warn everyone."

Ella's gut plummeted. "Is this about Deputy Fremont?"

James sat up slowly. "Good. You have a buggy. We can still let them know. Gideon's on the list."

Ella peered down the road. The sheriff's car was long out of view. Even the dust it had displaced in its path had settled again.

It was too late.

⌁⊷❈⊶⌁

Margaret rapped on the workshop door before shading her eyes to look in a window and determine that Lindy was not inside. She paced to the back door of the house and knocked again.

When the door opened, it was David Kaufman's eyes looking back at Margaret.

"Is Lindy here?" Margaret asked.

David shook his head. "She went to Chardon. She called a

little while ago and said she decided to stay and have supper with a friend."

"So she's safe."

David's eyes flashed from side to side. "Did you see something?"

"How long have you been here?"

"Ever since school let out. I came straight home."

"Good. Just let Lindy know I was checking on her. You know where to find me if you need something."

David nodded. "Thank you."

"And David, look around. Make sure you don't notice anything missing from the house."

Exhaling, Margaret turned to cross the street. She had no appetite for supper. She only wanted to think.

And pray.

There had to be an answer to all this perplexity.

And there he was, Braden Truesdale still standing on the street a block and a half down. If he had good reason to be in the neighborhood in the first place, certainly he'd had plenty of time to finish his business and be on his way.

And what was in that ridiculous bag?

Margaret marched down the street. He saw her coming and made no effort to move.

"I feel compelled," Margaret said, meeting his eyes, "to ask you once again what your business is on this street."

"Does Gray know you're so nosy?" Braden said.

"We are not discussing Gray." Margaret gripped the handle of her satchel, prepared to swing it if necessary. "What's in that flour sack?"

"Not your business."

"I'll have a word with Deputy Fremont," Margaret said. "He may find it interesting that you were on this street on this day with that bag in your possession."

"Deputy Fremont is otherwise occupied," Braden said. "And if I were you, I'd stay out of the Amish problem, because it will soon be messier than you ever imagined."

"I demand that you explain yourself."

Braden laughed and sauntered up the sidewalk.

CHAPTER 32

Gideon put both hands on the back of Miriam's shoulders as she stood in the kitchen and leaned forward to speak softly into her left ear.

"Take a rest," he said. "I've given the girls chores to do upstairs. They won't bother you."

"Your *kinner* are never a bother to me." Miriam continued to layer cut vegetables around the chicken in the roasting pan.

"I know my children," Gideon said. "Savilla is settling down as she gets older, but Gertie can still be a handful. Go put your feet up for a few minutes while they're occupied."

Miriam laid her wooden spoon on the counter and rotated to face him. "I could do with a cup of *kaffi*."

"I'll make it." Gideon reached for the coffeepot on the stove before Miriam could get to it.

"It just needs warming," Miriam said.

"Then I'll warm it." Gideon pointed to the comfortable chair he and James had positioned in the kitchen weeks ago. "Go. Sit."

Miriam settled in with a sigh while Gideon added wood to the stove. "Don't get the stove too hot," she said, "or it will be too much to roast the chicken."

"Just enough to get the *kaffi* hot quickly," Gideon said. He set out two mugs. If he drank coffee with Miriam, she would rest a few minutes. If he left the room, she would set her mug aside after the second sip and discover a task that had transformed from unseen to urgent.

Gideon was pouring the coffee when a solid knock sounded at the front door.

"What in the world?" he said, standing.

Miriam tilted out of her chair. "I'll get it."

When the door did not open immediately, the knock became a pounding. Gideon followed Miriam through the dining room and across the front room.

Miriam opened the door, and Gideon stared into the eyes of Deputy Fremont.

"I paid the fine promptly," Gideon said.

"We're beyond fines." Deputy Fremont pushed Miriam aside and entered the house, leaving another uniformed man on the porch.

Indignation burned through Gideon. "You will treat Mrs. Lehman with respect." Behind him two sets of young feet clattered down the stairs.

"Gideon Wittmer," the deputy said, "you are under arrest for contributing to the delinquency of three minors, Tobias Wittmer, Savilla Wittmer, and Gertrude Wittmer."

"I know my children's names," Gideon said.

"Apparently the fines did not make you see the error of your ways," the deputy said. "Perhaps jail will make a stronger impression."

"*Daed!*"

Gideon looked over his shoulder at his daughters. "You listen to *Aunti* Miriam and do what she tells you to do."

"Don't worry about the children," Fremont said. "We have a plan for them as well."

"Miriam," Gideon said, "send Tobias to town to find Mr. Eggar."

"I'm afraid Tobias is not going into town," Fremont said. He cocked his head toward the bus parked in front of the house.

The back door creaked open, steps crossed the kitchen, and Tobias appeared. Confusion clouded his eyes.

"Take care of the girls," Gideon said. "Miriam, remember, Mr. Percival Eggar. He will know what to do."

☙❧

Ella helped James into the buggy and urged the horse to maximum speed. By the time they arrived at the Wittmer farm, only Miriam remained, tearful, leaning against a post on the front porch. She straightened when she saw James emerge from the buggy.

Ella took his elbow. "Are you sure you're steady enough to walk?"

"What in the world happened to you?" Miriam came down the steps of the porch.

"I have to admit I've never had such a headache in all my life." James divided his weight between Miriam and Ella until they got him settled in a chair on the porch. Miriam chipped ice off the block in the bottom of the icebox and wrapped it in a towel to press against her husband's head.

"We're too late, aren't we?" James said.

"The sheriff's officers took Gideon," Miriam said, "and they took the children in a bus—all three of them."

Ella's heart thudded. In one afternoon, intuition had grown into fear, and fear into reality.

"Your father is on the list," Miriam said.

"But the boys both have been going to school," Ella said. "Seth has only been in my class since last week."

"Before that, he wasn't doing his homework. That's negligence and delinquency according to the papers."

"Show me," James said.

Miriam produced the papers Gideon had left with her.

"Ella, you need to go," James said.

"But you're hurt," Ella said, trying to look over James's shoulder and scan the legal papers for herself.

"Take the buggy and go. Now."

His tone mobilized Ella. She raced back out to Gideon's buggy, picked up the reins, and clicked her tongue. The horse circled the yard to get turned before falling into a familiar trot up the lane.

Faster. We have to go faster.

The more she urged the horse, the more the buggy swayed. Finally she was at the final intersection, and she tugged the reins to make the turn.

Her father stood in the yard, twenty feet from the deputy's automobile. Ella urged the horse to pull the buggy parallel to the vehicle.

"Gideon!"

Smudged glass separated them, but at the sound of Ella's voice, Gideon turned toward her. Ella leaped out of the buggy.

"Step back." The voice was male, deep, unyielding.

Ella looked up now and saw Seth being loaded into the bus she had seen on the main road. Gideon's three children leaned out of the bus. Tobias had one arm around each sister. Ella ran to them, squeezing the girls' outstretched hands.

"God is with you!" she said. "God will not leave you!"

"They're taking your *daed*," Seth shouted.

Ella spun around in time to see her father pushed into the waiting vehicle. At least neither Gideon nor Jed was alone.

The engines of both vehicles sparked and caught, and Ella was left with her father's stunned wife trembling and falling back into her crumbling flower bed.

❧❦❧

"It's Ella," Miriam said.

James took the bundle of melting ice off his forehead and followed his wife's gaze out the wide front window.

"She brought Rachel with her," Miriam said.

"She wouldn't want to leave Rachel on her own," James said.

Miriam opened the front door before Ella could knock and admitted the two guests.

"I was too late—again," Ella said. "Deputy Fremont was already there."

"So they've taken Jed?" Miriam said, gesturing that Ella and Rachel should sit.

"And Seth," Rachel said. "I promised to put him back in their school if they would just leave him alone, but their minds were made up."

"James, how is your head?" Ella peered at the bruising lump.

"Never mind my head," James said. "I'm just sorry I couldn't warn anyone. They could have hidden. If I'd just had a horse."

"It wouldn't have made a difference," Ella said. "Even a horse could not have raced against an *English* automobile to get to all the farms."

"But some of them might have hidden their children. I can think of a dozen places Tobias and the girls would have been safe."

"Where have they taken them?" Rachel asked. "The men will go to jail. I understand that. But where will they take the children?"

James reached for the papers Gideon had left behind, shaking his head. "State custody. That's all it says. I suppose they will go wherever neglected children go."

"My son is not neglected!" Rachel moved to the edge of her seat.

"Neither are Gideon's children," Miriam said.

"We have to find out where they are," Ella said.

"'Mr. Eggar,'" Miriam said. "That's the last thing Gideon said.

218

Mr. Eggar will know what to do."

"Ella, go find this Mr. Eggar," Rachel urged. "Do you know where his office is?"

"Yes," Ella said, "right on Main Street."

James painfully shook his head. "He's not there. I tried. The young man in his office did not expect him back before he closed the office at six."

Ella studied the clock on the mantel. Chasing around half the county all afternoon had consumed more time than she anticipated. Dusk enveloped the house. "It's past six now," she said.

"Someone in town will know which house is his," Rachel said. "You'll just have to keep asking until you find someone who does. Start with Lindy, or that *English* teacher who lives on her street."

Ella's gaze went to James and Miriam. James was once again pressing ice to his forehead, and Miriam was ghastly pale.

"I will look after James and Miriam," Rachel said.

"I don't need looking after," James protested.

"Neither do I," Miriam said.

Ella met Rachel's glance.

"I don't want to wait alone," Rachel said. "We'll all want to know what Ella finds out."

"I should be the one to go," James muttered.

"Old man," Miriam said, "you're going nowhere."

Ella drew a deep breath. "I'll make sure the lanterns on the buggy have plenty of oil."

❦

"You knew this was going to happen?" Margaret could hardly believe her ears. It was all she could do to remain seated on the davenport in her parlor.

Across the room, Gray Truesdale's lanky form overpowered the chair he had chosen.

"It should come as no surprise," Gray said.

"It most certainly does come as a surprise," Margaret said, her pitch rising against her will. Fury roiled through her midsection. "The fines were ridiculous in the first place. But arresting the fathers? Taking well-loved children into state custody as if they were abandoned orphans?"

"The lawmen are only doing their jobs," Gray said mildly. "It has nothing to do with you. Don't let it get you into a bothered state."

"A bothered state?"

"Your tea is getting cold," Gray said.

Margaret was tempted to toss her cold tea in Gray's lap. How was it possible that he could maintain this dispassionate demeanor when children were being stolen from their homes under the guise of the law?

"The men will take care of it." Gray lifted his teacup. "Will you freshen this for me?"

Margaret glared but picked up the teapot and refilled his cup.

"You're overreacting," Gray said between sips. "You have to let things take their natural course."

And just what was the "natural course" of a situation as complex as legislators and sheriffs and school boards refusing to view the circumstances through a lens other than their own? Margaret did not waste her breath posing the question to Gray.

"I saw your brother earlier," she said instead. "He was acting quite odd."

Gray shrugged. "You met him at Sunday dinner. You know he's odd."

"He was right here on my street, carrying a flour sack I'm certain did not contain flour."

"People use old flour sacks for all sorts of things," Gray said, forking into a sliver of pie. "Potato sacks, too. When we were young, the Amish around here were always glad to have sacks my mother didn't want to use."

"He made me nervous," Margaret said. "I think I will have a word with Deputy Fremont about it. Perhaps there have been some thefts in the neighborhood."

Gray put down his fork. "You think my brother is a thief?"

"I'm saying he was acting in an eccentric manner. If you want me to put such confidence in the sheriff's department, wouldn't it seem prudent to mention my observations?"

Gray took a bite of pie and chewed slowly. "You have misunderstood me."

"Have I?"

"Margaret, we were having a pleasant evening before I mentioned the Amish problem. I'm sorry I brought it up. Let's forget about it."

"Those children must be frightened half out of their minds."

Gertie's face loomed in Margaret's thoughts. Then one by one the other Amish children who had stopped attending school marched through her vision like a moving picture.

"They'll be well looked after," Gray said.

"You can't know that. I have to do something."

"I must insist that you stay out of this."

Margaret raised her eyebrows.

"I know you are a woman of strong cause," Gray said, "and on the whole I find it an admirable quality. But when we are married, I hope you know it will not be your place to involve yourself in matters I do not approve of."

Margaret stood up now. "We have spoken around the matter of marriage," she said, "and I confess I had hoped we would find a common mind. But I think we both know now that we are not as well matched as we had supposed."

Speaking the words aloud jolted electricity through Margaret's body.

Gray stood. "I can give you a comfortable life. You won't get a better offer."

"No," she said softly, "I don't suppose I will."

A knock on the door startled them both. Margaret moistened her lips and answered the door. Ella Hilty stood under the porch light.

"I'm sorry to disturb you," Ella said. "I need to find Mr. Percival Eggar. I wonder if you know where he lives?"

"Come in," Margaret said.

Ella glanced at Gray. "I'm intruding."

"This is Mr. Truesdale," Margaret said. "He's finished his pie, and I'm certain he will understand your need for assistance."

"I'm grateful for any help you can give me." Ella's words lost their fluidity. "My father. . .Gideon. . .the children. . .I don't know where to begin."

"I think I know the basics," Margaret said. "I'm sorry I don't know where Mr. Eggar lives, but we can get the telephone operator on the line. She will know how to reach him."

Margaret picked up the telephone on the table at the bottom of the stairs. With heavy, deliberate steps, Gray Truesdale left the house and closed the door behind him.

CHAPTER 33

It's late. You must stay the night," Margaret said after Mr. Eggar left her bungalow with two sheets of notes recording Ella's account.

Ella shook her head. "Miriam and James and Rachel—they'll all worry that something happened to me as well."

"I'll drive you, then," Margaret said.

Again Ella shook her head. "James's wagon is already stranded in town. I can't leave Gideon's buggy here all night. We'll need it in the morning—and what would we do with the horse?"

Ella was just being practical. She wrapped her shawl around her shoulders and thanked Margaret again before stepping out into the darkness. On most evenings, Amish farms would have quieted by now, lanterns turned low for one last look at sleeping children before parents retired themselves. Morning light would soon enough usher in the labor of another day of farm chores.

On this night, though, the lanterns would burn deep into the darkness, beacons of hope for what the new day might bring.

James, Miriam, and Rachel had hardly moved from where Ella left them hours earlier, though Rachel said she had been out to milk the cows for the night. The Hilty cows were long past their evening milking, so Ella spoke rapidly. There had been little Percival Eggar could do with state and legal offices closed for the evening. He promised to give his full attention when the business day began and to find out where the children had been taken. It was sure to be one of the state orphanages, he said. The men would be in the county courthouse in Chardon, and he would bargain for their release. In the meantime, Mr. Eggar suggested, they should all hope and pray for a firm legal outcome in their favor.

Hope and pray. After milking the Hiltys' cows—a task Seth normally assumed—Ella dragged herself back into the house, where she sat on her bed to sort out which came first—hope or prayer. Did she pray because she had hope for the answer she sought, or did she hope because of the comfort of prayer?

In the morning, the women descended on the Hilty farm before Ella cleared away the dishes of Rachel's uneaten breakfast. At last Ella had her answer about how many fathers had been arrested and how many children were deemed neglected.

Gideon Wittmer; two girls, one boy.

Jed Hilty; one boy.

Cristof Byler; one girl, three boys.

John Hershberger; three girls, one boy.

Isaiah Borntrager; two girls, three boys.

Chester Mast; two boys.

Six men and nineteen children. How the women had known to come to Ella, she did not know. Perhaps they had found each other one by one because they knew the men who chose to send their children to Ella to teach.

"Mr. Eggar is working hard for us," Ella assured the circle of anxious mothers.

"When will we know where our children are?" Mrs. Hershberger jiggled her restless infant on one knee.

Ella swallowed a lump of impossible words. "Most likely, they are at an orphanage."

"But they are not orphans!" came the nearly unanimous response.

"My Ezra was not at home when they came," Mrs. Borntrager said. "Will they come back for him?"

"They'll be back," Mrs. Byler said. "They'll accuse us of neglecting the little ones as well."

"They'll take my baby." Mrs. Hershberger held the child tightly to her chest.

"They could come for David," Mrs. Byler said, looking at Rachel.

"David goes to school," Rachel said.

"But they'll wonder what neglect caused him to run away from home."

"We'll have to hide the *kinner* still with us," Mrs. Hershberger said. "The *English* cannot steal children they cannot find."

Ella put up her hands, palms out. "Let's not jump ahead of ourselves. We have God on our side, and we have Mr. Eggar. He will come to the schoolhouse at three this afternoon to tell us what he knows."

Everyone's eyes moved to the clock on the mantel, ready to count down seven and a half excruciating hours.

"I have to take James into Seabury to fetch his horse and wagon," Ella said. "And we must care for the animals. Let us not be afraid to ask for help when we need it."

She wanted to add, *I'm sure they'll all be home soon.* This was the prayer of her heart. But could she sustain hope if the prayer went unanswered?

⋘❋⋙

The Wayfarers Home for Children. That was the name Percival Eggar uncovered in the legal documents he had demanded. At least—as far as they could tell—all of the children had been taken to the same location. They might have been scattered around eastern Ohio. For now they were together.

It was Saturday. Margaret owed no time to the Seabury Consolidated School District.

Three days after their arrests, the Amish fathers were still in jail in Chardon, and their children were still temporary wards of the state.

It was unconscionable.

Margaret had heard nothing from Gray since Wednesday evening, nor did she expect to. He had wanted her for his wife. Margaret had no doubt of this. He was courting in polite stages, and Margaret had given him every encouragement.

Until this. Until the Amish mystification.

The pressure in her chest waxed and waned through the days and nights. Seeing Gray around town would stir up visions of what might have been.

It was better to find out now, she told herself.

The children were what mattered. The Wayfarers Home for Children was thirty miles from Seabury. Margaret supposed few of the Amish families ever had reason to be thirty miles from their own farms. Had the sheriff's department done this on purpose—taken the children beyond reasonable reach of their mothers?

Margaret owned a car and could afford the gasoline. The least she could do was drive thirty miles and ascertain the welfare of the children.

She found the building without trouble. A blockish brick structure, it was set back from an entrance arched in wrought iron. Despite the expansive lawns calling for tumbles and giggles, Margaret saw no sign of children. She scowled at the thought that residents of the Wayfarers Home for Children attended classrooms even on Saturday. The driveway wound toward the building, and Margaret saw no reason not to park as close to the front door as possible.

At a reception desk a few minutes later, Margaret politely explained the nature of her visit. She wanted only to take assurance to the mothers of the Amish children of their well-being.

"The children are being suitably looked after," said the graying woman behind a narrow desk, "which is a great advancement beyond the actions of their parents, as I understand it."

Margaret bit her tongue. "I would like to see them. Many of them will recognize me from their days at the Seabury school where I teach."

"This is an unorthodox request. I would have to consult the director."

"Please do." Margaret seated herself on the edge of a wooden chair that rocked on one uneven leg. "I will wait."

"He may be engaged." The woman pushed spectacles up her nose.

Margaret smiled. "I teach six-year-olds, so I am well acquainted with patience."

The woman's chair scraped the tile floor, and her buttoned shoes dragged down the hall. Margaret's investment paid its return in the arrival of a man who was perhaps forty years old.

"I understand you want to see the Amish children," he said.

Margaret stood. "That's correct."

"I'm afraid children are not allowed visitors so soon after their arrival," he said. "We find it only distresses their adjustment."

"Surely they won't be here long enough to have to adjust," Margaret said.

"We have our policies." He gave a tight smile.

Margaret's blood raced. "You don't mean to tell me you would withhold them from their own mothers."

"The policies are quite clear on this matter. The children are here because they were neglected. Any visit would have to be closely supervised."

A supervised visit would be better than no visit.

"So if I return with the mothers on another day," Margaret said, "have I your word that they would be permitted to see their children?"

"Briefly," he said, reluctant. "No more than one hour, and only if I have adequate staff available to meet the supervision standards."

Margaret met his eyes and held them hard. "I will be back."

Getting there had been easier than James imagined it would be. The first glimmer of opportunity came when Miriam insisted on going with Ella to a meeting with the women, leaving James alone in the *dawdihaus* with his bruised forehead. Regardless of what he might look like, he was not seriously hurt. Without Tobias and Gideon, the farm chores had fallen to him. If he could handle that work, he was fit enough for what he had in mind.

In the unexpected solitude, James scribbled a note and left it in the middle of the table, where Miriam would find it easily. He would not be home for supper. Only the fingers of one hand would be required to count the number of times he was not home for supper with his wife in the last forty-four years.

Once he heard Margaret's news, James wanted to see for himself. But thirty miles was a long way to take a horse and buggy. James might find a train for part of the way, but he would be tied to schedules he did not know. David's method seemed more direct and efficient. If *English* drivers would stop for David when he sought a ride into Seabury, why would they not stop for James as well?

He had changed automobiles twice, but here he stood in a gently descending expanse of shadows behind the Wayfarers Home for Children. One by one, lights flickered on inside the building as late afternoon slid into evening. James suspected an approach to the rear of the building held more potential for his goal.

James waited under the spreading barren branches of an elm tree, breathing in and out with care and surveying the ground-floor exits.

A door opened. A woman came out, her arms filled with a basket of undetermined contents, and followed a path toward the corner of the building. It mattered not what she carried, only that she had left the door ajar. In a stealth moment, James found himself in a small pantry.

He stood still and listened for movement in the adjoining room, which he reasoned must be a kitchen, large enough to prepare food for hundreds of children and staff. Hearing nothing, he padded out of the pantry and across the kitchen. Voices came to him now. Children's voices. One lilted above the others.

James had known that voice when it was nothing but the babble of a *boppli*. A half inch at a time, he pushed open the door that separated him from Gideon's children—at least Gertie.

He almost did not recognize her. Gone was her prayer *kapp*. Rather than braids coiled against her head, her blond hair hung loose around her shoulders. A pink ribbon at the top of her head matched the pink dress she wore with a splash of lace down the front.

The children's voices settled as a woman at the front of the room clapped for their attention. Rows and rows of children. As his eyes adjusted to the reality of looking for Amish faces above *English* clothing, James spotted them one by one. Savilla and Tobias—with his hair trimmed in *English* fashion—and Seth Kaufman beside him. The Hershberger girls and their brother, Isaiah Borntrager's children, the Bylers, the Masts. They were all there, but separated, each of them seated with other children their own age rather than with their siblings.

The woman explained the next day's schedule. A Presbyterian minister would come in to hold a morning church service. Children assigned to set up and clear after meals should be prompt. In the afternoon, if the weather was fine, there might be organized outdoor games before the evening prayer meeting.

James settled his gaze again on Gertie, who sat at the end of a row. Her eyes began to wander, and she turned her head toward him. When her blue orbs widened, her lips also parted and she drew in breath as if to speak.

James put a finger to his lips. Gertie clamped her mouth closed. He stepped back into the kitchen, determined to find a way to get the children back. For now it was enough to see that they were unharmed—except for the silly clothes and hair arrangements.

"Who's there?" a voice called. The weight of a box thumped against a butcher block table.

"It's dark in here," another voice said. "Turn on the light."

"I can't find the string to pull."

James slithered back through the pantry.

CHAPTER 34

Hustling out the rear door, still ajar from his entrance, James plunged into the surrounding darkness. Most of his white shirt was covered by his black wool coat, one that Miriam had made for him only last year. For a few minutes he pressed himself up against the same tree that had sheltered him on arrival, waiting for his breathing to compose its rhythm enough that he would be able to find his way around the building without fearing collapse.

James could hear the words Miriam would speak to him if she were there. *"Old man, what have you done now?"*

By now he had missed his supper, but food was far from his mind. The pleading expression on Gertie's face lingered in his mind. Would she have a chance to tell Savilla or Tobias she had seen James? He hoped so. He wanted Gideon's children to know they were not abandoned.

"Gottes wille," he muttered. "Lord, keep them safe."

As soon as he got home, James would sketch what he had seen—the corners of the mammoth building, the doors opening in the back, the path to the large room where the children gathered. As soon as tomorrow's Sabbath was over, James would find a way to get to Chardon to visit Gideon and the other men. And he would visit Percival Eggar in Seabury every day if he had to.

James prayed it would be God's will for an obliging driver to happen by just as he arrived at the road. An even more gracious answer to his prayer would be a driver whose destination was Seabury and who could carry an unexpected passenger safely to his home. He took off his black jacket now, exposing his white shirt and hoping it made him more visible in the headlights of passing automobiles. Miriam would disapprove of his shivering in the night wind, but Miriam would disapprove of most of what James had done today.

Two cars passed without stopping. James began to walk in the general direction of home. If God did not send a ride, it would take him all night to get to the farm.

The lights of another automobile swung around a curve, accompanied by a particularly noisy engine. James waved one arm in a wide swath, expelling his breath again only once it was clear the driver was slowing. James paid no attention to the variations in *English* automobiles. He supposed this one was one of Mr. Ford's inventions. A young man with a broad smile and wavy hair leaned across the seat to look out the window at James.

"Are you stranded?" the man asked.

"You might say," James said. "Are you by any chance headed to Seabury?"

"I could be. Is that where you're headed?"

"A farm near there."

"Get in," the man said, pushing the handle so the passenger door would open. "I'm Edwin."

"James Lehman." Grateful, James settled into his seat. He had been in Lindy's car a time or two, but it still seemed an adventure to ride through the night behind a motor.

Edwin cocked his head as he put the car back into gear. "You're one of those Amish."

James slipped his arms back into his jacket and nodded. "How long do you guess it will take to get to Seabury?"

"Less than an hour," Edwin said. "Do you mind if I ask a question?"

"Of course not." James could hardly deny conversation to God's answer to his prayer.

Edwin accelerated. "What brings you so far from home at this hour?"

≈✻≈

Ella had no students. She had returned to the schoolhouse on Monday long enough to put away what little there was of value and to make sure the windows and doors were closed securely. Each day winter howled a few degrees colder.

Monday. The children and the fathers had been gone five days. Households with older sons sent them around to be sure women with younger families had enough help with the animals, and each day the women seemed to find each other and congregate in another home.

Percival Eggar filed documents with Latin names at the courthouse in Chardon and assured the families that he had seen their men and they were fine. But the judicial process seemed to be in no hurry to come to the aid of a handful of rural farm families, and Mr. Eggar offered no estimation of when the case might come before a judge.

Leaving Rachel in the gentle care of Mrs. Glick, Ella took the buggy into Seabury to turn in her pile of library books, and because the slow ride to town would give her time to think about all that had transpired in the last few days.

Mrs. White, the cheery librarian, checked in Ella's books. "Your bird book is back on the shelf, in case you're looking for it again."

"Thank you." Ella was not much in the mood to contemplate what to read in her shrinking leisure hours. She was tempted to ask Mrs. White if the library had any books about the legal system.

"I have to say," Mrs. White said, "I was surprised by that article in the newspaper, weren't you?"

"Our people don't read the newspaper," Ella reminded the librarian.

"That's what I thought," Mrs. White said. "I was doubly surprised to find that one of you had given an interview to a reporter."

Ella rubbed one tired eye. "I'm sorry. What did you say?"

"There's a long article in the paper out of Cleveland." Mrs. White pushed a neat stack of books to one side of the desk. "You should read it."

"No, I couldn't." An interview? A Cleveland newspaper? Ella could not make sense of Mrs. White's words.

"Follow me." Mrs. White came out from behind the desk and with short, clipped steps led the way to a section of the library Ella had never before explored. Two rows of racks had newspapers hanging over them. Mrs. White plucked up the one she wanted and swiftly opened to the page of interest.

Amish Children Victims of Neglect, the headline said.

Ella gasped and took the newspaper into her own hands. "I don't understand."

Mrs. White pointed to a phrase in the first paragraph. "An exclusive interview with a Geauga County Amish man."

"No," Ella said. "We wouldn't do that!" She scanned the article. *Children kept out of school. Fathers stubbornly defy state laws. Illegal private school.*

"Well, someone did." Mrs. White flipped the paper to show Ella what lay below the fold.

Ella stared into the faces of her father and her fiancé, bearded and behind bars.

"I don't know how a reporter got that picture on a Sunday," Mrs. White said. "I guess he was determined to get the scoop for the Monday morning edition. Some people have no respect for the Sabbath."

⁓✦⁓

"Perhaps we need to pay Mr. Eggar a larger fee," Isaiah Borntrager said.

"He's doing all he can," Gideon said. "He's been to see us every day. We can't blame him for how slowly the court system works."

The six Amish men occupied two jail cells side by side. Gideon and Jed tended to pace the limited square footage, while Isaiah sprawled on a lower bunk in a prolonged sulk. On the other side of the wall, the restless shiftings and murmurs of John, Cristof, and Chester told a similar story from the other cell. A guard walked past them every hour or so, but in between they were free to lean against the bars of the jail cells and speak so all could hear.

"Five days," Isaiah muttered.

"And we still don't know what happens next," Jed said. "Whatever happens to me, I want Rachel to have her son home."

Percival Eggar had brought enough news for the men to know that no further harm had come to their families—no more children taken, no threats against wives left behind. But what of the children already removed from their homes? No matter what flowery language Mr. Eggar constructed about the safety of the Wayfarers Home for Children and the competency of the staff who served there, every father in the jail cells thought constantly of their children foundering in a sea of *English* expectations without even the comfort of coming home to their own farms and families at the end of the day.

"We should pray," Gideon said.

"All I do is pray," John Hershberger said from the other cell. "My every thought is prayer."

"Together," Gideon said. "We have already seen how prayer together, aloud, brings us encouragement. Let us not fall away now. Remember the faithfulness of the martyrs in our hymns and learn from their steadfastness in times of trial."

Isaiah swung his feet off the bunk. "We've cowered long enough, depending on the *English* lawyer to free us. Only God can free us."

The six men lined themselves up along the iron bars, hands hanging through the openings as if grasping for the freedom on the other side.

Gideon spoke aloud. "Lord God, You ordain our lives. You ordain our moments. We cleave to You in this our time of trial. Keep us free from the night of darkness of temptation and sin. Instead, lead us in the light of Your divine mercy. The psalmist tells us, 'The Lord God is a sun and shield: the Lord will give grace and glory: no good thing will he withhold from them that walk uprightly.' We depend on You to keep our steps upright and lead us into Your goodness and glory."

John cleared his throat. "May Your merciful eyes be upon us even in this place where we cannot look on Your beauty in the land. Forgive us our weaknesses for the sake of Your dear Son. Turn darkness to light before our very eyes."

Booted footfalls thudding against the hall floor pried Gideon's eyes open and he put a hand on Isaiah's arm.

"Praying again," the guard said. "Doesn't it occur to you that it might be God's will for you simply to obey the law?"

Gideon said nothing, instead moving his eyes to Percival Eggar standing beside the deputy.

"If you would please," Percival said.

The guard rattled a ring of keys. "I know. You want a confidential conversation with all of your clients in one room." He unlocked both cells and herded the prisoners together in one cell. Once the attorney stepped in as well, the guard locked the cell and retreated from sight.

"I had hoped," Percival said, "that the authorities simply wanted to make a point by detaining you through the weekend when the courts would be closed. I'm afraid the news I have today is not encouraging. They are prepared to jail you indefinitely, right up until trial."

"When will that be?" Gideon asked.

"The dockets are full." Percival shook his head. "Weeks. Months, perhaps. We'll use the time to prepare our case."

Jed separated from the group. "And if we lose the trial?"

"Let's not jump to that," Percival said. "We can make a strong case on the grounds of the free exercise of religion."

"What are our wives supposed to do in the meantime?" Chester asked.

"I'll try to arrange a visit," Percival said. "And there are rules that will allow them to see the children."

"What will it take to end all this?" Gideon slowly paced toward the rear wall of the cell.

Percival shrugged one shoulder. "Agree to put your children in the consolidated schools until the age of sixteen. And I'm sure there will be another fine."

"No compromise?" Chester said. "No reasoning together?"

"I'm not giving up," Percival said. "The question is how long you want to persist on the path to lasting justice for your people."

<hr />

Gray startled Margaret. She had stayed late in the school building on Monday, hearing other teachers close their classroom doors and fall into step with one another down the back stairs more than an hour ago. It was essential that lesson plans were clear and specific for the following day and all supplies arranged in an orderly fashion. When Margaret finally left the building, exiting through the front door so the woman who worked in the office would know the last teacher was gone, she did not expect to find Gray Truesdale waiting for her.

He leaned one shoulder against the brick of the building, straightening when he saw her come through the door.

"Mr. Truesdale," Margaret said, reverting to the neutral cordiality of the early days of their acquaintance.

"May I speak to you?" Gray said.

"Of course." Instantly, a lump formed in Margaret's throat.

"I may have spoken harshly the last time we met," he said. "And I missed sitting with you in church yesterday. I looked for you after the service."

"I didn't feel up to attending," Margaret said.

"It's your church, too," Gray said. "I would never want you to stay away because you are angry with me."

"I'm not angry," Margaret said. She ached with disappointment over his views, with grief for what might have been.

Gray ran his thumb and forefinger over the brim of the hat in his hand. "The preacher spoke about humility. Maybe I need to learn some."

Optimism flickered, struggling against the harsh wind of the words they had spoken to each other.

"I'd like to come for pie on Thursday," Gray said.

Margaret shifted her satchel to the other hand. "I have preserves made from the blackberries you brought me. It seems only right that you should help eat them."

He offered that crooked smile Margaret found so difficult to resist.

The lump in her throat softened. She would make pie. It was a small town and they attended the same church. One last evening of pie might make it easier to find the necessary geniality for an amicable break.

If Margaret had told Gray what she intended to do the following day, she was certain he would have changed his mind about the pie.

CHAPTER 35

Margaret pulled the car up close to the Hilty farmhouse and checked once again to be sure she had not left clutter on the seats. Living alone and driving alone most of the time cultivated a habit of leaving books and papers on the backseat as if it were an ordinary storage shelf in her bungalow. But today the seats had to be cleared. Today she needed space for six passengers. It would be tight, but Margaret was certain the Amish mothers would do whatever it took to see their children.

Rachel and Ella were waiting on the porch and descended the steps. Margaret scurried around the car to hold a door open for them.

"What about your class?" Ella asked once they were on their way.

"I arranged for a substitute teacher," Margaret said. "It's allowed under extenuating circumstances."

"I'm surprised your principal would consider this extenuating circumstances," Ella said.

"I said I had a personal matter that required immediate attention." It was none of Mr. Tarkington's business what Margaret did with her day. In four years of teaching at the Seabury school, Margaret had only availed herself of the services of a substitute on two other occasions, both involving abrupt illness. By now the substitute would be reviewing the clear and specific lesson plans Margaret had left. Her pupils would notice no difference in classroom routine.

"I don't have the words to thank you for taking us." Rachel was squeezed in between Ella and Margaret, leaving the backseat available for four more mothers.

"It's the right thing to do," Margaret said. "Where do we go next?"

"To the Glicks'," Ella said. "Mrs. Hershberger is leaving her *boppli* there. The littlest Borntrager boy will stay with Mrs. King."

Margaret nodded in satisfaction with the plan. Margaret had warned the mothers there would not be room in the car for their small children still at home and that she was uncertain whether young ones would be admitted at the Wayfarers Home. The Masts and Bylers did not have any children younger than those who had been removed.

"I'm so worried about Seth," Rachel said, rubbing a hand over her eyes.

"He and Tobias are close in age," Ella said. "They're probably together. And the Mast brothers. They'll all help each other."

Just like their parents. Some of the boys were old enough to be in high school. They would be fine. The girls were younger, though. Margaret couldn't think of any Amish girl at the Wayfarers Home older than eleven or twelve. Who was looking after them?

After several more stops, four mothers crammed into the backseat and settled care packages on their laps. Margaret did not have the heart to tell them they might not be allowed to leave gifts.

This time she knew just where she was going and drove confidently up the long driveway before parking outside the front doors and turning off the engine.

Rachel's eyes widened at the enormity of the brick building. "It would take three or four of our church districts to fill this place."

"This is no place for children," Mrs. Hershberger muttered from the backseat. "Couldn't an *aunti* or a *grossmudder* take in a child who is truly orphaned? Have they no families at all?"

"I don't know," Margaret said. "Let's focus on the nineteen children whose mothers are right here in this car."

"Do they know we're coming?" Ella asked.

"I phoned ahead." Margaret opened her car door and stepped out. "Let me speak on your behalf while you pray to see God's mercy in the faces of your children."

⚜

Margaret led the way. Ella intentionally fell to the back of the line, watching to be sure the other mothers were holding themselves together as they approached a structure that could have contained all their homes and still had room for chickens and cows.

Other mothers. Ella loved Tobias, Savilla, and Gertie. Together with Gideon, they were going to become a family in a few weeks. She would throw herself in the path of danger for any one of them. If Ella's maternal instincts surged as hard as this, she could only imagine what this day was like for the women whose wombs and arms had carried their children since the first spark of life.

Margaret held open the front door, and the Amish mothers shuffled inside, uncertain.

Margaret pointed. "We'll go to that desk. They are expecting you."

A man met them in the hallway. While the gray-haired woman Margaret had met on her first visit stared at the huddle of rich-hued dresses and black aprons, Margaret introduced him as the director of the children's home. One by one the mothers gave their names and the names of the children.

"I'll Ella Hilty," Ella said. "I'm here to see Tobias, Savilla, and Gertrude Wittmer."

The director arranged his glasses on his nose and consulted his list. "My information indicates that the Wittmer children have no mother."

"I'm engaged to their father," Ella said quickly. "Our wedding is only a month away."

A wave of sympathy flushed through the man's face, but his words were firm. "I'm afraid we have no provision for such a circumstance. Anyone might come in and make such a claim. It's for the safety of the children. You understand."

Ella's mouth fell open, her heart beating its way up her throat.

"We most certainly do not understand," Margaret said calmly. "The children know Miss Hilty well. They understand that their father will marry her soon. I have observed no discord between them on this matter."

Ella forced herself to breathe, and the air flowing out of her lungs cradled a prayer of gratitude for Margaret's presence.

"Think of how the Wittmer children will feel," Margaret said. "The other Amish children will see their mothers, and the Wittmers will know someone came for them as well and you prohibited the visit."

The director cleared his throat. "I will have to consult the state guidelines, but I make no guarantee."

"What about our children?" Mrs. Hershberger wanted to know. "Where are they?"

"They'll be brought to you," the director said. "They are in classes throughout the building, so it will take some time to gather them."

"We had an appointment," Margaret said. "Why are the children not ready?"

Ella put a hand on Margaret's arm and said to the director, "Just tell us where you'd like us to wait."

He turned to the woman at the desk. "Will you please take the mothers to the visiting room where they may wait more comfortably?"

"And the others—Miss Simpson and Miss Hilty?" the woman asked.

The director sucked in his lips slightly and turned to Ella and Margaret. "I'll have to ask you to wait out here until I have ascertained your status."

"I will gladly wait out here," Margaret said, "but I will insist that Miss Hilty see her children. Otherwise you will hear from Mr. Eggar, the attorney representing the children's fathers."

"Mr. Eggar has already been in touch," the director said. "We are both responsible to the court for our actions. I intend to be above reproach."

"I hope that does not also require you to be above compassion," Margaret said.

Again, Ella touched Margaret's arm. One might think the director held hostage Margaret's own offspring.

"I'll wait out here," Ella said. "Is that bench acceptable?"

The director gestured toward the bench directly across from the reception desk. "Please make yourselves comfortable. The rest of you may follow the receptionist, but let me remind you that this visit will be closely supervised."

The director withdrew to his office.

Ella and Margaret sat on the backless bench. Ella did not even wish for a chair with a back or any other comfort that might compromise her vigilance. She watched the five mothers trail after the woman to a door, which she held open for them. Ella leaned forward for a glimpse of the space where mothers and *kinner* would be reunited.

"This is not right," Margaret muttered.

Though her heart begged for release from captivity within her rib cage, Ella sat with her hands calmly crossed in her lap. A moment later, three young women left the director's office, dispatched—Ella hoped—to bring the children from their classrooms.

"If the director does not return promptly, I will advocate once again for you to see your children."

Ella's shoulders softened and gratitude again overflowed for the *English* who understood her heart. Perhaps Margaret's own experience as a teacher helped her know how quickly and firmly affection might grow with a child.

One by one, the young women returned, shepherding children into the visitation room. Most of them moved quietly through the halls.

The first time the door opened, Mrs. Mast shrieked at the sight of her boys.

The second time, it was Seth who came down the hall and Rachel's sobs that escaped the visiting room.

Then Mrs. Borntrager.

The young women returned to the classrooms, returning each time with one or two children. It seemed to Ella that they had begun with the older grades and were working their way down to the younger classes.

"They didn't bring Tobias," Ella said.

Margaret took her hand. "You *will* see your children."

The students grew younger with each escort. Mrs. Hershberger's voice went shrill at the sight of her children.

"They skipped Savilla, too," Ella said.

"Has the man no heart?" Margaret said. "Gideon's children are bright. They will see that the others are going and know that someone has come for them."

The Byler children came at last, Hans trailing after his older siblings. Ella swallowed hard.

The sound she heard next was the most beautiful cacophony ever to reach her ears. Down the hall, a child's demands grew more insistent with each clattering step.

"If Hans gets to go, why can't I?"

Margaret and Ella grinned at each other and stood up.

"Gertrude!" The young escort spun on one heel, holding tight to Hans Byler's hand. "Go back to class immediately."

"Is Hans in trouble?" Gertie asked.

"No. Go back to class."

Ella's eyes widened. Gertie's yellow hair fell around her shoulders above a blue plaid jumper and white blouse intended for a girl at least two years older.

"What have they done to our children?" Ella whispered.

"I won't go back without Hans." Gertie stomped a foot, something she never would have done at home.

The young woman escorting Hans opened the door to the visiting room and gave him a gentle push between the shoulder blades through the door frame before sealing the room again.

"What's in there?" Gertie wanted to know.

Then, in a moment that Ella wished she could ponder in her heart for the rest of her life, Gertie's curls bounced with the rotation of her head and her gaze found Ella.

Ella started toward Gertie. The receptionist was on her feet. Gertie was already hurtling toward Ella, out of reach of the young escort's efforts to contain her.

"Go," the receptionist whispered. "Hurry."

Ella raced down the hall and scooped up Gertie in her arms.

The director appeared from his office. "What's going on?"

Ella ignored him. It was quite obvious what was going on. Gertie buried her face in Ella's shoulder.

The clipped steps behind Ella belonged to Margaret.

"Now if you would please send someone for Miss Hilty's other children," Margaret said.

"This is thoroughly unorthodox," the director said.

Ella took Gertie's face between her hands to examine every inch of it. "Are you all right?"

"I don't like it here," Gertie said loudly. "They never let me talk to Tobias and Savilla. I only get to see Hans when it's time for our reading lessons. And they won't tell me why Hans went in that room."

Tears blurred Ella's eyes. "Hans went in there to see his *mamm.*"

Gertie kept her hands clasped behind Ella's neck.

"You can see their affection is genuine," Margaret said to the director. "If you care for these children at all—"

The director tilted his head, and the young woman awaiting his bidding started down the hall. She opened the door to the visiting room.

"You won't have long," he said.

Inside the room, tears and laughter intermingled. The children hated the clothes they were forced to wear, and no two of them had been assigned to the same dormitory room. They sometimes saw each other across a classroom or the assembly room, but rarely were they allowed to speak freely with each other and it must always be in English, not Pennsylvania Dutch. Ella's chest felt as though it might cave in with the isolation they described. Sitting in opposite corners, two women in navy blue wool dresses watched the movements in the room. Every few seconds, Ella's eyes went to the door, looking for Savilla and Tobias.

When the door opened, it was Gertie who saw them first and shot off to greet her siblings. Whatever manner in which they might have irritated each other at home dissolved in the embrace. Ella waited for their eyes to lift and opened her arms to Tobias and Savilla.

Questions spewed from all three of them, and Ella had few answers. She could only tell them that Gideon was with the other fathers. She hadn't been to see them—none of the women had managed a visit to Chardon—but Mr. Eggar brought news that they were well. Tobias promised to pray for his father.

The large round clock opposite the door seemed designed to greet everyone who entered the visitation room and remind them that their minutes were few. As if on cue, exactly one hour after the mothers had entered the room, the two women in blue stood up and announced it was time for the children to return to their classrooms. One of them opened the door to reveal the three younger women who would escort their charges on their return.

Ella held on to Gertie as long as she dared. In the end, it was sensible Savilla who wordlessly pried Gertie's grip off of Ella's neck while a visible lump formed in Tobias's throat.

And then they were gone. The room fell into a choked hush.

Margaret drove most of the way home hearing only the machinations of her automobile, the shifting gears, the rhythmic thump of tires, the engine threatening to sputter for more fuel.

"I want my children back," Mrs. Hershberger finally said.

"And my husband," Rachel said.

"I never thought I would say this," Mrs. Borntrager said, "but it's time for them to do whatever is necessary."

"Whatever is necessary for what?" Mrs. Mast challenged. "To bring our families home, or to do what is best for them in the long run?"

Margaret kept her eyes on the road. Beside her, Ella took in a long, slow breath.

CHAPTER 36

It's the bishop!" Isaiah lurched toward the bars of the jail cell.

Gideon, who had been praying silently at one end of the bottom bunk, opened his eyes immediately and pushed himself off the bunk. Men in both cells lined up along the cell doors and watched a uniformed guard escort their spiritual leader into this forgotten corner of the *English* justice system.

"This is our pastor," Gideon said. "Please admit him."

The guard shrugged. "He's not on the list."

"What list?"

"I have a list of approved visitors on my desk," the guard said. "He's not on it. He stays on this side until your attorney comes."

Bishop Garber nodded. "It's all right. Mr. Eggar brought me in his automobile. He will park and then come in."

The guard withdrew to the end of the hall, and through the bars the bishop shook each father's hand with a prolonged grip.

"Bishop," Isaiah said, "have you come to tell us what we must do?"

"I have come to pray with you and for you," the bishop said. "You are caught between obeying God's command to submit to the government He has ordained and obeying God's command to train up your children in the way they should go. I don't make light of the decision you face."

The decision had become considerably more complex after six nights in jail. The men's resolve to act as one faltered more with each day away from their wives and children.

"When we were baptized," John Hershberger said, "we all promised to submit to the church. Bishop, if you tell us what to do, whatever it is, none of us would find shame in submitting to you."

The bishop shook his head. "I've never been that kind of bishop, and you know it. I didn't ask to be a minister, much less to have the bishop's lot fall to me. You also promised to be willing to serve as a minister, if called upon. In this situation, we must all minister to each other."

John sighed and stepped away from the bars. "It all seemed so clear in the beginning—at least to me. I didn't want my children in that town school. Now they will go to an *English* school whether or not I like it, so I might as well have them at home with me at night."

Chester Mast shuffled his feet.

"Chester?" the bishop said. "Would you like to speak?"

"We've come this far," Chester said. "We'll never know what might come of it in the end if we don't see it through."

Determined footfalls approached.

"Here's your Mr. Eggar," the bishop said.

Two guards accompanied the attorney and allowed all the men to file into one cell before withdrawing down the hall to monitor from a distance. The fathers leaned against the walls, eager for Mr. Eggar's report.

"I continue to work toward your release," Mr. Eggar said. "We have an arraignment hearing on Thursday morning. I've confirmed with the judge's clerk that we are on the docket and stressed that the delay is approaching the outside limits of 'unnecessary delay.' "

Gideon worked his lips in and out as he listened. The sheriff's department seemed to rely on the general ignorance of the Amish about specific rights within the legal system.

"What does that mean?" Jed asked.

"They'll formally read the charges, and we'll enter a plea of not guilty," Percival said.

"But we are guilty, aren't we?" John asked.

"We're not giving up," Percival said. "We want this to go to trial. That's where we get to make our case."

"What if we lose at trial?" Jed asked.

Silence fell.

"What if I said I would pay the fine and send my children to school?" John asked finally.

"Then you would plead guilty," Percival said. "Is that what you wish to do?"

"I know I want to go home to my family," John said. "What if the long way around is a lot longer than any of us imagined?"

Gideon stepped away from the wall, paced the center of the small cell, and turned in a complete circle.

"If Mr. Eggar determines that it is an option to pay the fine and obey the school laws," Gideon said, "then each man must decide whether this choice is in the best interest of his family."

"I want to go home," John said.

"I want to see it through," Chester countered.

The others stared at one another, silent.

❧

Margaret slept more deeply on Tuesday night than she had in weeks. It might have been simply because the day's emotions had exhausted her, along with the Amish mothers, but she preferred to believe she slept the sleep of the righteous. She had done the right thing. She had acted on behalf of the defenseless. She had cared for the—temporary—orphans and widows, just as the Bible told her to do.

The morning sky was still gray when Margaret left her home on Wednesday morning ready to resume her normal responsibilities at the school. If the substitute had encountered any difficulties or been unable to get through all the lesson plans, she would have left notes. Margaret wanted to review the situation long before her pupils arrived. The woman who worked in the school's office was always first to the building, making her rounds with the keys, and Margaret intended to be the second arrival.

In her classroom, she reached for the switch that would rouse the electric lights to overcome the dim gloom of early morning. Margaret had taught long enough in a one-room schoolhouse that was never electrified to be grateful for the transformation that came with the simple touch of her fingers. She scanned the room. The rows of desks were in satisfactory alignment, and on the center of her own desk was one white sheet of paper with neat script. Margaret pulled out the chair and sat down to read the substitute's report.

Four students absent on Tuesday, it said. One more than on Monday, and all with influenza. At least that was the substitute's opinion.

Steps in the hall so early—well before she expected any of the other teachers—startled Margaret, and her spine straightened as she cocked her head toward the open classroom door. A moment later, a man's form filled the space. Margaret rose to her feet.

"Mr. Brownley," she said. "Good morning."

"Good morning." Brownley stepped into the room. "I understand you were not present here yesterday."

"That's correct." Margaret's throat went dry.

"Now, Miss Simpson, you and I have known each other for some time now."

Brownley began to pace the perimeter of the room, a habit that irritated Margaret more each time she witnessed it.

"Four years," she said, though only in the last few months would the superintendent have recognized her as one of his teachers in any circumstances outside her classroom.

"And you are happy working for our school district?"

Margaret stretched her lips into a wan smile. "Quite."

"Then I must admit I find it confounding why you would put your position at risk as you have." Pace. Pace.

"I'm afraid I don't understand."

"Ah, but I believe you do." Brownley stopped moving at last and turned to face her, hands behind his broad back. "I have it on good report that you were seen yesterday driving off one of the Amish farms with a number of Amish passengers. This happened at a time of day you should have been here discharging your duties."

"I followed protocol in requesting the time away," Margaret said, "and made suitable arrangements for my classroom."

"I originally engaged your help to be sure the Amish students consolidated with minimal disturbance," he said. "I'm sorry to say your efforts disappointed me."

"Perhaps," she said, "if you had not taken matters back into your own hands without waiting for the benefits of the woman's touch you espoused to desire, I would have succeeded."

There. She'd said it. She might as well continue.

"You asked for my help, and I gladly rose to the challenge," Margaret said. "With a bit more time, I might have been able to assure the Amish families that our school administrators were capable of listening to their very reasonable concerns. Instead, you ensured that they would see me as no more than a puppet without even the strength of strings to do as it was told."

"Your job was to serve the interests of the committee." Brownley glared.

"I am a teacher, Mr. Brownley. My job is always to serve the interests of the children." Margaret returned the glare.

Brownley resumed pacing. When he reached the door, he turned once again to face her. "Miss Simpson, when is your contract due to expire?"

"Not until June 30."

"Ah." He put one hand on the door. "You do understand that there are always extenuating circumstances that may void a contract."

The door closed behind him. Margaret dropped into her chair, trembling but without regret.

CHAPTER 37

"My advice is to accept the offer." Percival Eggar looked at each man's face on Wednesday afternoon. His eyes settled finally on Gideon.

"It's what they always wanted," Chester Mast mumbled. "We've sat in jail for a week for nothing."

"I've spoken with your wives again as well," Percival said. "They are most anxious to have the children home."

"And the only way the children can go home is if we give in and put them in the town school," Gideon said.

"This is not the end," Percival said. "Everything that happened during the last week can work in our favor when we take the case to court."

"Court. I don't know." With seven people in the cell, there was no room to pace. Instead, Gideon lifted himself up on his toes and then lowered his heels.

"It's the next step," Percival said, his eyes insistent through his spectacles. "You file your own suit to establish infringement of your religious liberty and free speech rights. Sending the children to school will take the focus off the truancy question and allow us to explore the issues that can settle this question once and for all."

"Can we make an offer of our own?" Gideon asked, pushing up on his toes again.

"I'm not sure we're in a position to counter," Percival said. "We want to get you out of here."

"I want their promise that if we do this, our children will also be returned to our homes—today."

Percival nodded. "More than reasonable."

"Do they know you are thinking of a court suit?"

"I have not said so overtly," Percival answered.

"Then we do have something to bargain with. Tell them we will pay the fines and send the children to their schools. Then tell them you will delay the suit if they agree to sit down with our bishop and a few of our men to listen to our viewpoint. Perhaps we can still avoid starting our own legal action."

"Don't you want to settle this permanently?" Percival said. "This could be a landmark case."

"I do not wish to be a landmark," Gideon said. "I wish to be a father whose children are brought up in the nurture and admonition of the Lord."

"And if the authorities do not agree to such a meeting?" Percival said.

Gideon shrugged and looked around the cramped cell. "Then we speak of the court question again."

Murmurs circled the room.

"You all agree?" Percival asked.

The men nodded, and Percival called for the guard to let him out of the cell.

"I'll have to speak to the sheriff," he said, "and then see the judge. I don't know how long it will take."

"We'll wait."

A minute later, Gideon watched Percival disappear through a door.

The six fathers remained in one cell, some sprawling on bunks, some leaning against walls, some shifting their weight from one foot to the other and back again in a slow, swaying rhythm.

"Will we really go to court?" John Hershberger asked. "Will the bishop allow that?"

Gideon took in a slow, deep breath, praying it would not be necessary to answer John's question.

They waited.

Lunch arrived, and they picked at the trays.

They waited.

Someone came for the abandoned trays.

They waited.

Finally Percival's solid footsteps approached. All six men crowded against the bars.

"Get out of the way," the sheriff said, turning a key in the lock. He swung the door open. "Your attorney has taken care of the fines. You're free to go."

"And our children?" Gideon said.

"The paperwork is already in progress," the sheriff said. "We'll take you all home in a bus and send another for them."

"Thank you." Gideon was the first of the men to step out of the cell.

The sheriff pointed a warning finger. "Those children had better be in school tomorrow. I've already notified Superintendent Brownley. The principals will know to expect the return of their wayward students."

❧❦❧

"How long?" Ella asked David. She laid a hand against Lindy's hot cheek.

"She felt fine yesterday," David said. "Then this morning, she didn't get up. I couldn't go to school and leave her like this."

"Of course not."

"I'm fine," Lindy muttered. "Just a little under the weather."

"A lot of students have been absent with influenza," David said.

Ella moistened her lips. She did not have to read *English* newspapers to know that influenza had decimated Cleveland, thirty miles away. Authorities had closed schools, theaters, and even churches in an effort to contain the disease. She looked again at Lindy. Perhaps it was not influenza.

"We should call the doctor." Ella glanced toward the telephone in the front room.

"No doctor," Lindy said. "I'll be right as rain tomorrow."

Ella doubted this. And if David stayed out of school, the authorities might take him to the Wayfarers Home for Children along with the others.

"David," Lindy said, gasping for sufficient breath. "I want the new birdhouse. I'll feel better later, and I can paint it in the kitchen."

"I'll get it when you're ready," David said.

"Get it now, please."

Ella nodded at David, certain it would do Lindy no good to get worked up in a minor argument.

"I'll get another cool cloth," Ella said. She went into the kitchen, found a drawer of small towels, and tentatively turned the knob next to the faucet. Water coming straight into the house certainly would have advantages. Cold water drenched the towel, and Ella wrung out the excess. As she filled a glass with water as well, she wondered how quickly influenza might infect the Amish. Had she already invited germs into her own body by touching Lindy? What about the men in jail? The children at Wayfarers? The students in the consolidated schools already experiencing absences? When Cleveland closed its schools, towns like Seabury ought to have done the same.

Ella was not going to leave Lindy suffering because of her own fear that she might catch the disease—if it even was influenza. Without hesitation, she carried the damp cloth and the glass of water to Lindy's bedroom.

David returned just as Ella coaxed Lindy to sip the water.

"It's not there," he said.

"My birdhouse is gone?" Lindy pushed away the glass. "Has someone smashed in *again*?"

"No," David said. "There's no sign of vandalism this time. But there are a few things missing. And I found this on the workbench."

He handed a note to Ella.

You're getting what you deserve. Stop helping those people.

"That's it," Ella said. "I'm going to see Deputy Fremont."

"What does it say?" Lindy asked.

Ella ignored the question and turned to David. "You're staying here, right?"

He nodded.

"Fluids," Ella said. "Whether or not it's flu, she needs fluids. I'll be back."

Ella marched through the Seabury blocks until she reached the sheriff's outpost. Deputy Fremont looked up and raised an eyebrow. Ella pressed the note flat on the desk in front of him.

"Someone left this for Lindy Lehman," Ella said. "Is this not grounds for further investigation?"

Fremont glanced at the note. "How do I know where the note came from?"

"I just told you. Someone left it for Lindy. David Kaufman just found it on her workbench—and more items are missing from her workshop."

"Why isn't Lindy here on her own behalf?" Fremont asked.

"She's ill."

"Not the influenza, I hope."

"'I suppose that would be for a doctor to say."

"Is the boy ill?"

"No," Ella said. "Not so far."

"I can't go where there's flu," Fremont said. "That will only spread the sickness."

"But someone is threatening Lindy," Ella said, "and it's because of her kindness to the Amish in the school question."

"That's a moot point now." Fremont nudged the note to one side of his desk. "I just had a phone call from Chardon. The men have agreed to send their children to school."

❧✽☙

Finally Gideon's farm was in sight, the familiar roll of ground under barren trees wrapped in a warning of the winter to come. Had it snowed while he was in that windowless cell picturing his children crying themselves to sleep or his betrothed hustling between Rachel's bereft spirit and Miriam's frail health?

The truck did not make the turn down his lane. Instead, the driver, wordless, stopped where the paved road gave way to gravel in one direction and simply waited for Gideon to disembark. Gideon shook the hands of the two remaining passengers, supposing their throats to be as thick with anticipation as his own. He had taken nothing with him when the sheriff came last week, and he carried nothing with him now. One of three horses in his pasture noticed him and trotted to the fence, where Gideon scratched its neck. Then he turned his head toward the house. With each step, he hoped for an outburst of some sort. Savilla impatient with Gertie. Pans clattering from the kitchen. Miriam chastising chickens who had dared too close to the front porch.

But he heard nothing, which only made his chest clench more deeply.

Without going in, Gideon rounded one side of his home and followed the path to the *dawdihaus*. He knocked softly. The door swung wide, and Miriam tumbled into his embrace. When she pulled her neck from the curve of Gideon's neck, she shouted for James, who emerged from the bedroom and strode across the sitting room.

"A cake!" Miriam pronounced. "We need a cake. I'll put jelly between the layers."

Gideon laughed and tried to pull her back, but Miriam was already headed out the door to the main house where she kept her best baking dishes.

"There's no stopping her now," James said.

"I was afraid she might be unwell," Gideon said.

"She is," James said quietly. "In an hour, she will refuse to admit how tired she is."

"Then we should stop her," Gideon said. "I don't need a cake."

"No, but she needs to make you one."

They had ambled outside as they spoke, and now Gideon raised his head to the welcome sight of the Hilty buggy traversing the hardened cold ground. He ran to greet Ella, and she leaped off the bench into his arms and leaned fully against him. Her winter bonnet slid off her head, and even through her prayer *kapp* Gideon could smell the invigorating scent of her hair. He inhaled and wrapped his arms around her, resolving not to be the first to disturb the embrace.

Finally, without letting go of him, Ella turned her face up. Gideon kissed her mouth before she could release the torrent of questions rising through her throat. She tasted of the brisk air she must have been gulping all the way to his farm.

"The children?" she finally said.

"Not yet," Gideon said. "But they promised today."

Arm in arm, they went inside the house, where Ella deftly took over the responsibilities of stirring cake batter, arranging wood to produce the proper temperature, and setting the pans in the heat.

When the pans came out of the oven and the children were not home, the mood sobered.

When the cake was cool enough to frost and still the children were not there, silence shrouded the darkening kitchen.

Gideon watched the sky grow gray. James coaxed Miriam into the front room where she could rest more comfortably. Ella frosted the cake and sat down at the kitchen table beside Gideon.

"I want to be here," she said, leaning against his shoulder, "but. . ."

"But Rachel is waiting alone," Gideon said. He kissed the top of her head. "Go. If Seth comes home, you will know my children are also home."

"I'll come first thing in the morning," Ella said. "I know they have to go to school, but I can't wait all day to see them."

Gideon walked Ella to her buggy for a reluctant good-bye. Then he followed the buggy up the lane and watched her disappear around the curve in the road. He stood for ten silent gloomy minutes, praying that it would be God's will for the sheriff to keep his word, before he saw the flicker of an automobile headlight.

Then came the sound of the motor.

Then came the shadowed shape of a bus.

Then came the cries of his children's voices.

Then came the tumble of arms and legs of his offspring safe in his embrace.

❦

Margaret never liked to admit to favorites among her pupils, but the sight of Gertie Wittmer back in her seat, swinging her feet, warmed Margaret with satisfaction. Beside Gertie, Hans Byler sat straight and attentive. Even with his hat on his head, Margaret could tell it would be weeks before his hair would grow back out to a proper Amish boy's haircut. At least they had not cut Gertie's hair. Her braids still wound neatly against the sides of her head.

But even with Gertie and Hans back, the number of students absent from Margaret's classroom had risen to five. In a sober impromptu meeting with all the teachers after the final bell, Principal Tarkington relayed the somber news that Geauga County officials were dispatching nurses to make the rounds and determine the severity of the influenza outbreak that had reached even Seabury.

Margaret gathered her things and walked the six blocks to her house, which had grown cold in her absence. She turned the knob on the radiator in the front room and heated the oven in the kitchen.

She had promised Gray a pie. Probably the last one. Perhaps

they would not even get so far into the evening as to eat it. His last visit to her home had ended in an argument. What might he be expecting tonight?

When she had the pie in the oven, Margaret found she could not bring herself to sit quietly and wait for Gray. The sun was long set, but Margaret did not care. She donned a coat, took a bushel basket from the back porch, lit a lantern, and pulled dead growth from the spent flower bed along the side of the house.

She had expected to have time to straighten herself up before Gray's arrival, but he startled her with an early appearance. Surely it was not seven thirty yet. She pulled her gardening gloves from her hands and raised her fingers to her cold cheeks. In the darkness, he drew near.

Margaret wanted him to kiss her. This might be the last kiss in her entire life, and in this moment, she wanted it very much. His warm breath settled on her face as he leaned in, and she willingly raised her lips to meet his. His kiss deepened, more than ever before, and she allowed it. Once they began to speak, the exquisite moment would be gone, and she might never know another like it.

Finally, dizzy with the truth she must speak, Margaret pulled away.

"I have to tell you something," she said.

His hand on her waist, he sought her mouth again, but she stepped back, her knees weak.

"It's important," she said. Her words raced. "I took the Amish mothers to the Wayfarers Home for Children. I didn't think it was right to keep them apart, and I went to their farms to pick them up and drive them over there."

He put a finger on her lips. "I can forgive that."

Margaret took another step back. She had not asked for his forgiveness. In fact, she felt no need for repentance. Her lips parted in preparation of saying so when the thrash in the bushes made them both turn their heads.

Margaret bent to lift the lantern on the ground beside them. Gray lunged toward the noise. Someone had stumbled and fallen into the overgrown hydrangea bush and was now flailing in a foiled attempt to find the way out. Gray reached into the shadowed mass with one long arm.

"Braden!" Gray said as he pulled the intruder into the light of Margaret's lantern.

Margaret's eyes rolled to the flour sack Braden gripped in one fist. This time she did not hesitate to snatch it away from him and pull it open.

"These things belong to Lindy," she said. She tipped the open end toward Gray.

Gray pulled the lapels of his brother's jacket. "What are you doing with someone else's property?"

"What is it to you?" Braden's eyes flashed. "The Amish are no friends of yours, either."

"Whatever happened in the past," Gray said, his jaw barely moving, "there is no call for this."

"If Lindy Lehman had married our farmhand, he never would have run out on me."

"That's water under the bridge," Gray said.

"I'm just paying her back for ruining my life. I could still be on the farm instead of selling for half what it was worth."

"You could have hired another hand, but you're so mean no one wanted to work for you."

"Do you mean to tell me this is all over some old grudge?" Margaret twisted the top of the flour sack closed. "I'm going in to telephone the sheriff's department."

CHAPTER 38

Saturday's quilting bee had even more children underfoot than usual. None of the mothers whose children had been away wanted them farther than the women could call. Even Seth, Tobias, and the Mast boys were there on the Glick farm with instructions not to wander off. Fortunately for the older boys, a creek ran through the Glick property, and as long as they could stand the brisk temperatures, Ella was certain they would occupy themselves. If they got cold, they could retreat to the barn and find something to do there. Hans Byler, though, was required to remain at his mother's side in her place around the quilting frame that filled most of the room. He leaned against his mother with one hand on her back. Under ordinary circumstances, he might have been whispering in her ear that he wanted to go play with the bigger boys, but Ella was fairly certain that the six-year-old was right where he wanted to be.

"They're not required to ride the bus," Mrs. Mast said. "They're only required to be in school."

"It's a long way to walk." Mrs. Hershberger held up a needle to the light to find its eye with her strand of white thread.

"My boys are old enough to take a buggy on their own," Mrs. Mast said. "They would have room for others."

Gertie sat on a chair between Ella and Miriam with a square of fabric on which to practice her stitching. Hans was nearby. The stair-step Hershberger children dotted the room. Perhaps the *kinner* ought not hear this discussion.

"Isaiah said he is going to take ours himself," Mrs. Borntrager said.

Gideon had said the same thing—either he or James would transport the three Wittmer children. Tobias had handled his first two days in the consolidated school well. The teachers had given him a long list of assignments to get him caught up to the other pupils. Gideon still hoped it would only be a matter of a few weeks before the Amish would be in their own school.

"Let's talk about something else," Miriam said, for which Ella was grateful.

"We have a wedding coming up." Mrs. King's eyes twinkled. "Less than a month to go."

Mrs. Hershberger smiled behind one hand. "Shh. We aren't supposed to know until the banns are published in church."

Ella carefully poked her needle through the block she was quilting. Mrs. Hershberger was right, according to tradition, and Ella usually shied away from being the center of attention. Maybe her wedding memories would always include the shadow cast over her engagement by the new education laws, but she hoped not.

Rachel laughed heartily aloud, a sound Ella had not heard for weeks. "Of course the banns will be published," she said, "but it's time to buckle down and get the house ready, so it will hardly be a secret what's going on."

From there the conversation turned to the usual tasks of preparing a home for a wedding—moving the furniture, scrubbing down the floors, arranging the food. Ella listened but said little. Everyone seemed relieved to be talking about something normal.

Ella pulled her needle up through the layers of backing, batting, and quilt top and turned to glance at Gertie.

The girl's chair was empty.

"Miriam," Ella said, "where did Gertie go?"

They both looked around.

"I'm surprised she sat still as long as she did," Miriam said.

Ella pushed the end of her needle into the quilt to mark her spot. "I'm going to find her."

Gertie might have gone outside, and she didn't want the child playing alone along the frigid creek. Instead, she found Gertie swinging her feet below the kitchen table while the tip of her tongue poked through one corner of her mouth. Gertie was bent over a sheet of paper, pushing a thick pencil.

"Gertie, did you get into Mrs. Glick's things?" Ella sat down across from Gertie.

"It was on the table," Gertie said. She stilled her hands in her lap.

Gently, Ella slid the paper away from Gertie. "You should have asked if you needed something."

"It's just a list for the mercantile," Gertie said, "and everything was crossed off."

Ella didn't see the mercantile list on the back side of the sheet. She saw only a meticulous rendering of the quilt pattern the women were working on in the other room. Ella knew little about art, but she had studied enough drawings of birds to recognize a close likeness when she saw one. The detail. The shading. The proportions.

It seemed to Ella to be as close to the real thing as one might hope for, apart from a photograph that an *English* might take.

"Are you going to show it to *Daed*?" Anxiety crossed Gertie's face.

Ella licked her lips. She wasn't sure. Gideon would not be pleased, but she was on the brink of marrying him. Keeping secrets about his children hardly seemed the right thing to do.

The kitchen door opened, and Rachel bustled in. "I've got to go. Mrs. Byler is not at all well. I'm going to take her home."

Ella stood up. "I'll go with you."

"No need," Rachel said. "I'll just make sure she gets home and come back. There's plenty of quilting yet to do."

Rachel left, and Ella turned to Gertie. "Let's go back and help with the quilt." She folded the drawing in half and tucked it under the bib of her apron.

"It's the flu the soldiers have been bringing home from Europe, now that the war has finished," Mrs. Mast said as Ella took her place around the quilt frame.

Ella thought of finding Lindy hot and clammy a few days earlier. James had been to see Lindy and assured Ella she was mending. If Mrs. Byler had the flu, how many others would fall to it? A quilting bee had seemed like an innocent return to Amish friendship after the tension of the last few weeks. Now Ella was not so sure.

Gideon hardly knew what to think. His six-year-old daughter had created a stunning drawing of a traditional Amish quilt pattern. As a boy, he had slept under one very similar that his own mother had stitched.

"It's like a picture in a library book," Ella said.

The children were upstairs. The girls were supposed to be sleeping, and Tobias working on school assignments. James and Miriam had just withdrawn to the *dawdihaus*. Soon Gideon would tell Tobias that he was taking Ella home.

Only a few more weeks, she told herself, and no one would have to fret about how she would get home on a night heavy with winter air. She would already be home. Right here in this kitchen, with her husband beside her. Then they could talk all night if they wanted to.

"She has a gift, Gideon," Ella said.

"It's not the kind of gift our people are used to," he said. "It's the kind of gift that may lead to pride in what she has done—something that others cannot do."

"But it's beautiful, just as the quilt itself is beautiful," Ella said. "How is it so different?"

"The women quilt for practicality," Gideon said. "We need warmth."

"Then why don't we just sew together squares of burlap?" Ella countered. "Couldn't we stuff them with old copies of *The Budget* and be just as warm?"

"The beauty in a quilt is a thanksgiving for God's provision of our need," Gideon said. He put a finger on the drawing. "This is a vain display."

"We hang quilts over racks," Ella said, "or on walls. Even spreading a quilt on top of a bed is a way of displaying it. It's all beauty that comes from God's hand. Is it so wrong for Gertie to learn her own way of this same beauty?"

Gideon scratched under his beard. "Last summer she was drawing in the dirt with a stick. Even then I could tell she saw more than other children. And then there was the picture from school."

"What picture?"

Gideon left the room and returned a moment later with Gertie's self-portrait. He laid it on the table beside the quilt drawing.

"We must help her know what this means," Ella said, looking from one drawing to the other. "If she grows up afraid of it, we may lose her."

Gideon took the hand Ella laid open on the table. "You are the mother's heart my children need."

She smiled, and he leaned across the table to kiss her.

"Now I must go check on Miriam," Gideon said. "Then I'd better get you home."

With their coats buttoned up against the dropping temperatures, they walked together to the *dawdihaus*, where lamps still glowed within.

James and Miriam were sipping tea in the sitting room. Miriam was sitting up, and her bright eyes greeted them. Ella exhaled relief. She had been afraid that the long day of quilting, which Miriam had refused to curtail, would have worn her out.

"I trust Mrs. Byler will recover quickly," Ella said.

"I hope it's not the influenza," Miriam said. "It would be so much nicer if she is unwell because she is with child."

"Time will tell," Ella said.

"Speaking of influenza," James said, "I wish we had word about Lindy. I'm going to town first thing Monday, as soon as the Sabbath is over."

"David would let us know if she took a turn for the worse," Gideon said. Even without using a telephone number to call, a boy savvy enough to find a way to school in town right under his parents' noses would find a way to send a message to Lindy's family.

⚜

James scrutinized Lindy's movements on Monday. She hardly limped at all. The forced bed rest necessitated by the flu had probably been good for her injured ankle. And five days after Ella found her stricken with sudden illness, Lindy seemed determined—and able—to return to her routine. She poured coffee for both of them while she told the story of Margaret Simpson catching Braden Truesdale red-handed with a bag of wooden toys from Lindy's workshop.

"It's as if he thought he was invincible," Lindy said, "parading around the neighborhood like that a whole day after we discovered the items were missing."

"And the note?" James said.

"It was handwritten," Lindy said, "so it was easy enough to match up to Braden's handwriting. Even Deputy Fremont managed to get a confession."

"But why?" James wanted to know.

"Braden doesn't like the Amish, and I'm the closest person he knows to the Amish." Lindy added milk to her coffee.

"Lindy," James said. "I'm you're *onkel*. I know when you're not telling me everything."

Lindy stirred white milk into black coffee, her eyes set on the resulting caramel color.

James waited.

"I could have married, you know."

James would wait, no matter how slowly Lindy wanted to unfold the truth.

"When Peter Kaufman was courting Rachel, I used to go riding with a young man named Ezekiel. His father had all sons and Ezekiel was the youngest. He had no land left to give Ezekiel, so Ezekiel looked for other work so he could save up a down payment on his own. He hired himself out to the Truesdale farm."

"Truesdale? A farm?"

Lindy nodded. "Ezekiel worked there for years. Gray moved into town, and his parents died within months of each other. The truth is, Braden wasn't much of a farmer. He just liked living out in the middle of nowhere all by himself. It was Ezekiel who kept the farm running."

"So what happened?"

Lindy looked down into her coffee. "He wanted to marry me. I said no. He moved to Kansas. I moved into town."

"And the farm?"

Lindy shrugged. "Braden lived out there on his own, I guess. But he never found another man who would put up with his eccentric ways. Last year I heard that the farm sold to a young Amish couple from Illinois."

James folded his arms across his chest. "Braden must have known who you were."

"I don't know why he would."

"I'm sure Ezekiel talked about you," James theorized. "Braden knew your name. He blames you for losing his farm."

"That's ridiculous."

"Of course it is. That doesn't mean it's not true."

"But *Onkel* James, I never even met Braden Truesdale. I would not have known him if I met him on the street."

"That's what he was counting on. When he moved into town, he discovered you were here. Everyone in town knows you and your crafts. It can't have been hard to find out where you live, especially after David moved in. He still dresses Amish. Anyone could have followed him."

"I would never do anything to endanger David." Lindy's voice cracked. "He's the closest thing I'll ever have to a son of my own."

"I know."

"Even if you're right, it's over." Lindy pushed her coffee away, untouched. "He's not out there skulking anymore. I won't need to look over my shoulder every time I leave the house."

"Where is Braden now?"

"He spent a night in the jail in Seabury before being transferred to Chardon to see a judge. I suppose that will happen today or tomorrow. He already confessed, so it's only a matter of what his sentence will be."

Braden deserved to be in jail for a long time. "Perhaps he will leave town when he gets out," James said.

"Margaret will certainly be watching out for him."

"She's done so much for us," James said.

"It has cost her dearly. I don't expect to see Gray around the neighborhood anymore. He may not be the unstable brother, but he's no friend of the Amish, either."

James sipped coffee and then set the cup down carefully. "What have we done to offend them so?"

Lindy shrugged. "Sometimes all it takes is being different."

James sat silently, looking over Lindy's shoulder to the view outside her window.

"One day we will forgive them for all they have done," Lindy said softly. "Braden, Brownley, Fremont—all of them."

"You have a big heart," James said.

"I'm not so un-Amish that I don't understand the power of forgiveness."

James pushed his cup away. "The important thing is that you are on your feet again. I promised to make deliveries."

"I have a few things that Braden didn't find," Lindy said. "But before you go, tell me how *Aunti* Miriam is."

"Good days and bad." James stood and adjusted his hat. "I don't like to leave her for too long. I'll make the deliveries and then head back to the farm."

"There's a meeting with the school board this afternoon." Lindy set her coffee cup in the sink. "Will you be there?"

"I'll have to see." James doubted he would leave Miriam on her own again that day.

CHAPTER 39

Margaret had not been invited to the late-afternoon meeting of the school board and representatives of the Amish families, but that was the least of her concerns. She closed up her classroom—still five pupils absent—and marched down to Main Street to the building where Mr. Brownley conducted such meetings. In the hall, she paused to compose herself before slipping into the room where the meeting was already in session.

"This is a closed meeting," a young man said.

Margaret recognized him. He worked in Mr. Brownley's office. He had popped up from a seat in the rear of the room where he had been taking notes on a yellow pad.

She smiled pleasantly and said, "I believe I'll stay."

"The men in this room are quite capable of conducting themselves without your assistance," he said.

Annoyance welled, but Margaret contained it.

"I am an appointed member of the consolidation committee," she said. Her official resignation letter was folded in an envelope in her satchel, but she had never submitted it. "I'm quite sure you know who I am, and I assure you I will not bite if you simply permit me to sit beside you."

Margaret lowered herself into a stiff-backed chair against the back wall. With a huff, the young man picked up his pad and began scribbling, no doubt documenting her unwelcome intrusion.

She was relieved to see that Percival Eggar had insisted on meeting around a table, rather than the usual arrangement for school board meetings, where the board members sat in elevated chairs behind a long wooden desk and townspeople were left to present their positions from behind a railing, as if in a courtroom.

Mr. Brownley spoke from the front of the room. Naturally he had taken the seat at the head of the table.

"We agreed to this meeting," he said, "and we will keep our word. But I must warn you that I see few grounds—if any—for altering the arrangement the law demands."

Margaret ground her teeth. He had gotten what he wanted. The Amish children were in school. Now he had the gall to persist in his unflinching position even after he agreed to hear out the Amish fathers.

Percival Eggar spoke from the other side of the table. Margaret was glad to see he had chosen his seat in a manner that balanced Brownley's position.

"We will now begin presenting our case," Percival said. "We understand this is not a courtroom, and we trust that you will honor your word to hear us out."

"I don't have all day," Brownley muttered.

Percival was unperturbed. "We have a number of people who wish to speak, beginning with Bishop Leroy Garber."

The bishop rose and stood behind his chair. "Thank you for agreeing to meet with us. We are peaceful people and have no wish to antagonize anyone. You have acted in what you believe to be the best interests of children for whom you are responsible—on one level. This motivation is one we can admire. However, we respectfully disagree with the belief that what is best for your children is also best for ours. We ask that you hear not only our words, but also our hearts. I have asked Gideon Wittmer, one of the fathers whose children are affected by this crucial decision, to present the substance of our religious views and how they bear on our views of public education."

Margaret wanted to applaud. She had never met the Amish bishop before, and no doubt Percival Eggar had coached him carefully, but she found his speech stirring even if it was merely a preamble to what Gideon had to say.

The bishop seated himself, and Gideon stood. Margaret laid her satchel flat in her lap and settled her hands against the leather.

"We find joy in work," Gideon said simply. "We find joy in

working with our hands, in laboring along with animals created by God, in tilling the soil, in cultivating our gardens. And we find joy in caring for one another, worshipping together in our church district, building together, harvesting together. We find joy in living apart from the ways which seem more 'normal' to you so that we may seek with all our hearts to be closer to God."

Margaret leaned forward, watching Gideon closely as his feet began to wander away from the table.

"Nature is a garden," Gideon continued. "Man is caretaker. God is pleased when man works in harmony with nature, the soil, weather, cares for plants and animals. Christian life is best maintained away from cities.

"We are preparing our children for eternity. Your concern is to educate them for life in the twentieth century, but our concern is that they be prepared to serve God both in this world and the next. The education you propose to offer them—to demand for them—will teach our children to despise the work which we have thrived on for hundreds of years. Colossians 2:8 warns us, 'Beware lest any man spoil you through philosophy and vain deceit, after the tradition of men, after the rudiments of the world, and not after Christ.'

"It is our firm conviction that education beyond the eighth grade, which will lead our children into philosophies of this world, will not prepare them for eternity. Instead, it will lead them away from the ways of the people who know them best and love them most. How will advancing in the ways of this world be in their best interests if it takes them away from their own people?

"Because of these convictions, we cannot separate what we wish our children to learn in school from what we also teach at home. We do not put our religion in one stall of the barn and our learning in another with a wall in between. All of life is in God's hands, and it is there we wish for our children to abide."

Gideon found his chair again. Margaret let out the breath she had been holding, lest even this slight sound distract from Gideon's message. It was Percival Eggar's turn to stand.

"Gentlemen, as you can see, the Amish religion is not about believing something on Sunday and setting it aside for the rest of the week. The Amish truly *believe*. The course that Mr. Wittmer has so ably described is their way of following God. It is their deeply felt faith. I ask you, how can the freedom to demonstrate their beliefs in their actions be denied them in a place like America, which was founded on such liberties?"

⊷❦⊷

"You should have gone," Miriam said to James. "It would have made the most sense for you to stay in town all day."

James shook his head. "What would I have done all day?"

"You could have stayed at Lindy's and you know it," Miriam said. "You should be at that meeting. You only came home because you think you have to look after me."

James lifted the lid on the soup pot, trying not to think about how much of the afternoon Miriam had spent chopping the vegetables and browning the meat. At least she had done most of the work in the small *dawdihaus* kitchen. If she needed to, she could go lie on the bed for a few minutes. But moments ago the bus had dropped the children off at the top of the lane, and now Gertie pressed up against him.

"Are we going to make biscuits to go with the soup?" Gertie asked.

"Maybe there's some bread in the bread box," James said.

"But I like biscuits," Gertie said. "I like when they are fresh from the oven."

"We can make biscuits," Miriam said. "But let's do it in the big house. Then we can put them in the oven the minute your *daed* and *Onkel* James come home from the meeting. By the time they get washed up, it will be time to eat."

Over Gertie's head, James narrowed his eyes at his wife. He had planned to be at the meeting alongside Gideon, but he had already seen Miriam pausing to catch her breath three times that afternoon.

Gertie tugged on Miriam's hand. "Let's go now."

Miriam stumbled slightly, catching herself against the sink.

"Gertrude," James said softly. Instantly, she dropped Miriam's hand and crossed her wrists behind her waist.

"I didn't mean it," Gertie said.

"I know." James reached for the girl's hand. "Let's go see what your brother is up to."

"Lessons and lessons and more lessons," Gertie said.

This was true. Gideon had spoken somberly with Tobias about

his responsibility to represent the Amish well by working hard to catch up with the weeks of school he'd missed, even though they all hoped he could leave school soon. But between Tobias and Savilla, surely they could manage Gertie for a while.

"I'm fine," Miriam said. "Leave her be."

But James led Gertie back to the main house. He would get her settled within eyesight of Tobias and then he would make sure Miriam rested for a few minutes.

❧❀❦

"I'm sorry, but Rachel isn't home," Ella said when Lindy turned up at the Hilty farm. "I know she'd be so glad to see you well enough to make a visit. Can you wait for her?"

"When do you expect her back?"

As she always did when she visited Rachel, Lindy had exchanged her *English* men's trousers for a modest skirt and blouse. It seemed to Ella that despite living in town among the *English* and taking up a livelihood usually left for the men, Lindy never strayed too far from the rich hues of Amish dyes in her clothing.

"She took a meal out to the Bylers," Ella said. "Mrs. Byler was feeling poorly on Saturday, and none of their children is old enough to cook properly."

"I pray she is better soon," Lindy said. "I admit I'd like to rest a bit myself. I feel so much better than I did that day you found me, but between you and me, I'm not quite myself yet."

"Please sit down," Ella said, gesturing toward the davenport.

Lindy sank into the cushions. "I wanted to tell Rachel in person how well David cared for me. I had to insist that he go back to school this morning. He's such a tender boy."

"Let me get you a glass of water," Ella said. It couldn't have been wise of Lindy to drive all the way out here on her own.

"Actually," Lindy said, waving off the offer of refreshment, "I'm glad I caught you. James came to check on me this morning and make a few deliveries. I got the idea that Miriam is not as well as she might be."

Ella sighed. "I'm not sure what to make of her. James says she has good days and bad days, but I think more likely she manages to push through better on some days than others. I do as much as I can. It will be easier after the wedding."

"Let's go see her," Lindy said. "I have my car. It won't take us ten minutes to drive over there."

"Are you sure you're up to it?"

"It's only a few miles. I'll rest better myself if I know Miriam is all right."

Ella nodded. "Let's go."

Ella felt as if she had barely settled herself into the automobile seat before Lindy pulled onto Gideon's farm.

"Let's try the *dawdihaus* first," she suggested.

James answered the door, but Miriam was right behind him.

"Well, now, there's a sensible solution," Miriam said.

Ella and Lindy looked at each other and then at Miriam.

"This old fool ought to be at that meeting in town," Miriam said, "but he refuses to leave me. He thinks I'm going to fall into the soup pot or something."

"It's too late now," James said. "By the time I get there, the meeting will be over."

Miriam rolled her eyes. Ella laughed nervously.

"Ella can stand guard," Miriam said. "You'll have no excuse to stay. We'll go over to the big house and make sure Gertie minds herself."

"I'd be happy to," Ella said.

Miriam pointed at Lindy. "And you, my dear niece, can drive your stubborn *onkel* into town in your motorcar while there's still a chance for him to hear what is happening at that meeting."

Lindy grinned. "I'll crank it up."

CHAPTER 40

Had the young man always been so arrogant?

At the whispered pronouncement that the meeting was nearly completed and spectators were not being admitted, James merely stared at the young man. No one could mistake James for anything but an Amish man, and denying admittance to the Amish would defeat the point of the meeting. James nodded slightly at Margaret Simpson and stepped past the young man.

As he approached the table, his eye on an empty chair, Superintendent Brownley scowled.

"You have presented some interesting ideas," Brownley said, "but I am afraid I've heard nothing that allows me to interpret the law in a way that excuses your children from regular school attendance at least until the age of sixteen."

James watched the faces of the other members of the school board. At least one of them appeared sympathetic, though James could not be certain what was going through the man's mind.

Percival Eggar cleared his throat. "You may be right, Mr. Brownley."

Amish brows furrowed around the table.

"You may be correct that this question is beyond the scope of your authority to decide."

"I have wide authority," Brownley said. "I assure you I don't take my responsibilities lightly."

"I would never accuse you of such a thing," Percival said. "But it seems clear after today that the question is one for the courts."

"That's an extreme measure." Brownley shifted in his chair.

"I am prepared to represent my clients right through to the Supreme Court of the United States, if that is how they will find justice and the freedom to exercise the religion of their choice."

James blew out a loud, heavy breath, and attention turned toward him.

"I don't believe this guest has been introduced," Brownley said.

Percival answered, "This is Mr. James Lehman, the man who first engaged my services on behalf of the Amish. I would be quite interested in what he has to say at this juncture."

Brownley leaned back in his chair. "Very well."

Percival nodded at James, who looked from Percival to Gideon. What had the others already said?

"I'm at a disadvantage," James said. "I was not able to be present for the earlier portion of the conversation."

"That's no problem," Percival said quickly. "We will all benefit from your individual expression of your views."

"All right, then." James adjusted his hat. Miriam hated that nervous habit. "We accept that others do not believe as we do. We do not judge or try to convert anyone who does not come to us sincerely seeking to follow God and with a willingness to make whatever sacrifice that requires.

"Our work, whatever it may be, is for the welfare of the community we share. We do not seek individual prestige. Jesus said, 'My kingdom is not of this world.' The apostle Paul said, 'Be not conformed to this world.' Our people seek to believe these statements wholeheartedly, as the true word of God."

James glanced at Percival, uncertain whether to continue. He had not intended to speak at all. Surely Gideon and the bishop had explained these matters.

"Please go on, Mr. Lehman," Percival said.

"As I'm sure you have already heard," James said, "we do not separate school from life. But how can our children know this connection if we send them from our world into a world far from our homes to learn from teachers who know nothing of our ways? And if they are trained for a way of life that is at odds with our community, then how are they to know where they belong? Have any of us served the best interests of the children if we create this confusion for them?

"It is our firm belief that eight years of schooling, close to home and focused on the basics of reading, writing, and mathematics, suffice for preparing our children to contribute to the community to which they belong. Beyond this, public schools impart worldly knowledge that is not useful for living spiritually in this life and for all eternity."

James swiftly pulled out the empty chair and occupied it. From the back of the room came the sound of two hands patting each other with enthusiasm.

⊰⊱

Margaret rose to her feet, letting her satchel slide to the floor, and applauded with as much gusto she could muster. Around the table from which she had been excluded, every head turned in her direction. One pair of startled eyes after another fixed on her.

"Bravo, Mr. Lehman," she said. "Bravo."

Mr. Brownley let one hand fall heavily against the table. "Miss Simpson, please contain yourself."

At first, Margaret pressed her lips together, but before a single second passed, she began to march to the front of the room.

"I cannot hold my tongue any longer," she said. "Have you not heard the fine rhetoric of Bishop Garber, Mr. Wittmer, and now Mr. Lehman? Does it not strike you that each of these men has achieved an impressive level of articulate expression without the benefit of education in a consolidated school? I cannot think of a more remarkable illustration of the power of values that come from the heart, rather than a textbook."

"Thank you, Miss Simpson." Mr. Brownley glared, as he always did. Scowl and glare, scowl and glare.

Margaret ignored him. "Mr. Brownley originally asked me to serve on the consolidation committee. My approach was very different than his, however. While at first I was eager to present the virtues of our town schools and the many benefits the rural students would enjoy, gradually I realized the error of my way. If the Amish children are to have any benefit from attending our schools, it can only come if we make an effort to understand them.

"I am a classroom teacher, and I have spoken with teachers of other grades. It has been clear to all of us that the Amish children are more than capable of completing the work we assign, which is a credit to the Amish families and a testament to the schooling they received in the smaller settings that we have arrogantly come to regard as insufficient. I have not heard one account of an Amish child instigating a disturbance among the students. In contrast, I am ashamed of some of the town children, who have been rude bullies intent on ridiculing people they don't know just because they are different. And where, I ask you, did they learn such behavior?"

Margaret stared hard at Mr. Brownley, then moved her eyes with deliberation to the other members of the board.

Mr. Brownley pushed back from the table and stood up. "Miss Simpson, I must ask you once again to contain yourself. This is not a matter for you to decide."

"Isn't it?" Margaret retorted. "Would you rather it go to the Supreme Court, as Mr. Eggar suggests, than we learn from our Amish friends and find a way to care for our own? If the state truly wants what is best for the Amish children, we will listen to what the parents have to say. We will find a way to work together, rather than at odds."

"Please take your seat." Brownley nearly growled.

Margaret glanced at the chair she had abandoned against the back wall. Then she walked to an empty chair between two board members and sat down.

CHAPTER 41

Gideon could hardly believe that Miss Simpson was capable of such oratory, and in the presence of men. He watched Brownley carefully.

"I must insist that we return to some semblance of order." In his chair again, Mr. Brownley shuffled papers in front of him. "I fail to see how threatening to take a local matter to the Supreme Court of the United States accomplishes anything. We all know that such a process takes years."

"I have all the patience in the world," Percival Eggar said. "I will ensure that my clients receive due consideration."

"My hands are tied, Mr. Eggar," Brownley said.

"We would be glad to help you untie them, Mr. Brownley."

Gideon moistened his lips. "May I suggest what I consider to be an ideal solution?"

"Please do, Mr. Wittmer," Brownley said. The words were correct and polite, but Gideon had no confidence the superintendent would see the virtue in his proposal.

"As you know, we already have a school building that was constructed at no cost to the public school district, the town of Seabury, or the county of Geauga."

Brownley's eyes narrowed, but he was listening.

"All we ask now," Gideon said, "is permission to operate a private school to serve Amish students."

"It seems to me that is what you already attempted," Brownley said.

Gideon nodded.

"But your teacher was not qualified."

Actually, Ella was well qualified. Gideon said, "It has been our intention all along to attract a teacher whose credentials the state would recognize. I regret that this process has taken longer than I had hoped, but it is still the course of action we intend to pursue."

"Surely," Margaret said, "this is a reasonable compromise at least for the younger children."

"But this teacher would not be Amish," Brownley said.

Gideon kept silent. This gathering was not the place to reveal the fullness of his middle-of-the-night wrestlings with almighty God.

"Perhaps," Percival said, "all we need at this point is your agreement that the Amish families will be unhindered in their pursuit of establishing a private school. I will work closely with them on the necessary legal details."

"Suppose we were to agree to this proposal," Brownley said. "Am I correct in assuming that such a school would only go through the eighth grade?"

All the Amish fathers at the table were quick to nod.

"Then we will have solved only half of the problem," Brownley said. "I cannot recommend to the state authorities a solution that does not guarantee that the older children will also receive an appropriate education."

Gideon was well aware of this dilemma. Next year Tobias would be old enough for high school. Even if the girls were safely in the care of a teacher who understood the Amish ways, Tobias would be expected to enroll at the high school—unless Gideon insisted that his son remain in the eighth grade for three years.

"With all due respect," Percival said, "the point my clients—and Miss Simpson—have argued today is that for Amish children, completing the eighth grade *is* an appropriate education."

Brownley shook his head. "But the law is specific. Students must attend school until the age of sixteen."

"Unless they have work permits," Percival said.

Gideon's shoulders straightened.

"We are not talking about children who will be idle or unsupervised," Percival said. "They will not be lurking around the streets stirring up trouble or burdening society. When the Amish students leave school, they take up their share of work on the farm or in the family business. In fact, it is my understanding that the labor they provide is essential to the financial success of Amish enterprises."

Percival glanced at Gideon and the bishop, who both nodded.

"If they have work permits and demonstrate that they are in fact working, students between ages fourteen and sixteen may be excused from school."

Gideon marveled that Percival had not mentioned this to him before.

"That seems a stretch," Brownley said, predictably.

"Not to me." For the first time, a new voice spoke.

Gideon looked across the table at a member of the school board who had remained in Brownley's shadow for the duration of the meeting—and for all the weeks preceding.

"I think we should consider that possibility," the board member said.

Gideon looked around the table. Chester Mast and Isaiah Borntrager had allowed smiles to form behind their beards. Miss Simpson was grinning.

"I will prepare a full presentation," Percival said. "My assistant will contact you to establish a date to meet and ensure that every point of law has been adequately covered in our agreement."

❧

"I heard what you did."

Gray's words did not surprise Margaret. That he would speak them at all had been uncertain in her mind for all of the preceding twenty-four hours, but she had known he would hear of her bold actions on Monday afternoon. All of Seabury must have heard by the time they finished dessert on Monday evening. Margaret would not have been startled to discover her presence at the school board's meeting had made the headline of the Seabury newspaper.

And now here was Gray, leaning casually against the brick wall of the school as he often did, as if he just happened to be there when she exited the building.

Few occasions in her life had stolen her words, but this was one of them. She stepped an extra foot away from him, out of the circle of his scent. She would need her wits about her.

"I had hoped you'd gotten it out of your system when you took those mothers out to the home," he said.

Margaret's throat went dry. "I've only done what I truly thought was the right thing to do."

"Speaking at that meeting, Margaret? What were you thinking?"

In their last conversation, he had said he could forgive her for getting involved with the mothers. They had not gotten so far as establishing that she was not sorry. She wasn't sorry then, and she wasn't sorry now.

"If I. . .caused you any. . .embarrassment," she said, "please know that was never my intention."

He turned his head to one side and chuckled. "And we thought the ladies at church were gossiping about us just for sitting together in worship."

"Yes. I suppose they've moved on to more consuming matters now."

"Why is it so important to you that you would. . ."

"You can say it, Gray. Why is it so important that I would risk the fondness that has taken such gentle root between us?"

"You have a prettier way with words than I ever will," he said, "but that's the gist."

Margaret gripped her satchel handle with both hands, bracing herself to look Gray in the face without wishing he would take her face in his hands and kiss her persuasively.

"Who else was standing up for them?" she said.

"Maybe they didn't need anyone to stand up for them." Gray shuffled his feet. "I thought they liked to mind their own business."

"I wish you could have heard them speak yesterday," Margaret said. "They want nothing more than to care for themselves and do what is best for their families and their church. *We* are the ones who wouldn't let them."

"Things change, Margaret. This is not the sixteenth century anymore—or even the nineteenth."

"I know. But their *children*, Gray. The sheriff's department took their *children* just to send a message about who was in control. I suppose that was the last straw for me."

"It's over now, isn't it?"

"I hope so. We'll see if Mr. Brownley will keep his word."

Gray shrugged. "They have Percival Eggar now. They won't need you."

Margaret reached into her satchel and pulled out an envelope. "I'm going to drop this off with Mr. Brownley now. It's my official letter of resignation from the consolidation committee."

"Does it even matter now?"

"Maybe not to the superintendent. It matters to me. I don't want anyone thinking for even one more day that I in any way approved of the tactics used against the Amish."

"Then that's that," Gray said. He inched closer. "We won't ever have to talk about this again. We'll look back on it as a disturbance and nothing more."

"We'll look back on it." He still offered hope. He would still have her.

But the strings already constricted her heart. He would have her because he believed nothing would ever prompt such behavior from her again, or because he believed that once they married she would better adapt to the decisions he would make for the both of them. That he would indulge in this wishful thinking revealed how firmly he had begun to regard their futures as intertwined, and this thought softened her posture.

"I'm sorry, Gray." As soon as Margaret spoke the words, she recognized the space they left for misinterpretation, so she continued quickly. "I'm sorry to disappoint you. I'm sorry I hurt you. I'm sorry that I won't get to bake pies and wait for you on Thursday evenings or sit beside you in church."

I'm sorry I won't be your wife.

I'm sorry we won't grow old together.

I'm sorry I let you hope for this long.

The Amish children would never be behind them, but between them.

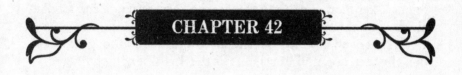

CHAPTER 42

Ella stood for a moment on Wednesday outside the schoolhouse before going in, savoring her mind's image of children carrying their lunch buckets and books, arriving to greet the teacher and begin the day.

She turned toward the touch on the back of her shoulder. Gideon's approach had escaped her perception, but the sight of him warmed her.

"What are you thinking?" Gideon asked.

"I was imagining the school open and thriving," Ella said, looking at the man who would soon be her husband. How good God was to turn Gideon's heart toward Ella.

"We *will* thrive," he said.

"We just need a teacher."

His answer came a few seconds later than Ella expected. "God will provide."

She allowed silence to linger as they gazed at the schoolhouse and Gideon's fingers grazed hers. Only three more weeks and she could be in his arms every day. Every night.

"It will be odd not to have *English* students like the ones we knew when we were children," Ella said. "Sally Templeton and I sat side by side for four years. I sometimes wonder whatever happened to her."

"High school, I suppose," Gideon said.

"Yes, no doubt." Sally would have gone to high school in town about the time Ella's mother passed away. Ella had always expected to take her share of the farm chores after she finished school, but having to keep house for her father on her own was a startling surprise. Not a day had passed in the last twelve years that Ella did not think of her mother and how her own life might have been different if her mother was still the woman keeping house and tending children on the Hilty farm.

Ella looked around. "Where are the *kinner*? I thought they had the afternoon off of school for the Thanksgiving holiday tomorrow."

"Miriam insisted Gertie would be underfoot here," Gideon said. "The sensible thing was to keep them all home. James is coming later."

"In time for the meeting?"

Gideon nodded. "We should go in."

They walked together down the gentle slope. Chester Mast had propped open the door, and his sons were carrying in a set of shelves.

"A place to put the lunch buckets and coats," Gideon said. "This time when we open, we'll be more than ready. Percival says we must not give Mr. Brownley any reason to suggest that we are falling short even in a small way."

Inside, while the Masts debated the most useful position for the heavy shelving, Ella and Gideon exchanged one last smile before parting. Gideon crossed the room to join the men stacking wood for the stove in one corner, and Ella joined the women organizing supplies.

"Here's Ella now," Rachel said.

Lindy stood beside her friend, looking more stable on her feet than Ella had judged her to be two days ago.

"Ella," Lindy said, "did you find it more useful to keep extra paper for the pupils in the teacher's desk or in a separate cupboard?"

Lindy gestured, and Ella's eyes widened at the wide cupboard on the side wall.

"It's lovely!" Ella said. The young woman who accepted a position teaching here would have every reason to be pleased with the schoolhouse and its furnishings.

"It's probably a good thing we had nothing like this when we were girls," Rachel said. "I would have hidden in the cupboard to avoid spelling tests."

Lindy laughed. "And I never would have told the teacher you were there."

"What about when you were a teacher?" Rachel asked. "Did you have students like that?"

Ella drew a startled breath. How had she forgotten Lindy's years in the classroom? Ella had been ten or eleven, old enough to remember her teachers. What else had she blotted out in the years after her mother's death?

"I was never a teacher." Lindy waved a hand. "It was all my parents' idea. The *English* teacher needed an extra pair of hands with the little ones, so I came in to help. I was sixteen, and my parents didn't know what to do with me after. . ."

Ella knew the unspoken end of Lindy's sentence. After she decided that she did not want to be baptized and join the Amish congregation as an adult member.

"Did you think about becoming a teacher?" Ella asked.

Lindy shook her head. "Rachel married Peter Kaufman when we were nineteen, and it was time for me to make my own way. Marriage was not for me. I moved to town and started selling small crafts."

"You've done well," Ella murmured. She stepped toward the cupboard and ran her fingers over the smooth pine finish. Surely Gideon knew Lindy had once assisted a teacher. He must. Lindy was his sister-in-law. Betsy would have told him. Ella glanced across the room at Gideon, who was stoking the woodstove. The room was chilly, and he would want it warm enough for the meeting that everyone would be attentive.

Someone opened the front door again, and cold air whooshed into the schoolhouse. Ella shuddered against the sudden sensation and, like everyone else, looked to see who had arrived.

"It's Miss Simpson," she said, surprised.

Margaret's arms overflowed with books and binders, and Ella rushed to catch the items threatening to topple off the precarious stack.

"I've brought things a teacher might like to have," Margaret explained as she divested her load on the nearest desk. "This will be such a nice place to teach. So cozy!"

The room was warming nicely, and Margaret shed her coat.

"I have some old textbooks for the younger children that have plenty of wear left in them. After all, learning to read doesn't change much, does it?"

Ella picked up a thick gray binder. "Neither does making sums, I guess."

"Those are old lesson plans," Margaret said. "They worked well for me when I taught in a one-room schoolhouse. Maybe another teacher would find them of help in getting started."

"I'm sure any teacher would be grateful to have all this," Ella said. "Any progress on the search?"

Ella shook her head. "The teachers college has no candidates to recommend at this point in time. Apparently Gideon was about to respond to an inquiry when Deputy Fremont arrested him. When she didn't hear back from him, the candidate took another position."

"That is unfortunate," Margaret said.

Margaret flipped open a binder and began explaining its contents. Ella listened politely but not attentively. All of this would make sense to a trained teacher, so Ella did not need to absorb the information. Instead, she wondered whether Margaret had burned her bridges with the school district. Would she be seeking a new position? After all Margaret had done for the Amish families, Ella could think of no solution more perfect.

"Margaret," she said.

"I know what you're thinking," Margaret said without looking up from the binder. "But I don't expect Mr. Brownley will be eager to continue our association, and if this school is going to succeed, the last thing you need is a teacher he regards as an adversary."

Ella swallowed back her hope. Margaret was right.

"What will you do?" Ella asked.

"My sister writes me letter upon letter about how much she misses me," Margaret said. "I'm thinking of returning to Columbus next summer."

A stone of disappointment sank down into Ella's abdomen. She raised her gaze at the somber sound of Gideon's voice.

"Let's gather," he said.

❧

"As you know," Gideon began, "we are here today because all of us would like to see our own school open as soon as possible."

The nods Gideon expected greeted him.

"An Amish teacher would be best," he said, "and I'm sure you would agree that we are opening a school in the first place because we want the best for our children."

He dared not meet Ella's eyes. Not in this moment. Not when his resolve must not fail.

"That's a cockamamy idea," Aaron King said. "We tried that. It got us arrested."

"A *qualified* Amish teacher," Gideon said. "Even Mr. Brownley would not object to this teacher, because she would demonstrate beyond question that she is more than capable for the job."

Lindy stood up. "I would like to volunteer to teach."

Chester Mast shuffled his feet. "I don't understand," he said. "What qualifications do you have?"

Gideon hoped that having the school on Chester's land would not make him feel he had a particular role above the other parents in the decisions they faced. They would need to form a proper school committee made up of several fathers.

"It's true I haven't been to teachers college," Lindy said. "But for two years I did assist an *English* teacher. I went to a one-room school myself. I understand the environment. I am willing to become qualified if Mr. Eggar can determine a route to qualification other than the teachers college. I might be a bridge between the school board and the church."

"But how long would that take?" Joshua Glick asked.

"Perhaps there is some sort of probationary status," Lindy said, "some way they could let me teach while I prove myself."

Gideon had not expected Lindy's offer. He let his eyes drift to Ella now. Even when she began teaching his daughters and a few others, the plan had always been to find a permanent teacher. The stack of correspondence with the teachers college, on his desk at home, proved this intention. Only the last letter mattered now.

We are unable to assist you further at this time, it said. *We will of course retain your inquiries, and perhaps next summer we will have a recommendation for you when we have new graduates.*

When Gideon began writing to the college, he had hoped for any teacher who might come to a classroom where all of the students were Amish. Only later, within the confines of the small cell he shared with the other men, had his thoughts turned in another direction.

When the church gathered next and the worship service ended, Jed Hilty would rise and invite the entire congregation to his youngest daughter's wedding. How could Gideon speak aloud the thought that pressed more firmly into his mind each day?

He did not want to break Ella's heart.

***

Leaning against the wall, James watched heads angling toward each other and listened to the buzz that rose.

It was an enthusiastic buzz, the sort of sound that filled a space with hope. And after the last few weeks, the people in this room deserved hope.

"I know some of you are uncomfortable with me," Lindy said. "You may even wonder why I am here. I chose not to be baptized into the Amish church. I moved to town. I drive an automobile. I have a telephone. But a teacher from the teachers college would do all those things as well. The difference is that I understand you. I *know* you. I *know* what is in your hearts for your children. You may see the differences between us, but I see the ways our hearts are still one."

It was a speech that made James's chest swell. This was his niece generously offering to set aside the quiet, orderly life she had made for herself to serve the community that had raised her.

But it would not do.

"Well," Isaiah Borntrager said, "we ought to carefully consider this matter. Mr. Eggar has assured us that he will help us see this through. Surely he will uncover some provision in the law that would work in our favor."

Mrs. Hershberger spoke up. "It does seem the next best thing to having one of our own members teach."

"And it might go well for her because she is not Amish," Aaron King said. "Mr. Brownley might be more willing to come to an agreement with a teacher who is not Amish, but Lindy would not teach what we do not wish our children to learn."

"I promise to work closely with the parents," Lindy said.

James caught Gideon's eye. Gideon's nod was so slight that no one else would have discerned it, but James did.

"Might I speak?" James pushed his weight off the wall and

turned his face toward his niece. "Lindy, you are offering a sacrifice that tells me once again what I have always known. Your spirit is right with God, and you love His people."

"*Onkel* James," Lindy said. "I want to do this."

"I believe your heart. But in my judgment, if we are going to demonstrate that we are capable of educating the children of our own community, we must have an Amish teacher from the start."

"I am Amish," Lindy said, "in language and culture and history—all the ways that will matter in the classroom."

James said nothing. Telling his niece that she lacked one qualification, the most essential one in his mind, did not come easily.

"A member of the church," Isaiah said. "That's what you mean."

James met Lindy's eye and nodded.

"I don't see a problem," Isaiah said. "Lindy did not break her baptismal vows. She never made them. She can still be baptized and join the church."

Still James said nothing.

"I have a strong faith," Lindy said quietly.

"Then you will have no trouble with the baptismal vows," Isaiah said.

"If Lindy wants to join the church," James said, "of course we will welcome her. But it's a serious decision. We cannot ask her to stand among us now and make such a promise."

Lindy sat down.

"I'm tired of fighting," John Hershberger said. "If we can have our own school and an understanding teacher, that's enough for me. In my mind, she doesn't have to be a church member."

"We cannot keep having the same discussion—dispute—with Mr. Brownley on this matter," James said. "It is imperative that we prove once and for all that we can teach our own children. Then let him test them and see how well they have done. We must be above reproach. If we have an Amish teacher and the children do well, the matter will be settled."

"Teachers get married," Cristof Byler said. "That's what started us down this road in the first place. We'll just end up back here."

"Right now all we need is the first Amish teacher," James said. "That will give us time to prepare other young women who might feel the call to serve God and the church this way."

The heads turning toward Ella did not escape James's notice.

The door opened and cold air gusted the length of the structure.

"Tobias," Gideon said.

James lurched two steps away from the wall.

"You said to come if *Aunti* Miriam. . ."

CHAPTER 43

They kept vigil. James and Gideon and Ella.

Miriam had appeared well enough on Wednesday morning, other than the fatigue that had been growing for months, but was stricken suddenly in the afternoon, moments before Tobias turned up at the schoolhouse. The ache in her legs had made her surrender to the comfortable chair in the corner of Gideon's kitchen. James had found her there when he rushed home from the schoolhouse meeting. She made a pretense of irritation that Tobias had raced off needlessly, but her protest was insincere when James half carried her to her own bed in the *dawdihaus*. Still, if Miriam had a choice in the matter, she would not have sent for the *English* doctor. But James insisted, and Gideon rode into town and the doctor arrived.

Unquestionably, it was influenza.

Even robust young men were felled within hours by the virulent strain that had circled the globe in the waning months of the world war. In fact, the doctor reported, the young experienced more severe symptoms than the elderly. The important point to remember, the doctor emphasized, was that most people made a full recovery.

Lindy had recovered.

A week after her illness, Mrs. Byler was still weak but recovering.

In the throes of watching his wife's suffering, James prayed for God's mercy. *Most people* did not give him the reassurance he sought. The medicines the doctor left seemed to bring no benefit.

No Thanksgiving turkey baked in the oven on Thursday. Miriam's fever raged. Her arms ached, she said. Her head ached. Her legs ached. No, she did not want to eat. She wanted another quilt. She wanted no quilt at all.

On Friday, Gideon encouraged the children to eat the food Rachel carried over, but the adults had no appetite. Miriam coughed most of the day. When she spoke, raspy, it was to complain how sore her throat was.

James left Miriam's bedside only when he had to and only for a few minutes at a time. Gideon tended to the animals. Ella kept Gertie occupied and periodically set out cold food for the children. James, Gideon, and Ella rotated through the bedroom of the *dawdihaus* determined that Miriam would not spend a moment alone, even when she slept. When she woke, and was not thrashing against the pain of her ailment, they coaxed water, tea, or a bit of bread into her.

James sat alone with Miriam in the abating shadows of Saturday morning, his elbows propped on his knees and his head hanging between his hands.

Had he brought this home after visiting Lindy in town or going to the meeting with the school board? Had someone coughed on him in the mercantile, and he carried the disease home to Miriam while his own body fought it off? Had Miriam been too close to Mrs. Byler, who had succumbed last weekend but was improving?

Gottes wille.

He prayed to accept God's will. But he prayed for God's will to deliver his beloved.

Gertie whined about not being allowed to see Miriam, but somber Savilla understood the gravity. If Gertie turned up at the *dawdihaus* door, Savilla would be right behind her to tug her back to the main house. Ella scrubbed everything she could think to clean in both structures.

James had always worried what would happen to Miriam if God should call him home. Somehow he had never imagined that Miriam would be the first to see the Savior's face.

Gideon slipped into the room. James looked up.

"She seems to be resting better," Gideon whispered.

"In and out," James said. "I persuaded her to sip some tea before she fell asleep again."

Her breathing was too shallow. James's hand on her cheek told him her temperature was climbing again.

"Maybe you should have something as well," Gideon said. "Mrs. Borntrager brought food."

James shook his head. He would not leave. Not now.

A gasp from the bed startled them both. Almost immediately, Miriam exhaled heavily. James knocked over the chair in his rush to get three inches closer to Miriam. Her eyes fluttered but did not open. James waited for her to take another breath.

"Miriam," he said, jiggling her arm.

She moaned, but she opened her mouth and inhaled.

The door opened. James did not take his eyes off Miriam. In his peripheral vision he saw Gideon reach for Ella's hand.

Miriam's chest fell slowly. James inhaled in harmony and held his breath, waiting for Miriam to release hers.

No rush of air came, no leaking breath, no rise of the rib cage. Finally James could hold his breath no longer and emptied his lungs against his will.

This time when he jiggled Miriam's arm, she did not moan.

Outside, the sun broke the horizon.

⋰⋆⋱

Gideon's tears burned the backs of his eyes. They had burned this way five years ago, when it was Betsy's eyes that fluttered but did not open, Betsy's chest that fell but did not rise.

Grief blurred memory then as it did now.

Had it been fair to send a boy not quite fourteen years old to tell the nearest neighbor? Ella had offered to go, but Gideon wanted her near. Tobias had done the job well, and the news spread across the Amish farms rapidly enough that church members streamed to the Wittmer farm in a steady flow throughout the day. They came first to the main house. Ella somehow enticed them to remain there, with only a few at a time walking to the *dawdihaus* to see James.

Some were relieved by the separation, lest they unwittingly take the influenza home from the *dawdihaus* to their own households. They preferred instead to express their condolences to Gideon. James made brief polite appearances at the main house between his long stretches of vigil beside Miriam. Ella and Rachel had bathed and dressed Miriam in her blue wedding dress and prepared her for the viewing. Gideon had seen for himself how most of the people who ventured to the *dawdihaus* to pay their respects chose to do so from a distance.

How many tens of millions had the influenza taken as it circled the globe? Why, in God's will, should Miriam, on a remote farm near a small town in eastern Ohio, be one of them?

Four men organized a crew to dig Miriam's grave not too far from where Betsy was laid to her final rest, and Chester Mast and his sons were building the pine casket.

The details had to be looked after. Later, James would be grateful that church members executed the traditions swiftly and capably, just as Gideon had been five years ago.

Unabashedly, after Ella pulled the sheet over Miriam's face, the two men embraced. Grief had brought them together when Betsy died and Miriam insisted she and James must help Gideon with his young family. Now grief bound them once again in the vacuum where Miriam's voice belonged.

The touch at Gideon's elbow made him jump, but it was Ella. Was it only eight hours ago that they had together witnessed a soul leave this world while they gripped the flesh-and-blood future they dreamed of together? Ella's face was drawn with exhaustion, emotion, efficiency. Gideon conjured a wan smile.

"Look." Ella tilted her head across the room.

Rachel, Lindy, and David were huddled in a triune embrace.

"Have they. . . ?" Gideon asked.

"Life is precious," Ella said. "Why should we waste any of it separated from people we love?"

"I'm happy for them," Gideon said. Even James would give thanks if reconciliation came out of this day that had wrenched his life inside out. Gideon had a vague awareness that he had not seen any of his own children in some time. He said, "Where are my girls?"

"Savilla has the Hershberger girls upstairs," Ella said. "I'll look for Gertie."

She started to move away but paused as the front door opened for the umpteenth time that day. Margaret Simpson stepped tentatively into the front room.

❧

Margaret felt out of her element. She knew nothing about Amish traditions upon the death of a loved one, and the extent of her relationship with Miriam Lehman was the conversation they had at the

Wittmer door last summer when Margaret had called and Gideon was not home. But in recent weeks Lindy had progressed from being a neighbor Margaret waved at to a friend she cared for, and Miriam was Lindy's aunt and Gertie's great-aunt. And Margaret felt some affinity for Gideon and the battle he led for the education of the Amish children.

Lindy crossed the room toward her and said, "I didn't know you'd come."

"It seemed only right," Margaret said.

After Lindy stopped long enough that morning to give Margaret the news before heading out to the Wittmer farm, Margaret reasoned that grief was grief. She did not have to be closely connected to Miriam to know that many others would feel the weight of a boulder on their chests today—and probably for weeks or months to come. In a black skirt and shirtwaist, at least Margaret did not introduce thoughtless color into a somber occasion. The men were in black suits and white shirts, and the women in black dresses and black aprons.

"You know a few people," Lindy said. "The mothers you drove out to the children's home will never forget your generosity."

Margaret spied Mrs. Borntrager standing next to the fireplace and Mrs. Byler firmly holding the hand of her young son. Hans shyly waved at Margaret, and she gave him a smile.

"I'll bring you something to eat," Lindy said.

"I don't need anything," Margaret said.

"There's plenty. Everybody shows up with food. In this way the *English* and the Amish are not so different."

And in which category did Lindy put herself? Her faith had been formed in the Amish church, yet she had not joined. And would not. If Lindy had decided that her offer to teach was a good enough reason to join the church after all these years, Margaret would have heard by now.

Margaret didn't see James, but Gideon appeared purely stricken. Perhaps by the time she reached him, the words she ought to speak would come to her.

"Margaret," Lindy said, her eyes filling, "it really was kind of you to come."

Margaret ran her tongue across her teeth behind her lips. "Is there something special I should say?"

"Speak your heart," Lindy said. "I'll be back with something to refresh you."

Margaret reminded herself that she was the same woman who stood up to Superintendent Brownley, the same woman who drove mothers desperate to see their children across the county, the same woman who said good-bye to a man she might have loved for a long time to come—because she had done what she thought was right for the people in this room.

Gideon never seemed to be left alone for more than a moment at a time. Margaret made her way through the crowd in his front room, listening to snippets of conversation. Most of it was in Pennsylvania Dutch. Occasionally an English phrase fell on her ears as someone slipped back and forth between the two languages. But Margaret did not need to understand the language the mourners spoke to understand the language of their hearts.

Words of hope.

Words of love.

Words of loss.

Words of tenderness and compassion and care and encouragement.

Why would anyone want to interfere with creating this sense of belonging for another generation? If she never did any other good thing with her life, if she never found another teaching position, if she never loved another man, Margaret would always know she had done the right thing for the families in this room.

❧❀❧

Ella first looked upstairs, supposing Gertie would want to be with Savilla and the other girls. But Gertie was not among the growing assembly in the girls' bedroom. Savilla's eyes bore a stunned stare. Ella had seen Savilla go upstairs with two Hershberger sisters, but now there were eight girls. Several of them, too young to discern what Savilla might be feeling on this day, giggled about something or other.

Rescue me, Savilla's eyes pleaded from the center of her bed.

Ella stepped into the room. "Savilla, would you help me find your sister?"

The nine-year-old swiftly unfolded her feet and took Ella's hand.

"It's a hard day," Ella whispered in the hall. "They don't know."

Savilla nodded, sedate. "I didn't get to say good-bye."

"I know. It was too dangerous."

"I don't care if I might get influenza," Savilla said. "You and *Daed* might get sick, and you were there."

Ella squeezed Savilla's hand. How could she explain that parents sometimes took risks themselves that they would not allow for their children? How could she explain that she and Gideon couldn't leave James alone? How could she explain that it might have frightened Savilla if she had seen Miriam at the height of her illness?

They started down the back stairs.

"I think I know where Gertie is," Savilla said.

"Let's go there together, then."

Savilla led the way through the kitchen and out the back door. On the final day of November, as the sun arranged its setting glory, the air was cold. As they passed the hooks on the back porch, Ella snatched a couple of shawls.

"She goes to the loft," Savilla said. "*Aunti* Miriam always told her not to go up there by herself."

Ella swallowed. Gideon would not approve of his rambunctious six-year-old climbing the ladder on her own. Even Ella didn't like to make the ascent.

Savilla was right, though. As soon as they entered the barn, Ella caught sight of Gertie's prayer *kapp*, a bright spot against the yellow and brown hues of the hay loft.

"I don't want to go up," Savilla said.

"You don't have to."

"Do I have to go back in the house?"

Ella shook her head. "Not if you don't want to."

"Can I go in the *dawdihaus?*"

Ella glanced out the open barn door. "Maybe we should talk to your *daed* about that first."

"I'll wait here, then." Savilla sat on the bench under the tack rack at the entrance to the barn. Ella wrapped a shawl around Savilla before taking in a slow breath, slinging the second shawl over one shoulder, and gripping both rails on the ladder. One step at a time she proceeded upward, resisting the temptation to look down.

Gertie sat up straight, surprised to see Ella come over the top of the ladder. Damp streaks striped her cheeks. Ella crawled around a bale and opened her arms. Gertie trembled in them as Ella wrapped her in the shawl. Ella pulled off the girl's loose *kapp* and stroked her head. They sat silently. Ella would wait as long as it took for Gertie to stop sniffling.

"Is it my fault?" Gertie finally said.

"No, sweet girl. It's not your fault."

"Maybe it happened because I didn't obey. That's what made *Aunti* Miriam so tired."

"No, Gertie, no. That's not why people get sick."

Gertie leaned into her, silent again.

"Why do people die?"

Ella knew she should say that everything that happened was God's will, but she could not make herself speak the words to a grieving child.

"I know my *mamm* died," Gertie said, "but I don't remember her."

The truth of the statement stabbed Ella.

"I don't remember her, so I don't feel sad. Sometimes that makes me feel naughty."

Ella kissed the top of Gertie's head. "That's because Miriam came and took such good care of you."

"Am I going to forget *Aunti* Miriam, too?"

"You're much older now," Ella said. "You'll remember more. And your *daed* and I will help you remember—and Savilla and Tobias and *Onkel* James."

Ella had feared she would not know what to say when she found Gertie, that it should be Gideon's role to comfort his child.

"Is your *mamm* dead?" Gertie asked.

"Yes, she is."

"Do you remember her?"

"Yes, I do. But I was a big girl when it happened—older even than Tobias."

"Do you miss her?"

"Every day," Ella said, her throat swelling. "I miss her because she doesn't know how much your *daed* loves me. I miss her because she doesn't know how much I love you."

Gertie snuggled in. "I'll help you remember your *mamm* if you help me remember *Aunti* Miriam."

"We'll take care of each other."

"You'll be my *mamm* now, and I'll be old enough to remember you."

"That's right. We'll be together a long time."

"Twenty days?"

"Much longer than that."

"No, silly," Gertie said. "*Aunti* Miriam told me you and *Daed* would get married on December 19. I've been counting, and it's twenty days."

"That's right," Ella said. "December 19."

CHAPTER 44

*D*aed!" Savilla jumped up from the table. "The eggs are burning."

Gideon dropped the fork he was using to so patiently toast a piece of bread over the front burner. The implement bounced once and skittered across the kitchen floor while Gideon reached for a towel to wrap around the handle of the iron skillet where the eggs had quickly become inedible.

Before today, he had never felt unable to feed his own children. Fried eggs and toast hardly constituted a challenging menu.

His mind had been on James and whether, once the children were on the bus to school, he would be able to coax their great-uncle to eat something. The counters and icebox were still mounded with food left from the visitation on Saturday and the funeral on Monday. He should have let the children have whatever they felt like for breakfast rather than feeling obliged to prepare the breakfast Miriam would have given them.

It was bad enough that he was sending them to school today—and on the bus. Now their bellies might be empty as well.

Gideon set the skillet in the sink, where it sizzled in the half inch of water he'd forgotten to drain last night.

"How would you like ham sandwiches for breakfast?" he asked, tossing a loaf of Mrs. Glick's bread to the table and spinning around to get Mrs. King's ham from the icebox. He had already packed Mrs. Glick's roast beef in the lunch buckets.

Tobias picked up a knife and began slicing ham.

"Will Ella be here when we get home from school?" Gertie asked.

"I think so," Gideon said. After yesterday's service, she said she would be back to restore order to the kitchen, but Gideon maintained that there was no need for her to come as early as breakfast. He could manage.

And he would have, if he were not worried about James.

What words would suffice?

What words would have sufficed when Betsy died?

None.

But James must eat before he endangered his own health.

"Is it sixteen?" Gertie asked.

"Sixteen what?" Gideon muttered.

"*Daed*!" Savilla said for the second time in as many minutes. Gideon looked from one daughter to the other.

Tobias plopped a slice of ham on a plate and slid it toward Savilla, who cut a clumsy chunk of bread from the end of the loaf before passing both items to Gertie.

"She means the wedding," Tobias said. "Sixteen days until the wedding."

"Am I subtracting right?" Gertie asked. "December 19 minus December 3 equals sixteen days.

Gideon opened the icebox again, looking for nothing in particular but hiding his face from his offspring.

"Yes, you're subtracting correctly," he said.

"And then Ella will cook our eggs?" Gertie said.

Gideon dodged her question. "I promise not to burn them tomorrow."

"Maybe we should just have leftover apple strudel tomorrow," Gertie said, unconvinced.

"Finish your breakfast," Gideon said. "I'll drive you to the bus stop today."

When they climbed out of the buggy at the bus stop twenty minutes later, the bus already rumbling toward them, Gideon scrutinized his children once again and hoped he was not forgetting something that might embarrass them later. They had their lunches. The girls' hair was not as tidy as Miriam would have managed, but neither was it as disastrous as it might have been. Their *kapps* covered most of the mess anyway.

"We'll be all right, *Daed*," Tobias said. "I'll make sure they're all right."

"We'll get better at this," Gideon said.

"Sixteen days!" Gertie said.

Gideon pulled over to the side of the road and waited for his three to board the bus with the other children. Watching the bus grow smaller as the distance increased hardened his stomach, and he puffed his cheeks and exhaled slowly at what he was about to do.

"Gideon."

Ella's voice startled him as she stepped out from behind a tree on the side of the road. He had planned to go home first, to check on James.

And to muster his resolve.

But here she was. He saw now that her horse and cart were nearby.

"I told you to rest this morning," he said, "and not to come for breakfast."

"I didn't come for breakfast," she said. "I just wanted to make sure. . ."

"I know. Thank you." He got down from his buggy bench. "I want to talk to you."

She glanced around before turning her face up for a kiss. Gideon obliged, hoping Ella would not sense the regret in his lips.

"What's wrong?" She stepped back.

He held her hand, studying the spread of her fingers in his palm. "Ella, I think you should be the person who becomes qualified to teach at our school."

She pulled her hand out of his grasp and stepped back farther. "But Gideon—"

"I know. Sixteen days. Gertie is counting."

"Don't you want—"

He reached for her hand again and pulled her toward him. "Of course I do." With his hand cupping her chin, he held her face and her gaze.

"I don't understand. We can't. . .not if. . .especially now. . .after Miriam. . ."

"I know it's not what we planned," Gideon said quickly. If she came to his house today, she would see for herself the mess he had made of things, and it was only the first morning on his own. What would it be in a month or a year? "I wanted to talk to you last week, on the day of the meeting, and then Miriam got sick."

"We've hardly had a moment alone," she said.

"James is right. We need an Amish teacher, and it would be wrong to ask of Lindy what Isaiah suggests."

Fright passed through Ella's eyes.

Gideon inhaled and exhaled with deliberation. "I love you, Ella Hilty. And you will be my wife. We have our whole lives ahead of us. We must think about the community right now. Can we live with ourselves if we do what we choose only for ourselves at the cost to so many others?"

"But I've never heard of a woman who continued to teach in a one-room schoolhouse after she married. Even the *English* would not do that."

"I know," he said softly.

"But the children," she whispered.

"We'll talk to them together. Gertie will see you every day. You'll be her teacher!"

"Oh, Gideon."

Disappointment racked her features. What had he done?

"I'm not qualified," Ella said. "They'll never approve me."

"Mr. Eggar tells me there is a test you can take. Mr. Brownley has agreed to administer it next week."

"Next week!"

"If you pass it, you will receive provisional qualifications. They will test the children in June to determine their progress. I *know* you can teach the children what they need for their test."

"Next week, Gideon?"

He kissed her. "This changes nothing between us except the date that will appear on our marriage license."

⚛

"I have to think. To pray."

Even in the morning chill, heat flooded Ella, and she let her shawl drop from her shoulders. Gertie was not the only one counting down the days until the wedding. Her trunk was half packed to move to Gideon's. They had waited for Jed and Rachel to marry and settle in. They had watched other couples marry as soon as the harvest ended. It was their turn. Ella was ready to marry. Her siblings, scattered in other districts, had made arrangements to travel. Rachel, even amid the distractions and travails of the last few weeks, was slowly scouring and rearranging the house for a winter wedding.

This winter.

Now Gideon wanted to wait—how long?

"Of course you should have time to think," Gideon said. "I'm sorry that circumstances mean I had to blurt out my thoughts so clumsily. But Mr. Brownley will want a prompt answer, or he may put off the test date for weeks, even months."

"I don't even know what I need to study to be ready for a test next week," Ella said. Panic welled. "Even if I did agree to finish out this school year, what about next year?"

If Gideon and James were set on an Amish teacher, would they not merely postpone the question? How long did Gideon expect Ella to wait? Who else was willing to take the test next?

"You ask wise questions. I wish I had all the answers," Gideon said. "But sometimes we must walk along the path looking only at the light on each step."

Ella's chest heaved, and her narrowing throat held captive the words spinning in her mind.

"No Amish teacher will have the formal training the state looks for," Gideon said. "The point is to demonstrate a teacher doesn't need it—that she can teach what the children need in her own way. Perhaps all your years of reading library books, and all the times your father allowed it when others might have disapproved, have brought us all to this moment."

Ella's lungs burned.

"I'll go," Gideon said. "You asked for time."

She nodded.

"Will you come to the house later—whatever your answer?"

Another nod. Sentences collided in Ella's mind, their phrases tangling up in each other. Gideon turned to his buggy, hoisted himself in, and picked up the reins. As his horse began the habitual responses to Gideon's signals, Ella slowly walked back to her own horse and cart.

The horse neighed and she scratched its ear before arranging herself on the bench. Gideon had turned the corner and was out of her range of vision.

Ella squeezed her eyes shut, flushes and chills taking her by turn.

Gottes wille. How could she know God's will? Was it even possible?

Was it God's will for Nora Coates to marry and stop teaching, or her own desire?

Was it God's will for the roof of the old school to fall in? Would it have been God's will if Gertie had been hurt that day?

Had it been God's will for Chester Mast to build a school on his land, or stubbornness to have his own way?

David's rebellion. The vandalism in Lindy's shop. The arrests. The children taken to the home. Influenza. Miriam.

Was it all God's will? Would this precise moment have come if any of these things had not happened?

The horse began to move, tugging the cart to the left. Ella opened her eyes.

"Whoa," she said, fumbling for the slack reins.

But the horse continued, and by the time Ella had a firm enough grip on the reins to pull the horse where she wanted it to go, she laughed aloud.

The horse knew the way to Gideon's farm, a route Ella had taken countless times, especially in the last few months. Perhaps even this moment, when a restless horse presumed to know the human mind, was part of God's plan.

Ella had never known such a prompt answer to prayer.

She and Gideon could have forty years together, a dozen children, dozens of grandchildren.

CHAPTER 45

Y ou can do this." Margaret shifted a pile of books to the right.

Ella had moved into Margaret's house three days ago when she agreed to take the examination. Every morning, before Margaret left the house to teach her own class, she assigned Ella new topics to study and arranged the relevant books on the dining room table.

"My mind is overflowing," Ella said. "I can hardly tell the difference between the seventeenth century and the eighteenth."

"You're doing very well," Margaret said.

"I have to sleep sometime." Ella squeezed her head between her hands. She had expected this week to be busy and next week to be worse—with wedding plans. Instead, she spent three solid days reading and making notes. In the evenings, under electric lights, Margaret quizzed her.

"We'll rest on the Sabbath," Margaret said. "Or at least we'll limit ourselves to conversing on these matters without resorting to opening the books. But it's only Friday evening. We have all day tomorrow, and then Monday and Tuesday before the exam on Wednesday."

"I can't learn all of this," Ella protested. "You went to high school and then the teachers college. You had years to absorb all of this."

"And you check out more books from the library than anyone in Seabury," Margaret responded. "It's only a matter of organizing what you already know."

Ella had always thought of herself as one of the most organized people she knew. Looking around at the piles of paper on the dining room table, she concluded she had misjudged the last twenty-six years.

"We have the questions that have been published in the newspaper for the last five years in three different counties of Ohio." Margaret thumped the stack of old newspapers that the library had allowed them to borrow. "We are not shooting arrows in the dark. The questions on your test will be very similar."

"That doesn't help!" Ella said. " 'Trace in early American literature some influences of its English origin.' When I was in school, our parents approved everything the teachers assigned. I didn't learn how to answer a question like that."

Margaret slid three sheets of paper out of an American history textbook. "You've already studied my college notes and outlined a fully suitable answer."

"But I haven't actually read any early American literature." Ella picked up a newspaper and said, "And how about this one? 'How does the knowledge of a scratch on the hand reach the brain? Would knowledge of an injury to an internal organ locate so accurately the place and nature of the hurt? Does the brain control the processes of the internal organs?' "

"Basic science," Margaret said. "You read veterinary books all the time because you find them relevant to caring for farm animals. Think about how you would care for an animal showing signs of sickness."

"At least I know this one," Ella said. " 'Name three kinds of corn and discuss each in such a way that they may be recognized by the description.' Now that's something every Amish pupil needs to know."

"You'd be surprised how many teachers would have to study for that one, yet you know the answer. You can do this."

Ella blew out her breath and set a fresh sheet of paper in front of her. "Let's keep going."

"That's the spirit."

They pored over the questions listed in the newspapers, reviewed basic mathematical formulas and their applications, and studied standard vocabulary lists. Ella filled one page after another with notes.

Mark diacritically: cafe, sacrifice, Panama, Sahara, Colorado, psychology, perfected.

A piece of work costs for labor $233.75, the workmen receiving wages *at the rate of $1.50 for a day of 9 hours. What would the same work cost if wages were $1.40 a day of 8 hours?*

Show how the environments of the American colonies were conducive to union.

Mention three principal mineral products of (a) England and (b) the Rocky Mountain region of the United States.

Discuss distillation and fermentation.

A man bought 50 cords of wood for $225 and sold 15 percent of it for $45. What percent was gained on the part sold?

Why was the destruction of the public buildings of Washington in 1814 by the British condemned?

What cargo would a ship be likely to carry from Odessa to London?

A and B engage to do work for $170. A worked 3 days more than ⅝ as long as B, and received $70. How many days did each work?

Show accent and sound of vowels of the following adjectives: reputable, estimable, Philippine, recreant, imitative. Use correctly in sentences the five words.

Give a model for parsing a noun, an adjective, and a verb.

Explain Standard Time.

Describe muscles as to uses, kinds, forms, structure, and motions produced.

For every question that gave Ella confidence, another drained hope. Science, mathematics, history, language. The arithmetic question bouncing constantly to the front of her mind was how many hours remained until the time of testing.

⤜✦⤝

On Saturday, Margaret cooked a hearty, filling breakfast. Lindy joined them for constant quizzing and looking up answers. They drank one pot of coffee after another.

Ella wondered what Gideon was doing that morning. What Gertie really thought about the idea that if Ella passed this test, she would be Gertie's teacher rather than her *mamm*. Whether Percival Eggar had another legal strategy up his sleeve if Ella failed. How dreadful it would be to learn that she failed only by a point or two.

On Sunday, Ella stayed home while Margaret went to church. Then they bundled up against the brisk wintry air, donned sturdy shoes, and went for a long constitutional, which Margaret claimed was refreshment for the mind as well as the body and during which she worked a range of academic topics into conversation.

On Monday, Margaret returned to her own school, leaving Ella once again to study amid the stacks of textbooks and notes written in Margaret's neat script from her college years.

By Tuesday morning, Ella could not absorb one more new sentence. She stacked the books tidily at one end of Margaret's dining room table, sorted her pages of notes according to topic, and began reading through them line by line.

Margaret topped off Tuesday's supper with a pie as delicious as any baked by an Amish woman and sent Ella to an early bedtime in the spare room.

On Wednesday, Margaret walked with Ella to the superintendent's office before proceeding to school.

"Don't let Mr. Brownley intimidate you," Margaret said.

"I'm sure he would like nothing more than for me to fail," Ella said.

"Don't give him any reason to think you might. And remember, he is only proctoring the exam. He didn't write the test, and he won't be grading your answers."

Ella nodded. Her heart pounded, pushing adrenaline through the physiology system she had learned so much about in the last few days.

"I'll come back as soon as school is out for the day," Margaret said. "I'll be here waiting when you finish."

Ella moistened her lips and pushed open the heavy door.

CHAPTER 46

I'll go to the bus stop," James said.

"I can do it," Gideon said.

"Or I will," Ella added.

James took his coat off the hook in the kitchen. "I want to be useful."

James's shoulders slumped more than they did two weeks ago. Over the last few days, Gideon had made several attempts to talk himself out of this observation, but each time he came to the same conclusion: James had aged five years in the two weeks since he buried his wife.

Gideon and Ella watched James go out the back door and head toward the buggy. Tobias would say it wasn't too far to walk from the bus stop to the farm, but each day seemed colder than the one before, and Gideon didn't want his children to suffer one moment more than necessary. They had suffered enough already in the bumpy fall months.

"I hope James believes me," Gideon said, "when I say he'll always have a home here."

"The girls would be heartbroken if he left," Ella said.

"Tobias, too."

"Besides, where would he go?"

"He still has a brother in Lancaster," Gideon said.

"We could invite him to visit," Ella suggested.

Gideon nodded. "In time, perhaps." He remembered those early days of being stunned that in a matter of hours the land under his life had rolled and reformed. Even after more than forty years together, James had been as unprepared to lose Miriam as Gideon had been to lose Betsy after eight. Gideon jerked his thoughts back from what it would be like to lose Ella, even after forty years.

"I should work on the casserole." Ella stood up and took a pan from a lower cupboard.

Gideon put out a hand, and Ella grazed it as she went by.

"It must be terrible for you to wait," he said. Her test results were due today—at least Mr. Brownley expected to have them today. How quickly he would pass them on to Ella was uncertain.

"It will be what it will be." Ella selected five large potatoes from a half bushel in the corner where Miriam's chair used to be.

The children had just spilled into the house and released their book straps and lunch buckets onto the kitchen counter when the sound of an automobile penetrated Gideon's consciousness and he got up to look out the front window.

"It's Lindy," he said.

Ella followed him, wiping her hands on a dish towel. "Were you expecting her?"

"No. She probably wants to see how James is."

"Or all of you," Ella said softly. She opened the front door to invite Lindy in.

"Come on," Lindy said. "Get in the car. Let's go."

"Where?" Gideon asked.

"Town. There's no reason Ella should wait another hour for the results. We all know Brownley probably got them first thing this morning."

Gideon and Ella locked eyes.

"I would like to know," Ella confessed.

"Then you should go," Gideon said.

"Come with me," Ella said. "James is here for the children. You heard him say he wants to be useful."

Gideon nodded. "I'll tell him we're going."

In the car, Gideon's hand kept wanting to reach for a brake lever to pull. Betsy always said that even when she was driving a buggy, Lindy liked speed, and this was Gideon's consistent experience with her. Ella showed no reaction. Perhaps she was grateful for the motor that would carry her to her test results and home again while there was still time to make supper.

Mr. Brownley kept them waiting. They arrived without an appointment, so Gideon had some sympathy for the time it would take for Mr. Brownley to rearrange his afternoon. The longer they sat in the reception area, though, the more Gideon resented the wait. How long would it take to say yes or no to the question of whether Ella had performed acceptably on the examination?

Finally Brownley opened the door to his inner office and gestured that they should enter and be seated.

"I understand you were to be married," Brownley said.

"We still are," Gideon said.

"Oh? I was given to understand that you realized that young women who marry cannot be teachers. It's not done."

"I do understand," Ella said evenly. "I am prepared to accept the responsibilities that come with a teaching position."

"Even at personal sacrifice?" Brownley said, one eyebrow raised.

"Yes."

Gideon's foot began to thump slowly.

"Miss Hilty, how did you feel about the exam?" Brownley asked.

"It was a privilege to be allowed to take it," she answered.

Gideon's foot thumped faster and more audibly.

"You didn't find it overly difficult, considering your own limited educational opportunities?"

"A person who loves learning will always find a way," Ella said.

"That is an admirable perspective," Brownley said. He settled back in his chair. "Was there a particular portion of the test that you found more difficult than another?"

Gideon interrupted the exchange before his foot would begin to stomp. "Mr. Brownley, it is our understanding that you have the results of Ella's test."

"Yes, I do. They arrived this morning. Of course, if you had a telephone, I might have saved you a lengthy buggy ride into town."

"Lindy Lehman was kind enough to bring us by automobile," Gideon said. "So if you also would be so kind?"

Brownley sighed. "Yes. Miss Hilty, your test score ensures that you will be duly credentialed as a teacher in Geauga County."

❦

Margaret answered the knock at her door.

"Ella!"

Margaret looked past Ella's grinning face to where Lindy and Gideon leaned against Lindy's car across the street. Her eyes came back to Ella's.

"You passed!" she said, stepping back to open the door wider. "You should all come in."

"I can't," Ella said. "James is at home with the children, and I've hardly seen them at all today, and I promised them supper, and Gideon will need to do the milking, and I—"

"Okay, okay," Margaret said, laughing.

"I just wanted you to know," Ella said. "I could not have done it without you."

"You earned this. You worked hard. You deserve the recognition."

"It is only for God's glory," Ella said.

"Then may His glory shine through the gifts He has given you," Margaret said. "I'll help you in any way I can. We can work on lesson plans and grading together, and I can give you a list of the books about teaching that I've found most helpful."

"Thank you. All of that would be wonderful," Ella said, "but I hate to impose. You've done so much for us already."

Margaret glanced at Gideon again.

"You gave up your wedding for this," Margaret said quietly. "At least you have a good man waiting for you once everything is resolved. He believes in you."

This was more than Margaret could say for herself.

"Yes, he does," Ella said, "sometimes more than I believe in myself."

"God has blessed you." Margaret squeezed Ella's hand. "When will you open the school?"

"In three days!" Ella put a hand to a cheek. "Three days! How can I ever be ready?"

"Why not wait until January—a fresh start in a fresh year?"

"Mr. Brownley will test my students in June," Ella said. "We have to be ready. Every day matters."

"Nora Coates would be so proud of you," Margaret said.

"No. No pride," Ella said. "Only obedience. A calling."

Margaret nodded. "I'll be praying for you."

"And I for you."

Margaret watched Ella scamper back to Lindy's car. She closed the front door and leaned against it.

"No pride. Only obedience. A calling."

Gray was gone. But like Ella, Margaret had obedience. Like Ella, she had a calling.

And she could ask God for no greater gift.

⚛

Ella would be the first to admit she was nervous. This time when the students arrived, there would be more of them. None of the families left their children in the town consolidated grade school because they feared retribution if they did not.

The schoolhouse was warm. The books were out, the chalkboard filled with assignments and instructions. Despite the outside temperature, Ella stood outdoors and welcomed her pupils.

The King children.

The Mast children.

The Glicks.

The Hershbergers.

The Borntragers.

The Bylers.

Her stepbrother, Seth.

Gideon's children.

Every family with school-age children was represented.

Ella welcomed each child by name.

Gideon sent his children inside. "Maybe we should make sure the window on the side of the building seals properly," he said to Ella.

"I've noticed no problem," she said.

His lips turned up on one side. "Let's be sure, shall we?"

Ella looked toward the door. "My pupils—"

"We wouldn't want one of the little ones to sit in a draft."

"No," she agreed. "We wouldn't."

She followed Gideon around the side of the building that faced away from the road. There, he took both her hands.

"This was to be our day," he said.

A lump stole her throat. "Yes."

"I promise you I will always remember this day."

"As will I."

"I don't want you to be disappointed."

"I'm not. I promise. I'm not."

"December 19, 1918."

Ella smiled. "The day I became a teacher."

"No," Gideon said, "the day you believed in yourself."

He leaned in to kiss her. The words tumbling around in Ella's mind told her, *Not here. Not now.* But her lips returned Gideon's soft pressure, and her fingers returned his grip on hers. The moment lingered, and Ella savored the sensation.

It was the giggling that made them step apart.

Gertie covered her mouth with a hand. "*Daed* is kissing the teacher!"

AUTHOR'S NOTE

I chose to set this story in Geauga County, Ohio, because this was the place of the earliest recorded conflict between Amish parents and state officials over the schooling of their children. Three Amish fathers were fined because they would not send their children to high school. My story is not a retelling of that incident, of which little is known. In fact, it is not a retelling of any one specific conflict over this issue but a fusion of principles and posturing that began in Geauga County in 1914 and continued until the Supreme Court of the United States ruled in 1972. Interestingly, in more recent decades Geauga County was again the site of discontent when a school superintendent attempted to eliminate the tradition of providing used textbooks and furniture to Amish schools. This was in hope of stirring up Amish parents to vote in favor of a levy rather than remain neutral and apart on the issue.

Because my story is a conflation, I have not strictly followed the chronology history gives us but have compressed events that happened over years or decades, and over several states, into a few months in one fictional town. Historically the Amish sent their children to school to study alongside non-Amish children through the eighth grade. Rural schools, often with mixed grades in one room, allowed Amish parents close involvement in what their children were learning. A movement that began in the 1910s to "consolidate" small rural schools into larger town schools, along with new compulsory attendance laws that took children past the eighth grade, gave rise to a sort of resistance movement among Amish parents. On January 12, 1922, eight children from Holmes County, Ohio, were taken to the Painter Children's Home and their parents charged with neglect because of their position on education.

Over the next few decades, Amish parents stood up against law enforcement because of the strength of their conviction. They paid fines, they spent time in jail, they kept their teenage children home to work on the farm, they established their own schools in defiance of standards of state law, they were charged with child neglect and contributing to the delinquency of minors. Fathers who were convicted used the court system to appeal. School districts that lost also appealed. Multiple issues emerged: Was the instruction untrained Amish teachers offered equivalent to the instruction given in public schools? Which was paramount—the state's interest in educated citizens or parents' religious convictions? Did the state have the power to close private schools?

In 1972 the determination of the Amish to educate their own children—and only through the eighth grade—reached the Supreme Court in *Wisconsin v. Yoder*. Chief Justice Warren Burger wrote: "A State's interest in universal education. . .is not totally free from a balancing process when it impinges on other fundamental rights and interests, such as those specifically protected by the Free Exercise Clause of the First Amendment." The Amish had successfully argued that enforcing the state's compulsory education laws would gravely endanger the free exercise of Amish religious beliefs.

I find an issue like this one interesting to write about because similar questions linger a century after Ella and Gideon and their real-life counterparts. We continue to need to understand each other better and learn to see the world through someone else's lens. (And for a little fun, I borrowed names from a variety of legal cases on record to populate the Amish farms around the fictional town of Seabury.)

I am particularly indebted to *Compulsory Education and the Amish: The Right Not to Be Modern*, edited by Albert N. Keim (Boston: Beacon Press, 1975), especially the chapters, "Who Shall Educate Our Children?" by Joseph Stoll and "The Cultural Context of the Wisconsin Case" by John A. Hostetler, and *The Riddle of Amish Culture* by Donald A. Kraybill (Baltimore: Johns Hopkins University Press, 1989) for an understanding of the religious and legal issues at play.

Thank you to Barbour Publishing for allowing me to explore these historical questions and ponder intersections with modern public discussion. Their team of editors, designers, and marketers turn a manuscript into a book. And as always, thanks to my agent, Rachelle Gardner, for walking this publishing journey with me with the grace and encouragement of the good friend she is.

ABOUT THE AUTHOR

Olivia Newport's novels twist through time to find where faith and passions meet. Her husband and two twenty-something children provide welcome distraction from the people stomping through her head on their way into her books. She chases joy in stunning Colorado at the foot of the Rockies, where daylilies grow as tall as she is.

Coming in 2016,
the next title in
AMSH TURNS OF TIME. . .

Hope in the Land
BY OLIVIA NEWPORT

*While the Great Depression stalls the country in gloom, can neighbors in
Lancaster County grasp the goodness that will sustain hope?*

*Gloria Grabill's English neighbor, Minerva Swain, has been trying the
Amish woman's patience for forty years. And when Henry Edison turns up in
Lancaster County to survey Amish women about their domestic contributions,
the last thing Gloria has time for is Henry's unending questions. Her hands
are full with a farm to run alongside her husband and a houseful of children.
Her oldest daughter, Polly, wants nothing more than the traditional path of an
Amish farmer's wife, but everything she does seems to push Thomas Coblentz
further away. Despite her own hesitant attitudes, Gloria's grit weaves together
Minerva, Henry, and Polly.*

ALSO BY OLIVIA NEWPORT

VALLEY OF CHOICE
Accidentally Amish
In Plain View
Taken for English

AMISH TURNS OF TIME
Wonderful Lonesome
Meek and Mild
Brightest and Best

Hidden Falls (a 13-part digital serial drama)